BloodMining

Darling Norman,
Fuck the Haiku! Thank
you for being here.

Laura x

17 Oct 2011
Laura Wilson

BloodMining

by Laura Wilkinson

Bridge House

British Library Cataloguing in Publication Data

A Record of this Publication is available from the British Library

ISBN 978-1-907335-14-3

This edition published 2011 by Bridge House Publishing
Manchester, England

All Bridge House books are published on paper derived
from sustainable resources.

For Fred, Morgan and Cameron

Thanks to:

Jess Davies, Roz Hart, Phil Moyes, SR (you know who you are) and Helen Wilkinson for critical attention to early drafts. Members of the Jubilee Writers' Group, with a special mention to Mark Sheerin, and Tony Cook at ABCtales for support and encouragement. Debz Hobbs-Wyatt and Gill James at Bridge House for hard work and making it all happen. My mother, Marian Williams, and my fathers, Mike Williams and Brian Wilkinson, for giving me opportunities you never had.

Part One

2048 – 2052

Chapter One

'Megan, get out of Xinjiang as fast as you can. I will not have your life on my conscience.' Jack's voice was breaking up.

'Don't you order me around, Jack North. You are not my boss,' Megan replied, shouting.

'A request then, from a friend, a plea. Get out of there.'

The taxi driver flinched as she yelled, 'Don't worry. I'll see you tomorrow.' She fumbled in her bag and pulled out the last of her yuan, handing the notes to the driver, whose eyes flickered, liquid, petrified and keen to leave the terminal drop off point as quickly as possible. She removed the chip from her mobile multi-media device, placed it in the lining of her bra, took off the ring on her marriage finger, slipped it into her pocket, and took her luggage from the seat beside her.

There were four Mujahideen slouched against the frames of the departure lounge entrance. As Megan walked from the cab, dragging her battered rucksack behind her, they stood upright, legs astride, their rifles held across their chests. Casual, confident killers. Young and high on ideology and power, Megan had seen hundreds of boys like these in almost every corner of the globe. They were frightening, unpredictable and random, but she'd managed the fear, the not knowing. Until now. Megan was scared. She tugged at her hijab, pulling it tight under her chin, and looked at the floor. A puddle of yellowing liquid snaked across the paving slabs. It looked like a dog had taken a leak against the wall and Megan hoped the soldiers wouldn't force her to lie prostrate on the ground. There would be no way of avoiding the piss. She used her arsenal of pacifying techniques. She must not make eye contact. She must not aggravate them. They must not sense her terror. As she neared the doorway the sensor kicked in and the doors slid apart. She took another step forward.

Two of the Mujahideen barred her entry. One kicked the rucksack at her feet, the other jabbed his rifle at her hand luggage, an old suede bag slung across her torso. She pulled it off and opened it, offering it to the boy. He snatched her mobile device, rifled through her purse, then opened her passport. He smelt of cheap aftershave and sweat. A handful of rebellious hairs spiralled from the cream skin of his fingers, the texture of pubic hair. Unusual for a Chinese. She held her breath. She felt the barrel of a gun touch her chin. It was cold, sharp, like a knife, and she lifted her head without lifting her eyes. The soldier tugged at her hijab, freeing her long black hair, and threw the cloth to the floor, before stamping on it. His boots were well cared for, polished and winking at her. He called her a slut, and spat on the floor, before hissing to his colleague that the white witch was a journalist. She wished she did not understand Mandarin.

The contents of the rucksack were all over the floor. A sparse collection of clothes, all black or charcoal grey, another larger multi-media device (mulmed), and a pathetic assortment of toiletries and cosmetics. Megan travelled light, taking nothing that she would not be happy to abandon at a moment's notice, aside from her ring, which she carried everywhere. Her words and pictures, her impression of a story, could never be taken from her, she etched them into her temporal lobes as well as her mulmed chip.

Her mind flooded with images of the two EBC journalists murdered in the borderlands between China, Pakistan and Tajikistan the previous autumn, and despite the chill beads of sweat gathered at the base of her spine and on her breastbone. She stared at her shaking, bony fingers.

They pulled at her jacket, opening it, and tapped at her jean pockets, and she felt a quickening in her belly. Just as she thought she might collapse there was a shout and the two boys stepped aside. Megan fell to her knees, centimetres from the rivulets of liquid – it was definitely urine, she could smell it now, though whether it was human or canine remained uncertain – and stuffed her possessions back into the bag. A lip-gloss rolled noisily across the pavement, into the gutter. It was her favourite, her only luxury item on assignments, a little thing she used to remind herself that she was a woman after days of falling asleep fully clothed in makeshift beds to the sound of gunfire, dust and dirt ground into her hardened skin. She left the gloss where it lay, and wondered later if either of the boys collected it as a souvenir, a gift for a girlfriend, sister or mother.

The aeroplane perched on the runway was old and half empty. The seats were rickety, the upholstery frayed. The wings drooped like forest leaves heavy with rain. It didn't seem capable of carrying its grateful, dismal cargo back to London. Megan boarded with an assortment of grubby, ragged looking individuals, putting her ring back on before she took her seat. A handful of passengers she recognized as fellow journalists. She saw the way they took everything in, as she did, recording the detail for later tales and anecdotes, even books. There were aid workers, emotional and exhausted, diplomats and wealthy Chinese. They scurried onto the plane, tails low, heads straight ahead, rats deserting a sinking ship. The lucky ones, perhaps.

Despite Megan's misgivings the plane took off easily, a shuddering, a roaring of the engines, a judder and they were airborne. From her window seat she watched the world below turn into toy town, and took comfort in the knowledge that the boys, with their rifles and dreams and confusion, were small – splinters of humankind in the unimaginable vastness that was the universe. It was hard to believe that in a matter of hours all this would mean nothing to her, not really. Abstract suffering – another war in another troubled country thousands of kilometres from home. How lucky she was that she could escape, leave. She thought of those that she had met and befriended. Those whose very existence was bound to the land, the cause. People whose experience was so far removed from the average European's that sometimes it was difficult to remember that they too slept, and ate, and bled.

The forgotten people. The little people at the centre of massive and terrible events. I tell their stories so that they matter. So that we know. So that we can no longer use ignorance as an excuse for our inertia.

She remembered Jack's words.

13

It was why she did what she did. He inspired her. All those years ago, when she saw him on the mulmed back in Wales, reporting from the scene of a devastating earthquake. Vigorous, energetic. A powerful life force amidst death and destruction. Blue eyes radiating compassion, bearing witness, the resonant tones forbidding forgetfulness, worse still, indifference. She saw a more perfect image of herself reflected in those pools, and from that moment on, over ten years ago, she knew her destiny. She would be like Jack North. She would seek out the forgotten people and tell their stories. And so she had.

The air conditioning blasted from the funnels above her head. She hadn't expected it to work. All four filters were turned towards her – she felt clammy when she boarded the aircraft, there were no other refugees on the row of three threadbare seats. The cool air was so violent Megan shivered. She pulled a cardigan from her bag and threw it over her shoulders, and peered out of the window. The plains of Xinjiang were fading fast as the plane gained altitude. Soon China would be covered in a blanket of cloud and she would have to conjure it from memory. It would get harder and harder to do this as time passed, and a great sadness washed over her. She wasn't just saying goodbye to China, she was saying goodbye to Hisham. They had loved for over seven years, on and off, whenever their professional paths crossed. They spent months apart and then intense, passionate months together. But Hisham was increasingly wedded to the East, she knew she would never return, and she doubted he would ever really leave.

This thinking about Hisham, working down there, reminded her that she was still in danger. Goose pimples scattered across her arms. Until she reached European soil, she was not safe, and if she wasn't safe, neither was her precious cargo. She put her cardigan on properly and closed her eyes, attempting to sleep away the waiting. She did not expect sleep to claim her but, eventually, it did. She dreamt of the night.

It had been humid in the hotel room despite the cold outside. She was languid and remote though Hisham didn't seem to notice.

They made love to the sound of shellfire, another part of the city was under attack, and afterwards he lit a cigarette, stared at the ceiling and commented on her fuller breasts and the gentle swell of her belly.

'No more rice cake for you, Missy Megan, otherwise you won't be able to run away from the bad guys.'

'You'd protect me, wouldn't you?' She rolled over onto her side and took in his profile. Atavistic and youthful for his thirty-nine years, the arch of his brow had a faintly aristocratic whiff. He claimed his father was a French diplomat but Megan had never bought into this particular fantasy.

'You are asking me to look after you? That's a first! Meg-an who is always so independent, so resourceful. You are joking, yes?'

'But would you protect me, if I needed it?' She knew that he wouldn't and wondered why she asked.

'You'll never need it, baby. At least I hope you never do. It's what I like about you. You're not like other women. You take what you want, you ask for very little.' He turned and kissed her on the shoulder.

'You're a selfish bastard,' she said as she lay back down and stared at the ceiling. Paint peeled away, in giant, curling flakes, as if it had been painted in a hurry before the plaster had fully dried.

'It's true. I cannot lie about this. I am vain, self-centred and egocentric. You are an extension of my id and you love me for it.'

Megan laughed but her heart felt like metal. She had secrets.

She hadn't told Hisham about the memory card, about the pictures taken only hours earlier from the corner of their hotel balcony while he was out chasing confirmation of the imminent arrival of Mujahideen forces in the region's capital and, as it turned out, dodging bullets on his return.

Pictures of Mujahideen slaughtering civilians in the street, of government soldiers butchering Mujahideen, of a man riding his motorcycle through the square with the corpse of his wife and child strapped to him, his peaceful, silent passengers. She had tried to send the pictures through to Jack in London but all connection to the outside world had been cut.

Almost all foreigners had left Xinjiang days ago and, as far as she knew, she was the last western journalist in Kashi. She was determined to bring the story back. She knew Hisham would understand this need but if he guessed what she intended he would have made excuses to prevent her carrying the card.

So she left with two secrets.

A small child on its mother's lap in the row in front began to cry, waking Megan from her slumber. Through the gap in the chairs Megan made out his crumpled face, mouth wide open, red and livid, toothless gums. The other two seats in the row were empty. The woman and child were alone. She imagined what might have happened to the father and resisted the urge to cry.

Megan closed her eyes again. She was exhausted from the trials of the day and sleep was oblivion, a way to block the memories, the anxiety. She released her seat belt and curled up, arm draped across her stomach. The void claimed her hastily. She dreamt of bald streets, snipers, and mewling cats. A deserted town, dusty and broken. She was running. Running towards a building – her flat, Highgate, her home. But it was destroyed, smashed and blown to rubble. Sepulchre-like. A cat sat amongst the debris and purred, its yellow eyes fixed on her stricken face, dreamy and hypnotic. The purring grew louder and louder. Megan felt the vibrations in the pit of her stomach reverberating through her core. The ground shook beneath her feet, and a bottomless rift appeared as the earth slowly cracked apart. She woke with a start.

The plane was shuddering, rattling through a stormy sky. The fasten seat belt lights were flashing and the pilot was talking over the intercom. Children were moaning and crying, the adults hushing them. Megan could barely make out his words… turbulence, storm overhead, then hissing.

Silence shrouded the air, deafening in its emptiness, its life-lessness. The baby in front was calm. Through the gap in the seats she could see him, propped up over his mother's shoulder. He stared, bug-eyed, at Megan. She wondered why his mother had not secured him and then realized with horror that the mother thought they were about to die. The boy was secure, tranquil, why would a mother wish to alarm him?

Megan had confronted death many times before, prepared for it, and felt it slip away, passing her by, placing its invisible hand on the shoulders of others. She understood that certain death brought with it a certain calm resignation. That the deepest fear rendered one lucid, not hysterical. And it was in that moment Megan made her decision. She had been through the options many times, swinging from one to the other, fear resurfacing with increasing ferocity.

The urge to comfort and reassure the mother and child was overwhelming. She had shivered at the sight of this tired old plane on the runway at Kashi but she would have boarded it even if it had not been the last plane out. She had known it would not be a comfortable journey but had felt that the plane would make it. It was not her time.

And this time, here, facing possible death, she decided to accept the life within her if she survived.

She leapt from her seat and came round to face the woman. She was Han Chinese, small, square, with cropped hair and a narrow scar meandering the length of her forehead from hairline to left eyebrow, luminescent and glowing as if backlit by her terror. She smelt of evaporated milk and damp. Gripping the armrest, Megan pleaded in rough Mandarin, 'Secure your baby. Everything will be all right. I promise, everything will be okay, but if the landing is shaky he could be hurt. Please.'

The woman stared at her, shocked and traumatized, and allowed Megan to secure her child. For over an hour the tinny plane rattled and shook, was thrown amongst the cobalt clouds, thrashed by the rain, but it finally came to rest, as planned, in a wet and windy London. As they disembarked the woman turned to Megan and bowed.

Megan wanted to explain. 'I'm having a baby,' she said.

The woman looked blank, the child latched to her hip, pond-eyed.

Megan curved her hand over an imaginary swollen belly and repeated, 'I'm having a baby. I knew we were going to be okay.'

The woman smiled, kissed her son's head, and said softly in broken English, 'Good, this very good. You good mother, good woman,' before turning and walking down the aisle and out into the robust English weather.

Chapter Two

'Hello, baby. I hear you've been on the news again, you sneaky, sexy devil.'

'Hisham.'

Megan was sat at her desk in the European Broadcasting Corporation offices when the mulmed rang. She had gone straight there from the airport, starting her piece in the cab before abandoning it to devour the city. London looked so clean and beautiful, unspoilt by bombs and blood. The air was crisp, her nostrils tingled and stung at the shock of air unfettered by concrete dust and fumes. The street corners seemed almost naked without gun-wielding youths and underfed civilians with resignation etched across their faces. Trees swayed in the breeze, leaves glistening in the damp air, the river free of rubbish and bloated corpses.

When she'd finished writing and loading the article she'd laid her cheek on the desk's smooth surface. She relished the smell of the cleaning fluid, its artificiality alien and wondrous. She closed her eyes and took in the sounds of the newsroom. Tapping, talking, rushing excitement. What a buzz. She had been away almost two months.

She leant towards the mulmed and lowered her voice. 'I suppose you want an apology. I won't say sorry for not telling you,' she said.

'No worries, sunbeam. I'd have done exactly the same, given half a chance,' said Hisham.

'I know you would. How is it there?'

'Fine. You know me, baby, I'll always be okay. Anyway, an Arab in a Muslim state. Not likely to cause alarm, no? I'll call again when I'm back in Paris.'

'When will that be?' She tapped on the desk with her fingernails. An insubstantial tune, popular when she left, long since forgotten by all but Megan.

'Soon, I hope. I've had enough of this shit-hole. No booze, no women. No life for me. Where are you going next?'

'Not sure. I need to speak with some people, Jack, find out what's going on, where the gaps are...' Megan talked on before realizing that the connection had broken.

Megan had not decided whether she was going to tell Hisham about the baby or not. She did not expect him to be a big part of its life. So why tell him? It pulled on her conscience. She was still the fatherless child.

Besides, Hisham would almost certainly try and persuade her not to keep it. He would tell her that she was out of her mind, a little war-weary, that she needed a rest, and afterwards she would come to her senses and return to the field. Her mind was made up but he would never understand. She had never seen herself as the maternal type but she had made a promise, on that plane, and the feeling of optimism that her body offered delighted and surprised her.

She lifted her head and saw Jack in her peripheral vision, the sight of him interrupting her thoughts. She watched him cross the newsroom, sloping between the desks, authoritative, cutting an imposing figure in a tailor-made jacket and worn jeans. A crisp, collarless shirt, with a cotton handkerchief peeping out of the breast pocket. Jack was a colleague and her unofficial mentor. It was Jack who persuaded his editor to give Megan her first break. She was never quite sure why he did that for her.

'Hey, Jack, would you take a look at this before I send it through to the Ed?' shouted a senior reporter.

'How long you got, Mike?'

'Minutes. Less. She wanted it ten minutes ago. Need a second opinion.'

'Right.' Jack jogged over to the reporter's desk. Megan watched him peer at the screen, stand back, offer advice, before turning to resume his original course. He was heading her way.

The reporter called out again, 'You're a star, mate! What'd we do without you?'

Jack shouted back, 'Work harder!' and a few people laughed.

'Some of us are trying to concentrate here,' muttered a

reporter from Deptford. He sat opposite Megan; they shared a desk. She had never liked him, and was glad that she spent so little time office bound.

'What's your problem? If you want silence go work in re-search,' Megan said.

'Look, I know he's your mate and everything, but he does lord it a bit. It's not like he's an editor or nothing.' He dived back behind his screen, but Megan was up for a fight.

'He could have been,' she said.

'Could have been is not the same as is.'

Megan resisted the urge to reach over the desk and punch him. 'He doesn't want an editorship.' She knew she sounded over-protective and defensive but couldn't stop herself.

'I'll do this until someone tells me to stop,' Jack'd said when Megan asked him the same question when she was an ambitious cub reporter.

The reporter raised his eyebrows, and she thought how ugly he looked, with his ridged forehead and bulging bloodshot eyes.

'He enjoys what he does. You should be so lucky, you miser-able bastard.'

'Steady.' He backed off.

Jack had stopped to talk with another colleague, a researcher, who hung around the newsroom whenever Jack was about. Or so it seemed to Megan. Jack ran his fingers through his fringe and smiled his roguish grin. Megan detected a trace of false coyness in his manner and wondered if he fancied the young woman, and why she was bothered if he did. The girl was no match for him; he would tire of her quickly, Megan decided. Jack played the foppish, hopeless romantic well, but it was all an act – he didn't get involved with his conquests. The researcher was pretty, a safe variety: blonde and petite, with a sharp little nose and rosebud mouth, she would never be described as a beauty other than by her family. Her name was Julie Brookings and she was always immaculately groomed. Before Megan left for her last assignment Julie had asked her if she might put in a good word on her behalf. There was an assistant producer's post up for grabs.

'I want to get on, like you,' Julie said. 'The editor listens to you.' Megan agreed, but didn't mention it in the end. It wasn't exactly deliberate; she forgot. She couldn't put her finger on it, but there was something about the girl that Megan didn't like. Pushy, ambitious.

Was Julie his type? Megan wasn't sure if he had one. Jack was in his forties and divorced. As far as Megan could make out there were plenty of lovers though no one special. He was attractive, Megan had fancied him herself when they first met but never seriously thought she was in with a chance. He was charming, worldly and well-heeled. She had been an eighteen-year-old provincial geek. Later he was colleague and then friend, the older brother she dreamed of having as a girl.

As Jack approached her desk Megan's colleague leapt up, announcing that he needed a drink. Jack plonked himself in the empty chair and remarked, 'Something I said?'

'He hates you.'

'Feeling's mutual.'

Jack gestured at the enormous screen on the newsroom wall. Megan's piece was headlining in the foreign section. 'Good work, Ms Evens, I'm proud of you.' He rested his elbow on the desk, head supported in the crook of an expansive hand.

'Why thank you, Mr North. Praise indeed,' she retorted in her parlour maid voice. She was embarrassed by her filthy clothes, ashen skin. She glanced at her hands and noticed that there was dirt underneath her fingernails. His joviality unnerved her. The piece was written, recorded, uploaded, but she needed to be serious.

'New guy on Middle East thinks you're yummy.' Jack nodded towards the far end of the room where a fair haired boy of around twenty-one sat talking into his mulmed.

'Even like this?' She spread her arms, palms to the ceiling, feigning disbelief. She'd heard it all before, a thousand times. She was an odd looking child, then an ugly teenager who, at around seventeen years old, transformed into a quite beautiful thing. Observed separately, her constituent parts were all wrong, together they were stunning, she was told. Tall and thin, pale skin, black hair, wide-set grey eyes, like a fish, a long Roman nose and a top lip fuller than the bottom. 'Ugly-beautiful,' an ex-boyfriend said once, and Megan thought it a fair summary though she'd thumped him first.

'I told him he'd change his mind once he got to know you,' said Jack.

'Thanks a bunch.'

'Anyway, he's too young for you. You need a real man.'

She pulled a face.

Jack continued, 'A grown up. Someone who can control you. If such a person exists.'

'You've managed. Though you're not what I'd call a grown up.'

'I'm different.'

'Indeed you are.' She stared at her ring, the stone glinted, caught in the artificial light, hypnotizing her momentarily. 'Jack, can we talk?'

'I was about to ask if you fancied a drink or two at your favourite watering hole as soon as we can get away?'

'Privately.'

'I meant just the two of us.' He pointed to the window. 'This rabble's heading over to that law-abiding dump across the river.'

'If you're talking about a drink or two then a law-abiding establishment should be perfectly adequate, Mr North,' she replied tartly.

'I love it when you're cheeky, Ms Evens, but I always like the option of breaking the law even if I chose to abide by it. Damn these health fascists.'

'I've never known you to drink less than three measures in a sitting, wherever you are.'

'Would you care to join me or not?'

Silence. Then, 'I need to wash, change. I'm a sight,' she said.

'You look perfectly adequate.'

'I feel disgusting. I can still smell the fear on my skin.'

'Fear? You? Unusual.'

'Not lately. My numb button seems to have bust,' she whispered, afraid that someone might overhear.

'Maybe you need a break. Some home-bound stories. A holiday even.'

'Maybe. I can't remember the last time I visited Mum.' She lowered her gaze, fiddling with her ring, twisting it round and round her finger.

'So, what you do think, where shall we two meet?'

She didn't reply, lost in thought.

He leant in and said, 'We can meet near your flat. I'll take the tube to Highgate, it's only a couple of stops.' He stood to leave, tugging at the front of his jacket. 'I've a better idea, let's meet in Camden. Easy for both of us, and there are plenty of illegals there. I'll get some tobacco too.'

'A celebration indeed.'

'Only the best for you.'

'I've given up,' she replied apologetically, still playing with the ring. It had been her mother's, given to Megan when she left Wales. It was one of few possessions she treasured, though it was of little monetary value. A slim strip of silver with an oval disc on top, inlaid with a small emerald – green like the flag and fields of Wales, her mother had said. It was her good luck charm.

'I don't believe it. Megan Evens a non-smoker. Has the ministry of health and population protection got to you too? I'll believe it when I see it!'

It was dark when Megan left her flat. Tepid February rain ran down her sunken cheeks as she walked from the underground station. It was good to feel the rain again though she knew that in weeks' time, when it would still be falling, and falling, angry and wild, she would be cursing it like the rest of the population.

She headed north up the street, underneath the railway bridge where the pigeons sheltered from the weather and took a sharp left towards the lock. She snaked around the waterway until she came to the house. It had been empty for years, then squatted by impoverished survivors, and now it looked ordinary enough.

Enough not to raise suspicion. She pressed the intercom to the right of the brown door then waited for the 'hello'. When it came she repeated the password and a voice said, 'Hey, Megan. Good to see you. Bin a long time. I'll get your usual.'

'Don't,' she said, adding hastily, 'Thanks.'

The bar was at the back of the house in what was, to the untrained eye, a kitchen. Poky and dimly lit, it backed onto the canal. Groups of people sat huddled at fold-away tables cradling glasses of green, yellow and clear liquid. The air was thick with cigarette and candle wax smoke.

She remembered the first time she met Jack in the EBC bar. He was larger in the flesh than she'd expected. Most people looked bigger on screen but this wasn't true of Jack North. He stood over 190cm, only a few centimetres taller than her, slim-built without appearing light. Tanned and relaxed he appeared younger too. He'd held out a hand and said, 'Golly, you're tall.'

'So are you,' she'd replied. What a strange word to use – 'golly,' she'd thought.

'Enjoy it,' he'd said placing a glass in front of her. 'Last one of the day here in glorious, health conscious London.'

She'd laughed. They both knew the whereabouts of most of the illegal drinking dens in central London. Jack said he knew Megan was going to be a great journalist when she confided that she knew how and where to get hold of tobacco and copious amounts of alcohol. 'Your first investigative success, Ms Evens,' he'd said in his clipped public school educated tones.

'I always get what I want,' she'd replied.

Jack was nowhere to be seen in the kitchen. She popped her head round the door. Despite the disgusting weather he was sat outside on the only bench under a frayed canopy. The canal was fat with dirty water bursting from the concrete skin of the banks. The bar manager, Tay, a lanky guy in his mid-twenties, shuffled out and asked them what they wanted. Jack raised an eyebrow when Megan ordered a tonic water but said nothing.

'The air's too poisoned in there even for me,' he said as Tay left.

25

'You shouldn't have lit a tab out here. Too risky,' said Megan.

'This is not like you,' Jack said, staring at her. She dropped her head.

He spoke less harshly, 'I'm careful, Tay knows that. No one out tonight anyway. Bloody weather.'

'I heard that the flood centres are packed again. Most of the wash under water,' she said.

'Yeah, I was down there last week. Why these bloody people won't move to higher ground I'll never know,' he said, stubbing out the half smoked cigarette, looking up and down the canal.

'It's not that easy for some people. It's their home, family been there for generations...'

'Like your mother and her place.'

'Yes. Not that I know much about past Evens.' She smiled. It was true and it hadn't bothered her too much, until now. Family. History. She was more interested in history-in-the-making.

'How much does anyone really know about their family?' Jack said.

'Not much.' She stopped and said suddenly, 'Anyway, just as well for the authorities that they won't. There aren't enough new builds.'

Jack looked puzzled and then said, 'East Anglia, we're back to the floods. Can't keep up with you.'

They talked about the weather, the rioting in Shanghai, other newsworthy issues. It was displacement activity for Megan. She needed to tell Jack about her pregnancy but she didn't exactly want to. When he asked if she fancied accompanying him on a trip to America to interview residents of the former state of Florida she told him.

'I don't know what to say. If it was anyone else telling me this I'd think it was some kind of a joke.'

'But I'm not the joking kind.'

'Exactly.' He stared at her, until a drop of rain fell through the tarpaulin canopy and onto his face, distracting him. Though it wasn't cold, he pulled his thin jacket across his chest. The raindrop rolled down the side of his nose like a tear. There was a long pause, then he said, 'You're a bloody brilliant journalist, gifted even. You can't stop now, Megan. You have a brilliant career ahead – I can see books, awards...' he drew a billboard across the air with his hands.

'I'm not intending to give up completely. Once the baby is born and grown a little I'll work.'

'In Wales? You'll be bored stiff. Reporting on school sports days, local vineyard expansions, babies born in tractors on the way to the hospital. Don't go.'

'Remember the little people, you said. I'll be telling their stories. And there's Mum.'

'You could stay here. Get a nanny,' he said.

'A nanny that will do weeks or months at a time? Keep house, grow the food? On their own? Single parents join collectives, Jack, whether they like it or not.'

'Can't see you in one of those places. Move from foreign affairs then. Do national, political.'

'Too close. I need a complete change. It'll be hard enough without a constant reminder of what I've given up. I can't stand the authorities, you know that. I need to forget for a while.' Her voice broke.

'Need to forget? We don't forget. It's our job to make people remember.' He banged his palm on the bench. Megan thought it must have hurt. His colour rose as he spoke, and Megan thought he was angry with her. She thought she might cry. She never cried. She wondered what was happening to her and blamed the hormones racing around her body.

'Something happened. In Xinjiang. I can't do this anymore. Not forever, just for a while.'

'If you go it'll be impossible to get back in.' His voice was hard, it sounded like a threat.

'Never say never, Jack. You told me that.'

'What happened?' he demanded.

'You may have caught wind of it though it never made it onto the Christian news. A desert town, few civilians left, only the injured and interned remain. Many, many soldiers: British,

American, Russian, destroying everything that's left, which isn't much...'

'I see it.'

'A boy, maybe nine or ten, chubby, walks into the building that's laughingly called the hospital. I'm talking to an old man who's dying. Usual, awful stuff. He recognizes the boy, calls out his name – Lok – and the boy's eyes shimmer. Then soldiers pour in from everywhere, guns raised. The patients begin to cry, and I realize that the boy isn't fat, he's clothed in explosives. The sick and dying are praying to their God, and a European officer orders a private to shoot to kill. I look at the soldier, himself another boy, then the bomber, and I'm not sure that the soldier can do it. Time stops, my heart is racing and I think, shoot, shoot. Shoot him.' Megan felt the self-loathing rising again.

'So you're human,' said Jack.

'He didn't die straight away. He cried for his mother and asked for forgiveness. From whom I wasn't sure. Us? His God? His cell? I should have died there. We all should.'

Jack lifted his eyebrows. 'But you didn't. The boy was dead either way.'

'A child, Jack. A child. And I thought that's it – no way. And then, on the plane, coming home...'

'What?'

'I thought I was going to die again. And I thought this child is a gift.' She touched her stomach. 'As one soul departs another enters.'

'Christ. You sound like your mother.'

She cracked her knuckles. 'Maybe I'm more like her than I care to admit.'

'Crap. You're nothing like her. Your mind's made up?'

'I'll take the risk that I might never be able to get back in. That I'm condemning myself to confessional pieces about my life in the provinces at best.'

Tay shuffled onto the balcony, checking both ways, before pulling a bottle of bourbon from underneath his jumper. 'This just came in. Thought you might appreciate it.'

Megan shook her head.

'I'll have one,' said Jack.

Tay shrugged and poured him a glass, then breezed away.

Megan felt a pang. Would there be people like Tay in Bangor? God, she hoped so. There were a few odd balls at school. She hoped they hadn't changed, that they'd stayed, or returned.

'How long?' said Jack.

'What?'

'How long before you leave?'

'Long as possible. I need time before I go back. Long good-byes etcetera.'

'You're not sure.'

'I am.'

It was a long time before either of them spoke. Finally Jack said, 'I'll miss you.' Hands clasped he bowed his head as if in prayer, then reached across the bench and laid his hands over hers. It was strange to be held like this. He rarely touched her. When he lifted his head he looked almost lost and Megan saw the good-looking middle-aged man before her as a boy. His craggy features melted into smooth, shiny, freckled cheeks, the sandy locks intensified to a Titian blonde, the blue eyes expectant and innocent. She held tears at bay. They were not for him but for the loss of a way of life she had known and loved.

'I'll miss you too. But we'll still see each other. Maybe more – I won't be on the other side of the world. If you can bear to use your travel allowance on trips to Bangor that is…'

She was deceiving herself as much as him. Their lives would no longer be interlocked, interdependent. There would be no hour-long conversations in the middle of the night, discussing ideas, stories, life. No brief daily chats, no breaks in the canteen over rancid nettle tea, no drunken evenings, and cigarettes in secret corners of the city. She would miss him, more than he would miss her she imagined, but she never looked back, ever, and she would move on. She had to – she would have two souls depending on her soon.

*   *   *

29

Two weeks later she visited Wales to break the news to her mother.

'Stop crying. This is supposed to be good news, tidings of great joy and all that.'

'I am happy, Meg, I am. Happier than I've been since you… Oh, I don't know, happier than I've been in a long while.' Her mother wiped her eyes, a smile flickering behind her crumpled features. 'I can't believe it. Me, a grandmother, a nana. I never thought it would happen. If you had children at all, I thought it would be later in life. And that I would be dead and gone by then.'

Sat on the enormous sofa, spiky black against cream, Megan felt like the figure in a sketch on Elizabeth's bedroom wall. It had been drawn by Elizabeth's mother during a period inspired by Aubrey Beardsley. Fiddling with a hole in the upholstery she grinned at Elizabeth. It felt good to see her mother's face fill with delight. It was a face that looked as if it rarely smiled.

Elizabeth looked rusty, a little dented. She had enjoyed rude health for many years but there were signs that this would not last much longer. She was an old woman; she didn't move so fast, the arthritis in her knees slowing her down on even the driest of days. Megan wanted to care for her. But she was under no illusion, it would be hard to adjust. Bangor was provincial, quiet, the career opportunities limited, the people less sophisticated than Megan was used to.

As if reading her thoughts Elizabeth said, 'Won't you miss London though, Meg? Life is quiet here. Nothing much happens. Your friends? Work?'

'I don't have so many friends in London…'

'You never spent much time there,' Elizabeth interrupted.

'No. And quiet is good. I am grateful that I was born here and not in some war-torn nation where starvation and danger are never far away. People moan that life's not easy here, with the oil and food shortages, the flooding, our inept coalition, but we're lucky, Mum. We've never known disaster.'

Megan gasped and put her hand to her mouth. She regretted

her final comment. Her mother froze, eyes unblinking, pupils dilated. She saw the distant, veiled look in Elizabeth's eyes as she waved her hand dismissing the oncoming apology. The curtain was descending. It fell whenever the past, and Elizabeth's past in particular, was mentioned.

When Megan first learnt about 2015 she was fascinated, as most children were. On returning from school one spring afternoon, aged ten, she'd asked her mother what it was like to live through such a time. Elizabeth would not be drawn. She knelt down and gripped Megan's shoulders, gaze locked. She said, 'You can never understand. Never. I hope you never do. I hope you never have to go through what I did.' And then, like a snail threatened by inquisitive fingers, Elizabeth withdrew into her shell. She frightened Megan. Years went by before Megan asked again, only to receive the same fierce reply, the same withdrawal.

'I'll never understand 'cos you'll never let me,' she'd said at fourteen. In the end Megan stopped asking, though she read about it night after night, wondering what it must have been like to lose so much.

She loved her mother, but sometimes she felt that a part of her was missing. The hole wasn't created because she had not known her father – he died before she was born – but because she knew so little about him, and her mother refused to talk about him. Her father was a mystery, and this lent him a weight, and importance, that Megan felt he probably didn't deserve. Megan did not want her child growing up with a similar sense of loss, or a misguided impression of his or her father.

Megan knew her mother was close to tears again. And though Elizabeth didn't like apologies she was going to get one regardless. 'God, I'm sorry, Mum. I meant my generation not yours.'

Her mother ignored her. She touched the silver cross resting on her collarbone and said, 'Well, there's lots here, especially for children. I had an amazing childhood here.' And she looked at Megan.

'As I did,' Megan said. She saw her mother's eyes mist over and added, 'If only I'd realized how precious it was I might have appreciated you a little more. I was an ungrateful, spoilt, little witch.'

Elizabeth shifted in her chair, an upright leather armchair. Megan glanced at the elephants on the mantelpiece, their dark surfaces smooth and shiny; she longed to hold one in the palm of her hand as she did as a girl, feel the weight and comfort of it.

'Why don't you live here, Meg? When you come back.' There was ill-concealed desperation in Elizabeth's tone.

'At Tŷ Mawr?'

Her mother's eyes wandered to the mantelpiece. 'Why not? Some animals live together in family units all their lives.'

'Aren't elephants led by the oldest matriarch?' She laughed.

'You can have your own life. It's so big here, cariad. I rattle around this old house, it makes me feel so small, so useless. If you came back it would have a purpose, I would have a purpose.'

'I'm not sure, Mum. It's been a long time. We're both used to our own company. I'll get somewhere close by.'

'Nothing's cheap, Meg. It'll save you money.'

'What about a baby? Crying at all hours.' Megan wondered how she would cope, never mind her mother. Would she be able to block it out like the sound of bullets, bombs?

'I'll help out. Look after the babe.'

'Mum. The idea is that by moving back I can help you, not the other way round.'

'Then you'll move in? I'm a useless old woman these days mostly.'

Megan knew her mother wasn't useless, but she was old: almost seventy. She stared at Elizabeth and thought of the years she'd spent raising her, the work, the worry and heartache. It was payback time.

'That's not quite what I meant, but if you like, yes. The stairs must be hard enough. And the maintenance, the cleaning, the gardening… I never understood why you stayed here.'

Megan knew it wasn't easy for Elizabeth, living alone. She had no one aside from her daughter.

'Tŷ Mawr reminds me of you. Our life together.'

32

'And your mother, of course.'

There was a long pause before Elizabeth replied. 'Yes, it reminds me of Mam. Come home, Megan.'

'I will, Mum, I will.'

Chapter Three

It was August when Megan made the move back to Bangor. The blackberries were fat and shiny in the hedgerows, the lawns parched the colour of hay. The town was dusty and airless, shut up for the season, like an empty room, furniture covered in heavy sheets. The straights were still like a pond.

On the train Megan travelled with only a neat suitcase for company. She had sold what little furniture she had in her flat to the incoming tenants, and a couple of boxes of personal possessions, trinkets from her sojourns abroad, had been sent on. She rested her cheek in her palm and watched London fly by her eyes and into her past. She was unsentimental about her flat, she'd spend so little time in it, but the city had a pull.

When Megan first moved to the capital in 2038 she felt dwarfed by the buildings with their gargantuan stone shadows, by the people with their purpose and glamour. She was just eighteen. She remembered her first sighting of EBC tower. A monolithic glass needle, erect and defiant, it had been home to the dominant media empires of the past fifty years. The communications district sat in the bend of the river Thames, and, as a whole, was something of a ghost town. The population of London stood at five million, huge compared to Bangor's six and a half thousand, but still the size and scale, the ambition of the area, highlighted the lack of people on its streets and walkways. It had the look of an abandoned ant nest. But not in the tower. Staff buzzed, like worker bees, as she'd made her way to the office of the foreign affairs editor on the nineteenth floor.

As she stared out of the train window she wondered if it was the place itself that she would miss, or what it represented. Freedom, experience, anonymity, adulthood. Jack. There were so many places in the city associated with Jack. The EBC tower itself, the office, the bar. The day she returned from the Arctic assignment he sat on the edge of her desk and said, 'I never saw you as a 'share your byline' sort Megan. Hell, you even take your own pictures.'

'Hisham was my ticket in. You know that.'

The Blackfriar pub on the north side of the bridge. Jack rolling a scrap of paper between his fingers – he craved cigarettes when he drank – head down, intent on the action, his fringe obscuring his face.

The illegal den in Camden Lock. She remembered Jack's warning. 'He'll never love you enough.'

'I am not in love with Hisham Abdullah,' she'd said. And Jack'd smiled his lop-sided grin.

She was reminded of Hisham, though he'd never visited her in London. It was his fault she had to leave; she bit her lip.

The journey took less than two hours. Megan wished it was longer. She could have travelled all day and all night. When the train pulled into Bangor station only Megan and one other passenger disembarked. She stood on the platform and watched the train slide into the black hole of the tunnel cut into the rock, gathering speed for the final leg of its journey to Holyhead on the island of Anglesey. A prevailing westerly wind rattled round her ears. She decided to take a bus to Tŷ Mawr.

The municipal bus weaved its way from the station, stealing through the city. The roads were more or less empty of anything other than delivery vans, buses, state-run taxis and a handful of reckless individuals using their cars and precious mileage allowances. Others sailed past on their bikes. Megan looked for familiar faces but didn't see any.

She shuffled in her seat, uncomfortable in the heat with her ripe, heavy body. Part of her wished she had ordered a taxi but the slow ride to Tŷ Mawr gave her a chance to readjust. It was the strange little city of her childhood – if not exactly ugly, certainly not picturesque, unlike the surrounding area of mountains, falls, moorland, horseshoe-shaped passes and curling stone walls. It was a blemish in an otherwise beautiful face. It seemed so small after the drama and grandeur of London, but so comforting and familiar. This is where my roots are, she thought. Perhaps this where I belong after all.

The bus glided past the brown stone university, past the cathedral tucked in among the plain grey slabs of the shopping centre, the theatre Megan visited every Christmas as a girl to watch the pantomime. The hum of the bus resonated through her bones. There was nothing new, all the buildings were old, and some still stood empty. Nothing had been built in over thirty years.

The bus moved dreamily on, dropping passengers like trees shed leaves, leaving the town behind. Megan saw the vineyards she worked in over two school summer holidays, the farm where she picked sweetcorn. The bus climbed up the hill, groaning as it took the sharp curve at the brow, the smell of burning rape seed oil pouring from the rear, and then, there it was – Tŷ Mawr – looming in the distance, a grey obelisk. The guardian of her childhood. The house that reminded her of her roots, that even looked like her: tall, dark, out of place. The house with arched front windows, pointed rooms in the roof, curved chimney stacks standing guard over solar panels, and purple clematis weaving round the door frame.

Tŷ Mawr changed colour with the weather. Slate grey and shiny in the rain, lighter but more foreboding when dry. It was built by a Welshman who made a fortune during the early days of the Californian gold rush. He died soon after his return to the homeland from a sickness contracted in the west. Too expensive for the locals, a succession of childless foreigners lived in the house before it stood empty for decades. Some said that Tŷ Mawr was haunted but Elizabeth said that her father, Megan's maternal grandfather, a man she never met, believed that the house rejected the English visitors. It was waiting for a Welshman, and his family, and once they arrived the house would be happy again, he'd said. For him, Tŷ Mawr represented success, a generosity of spirit, a pathway to a new life.

She felt herself filling with a sense of belonging, and a deep, irrational affection. This is me, she thought. The house, the city, the country – they were part of her; she had forgotten it a while, that was all. It was like sliding into an old pair of shoes:

comfortable, moulded to every contour, even if she wasn't sure they suited her any more. She thought she might cry.

The bus stop was only ten metres from the door but the driver insisted on stopping right in front of the house.

'You take care, love,' he said as Megan clambered down the steps. 'Precious load you've got there.'

'I will,' she said, waving.

She stood at the door, hand on the brass knocker and took a deep breath. She had returned home.

'Come in, come in, cariad,' Elizabeth said, flinging open the door and waving her inside. Megan hadn't had chance to knock.

'I heard the bus! You remember how the house shakes when the buses go by? The foundations are weakening, one of these days it'll crumble, I swear it will.' Her mother stood on the doorstep in an ill-fitting floral shirt and wide-legged trousers. Her wavy, grey hair was pinned high on her head. Rogue strands broke free from a tortoiseshell clasp, giving her the dishevelled appearance of a farmer's wife. She was as wide as she was high.

Seeing her mother there, in the doorframe, Megan was overcome with emotion; she wanted to tell her how much she loved her, but couldn't. They simply didn't talk like that to each other. 'Of course I remember, Mum.' Megan started to lift her bag over the threshold.

'Let me, let me. In your condition!' She grabbed the bag from Megan, hoisted it over the draught excluder and wheeled it into the hall before turning and throwing her arms round her daughter.

'Oh, Meg, it's lovely to have you back, lovely.' She squeezed Megan tight, and Megan held on, relishing their closeness, though she thought it must be an uncomfortable position for her mother, given the difference in their height and the enormous swell of her belly.

Elizabeth stood back and beamed. She went to stroke Megan's stomach. Megan recoiled.

'I'm sorry, Meg. I should have asked.'

Megan's hands covered her face. 'I didn't mean it.' She reached for her mother, but she withdrew. 'You know how it is. It must have been worse when you had me. Strangers wanting to touch you all the time. Even now some people don't ask.'

'Come on, let's go through. We can't stand here all day! I've prepared some tea, it's a bit early for supper. Your favourite. Bread and cheese.'

'Isn't bread difficult to come by? It is in London. The wheat harvests have been terrible. Unless you've changed your mind about all the GM stuff.'

'Heavens, no! I will not touch that stuff. The bread was difficult to get, but I have contacts.' She tapped the side of her nose theatrically. 'Only the best for you two. Come on.'

They ate at the wooden table sitting under the apple trees near the bottom of the garden, the gnarled boughs and tatty leaves providing welcome shade from the sun. Elizabeth fussed, as she had always done, encouraging Megan to eat up.

'Have an elderflower cordial, Meg?'

Megan nodded, and leant over to top up her tumbler from the glass jug.

'Let me, cariad. Let me.'

'Mum, I'm pregnant, not disabled. I can do it.'

Megan wondered if her mother could let her be. Treat her like the adult she was rather than the eighteen-year-old girl she'd been when she left home. If they could live together like two adults house sharing, rather than mother and daughter. Is it ever possible to stop being a mother, she thought.

'I thought you'd like to sleep in the spare room tonight. We can choose your room proper tomorrow. I've made up the bed,' Elizabeth said.

'I figured I'd be in the attic room, Mum. There's the little bathroom next door, and we'll have some space from each other.'

'But it's so cramped up there, Meg. What about baby?'

Megan laughed. 'It'd be good for it to be away from you. It'll be tricky enough with one of us crotchety from sleep deprivation, never mind both of us.'

'Oh, it'll never do.'

'It's fine, Mum. Stop fussing.' She took another piece of

bread, the upturned side already hard, toasted in the afternoon sun.

Elizabeth shifted in her seat. 'Let's decide tomorrow, Meg. No squabbling. Let's enjoy the rest of the day. Have some more cheese.' She offered the plate. Megan smiled and shook her head. A fly landed on her arm and she swatted it away. She hated insects.

They sat in the shade for hours. Reading, enjoying the hum of the grasshoppers. Megan loved the garden as a child, even the old leylandii trees at the top end. She still did.

That night Megan lay on the single bed in the attic room gazing at the blue-black sky through the roof window. She had considered setting up the telescope that sat on a tripod in the corner, but decided her legs were too tired to support her any longer. The weight of the baby made it difficult to lie on her back, but she needed to take in the stars. The soft mattress folded up at her sides, enveloping her. She imagined her mother lying in the room, and her mother before her, and lots of other Evens.

After breakfast Elizabeth insisted Megan settled back home properly. 'You'll have this room,' she said, standing between the doors to the two double bedrooms on the second floor, pointing to the larger room.

'But it has so many memories for you, Mum.'

The bedroom had been Elizabeth's as a girl, she'd told Megan. And it had been hers when she moved back to Tŷ Mawr as an adult, just before Megan was born.

'I insist. These two rooms will be perfect for you and baby. I'll move down to the mezzanine, to the room with the en-suite. That way I won't disturb you at night,' she said.

Elizabeth had suffered periods of insomnia ever since Megan could remember. As a child when she woke from dreams or nightmares to hear the house moving, she would call out for her mother, crying that ghosts were walking on the landing. So many people, long dead and gone, had occupied the house it was natural that a girl with a vivid imagination would picture such things.

Elizabeth would say, 'It's me, cariad, me. The only ghost here is me, and I'm definitely of the friendly variety.'

'Surely it'll be us disturbing you, Mum? Babies can be very noisy.'

'A change of space will be good for me. Let's look to the future, Meg.'

'If it makes you happy.' Megan didn't want to argue, and the rooms were lovely, large and airy. Room to spread out in, get messy.

Megan went to get her bag from the top floor, and other boxes dumped in the cellar, while Elizabeth packed up her possessions, trinkets, photographs, jewellery and other items found on dressing table tops. When Megan returned there were two large boxes behind the door.

'One's to go to my new room, the other we'll store in the cellar,' announced Elizabeth. But the boxes were too heavy for Megan and her mother to haul down three flights of stairs.

'Let's empty them and transfer the contents into four smaller boxes,' Megan suggested. 'That way carrying them won't be too difficult.' Megan was pleased that the opportunity to rifle through some of her mother's private possessions presented itself so naturally. As a child she was barred from her mother's room, and after an ill-fated sojourn when she left an incriminating doll's shoe on her mother's dressing table, Elizabeth had a lock put on the door, and wore the small, intricately decorated metal key on a chain around her neck with her crucifix.

Initially, there was little of interest in the boxes: old costume jewellery, fussy ornaments, some romantic fiction, knitting magazines. Nothing worth hiding or protecting from small fingers and big eyes. Bundles of postcards and letters provided padding, and Megan longed to flick through some of them, though she knew Elizabeth would never agree to such a request.

'I didn't think people wrote letters even in your day, Mum.'

'They're Mam's, mostly, not mine,' said Elizabeth stuffing them into a corner of a box.

Then one object caught Megan's eye: a ceramic heart with a

faded pink rose painted on one side. The rose reminded Megan of the flowers on the walls of the attic room. She wondered which came first: the wallpaper or the strange heart with the gold thread handle. It looked extremely old.

'What's this?' asked Megan.

'It's called a pomander. An old-fashioned thing, to hang in wardrobes amongst clothes to keep them smelling fresh,' Elizabeth said, reaching over to take it from Megan's hands.

'How do you replace the fragrance?'

'You can't. It's why it stinks now.'

'How old is it?' said Megan.

'It belonged to my mother's mother, your great grandmother. She was fond of roses. When she died, my mother, Hannah, planted four bushes at the back of the patio in her memory.'

'They're still there.'

'Yes. Thorny old things.'

Elizabeth turned the pomander in her palm. 'It's not worth anything but I can't bring myself to throw it away.'

'Then you mustn't. Keep it.' Delighted that Elizabeth had revealed some family history, and sensing a rare opportunity to find out more, Megan pushed on. 'The rose reminds me of those on the wallpaper upstairs.'

'So it should. Hannah decorated the attic in her mother's honour. Pink, cream and white soft furnishing and a floral wallpaper chosen by a young me on all four walls. The paper was never covered over,' said Elizabeth, carelessly throwing the pomander in the box destined for the cellar.

'Why don't you keep it out? It's precious to you. All those memories.'

'It smells. Musty, ancient, decrepit. The stench reminds me of death. Too close for comfort.'

'You're seventy. Not ninety.'

Elizabeth ignored her. 'Some of my tops stink thanks to this. I don't even like it. Never did. I'm not fond of roses, they only look good in June, and the thorns are vicious. As to the heart shape, Lord!' Megan could feel her mother drifting away again. Closing the door to the past.

'But that's not the point. It was your mother's, your grand-mother's. It's your connection to her. It doesn't matter that it's ugly.'

'The past is the past. Over, done with, I must look to the future these days. I don't need ugly little keepsakes to remember Mam by. She's in my heart. Always will be,' she said, busying herself moving things from one box to another, quickly, without thought.

Megan returned to sifting through the box. She pulled out a sepia toned photograph of a woman who looked like Hannah and a tall man in a suit whose face had been spoilt by a stain, a raindrop or spilt drink perhaps. She wiped away dust with her finger, and realized that the man's face had been scratched away. 'But things help us remember. Prompt the details, spark other, faded, memories. We need to talk of our memories, to keep them alive.'

She lifted the image to her face, studying it closely. The man had his arm around Hannah's waist and there was an intimacy between them that Megan hadn't noticed at first. Elizabeth said nothing, rummaging without purpose.

'Who are they? This looks a bit like you, and a bit like your mum, but I don't recognize the guy. He's too tall to be your dad, if I'm remembering right. Like the one in this bedroom when I was little.' Megan was talking to herself as much as Elizabeth. She was intrigued, though not especially so. She was interested in the vaguely dispassionate way most people are in their distant ancestry, those characters unknown to them personally.

'It is Mam. Hannah...'

'My grandmother.'

'It's a lovely photograph of her. She was an attractive woman, even when she was older. I am like her, a tiny bit. I'm a skewed version.'

Megan looked at her mother and back to the picture. She could see the similarity but disagreed that Hannah was the more attractive. She was certainly more polished than Megan had ever seen Elizabeth, but there was something slightly odd about her. As if she was wearing someone else's nose. Megan kept these thoughts to herself and turned her attention to the man. She said again, 'This isn't your dad. Who is he?'

'I didn't say it wasn't my da.'

'You didn't have to. It can't be. Too tall, too skinny. Who rubbed his face out? Hannah after a row?'

Elizabeth laughed, and Megan thought she detected a slight rancour.

'I did. It was me. I didn't like him,' Elizabeth said.

'So who was he?'

'A friend of my mother's.' Elizabeth continued to move things from the large box into a smaller one.

'Why didn't you like him?'

'I can't remember now. It was a long time ago, Meg.'

'But you hatcd him so much you scratched his face out? With a knife from the looks of things.'

'A compass as a matter of fact,' Elizabeth corrected, always the teacher she couldn't help herself.

Megan thought it odd that her mother remembered the instrument she used to deface the image of this stranger, but not one reason why she disliked him so much. And why had she kept the photograph? She was withholding information. Megan knew her mother didn't like to dwell on unsavoury behaviour, to rake over former actions of her own and others in an attempt to rationalize, understand and excuse. She disapproved of therapy. 'No one ever got over trauma thanks to talking about it,' she'd said. 'Time cures, if it can, and some things we never get over.'

Questions whirled in Megan's head. 'Where was your dad, my grandfather, when this was taken? Was this man a lover? Why did you keep it?' The words were out before Megan could censor them. They weren't loaded in any way. After all Hannah meant nothing to Megan and neither did Robert. They were abstract figures, important only for their influence on Elizabeth.

Elizabeth dropped a hairbrush with a ceramic back. 'Good heavens no! Da was dead, Lord rest his soul.'

'I always thought your parents died within months of each other,' Megan said.

'No, no. Mam survived. She died later, years later. After you were born, though you were tiny. You won't remember her.'

'I don't.'

'Such a shame. You would have loved a nana, wouldn't you?' Elizabeth's voice caught.

'What you never have, you never miss,' Megan said, though privately she wondered if this was true. 'So Hannah met this guy when you two lived here together, after… everything, you know.'

'Yes.'

'Before you met my dad?' Megan scratched her stomach. She felt as if her skin would split apart, like an over ripe fig.

'Yes.' Elizabeth turned away.

It should have been Mum first, thought Megan. No wonder she resented this tall stranger, this interloper, imposter to her beloved father's throne. Megan ached to know more, but she held her tongue. She held the picture, resting it, along with her swollen belly, in her lap.

There was an awkward silence. Then Elizabeth picked up another treasured object. 'Would you look at this! How lovely is she here?' She held up a photograph in an ornate gilt frame. Hannah and Robert on their wedding day. Megan's maternal grandparents. She took it from Elizabeth, studied it and then handed both pictures back to Elizabeth who went to place them in one of the small boxes.

'It's a beautiful picture, Mum. It's the one from the wall, isn't it?' She looked up at the empty space. A faint brown outline stained the wall. 'It seems naked without it.'

'Yes, it's beautiful. She was beautiful. He was beautiful. Lovely, lovely Da.' Elizabeth's voice began to break.

'It should stay on display. Why pack it away?' Megan said.

'My room's too cluttered already. This place is packed with junk.'

'There's here.' Megan corrected herself. 'My bedroom. I've virtually no personal stuff. It's going to look so bland. Let it stay in its place. To be seen, not buried away, out of sight. It'll be something I can tell the baby about in years to come. Family history.'

Elizabeth looked unsure.

'I'd like that.'

'Very well.' Elizabeth closed the lid on the box.

The pomander lay on top of the postcards and letters. Megan picked up the framed photograph and hung it back on the wall.

Later, when she'd finished sorting out the room, making the bed, stacking her books, and hanging her clothes in the built-in wardrobe, Megan lay on the bed wondering if this would ever feel like her room. Despite the open windows it still smelt of her mother, her perfume lingered, the scent of her clung to the mattress. Megan felt like a child again, and she closed her eyes and drifted. As she sank into sleep the door creaked open. Megan jumped, sat up, startled. Oblivious, Elizabeth waddled across the carpet and placed a vase of flowers on the mantelpiece.

'God, Mum. You gave me the fright of my life.'

'I'm sorry, Meg. I should have knocked. I just thought you might like something to brighten up the room.' She fanned out the flowers, rearranging them. The green of the leaves picked out the colours in the tiles surrounding the iron fireplace. The design was elaborate and fussy, very Victorian, and not at all to Megan's taste.

'I guess we'll both have to work at changing our ways.'

'We'll manage.'

'The flowers are lovely, thank you.'

'You get some rest now. I'll wake you for tea.'

When Megan woke up she didn't know where she was. As the room came into focus she saw the picture on the wall next to the window overlooking the garden. It drew her in again. She studied it, fascinated. The colours were washed out, the faces yellowed. It looked hundreds of years old, not seventy-odd. Hannah wore a floor length cotton dress with a high neck and large frill round the hem. A floppy straw hat framed her straight, dark hair.

I must get my hair from her, my grandmother, Megan thought.

In her right hand Hannah held a white parasol. Robert looked uncomfortable in his brown flared trouser suit, large collared cream shirt and wide tie. They looked so happy. So naïve and expectant. Megan couldn't imagine such an innocent age.

Chapter Four

When Ceri had called suggesting the trip Megan had not long put Cerdic to bed. Her son had kept her at his bedside longer than usual, chattering about the story she'd read. Elizabeth was pottering in the garden and Megan had switched on the mulmed and demanded the news channel. As the footage of the major stories of the day flickered onto the screen she was caught by an image of an old woman perched on a pile of rubble holding a baby.

Sitting on what had only recently been her home the woman rocked back and forth. Disbelief filled her eyes. Megan didn't know if the woman rocked to comfort the child or because of the shock. Megan couldn't tell if the child was alive or not. A leg dangled from a filthy blanket. Tiny toes, encrusted with dirt and dust. It looked peaceful, as if it was sleeping, it might have been, and Megan mused that this creature knew nothing of this momentous event. As a child and an adult he or she would only hear of this day through others: the day that altered the course of its life. Father, mother, sister, brother would be words only, belonging to others. Maybe a few charred images retrieved from the wreckage of a former life, an alternative future. The old woman was bewildered, ancient. Eyes misty with tears and cataracts.

Megan was entranced and knocked by an unexpected feeling of loss. Not only for the woman, and the baby, but for her former life. She imagined how she might have covered such a story. She was obsessed by survivors, how they coped. How people dealt with the pain, the anger, the guilt and the sense of hope that emerges after long periods in the wilderness. She wondered why Elizabeth couldn't, or wouldn't, speak of her loss.

The soft purr of her mobile had broken her reverie. She ordered the mulmed to turn down the volume. It was Ceri, a close friend, and she was fed up of work, work, work. Not getting the time to spend with her son, jealous that her husband stayed at home while she earned. Megan scolded herself for her self-indulgence and self-pity.

She was lucky. The financial freedom to work part-time, to have her mother's help, to take part in her son's growing up.

'I thought – sod it, I'm taking the day off, I deserve it. Let them try and stop me. I work bloody hard for those gits. Besides I'll have to do the work when I get back. They'll not get anyone else to help out, oh no,' Ceri ranted, half in jest. 'So how about it, Tuesday next week?' she continued.

'I'm not sure. Cerdic gets so tired, and if I'm remembering correctly the walk to the beach is long. All those dunes. He struggles with distances, walking, really.'

'You could bring the buggy, Meg. I'll help you push it uphill.'

'He's nearly four, Ceri. He'd hate that. He's not daft.'

'We could say it's for the stuff. We could even put all the gear in it at first. Tip it out when he's shattered. Christ, it'll probably be useful anyway. It's a bastard lugging it all!'

Megan felt exhausted just thinking about it. 'I'm not sure…'

'Come on, Meg. We can talk.'

'Okay, you win. I've never taken Cerdic there. He'll love it. And we take the buggy, right?' said Megan.

'Right. That's settled then. I'll get a crowd together. And how are you, Meg?'

'Fed up.'

'Work?'

'What else? You know how it gets on my tits from time to time.'

'I sure do.'

'Reading how dreadful it is when the floods come, the stink of rape seed oil on Anglesey when a south westerly wind blows. My boss yelling at me that the headlines just aren't dramatic enough. I want to scream "Shut up. What have we got to bleat about? Try feeding kids in a conflict zone where rain hasn't fallen for three years and the soil is as hard and barren as granite. When your home has been reduced to rubble. When falling in love with the wrong guy means you face execution. We're lucky. Fucking lucky. We've got nothing to bleat about, not really." '

'I feel guilty for moaning now,' Ceri said.

'Please don't. I didn't mean to make you feel bad. We're British. We have to moan, it's part of us. In our DNA.'

'How is Cerdic? Have you been back to the doctor's?'

'I'm always hassling them. But they're good…'

'At fobbing you off…'

'It's hard to prove anything at the moment, he's so young. It could all be developmental.'

'He's happy and bright. That's the main thing.'

'It is. And he can jump now. Hop a little and run a bit too. He'll be fine, fine.' Megan was aware that she was attempting to convince herself more than her friend.

'Of course he will. They're all different that's all. He'll do things in his own time. He tickles me, Megan, that funny little walk of his. Tiptoe, tiptoe. Like he wants to surprise you, leap up on you,' she said. Then, almost to herself, 'Aren't they gorgeous?'

'They are. I'll see you next week. Something to look forward to.' And with that Megan logged off.

Ceri had been Megan's best friend at high school. In truth her only friend. They did everything together and once they even shared a boyfriend, giggling uncontrollably as they compared notes on his dry, characterless kissing. When Megan moved away they lost touch despite the tears and promises at the leaving ball. Ceri came to the capital once but didn't enjoy herself one iota.

'I'm just too Welsh, Meg. Like a fish out of water here. We'll see each other when you visit home,' she'd said as Megan waved her off at the train station. But they never did. Their lives went in different directions and they fell off each other's radar. Ceri continued to work at the vineyard, picking, bottling and labelling. Megan found it hard to believe that Ceri could be content with such mundane work and when she heard that Ceri was having a baby, at twenty-one, Megan realized just how far apart they had grown. The thought of being tied down like that was inconceivable; there was so much she wanted to do.

But now she realized that achievement comes in a variety of forms. Cerdic's first smile, first word, first step, were precious, unforgettable moments, no less wonderful than the day she saw her name in print for the first time, the moment she secured an important story. Better perhaps. Different. After all, she had pictured her name on a byline, a photo caption, for years. But she had never imagined the delight and pride she might feel the day her son rolled over, from back to front, and shot a gummy grin at his astonished mother. When Megan remembered how she had dismissed Ceri's choice – that of motherhood and staying put – as inferior to her own, she was ashamed. And it was Ceri Megan sought out first on her return to Wales.

Ceri worked at the same vineyard, but she was marketing director now and it was thanks to her innovations that the organisation enjoyed an almost unrivalled reputation. Her eldest son, who she raised alone after his father ran off to join the army, was approaching his eleventh birthday, and she had a two-year-old boy with a husband she met on a business trip. Her hair was still bleached blonde, though expensively done now, she still squeezed her curvaceous, compact body into impossibly tight clothes and her laugh could still shatter glass. Like an anchor with a long chain Ceri secured Megan whenever she felt herself drift, without ever restricting her, without asking her to be someone she was not.

Megan told the mulmed to close and went to ask Elizabeth if she would like to come on the trip. There would be plenty of room, and she might enjoy the journey; it was a picturesque route and it would be a leisurely one. Ceri's city car was larger than usual, with seating for six, but it ran on hydrogen and was slower than oil-driven vehicles. Elizabeth did not answer immediately. Instead she grabbed a piece of chalk and set about drawing up a list of what Megan ought to take on the blackboard in the kitchen. Megan took this as a yes and smiled as she reminded Elizabeth that Harlech was not the other end of universe.

'Not to you, Meg. Not to you. But most of us haven't travelled like you have. Not in a long time, cariad.'

Elizabeth's enthusiasm and excitement were infectious. Megan couldn't shake the feeling that it would be a day to remember.

*   *   *

The children marched into the retreating sun. In their hands they carried an assortment of buckets, spades, driftwood, and bedraggled, sand coated toys. Like ants they marched uniformly, in single file, the line broken only occasionally at the rear by the toddlers who struggled to keep up, all big heads, short legs and rounded bellies. Bursts of lopsided jogging and on they went towards the rock pools.

It was a baking hot day. Megan felt sure she couldn't remember a hotter summer. At twenty-seven degrees the day was cool compared to July's temperatures when the gauge hit thirty so often that it no longer warranted a mention on the news. It was an extraordinary summer. Her first glimpse of the golden sands running along the coast like a highway was magnificent; she wanted to run across the coarse yellow dust and throw herself at the black green sea, immerse herself in the fluid world of the deep. Another country. The sea was her first experience of otherness, of exploring a different world.

The tide was out, and miles of undulating damp sand, the colour of tea, spread out before the picnic party gathered in front of the dunes. The adults lounged, dozing, reading or taking in the view. Old windbreakers and faded parasols offered relief from the sun. Megan huddled in a patch of shade, wrapped in a towel, knees to her chest, dark shades obscuring half her face, a wide brimmed straw hat flopping over her forehead. Flinging off her hat, she grabbed the thick plait of her hair and pulled it over her head and face to air her neck.

'How long is your hair, Meg!' Ceri said.

'Too long. I need to get it cut. It's finding the time,' Megan replied, throwing the plait back. It fell with a satisfying thud.

'When was the last time you went to a hairdresser?'

'Oh, I don't know. Cerdic was a baby. Weeny. Maybe a year old?'

'Meg! That's years ago.' Ceri took care of herself and Megan knew that her friend would be horrified at her lackadaisical attitude to her appearance.

'I've chopped the ends off myself a couple of times.'

'You're unbelievable!' Ceri pushed Megan's shoulder. 'Doesn't look bad for a home job, though,' she added.

Next to the women was a pile of empty water carriers and apple cores half buried in the sand. Megan gazed out to sea watching sailing boats gliding on the horizon, eyes darting periodically in the direction of the children, and her son in particular. It was a typical beach scene, like a picture in a holiday brochure.

Sun block dribbled from Megan's sweltering flesh. She watched it forming a puddle of milky liquid at her feet before the sand absorbed it, leaving no trace. She looked into the hazy sky, ruminating why humankind feels the urge to leave something behind, something to be remembered by.

'I saw Hisham on the mulmed last night. In Tajikistan again,' Ceri said. Elizabeth was asleep and Ceri was taking the opportunity to delve into taboo areas.

'Good for you.' Megan stuck her tongue out at her friend. 'And before you ask, no I haven't heard from him.'

Ceri hadn't asked in many months so Megan figured she was due another interrogation. In an impulsive moment Megan told Ceri the identity of Cerdic's father. No one else in Wales knew. At least not to Megan's knowledge. Ceri skirted round the subject many times and eventually tempted Megan into disclosure with a reciprocal promise to reveal the father of her son, Dafydd, one of the best kept secrets in Bangor, she claimed. Megan already knew. Most people in the community did though they pretended not to.

'Do you think he thinks about his son, his child? What he's doing, what he looks like, his favourite game? I don't think I could bear not to know,' Ceri said.

'You're nosy, that's why.'

'So are you! You get paid for being a nosy parker, Meg.' Ceri poked Megan's upper arm.

'Not anymore. I'm a provincial sub, remember? I pick the fat off others' stories. It's a miracle there's anything left half the time. Making something of nothing. That's what most of the journalists do here.'

'Oh you're harsh, Megan Evens!' Ceri laughed.

Megan picked at her feet. 'He does know what he looks like.'

Ceri dropped the book in her right hand. 'Really. How come?'

'I sent some pictures to his Parisian apartment when Cerdic was three or four months old. I thought that despite what happened, his final, disgusting act of cowardice, the unsaid, ugly words, he might like to see his son. Have a memory. An impression.' She looked at the sea.

'Did you hear back from him?'

'Two years later. It took him that long to find the courage to write. Fucking coward. He thanked me for the photographs and went on to say that his father had been a lousy one, and he knew that he too would be rubbish at this most important of jobs.'

'I bet he would have been,' Ceri snorted. 'I can't believe you've kept this to yourself. I think I'd have exploded. You're such a dark horse.'

'You just can't keep anything to yourself, that's all.'

'You're right, I can't. But still, four years! Anyway, what did he say?'

'He asked me to tell Cerdic, sometime in the future, that his father died when he was young. "Tell him I was handsome, brave and clever. And that I love him very much. This way he will never face disappointment in the way I did, baby. He will never be crushed by the knowledge that his father is a useless shit. This is my gift to my son." Or words to that effect. I'll never forget the sentiment. I wobbled for a minute or two, unsure if the dominant emotion was sadness or rage. Which to choose.' She pushed her toes into the sand. Hard, forceful.

'You settled for angry?'

'I did. It's not like I was asking him to look after Cerdic or anything. Love me, like I'd loved him. Just write, talk, visit Cerdic occasionally. Make a connection. Oh, he can swagger on battlefields but he can't do emotion, true, deep emotion.'

'Tosser.'

'I always knew, deep inside, that he didn't love me like I did him. I mean he loved me, but he didn't care. If that makes sense. We'd been drifting apart. He was taking more and more risks, I was getting more and more fearful, like my luck was about to run out.'

Ceri picked up the book and fanned herself with it.

'You don't see too many of those outside Tŷ Mawr,' Megan said, looking at the book.

'Think I may have swiped it from your library.' Ceri pulled a half-apologetic face, then said, 'He's a wanker.'

Megan withdrew her feet and wiggled her toes free of sand. 'Maybe. Sometimes. He's human. I won't contact him again.' She swiped at her ankles, rubbing the grains away.

'That's my girl, forget him. And I promise never to mention him again. Cross my heart and hope to die.' Ceri licked her finger and crossed her chest. Megan gave her the thumbs up sign. They were fourteen again.

'You need to get out and meet people,' said Ceri, 'someone new would take your mind off him.'

'Maybe. It's hard to meet the right person.'

'You're too fussy.'

'I'd rather be on my own than in the wrong relationship. I've made that mistake once. I will not repeat it.'

'Don't you get lonely?'

'I'm less lonely than I was when I was seeing Hisham.'

'Oh, Meg.'

'Don't pity me, Ceri. It wasn't all bad. In fact, some of it was good. But I'm done with men.'

Ceri raised an eyebrow, a salacious glint in her eye.

'Well, I'm done with love. Relationships,' Megan said, smirking. She picked up a handful of sand and watched it running through her fingers.

'Meg, your shoulders are crimson! Shall I rub some cream in?'

Megan closed her eyes and drifted as Ceri massaged the lotion into her seared skin, focusing on the sensation, the intimate pleasure of flesh on flesh. Loneliness swam through her veins.

'Cerdic's down again, Megan,' Dafydd yelled between great noisy slurps of the remaining beef tomatoes and the last of the precious bread. He sucked juice from his chin and leapt to his feet. He was an unusual boy, happier in the company of adults than peers.

'I'll help him!' he announced.

'He'll get himself up,' Megan replied.

This was wishful thinking. Cerdic took ages to get up off a carpeted floor, but Megan hoped that he might find it easier on the sodden sand. Either he would sink into it, and it would bolster and support him, or he would find it harder than ever to work with the additional force on his feeble limbs.

Above the sound of the lapping waves, childish prattle, cricket balls on bats, she heard the distinctive wail of her boy begging for help. It was as hard as ever for him. She threw off the towel resting over her shoulders, clambered to her feet and strolled across the beach to where a solitary Cerdic sat moaning. The other children had marched on. By the time Megan had reached her son they were already poking about in the pools, leaping from rock to rock, seaweed popping under smooth wide feet.

'Mummy, Mummy, help me, help me.'

Megan bent over and held out her hand. She felt the sun boring into her unprotected flesh, through the top layers of her dermis and into her sinews, muscles and bone. Her mouth was dry and she regretted not having taken a drink of water. Cerdic looked at her, appealing with his deep set, penetrating eyes. He reminded her of an orang-utan.

'Come on handsome, you can do it. I'm not going to pick you up.'

The monkey-face shifted, eyes blazing, awash with rage and frustration. He slapped the ground with boxy fists. Goblets of sand and seawater splashed up, hitting Megan in the face, on her thighs. She wanted to lie face down and wait for the sea to wash over her. She smiled, licking her lips, tasting the sweat in the corners of her mouth, salty and raw it bit at her tongue.

'Come on, up you get. Push hard with your arms,' Megan said, sitting next to the boy and demonstrating.

Cerdic stopped crying and smiled at her clumsy efforts to show him. Leaning forward, on all fours, he bent his chubby knees and curled his swollen calves under his thighs, pushing from his arms with all his might. The supreme effort this took was palpable, and as he stood upright, like early man – vertical, knees bent, arms dangling loose – he looked triumphant. Then he faltered and promptly fell right back onto his bottom. Megan wanted to cry for him but she needed him to prove that he could do it. She knew it shouldn't be this hard.

'Can't, can't,' he screamed, furious now.

'No such word as "can't".'

This was one of many of Elizabeth's empty, meaningless expressions and even as a girl it drove Megan berserk. By nine years old she had worked out that some things are difficult, if not impossible, for some people. It was ridiculous to suggest anything otherwise, and yet here she was repeating the same useless maxim to a child who was too young to understand anyway. When, as a girl, she'd explained the madness of this saying to her mother she was called impertinent, and Elizabeth had questioned where her daughter got such a temperament. A precocious Megan retorted, 'From you, presumably, and Daddy, whoever he might be. And besides, it's two words.' She was sent to her room without supper, slamming the door behind her, kicking and screaming so hard on the bed that she didn't hear her mother enter and place a sandwich and a glass of milk on her bedside table.

Daddy. The word made her smile, and wince. Like candyfloss it was sweet and insubstantial and too much left her feeling sick. A father was an abstract idea, a vision. She could not imagine what a father actually did, sounded like, felt like and smelt like. Of course, she knew other people's fathers, but she imagined that her daddy would be different. He would have kissed her better when she fell, asked about her days at school, her friends, taken her swimming, taught her to ride her bike. Elizabeth did these things but Megan could not believe that she did them like a father might.

Megan would tell Cerdic everything about his father when he asked. Good and bad. She would tell of the adventures they had, the horrors they witnessed, the companionship they shared, of their rivalry and laughter, of the tenderness, and spats. A flawed, human father, not some idealized icon. Someone concrete, real, made of blood and sweat. Not a nebulous figure created by dreams and romantic yearnings, like the father Megan conjured.

'Help me, Mummy, help Cerdic.'

Megan wondered how long her boy had been yelling at her. Seconds, minutes? She threw her arms round her son and held him to her breast, his slipperiness reminding her of the minutes immediately after his birth, when he was in his raw, unanointed state. She hauled him onto his feet.

Megan regarded her boy, holding him by the shoulders, arms straight. He was tall for his age, like her, and plump, like his father. Skin the colour of butter fudge, straight brown hair, long in the fringe, so much so that the tips of his hair stroked the dark lashes which framed his almond shaped eyes. Megan often wondered where those eyes came from. Jade shot through with topaz, they were totally arresting and reminded her of a tiger. Dangerous, rare and precious.

'Hey, mab, let's catch up with the other kids.'

The boy stretched his hand up towards his mother. Megan grabbed it greedily and they ambled to the rock pools. All the time in the world. Cerdic fell down on several occasions. Megan dismissed her worries – he was tired, it was a distance for his four-year-old legs – and determined to enjoy playing with her boy.

They searched and scrabbled until their bucket was full, mostly seaweed and a few cracked shells, sea-life like crabs and shrimps were as good as extinct in these parts and had been for decades, and Cerdic handled his haul like priceless treasure, showing it proudly to an audience of fellow rock pool hunters. The seaweed was slimy and the stench overpowering. Cerdic and the other children didn't notice but the grown ups pinched their noses and groaned. Their disgust tickled the little ones and Cerdic pulled out a flat ribbon of weed, ruffled on each side like lace, and waved it round his head like a lasso. Laughter filled the air. On the second circuit his weight shifted and tipped him off balance, his feet sliding away from him on the green rock. He fell backwards suddenly and heavily. The dull crack of his skull hitting stone echoed in Megan's heart. He lay motionless across the jagged stone. Megan leapt to his side, almost slipping herself, and placed a hand to his brow, then his neck, searching for a pulse.

She tried to scream out, but sound needs air and her diaphragm froze, locking the breath in her rib cage. For all she had witnessed in war zones across the globe nothing prepared her for this. A trickle of viscous blood made its way from the base of his skull and into a pathetic rock pool. His blood seemed to float on the surface of the oily seawater.

Finding her voice at last, Megan hollered. She saw a woman racing over. Someone short, and nut brown, plentiful flesh quivering over the sands. It was only as she danced over the rocks towards her that Megan realized it was her friend. She thought how graceful Ceri was for a woman of such proportions. Ceri put her ear to Cerdic's chest before talking his arm and placing two fingers on his wrist.

'Call an ambulance. Now.'

A middle-aged woman with pendulous breasts and a rubber ring waist shouted into a mobile. Megan longed to hold Cerdic close, but she made do with resting her hand on his clammy forehead.

'Do not move him, not a centimetre, until the medics arrive,' Ceri ordered.

Megan was aware of a great cacophony of noise but she could not hear a thing. She watched him fall, over and over in her mind's eye, her arm reaching out, too short, too late. The iron smell of the sea sickening her, turning her stomach. Megan stared at Cerdic. Was she to watch him die, here, on the putrid rocks?

In the border region between Mongolia and Xinjiang Megan looked on as a child died in its mother's arms. The mother sat perfectly still, staring into the child's eyes. He was withering away after days of diarrhoea, weeks without clean water, and months of malnutrition. Then she raised her face to the sky and began ululating, wailing, like an animal caught in a trap, braying and screaming.

Onlookers bowed their heads, prayed or wept. But Megan did not. She became an automaton. Out came her camera, she pointed it at the woman and child, and clicked and clicked and clicked. Later, when she viewed the memory card, there were so many images, one after another, saying no more, and no less than the previous one, and the one before that, and before that, and she realized that she had been trying to click the child back to life. As if by recording the moments of its death she could somehow replay and rewind, raise the child from the grave, snatch it from Allah's arms and return it to the mother.

A paramedic led Megan from the rock pools to the ambulance, which sat incongruous on the wet sand. Cerdic was strapped to a grey stretcher. He filled less than a third of the length, and Megan wondered dispassionately why there weren't special stretchers for children. Shorter. To make them look stronger, longer, less vulnerable.

Inside the ambulance Cerdic regained consciousness and Megan reconnected with her body. No longer moribund, a large white swab taped to his skull, Cerdic even attempted to smile at her. An oxygen mask covered his coffee face, but Megan saw the smile and grateful tears rolled down her cheeks.

'Little toughie, this one,' remarked the paramedic in charge. 'You're going to be all right aren't you mate?' Ordinarily such forced joviality would have irritated Megan.

At the hospital Cerdic was allocated a doctor. He was podgy, cherry-cheeked and shiny. Megan wondered how he coped in the heat, with all that weight and a job to do. His stature was immense, and he was kindly rather than imposing. Megan trusted him. Cerdic's condition was improving, and as the doctor diligently gave him the once over Megan poured out a litany of concerns. She had not intended to do this; the words poured from her mouth unprepared and unplanned, and it was a strange sensation. The doctor listened patiently, never interrupting, nodding gravely at times, smiling at others.

'You must not concern yourself with these matters now, Mrs Evens. The important thing is to ensure that your son is comfortable. Talk to him, console him. He has had a nasty shock, a bad bump. He is concussed and will need several stitches in his scalp.' The doctor's head bobbed up and down as he spoke. He reminded Megan of a toy woodpecker fixed on a spring against her mother's board in the days when she taught at a lower school, pecking its way down, steady and unrelenting.

She took Cerdic's hand. 'Call me Megan.'

Then she turned to her son. 'Mummy's here sweetheart. Everything's going to be okay.'

'We will look into these things you speak of in more detail when we are sure your son has suffered no lasting damage from the fall, Mrs Evens. In the meantime I will take some bloods, have a nurse dress his wounds and order rest for you both.'

Megan smiled at the doctor though his words rang with foreboding. 'What a brave boy Cerdic is. Mummy's little soldier, eh?'

Megan stared at the tiled floor as a nurse shaved the back of Cerdic's head. Thick tufts of discarded hair hovered on the ground, like puff balls, no longer part of her son they were insignificant and dispensable. Almost. She picked up a lock, covered in salt and blood, and tucked it into a side pocket of her bag. Another doctor checked the nurse's handiwork, before sending Cerdic to neurology for a MRI scan. Afterwards he was admitted to the children's ward – for total rest and overnight observation. Megan slept by his side on a makeshift bed with crisp white sheets and a stiff pillow, sand scratching the tender flesh on her shoulders.

The next morning the kindly doctor appeared at Cerdic's bedside, clipboard resting on his expansive chest. Megan noticed his nametag this time: Dr Gabriel.

'Mrs Evens? You'll be delighted to hear that the results of the scan indicate that Cerdic has suffered no lasting damage to the brain from yesterday's tumble.'

Megan breathed a little deeper and then stopped. Dr Gabriel's face remained serious, unreadable. It made her feel uncomfortable, though she was sure the opposite effect was intended.

'I wondered if I might ask you some questions, with a view to running some tests on young Cerdic here? With your permission, of course.'

Cerdic sat in bed, playing with a toy figure.

'Of course.'

Megan was taken aback. She expected the doctor to have forgotten their conversation and had resigned herself to badgering their G.P. again to investigate possible reasons for her son's difficulties. She wondered why Dr Gabriel was still on duty, if he had slept since they last met. There were dark circles under his cyes, though she couldn't be sure if they were new or a common feature of his face.

'Mrs Evens, was there anything unusual about your pregnancy? Any problems at all? All was normal?'

'Perfectly.'

'How old was Cerdic when he sat up?'

'Six months. Like the manual said.'

'And when he started to crawl?'

'He never crawled. He went from bum shuffling to creeping around holding onto furniture to walking.'

'And how old was he when he walked independently? You did tell me but I'm afraid I need to make an exact note for the records.'

'Two and a half. Just over. Thirty two months to be exact.'

'And his first word?'

'It was car. He loved cars. Still does. And trains and planes. My mother kept lots of old cars from when she had boys.'

'I meant how old was he, Mrs Evens?'

'He was just short of his first birthday. He spoke early, he's a bright kid.'

'Excellent, excellent.'

Dr Gabriel asked question after question, took more blood – Cerdic screaming at the sight of the syringe – swabs and tissue samples. He ran eye tests and hearing tests, weighed him and measured him. Megan was relieved that finally the medical establishment wanted to get to the bottom of Cerdic's developmental difficulties but it troubled her. There were very sick children here, with needs much more pressing than Cerdic's, one night at the hospital had been more than enough to remind her of this. So why the urgency to check Cerdic?

Hours later they were discharged with a change of dressing for Cerdic's wound and the promise of an appointment for the test results as soon as they were available. Embarrassed, and clumsy with her words, Megan thanked Dr Gabriel for taking her concerns so seriously, for not treating her like a fussing mother, even though she hoped that was exactly what she was. She laughed: a phoney, overly enthusiastic laugh.

'No need to thank me, Mrs Evens. I am merely doing my job.' And though he smiled Megan detected a slight frown dulling his shiny features.

Megan did not sleep well for many nights after their return to Tŷ Mawr, and neither did her mother. Nightmares punctuated Elizabeth's oblivion. Megan heard her cry out at night, and her ashen cheeks and sunken eyes betrayed her lack of sleep. Elizabeth made light of her worries when Megan asked, drawing a cloak around her private life as always.

'It's the heat, Megan, the heat. Cerdic will be fine, fine. He's a strong boy, recovering well.' But Megan didn't believe her. She wondered if her mother dreamed of her little boys, the children she taught long ago, images of dying infants etched upon her mind. And though Megan didn't know it at the time it was the beginning of a long period of sleepless nights and anxiety-ridden days.

Long days later Megan sat alone outside the office of an eminent doctor resident at the hospital. It was nine-fifteen; her appointment was for nine o'clock. Megan had been watching the minutes flash by. She was grateful for the reprieve and didn't understand why she didn't want to go in.

She was wearing heeled sandals and a knee length dress, cut from black cotton with bracelet sleeves and a slash neck. Her cheeks were dusted with a soft pink blush and her lips coated in a sheer gloss. She had looked elegant and quite lovely in her bedroom mirror but now she felt overdressed and wished she had worn her regulation black jeans. She had been keen to make a good impression, but she resented this desire to impress. What was she trying to prove by dressing up? That she was a good and fit mother? Surely only a vain, selfish woman would be concerned about appearance when discussing her child's development? She wiped the gloss from her lips with the back of her hand. She studied her pale shins, the blue veins visible beneath the surface in the harsh hospital light.

The consultant was facing the window, his back to the door, looking out onto a pleasant garden bordered with hydrangeas, hebe and St John's Wort. The air was cool in the sparse, smart office though Megan felt perspiration gathering under her arms and across her brow with every click of her heels on the floor, the sharp sound trumpeting her arrival at his desk. The doctor commented on the fine weather, reminding her that each day comes but once, never to return, and as such should be treasured. Platitudes. She looked at the garden. It was beautiful. She saw Cerdic's caramel cheeks and honeyed smile.

When the doctor finally spun his chair to face her Megan knew the news wasn't good, and though her stomach churned she told herself it would not be anything insurmountable. After all, this wasn't oncology or the ER. After asking her to take a seat, Mr Barnet, a phlegmatic, saturnine individual, informed a trembling Megan that her son had a rare congenital condition, a hereditary disease, commonly passed from mother to son, which would slowly rob Cerdic's body of its ability to function.

'AMNA. It stands for Alekseyev Motor Neuron Atrophy, named after the Russian scientist who first discovered the defective gene in the twenty teens. 2013, if memory serves me well. For reasons that have never been quite explained the condition appears to be more prevalent amongst the peoples of the East, the Slavs in particular,' he said.

Megan's mouth dried up, her lips seemed to be welded together. She struggled to push the words out. 'How serious is it?'

'Very, Mrs Evens. I am sorry.'

'What will it do to him?' She could feel the thick white spit at the corners of her mouth like glue. She went to wipe it away and realized that her hands were shaking.

'It starts in the muscles as cells break down and are gradually lost. The muscles weaken over time. Your son has trouble jumping and climbing, yes?' He didn't wait for her reply. 'By five years old AMNA boys are unable to walk far, and by seven or eight most are in a wheelchair. Nerve cells in the brain weaken, eventually failing to send messages to muscles and other vital organs like the lungs. Sufferers lose control of their bodies and minds. The average life expectancy…' Megan watched his mouth move without hearing the words. He was like a reporter with the sound turned off, and she wondered if she had ever looked as foolish on the mulmed as the doctor did now. Sunlight illuminated his form and she felt angry with the sun for shining.

'How long do we have?'

He gazed at her and curled his lips inward. 'If he reaches sixteen, it will be a miracle, of sorts,' he said, delivering the news as if it were quotidian, finishing with a standard, 'Do you have any further questions?'

Megan experienced a sensation similar, she imagined, to being eviscerated. It was as if he had ripped out her intestines, thrown them to the floor and then squashed them underfoot, before asking if there was anything he could do to help.

She remembered the night Cerdic was born. Sweltering and still. Even the sea was silent after his arrival. She stayed up all night, her body throbbing, unable to take her eyes from him, afraid that if she blinked he would disappear as miraculously as he had arrived. She remembered how, when he was tiny and slept in a cot in her room, she would wake to the sound of silence and rush to his bedside, placing a palm in front of his mouth, checking he still breathed. Like all mothers in the black moments she imagined a hundred ways he might be taken from her but nothing like this. She never, ever, imagined this.

Reeling from the shock, and working hard to control her spiralling emotions and liquid gut, she said, 'There must be something we can do.'

'As you will appreciate much research was abandoned, or more accurately put on hold, after 2015. Cerdic's condition is, mercifully, extremely rare, and as such it has not been high priority for many, many years. In the past decade research has restarted. But it is a slow process, Mrs Evens.' He returned to his garden as he spoke, and Megan thought there was nothing merciful about this disease.

'Has this research thrown anything up yet?' she said, adding irritably, 'It's Miss Evens.'

Mr Barnet commented on a blackbird that hopped on the lawn before replying with indistinct mumbling ruminations.

Megan was losing her patience though she believed the consultant's rudeness was not deliberate. She pressed for a clear reply.

'There are signs to indicate that matching stem cell and blood plasma transplants, from suitable donors, can slow the progression of the disease. It works best if the donors are relatives, close relatives. Scientists believe they can stop the disease in its tracks altogether if administered early enough with a perfectly matched donor though there is no conclusive proof as yet.'

'It is worth a try, Mr Barnet.'

'Worth a try, yes.' He nodded absentmindedly.

'Then we try it.' Megan's tone was polite but firm – this was not a request.

'There is no sibling?'

'There's me.'

The consultant spoke of the viability of samples from her, Cerdic's father, compatibility. He explained that it was most unusual, unheard of, for the mother, the carrier, to match, to be a suitable donor. She knew he meant no malice or blame – why would he? – but it pained her nevertheless. He rambled on, explaining the minutiae of technical detail. She twisted the ring on her left hand. Her mind flooded with images of Hisham. She would have to contact him. She knew there would be no question of him not helping and then she allowed herself the irrational hope that contacting Hisham might not be necessary, that she might be the one in a million, in a manner of speaking. She left Mr Barnet's office brim full of fear and hope, clutching a referral and a name for her son's killer.

Back at Tŷ Mawr, Cerdic and Elizabeth were playing in the garden, digging for worms and picking gooseberries, the air plump with the sound of squeals of pain as fingers were pricked by thorny bushes, and delight as hairy fruits burst between milk teeth, squirting tart booty everywhere. Hidden from view Megan peered from the corner of the kitchen window. They looked so content she couldn't bear to go and say hello, to face Elizabeth's questions, though she marvelled how she could bear not to. She gave Cerdic an imaginary hug and walked from the kitchen through the adjoining room, complete with dining table, chairs, and desk, past the library door, to the front of the house.

Lego littered the living room floor, marbles hid in every corner, and metal cars, old-fashioned petrol cars, lay on their sides and upside down among the debris as if in a scrap yard awaiting demolition. Megan was amazed when Elizabeth produced toys from the loft soon after Cerdic's first birthday. They had belonged to her boys, Robert, Matthew, Luke, and she had intended to keep them for their children, her grandchildren.

'Never thought they'd be down in my lifetime. You were such a career woman, Meg,' Elizabeth had said.

Megan wondered what else her mother kept hidden in the eaves, her secret history in mildewed boxes and old suitcases. Megan hoped that this retrieving of the toys, this small but significant salvaging of the past would start an avalanche of tales, but it never did.

Keeping the house tidy was a permanent battle, but Elizabeth had adjusted remarkably well to the chaos and disruption that a child brings. When Megan was a girl Tŷ Mawr had been immaculate; she spent many weekend afternoons dusting, polishing and wiping.

'Come on, Meg. Grab the vinegar and some rags. Those windows need a good scrubbing. Cleanliness is next to Godliness!' Elizabeth said.

'I have homework to do,' said Megan looking up from a biography she was reading.

'Do it later. I know what you're like, you'll leave it till the last minute anyway. Come on, get going. We'll listen to some music while we're at it.'

'So long as I choose. I hate your stuff,' said Megan, dragging herself from the kitchen table.

'Oh you kids. You don't know good music when you hear it. We'll take it in turns, starting with some Nirvana.'

Megan groaned and said, 'I prefer your classic stuff to all that heavy rock.'

Cleaning the windows took hours, but once immersed in the task Megan could not stop until the glass gleamed, and Elizabeth had moved on long ago. It was the same when Elizabeth suggested cleaning the kitchen – she had in mind a wiping down of surfaces, a scrubbing of the agar surface. Though Megan moaned and groaned at first, she would spend hours emptying every cupboard, wiping every jar, bottle and handle. Everything else fell by the wayside.

Picking her way across the lounge floor, through the maze of plastic and metal, Megan set the mulmed console to internet and whispered her nemesis. There were thousands of links.

'It may be rare, but not unheard of,' she said aloud.

'Not unheard of, no,' replied the machine.

She worked obsessively and for the first time in years felt the craving for a daytime cigarette. She worked through the first links quickly, abstractedly. A couple of reports of research projects beginning again, a development in the strain of the disease. She skipped over the pages. She read, and read, and read. She read until her eyes started to sting. She cut and pasted words, phrases, diagrams, into a newly created file. Hours earlier she had never heard of this condition. By the end of the afternoon she was an expert. Her head span, her brain throbbed, her stomach turned. But most of all her heart ached. She had to speak with her mother, she needed to ask Elizabeth: Why? Why didn't you tell me? Did all your boys escape? Maybe they were affected? Maybe AMNA would have killed them had they not died. Maybe…

Megan was sure that whatever her mother might have said nothing would have prevented her from having Cerdic. But at least she would have known the risks. She recalled her spring visit of four years ago. Afterwards they sat in this same room. Megan on the sofa, Elizabeth in the leather armchair in the bay window, her face silhouetted, smudged sunlight stealing through the lace curtains, filigree patterns transferred onto the floorboards.

Megan looked at the armchair. She travelled back to that evening. She saw Elizabeth, champagne flute in hand, animated, delighted, toasting her daughter and future grandchild. Megan wanted to holler at her, 'Did you know? Why didn't you tell me?'

Instead, hot tears streamed down her cheeks, their bitter kisses stinging her lips.

'Maybe you never knew.'

Chapter Five

Sounds of hissing water, rattling pans, slamming drawers and high-pitched jabbering darted through the house, like a guerrilla army raiding the relative calm of Megan's camp. Elizabeth and Cerdic were preparing the evening meal. Megan knew that her son would be sat at the old wooden table, drawing with crayons, or chalks, or kneading and moulding homemade play dough. The table was a piece of family art, the many coloured loops, squiggles and primitive carvings a canvas of creativity and memories over several decades. Megan had sat at it, just as Cerdic did, scribbling and drawing, tapping or talking into her mulmed, practising her letters and numbers, her ABCs and 123s, Mandarin and responsible citizenship. She had smelt its earthy wax, stroked its bark, scratched at it with her knife when her mother's back was turned.

Megan wondered how long ago they had left their horticultural pursuits. They didn't realize she was home, and she had been unaware of anything other than the words on the screen.

Her stomach and head whirled; she would have to face her mother, she couldn't hide in here forever. And she didn't want to; she longed to pull Cerdic to her breast and squeeze, and squeeze, and squeeze. Press him into her bones and blood. Megan had no idea how she would react to her mother, but she knew that she would not confront her with questions, not yet. She would play for time, say nothing, give her mother the space and opportunity to tell her what she ought to have told her years ago, to explain. If she could. If she knew.

Megan tried to get up from her crouched position on the rug. Her left leg gave way, pins and needles stabbing and spiking. She rubbed her dead limb back to life as she resolved to alter her position when working or watching the mulmed. It was a bad habit, one of many, this sitting in awkward, bad-for-the-posture positions.

Megan hobbled to the kitchen doorway, paused, took a deep

breath and then pushed the door open. She loved the kitchen. Dark and warm, the stove humming in the space where an open fire might once have sat, bare bricks rough and homely on the chimney breast, the deep white Belfast sink, the table and its bench, the dresser with Elizabeth's collection of Portmeirion pottery and assorted teapots, the terracotta tiles, pots and pans hanging from the ceiling. It would have been oppressive and claustrophobic had it not been for the wide window stretching almost the entire length of the far wall. It looked onto the south facing garden and washed the room in light. The scent of tomato leaves stung her nostrils.

'Mummy!'

Arms outstretched, Megan smiled as Cerdic fell from his chair and tumbled across the tiles towards her. A clumsy, adorable boy.

'Someone's pleased to see you. We've had a super day though haven't we, bach?' Elizabeth said as mother and son hugged each other.

Megan watched her mother from over Cerdic's shoulder. She looked tired and old, her skin the colour of putty, shrivelled and dry. A wave of pity washed over Megan and doubt flooded her mind. Perhaps her mum knew nothing after all. Perhaps her boys were lucky, unaffected, all three.

'I knew you would,' Megan said.

'What did you and Nana get up to?' Megan glanced at her mother and threw her a reassuring nod. She wanted the few hours before Cerdic was packed off to bed to be fun, anxiety free. Too much wasted time already.

'We did digging, and worm catching, and there was poo.'

'Nice!' Megan waved a hand in front of her nose as she spoke.

The boy laughed and Megan pulled him to her again.

Elizabeth chopped and mixed at the workstation. The scent of basil wafted over the kitchen, mingling with the home grown tomatoes and freshly baked bread resting on the heavy pewter range. The air was heady with aromas, and Megan felt dizzy. She hoped that Cerdic would visit Mediterranean lands one day.

70

The meal was tense. Megan did not want to talk about the hospital visit. Cerdic wouldn't eat the greens, the carefully cultivated garden lettuces, cucumber, sage and fennel that Megan and her mother struggled to grow and prepare. Neither had green fingers and while Elizabeth was a competent, well-practised cook she lacked flair. Despite Elizabeth's passion for eating she could not master serious culinary skills, and Megan ate to survive on the whole. On another occasion Megan would have pushed Cerdic to eat something other than a slice of the bread, bribing and threatening in equal measure. That evening she didn't have the stomach for it.

'So how was your day?' Elizabeth said with forced brightness.

Megan looked up from her plate, around which she had been pushing the salad and bread, and said, 'Fine. Nothing much to report, really. Early days. Have you finished, Cerdic? Let's get you up for a play and a bath before bed.'

She sensed her mother's unease, and impatience, and chose to ignore it.

They left Elizabeth clearing the kitchen, but she followed them upstairs soon enough. While Megan bathed Cerdic Elizabeth hovered, fussing on the landing and in the bathroom, tidying a non-existent mess. Megan lingered when choosing the bedtime story. By this time of day Megan was commonly brisk, keen to dispatch the boy for the night and enjoy some time to herself. Usually, she gave Cerdic a choice of one of two or three short books, and as a rule he was tucked up by seven. But that evening Megan promised to read two whole stories, both of which were lengthy. Elizabeth retreated downstairs.

It was almost eight o'clock before Megan tiptoed down. The kitchen was warm. An open bottle of red wine stood on the table. It was only two thirds full, so Elizabeth had already poured herself a large glass Megan noted ruefully. Their alcohol allowance would be gone before the month was out and she'd have to suffer days without before new vouchers came through. She picked up the bottle and a glass and wandered through to the library, looking for something to read, to distract her.

The library was stuffy, rarely used in the years of Megan's absence from Tŷ Mawr, with a small window of frosted glass the only source of natural light. It had almost certainly been a utility room used by servants when the house was first built, and it was Robert, Elizabeth's father, who had it converted into a library. Back in the days when Elizabeth was a working mum and Megan a girl she preferred the study on the mezzanine to work in, a room Megan had now appropriated. But that evening Megan wanted to hide away for a while and this would be one of the last places Elizabeth would think to look.

If asked, most people would have said the kitchen was the heart of the house, but Megan knew they were wrong. The library was. Here, in this buried room, in these four book-covered walls, was everything anyone needed to know about the family: its memories, desires, secret lives. Coded clues to the past were here, in the titles, between the crumbling pages, in the messages of love and giving scribbled on inside front covers. Hidden in pages were train tickets from Naples to Rome, shopping lists, children's drawings, flowers, and even the occasional photograph. Book-marks of lives past. As a girl, after arguments and upsets, Megan hid in the library. Elizabeth never knew. And it was here that Megan pieced together fractured vignettes of her mother's past, the rest she conjured mostly from imagination.

Megan turned on a lamp and let her eyes drift over the book-cases. Row upon row of books, mostly paperbacks, but with an entire case devoted to hardbacks. Orange and white spines, more brown than white, austere black spines with cracked white lettering and a tiny penguin, racing green spines, a bitten apple, an archer, the serpent, the snowflake. Brightly coloured spines with detail and pictures, novels from the early years of the century. Novels, plays, poetry, short story collections, books on art, sculpture, gardening, and bird watching, history books, and books written in Welsh. Robert's books. Megan scanned the rows. She rarely read fiction but desperately wanted to find something appealing, an escape. There were rows and rows of romantic paperbacks. She pulled one out, *And the Bride Wore Red*, and opened the cover. Large, rounded letters in red biro formed the name: Elizabeth Evens.

Dusty spines stared at her, empty eyed; they had been there such a long time. Only weeks ago, when Cerdic was watching his favourite show on the mulmed and the presenter was showing pictures of himself as a boy, Cerdic had turned to her, cheerful and curious, and said, 'I wonder what I'll look like when I'm a man, Mummy?'

Megan laughed and replied that she honestly couldn't imagine him as a man but was sure that he would be very, very handsome. Shiny cheeks blemished with stubble and spots? She couldn't picture it. High-pitched lisp a deep resonant boom? She couldn't hear it. But there, in the library, she resolved to ensure that her son lived to groan at the sight of his first grey hair.

Her eyes rested on a collection of medical textbooks. Hannah's presumably. Hannah had been a doctor, one of the few facts she was certain of about her maternal grandmother. She pulled a medical encyclopaedia down, opened it up, poured a glass of wine, switched on the desk lamp and sat at the leather-topped table in the centre of the room.

When Elizabeth breezed in, clothed in an air of studied nonchalance Megan jumped and knocked the bottle over.

'Damn it!' The wine flowed across the table and onto the floorboards with a gentle splash.

'Don't worry, there's not much spilt, let me get a cloth,' Elizabeth said, her voice shrill.

'There's no need. It's only bloody wine, it won't stain,' Megan snapped, and then acquiesced with an apologetic, 'I'm tired.'

Elizabeth returned with two cloths. She handed one to Megan, an old t-shirt of Cerdic's. Megan threw it over the puddle of wine and watched the purple stain creep across the cotton like a bruise.

'Don't you like to watch your favourite programme about now? That miserable soap opera?'

'I'll call it up later,' Elizabeth said, placing her glass on the desk and pulling up the other chair.

'Go and watch it.'

'I thought you'd want to talk,' Elizabeth replied, hands resting on the backrest of the chair, still standing. Hovering. 'You were gone such a long time. I was worried.'

'It can wait. Go on.' Megan did not make eye contact with her mother.

'I don't much care about the programme really. I'm not sure why I watch it half the time.' Her voice burnt with desperation.

'You're morbid,' Megan said.

Elizabeth pushed the chair aside and bent down, clutching the spare cloth, and began scrubbing the floor.

Megan continued to ignore her, wiping imaginary wine off the floor. Megan knew she could wipe away the tension as easily as the wine. It was in her power to do this and, though it was uncomfortable to admit it, she was enjoying her mother's discomfort. Tension like this was common enough between them, though rarely was the air so freighted with avoidance. The silence was sure to snap.

Megan stopped rubbing. Her head flopped between her arms. The scent of sweat wafted past her nose. Fear mixed with deodorant. The pungent air hovered around her ears, her hair brushed up against her cheeks, blood rushed round her brain. Her knees hurt, and she exhaled deeply and loudly.

'What is it, cariad? What did the doctor say?'

'Cerdic will probably die before he reaches adulthood. He will be dead before I am. If we can't help him,' Megan said, without emotion. The words lingered like smoke, forming ugly shapes. Elizabeth fell backwards, banging her head against a bookshelf. She looked like a rag doll with the stuffing dragged out of it. Folded, with a fixed expression of shock. Megan stared at her until she took in a gulp of air, and tears welled in her eyes. Megan's eyes fell to the floor.

'How? How can this be?' Elizabeth's voice was shrunken.

'He has a condition called AMNA. A rare genetic condition passed down the mother's line. From mother to son. Daughters aren't affected. Not directly. They are usually carriers.'

The blood drained from Elizabeth's lips, her fingers quivered. Megan said nothing more. Tears stumbled down Elizabeth's cheeks. Megan remained dry eyed. The silence was all consuming. Finally Elizabeth spoke. 'There must be something we can do. Is there nothing they can do?'

'Stem cell and blood plasma donations given early, and often, can help. It has to come from relatives but there needs to be a match. Being a blood relative isn't enough. As a carrier it's almost certain I won't match.'

'But you might?'

'I might. But the possibility is extremely remote. Like a miracle or something.'

'Miracles do happen.'

'Do they? You may believe, Mum. I never have. I'll take the test but I'm not banking on divine intervention.'

'What about his father? Hisham?' Elizabeth hesitated.

'You know his name?'

Her mother had never asked about Cerdic's father. From the day Megan announced her pregnancy, she made it clear to her mother that the father would play no part in her grandchild's future.

'You never did talk much about your private life,' Elizabeth said.

'That's rich coming from you.'

'I'm sorry.'

'Why do we do this, Mum? Shut each other out, from big important parts of our lives. I will not repeat that mistake with Cerdic,' Megan said.

'I'm glad.'

'So what do you know? Or think you know.'

'That he was an important part of your life, this Moroccan.'

Megan raised her eyebrows.

'Do you know where he is?' Elizabeth said.

'Not exactly. But I can trace him. Wherever he is,' Megan replied. 'You might match.'

'Will they want old donors?'

'It's not ideal. The doctor implied that young is better. The chances of success are much higher.'

'I more than likely won't match. I must be a carrier, like you.'

'Unless the condition skipped a generation. I don't know if this is possible. We could ask.'

'Yes.'

'But you'll take the test if Hisham doesn't match?'

'Of course, cariad. What are the options?'

'Mr Barnet said that some couples try for more children, to find the match. They can test the foetus,' she laughed bitterly before continuing, 'though I suspect that won't be an option in my case. And there's always the European donor database, though donors are rare and there are more risks involved. It might not come to that.'

They looked at each other.

'Your boys, they were killed by the plague?' Megan said quietly.

'Yes.' The shutters rolled down over Elizabeth's face.

'Would they have died anyway?'

'What are you saying...'

'Did they have AMNA?'

Elizabeth's expression was blank, unreadable.

'That's the condition, the one that will kill Cerdic.'

'No.'

Exhaustion washed over Megan, she thought she might faint and she craved sleep. Her brain was scrambled, she was emotional and irrational. This was Elizabeth, her mother, Cerdic's grandmother. She would do everything she could to save his life. She would have said if she knew.

Silence descended once more, drooping over them like a fog. Long moments passed. Then Megan pushed herself from her knees. 'It has to be Hisham,' she said, wiping her eyes and looking at her mother who remained on the floor. She offered Elizabeth her hand. She waved it away.

'How did you know?' Megan sighed, flopping onto a chair.

She still wore the shift dress she had on to the appointment with Mr Barnet. She stretched her legs, rubbing her knees, studying them. They were red and blotchy from kneeling on the unyielding wood.

Elizabeth reached up to the table and took a sip of wine before she spoke. 'About Hisham?'

Megan nodded.

'When you came back from Arctic, you were different, softer somehow. Love does that to you.'

And Megan was transported back to her first meeting with Hisham.

He came out of nowhere. A dark oasis in an ice desert of tainted white. The blue air shimmered around the silhouette of his bulky frame, mauve-grey wisps of cloud formed haloes above an apricot sun that lay low in the sky behind him. She peered through the window, took another sip of vodka and watched him limping closer and closer, taking regular swigs from a bottle clasped in his left hand, as if mirroring her, the cream fur trim of his hood luminous against the caramel flesh of his cheeks. Less than thirty metres from the shack he stopped, took a long gulp, wiped his mouth with the back of his gloved hand and grinned. His teeth gleamed like the snow and for a moment she thought the stranger's smile was for her. He looked like trouble. Irresistible trouble.

She had been waiting for her source for over three hours in a make-shift bar at the lakeside in Tukoyaktuk. The Arctic Circle. A place on the edge of the map. The door wheezed, the trundle of tired legs echoed round the bar. A gust of deathly wind blew across her face. It was January, a time when temperatures barely reached minus fifty degrees celcius. She didn't turn, she continued to stare out of the window gazing across the ice. The footsteps headed towards her then came to an abrupt standstill. Without moving she dropped her gaze to the floor. The boots were scuffed and tatty. She turned as her eyes wandered upwards. A dirty parka, stretched uncomfortably across a corpulent frame, an enormous shoulder bag. She wondered what on earth could be in it. A wide grin. Warm and exotic in a bitter landscape, he brought something of the desert with him.

'You Megan? You expecting Eric?'

She nodded.

'He's not coming.'

'I guessed,' she slurred, adding, 'Thanks,' as an after thought.

Uninvited, he sat on the chair opposite her, slapped his gloves on the table, took her half empty bottle, raised it to his generous mouth and took a drink. Megan wondered what he had done with the bottle he had moments before, which spirit it contained, for she was sure it would have held strong liquor. Perhaps that was what the bag was for. She wanted to object to his impudence but didn't know how.

He closed his red-brown eyes as he drank, and she noticed that his hands were delicate, the nails clean and manicured, his cheerful half moons peeking at her. His coat pulled across his chest, the zip straining under the pressure. It could have split apart at any moment. Like a gutted fish. Megan wondered what might spill out.

He wanted to work with her on the story. 'We will make a good team. I feel it, baby. We will create something important. We can learn from it, about the world, about ourselves.'

'Lofty aims, Hisham Abdullah.'

He talked some more, and drank some more, and Megan watched the light disappear for the long night ahead. She wondered how it might be here in summer, when the light never faded. Darkness closed in and, against her better judgement, Megan agreed.

'My name first on the credits, the byline, whatever. And don't call me baby,' she said. Megan had no idea what possessed her.

'These are your only demands?' He offered his hand. His handshake was firm and strong, a force. Hisham was tempting and addictive, he oozed risk and pleasure. Like a powerful narcotic he promised highs and lows, he could seriously damage her health, and still she hadn't been able to stop it. He would change her life. She'd felt it.

And so he had, though she could never have guessed how.

Elizabeth interrupted Megan's thoughts. 'Much later, months later, I saw Hisham on the mulmed talking about the conflict.'

'What?'

'You asked me how I knew it was Hisham.'

'I was miles away.'

Elizabeth continued, 'I saw the way you looked at him. You love him.'

'Loved him.'

And Megan was surprised that Elizabeth recognized the signs of love; she was surprised by her own transparency. Megan found it hard to imagine Elizabeth in love. Romantic, sexual love.

'Cerdic looks very much like him. Even more when he was a baby,' Elizabeth said.

'All babies look more like their fathers than their mothers. Nature's way of proving their paternity, ensuring they hang around for a while. Doesn't always work of course,' Megan said.

Elizabeth clambered to her feet and sat opposite. She took another sip of wine. She seemed nervous. 'Did you ever want him to be a part of it?'

'Maybe. Not really. Sometimes. I loved him, I hated him. I sent him pictures once. I don't know. I knew he never would so I didn't allow myself to think about it.'

'You loved him.'

'For a time. It was a strange relationship, based on circumstance, rather than true, genuine love. I see that now. I didn't back then.'

'You love Cerdic and that's all that counts,' Elizabeth said.

Megan drank from her mother's glass. The wine was smoky and sharp. 'Did you love my father? You never speak of him. I mean I know what he did for a living, how he died. But I don't know what he was like. What you two were like together.'

Elizabeth's eyes misted over, and she went to that far away place Megan was never invited to. And it occurred to Megan that she didn't know her. It amazed her to think that she had lived with this woman for the better part of her life but she didn't actually know her.

Shadows drifted over the room, cooling the feverish air with their presence. Evenings were closing in, summer was on its way out, despite the heat. Elizabeth's face softened in the dusk. Megan saw her mother as a young woman. Youngish woman, a few years older than Megan was now.

She knew that it was painful for Elizabeth to speak of the past. That she had never got over it, or moved on completely. Megan was almost a teenager when she learnt that Elizabeth had lost her entire family, and then, a few short years later, lost again. Megan's father. Her husband, loved one, she supposed. Or was he? Later Megan thought Elizabeth had remarried with what might have been considered unseemly haste. He was more probably a rebound than another true love. It was clear to Megan that Elizabeth loved her first husband, Andrew, and their three sons dearly. It was definite, fixed, unquestionable. As certain as night following day. The same could not be said of Megan's father. He was called Christopher, her mother said.

They met, married and had Megan within two years, barely four years after the loss of Elizabeth's first family. And although the state was encouraging survivors to move on, breed, and rebuild the nation, this didn't quite explain such celerity.

Megan had seen one photograph of her father. She had found it in the library, tucked in the pages of a book on the life and work of Sir John Everett Millais, the date in the corner read 31.07.20, a name scratched in pencil on the back. She repeated the name, over and over. Christopher Bryant. Dr Christopher Bryant. She might have said that she bore no resemblance to him whatsoever but it was difficult to be sure. He was a middle-aged man. It was small, a head and shoulders shot, taken against a plain background. It looked as if it might have been used to accompany an article in a magazine or journal. Or even an ID card. It was formal and characterless. A serious, grey-haired man with gentle eyes and just enough laughter lines to suggest that he wasn't always so dour. He must have been clever. He'd been a doctor, Elizabeth had said. Why did she not carry her father's name? Why didn't Elizabeth? 'Because we are the only Evens left,' Elizabeth had said. Megan had imagined him witty, cultured, kindly. A man who saved lives by day and by night enjoyed a glass of brandy while he smoked a slim cigar. But it was impossible to read anything into an image. What he liked to do of an evening, what his favourite colour was, what made him laugh. Had her mother found him attractive? Had the book belonged to him? Megan wasn't sure, and she hadn't asked her mother.

'Did you love him?' Megan repeated.

Elizabeth cleared her throat before replying. 'Your father would have loved you dearly, been so proud of you.'

'That's not what I asked. Did you love him?'

'I think so. I barely remember him, Meg. It was a long time ago, and we had such a short time together.'

Megan knew her mother was lying but another wave of exhaustion washed over her and she knew she could fight it no longer. The wine had given her an emotional manicure, filed away the sharp edges of her despair, and perhaps Elizabeth was right, perhaps it didn't really matter.

She would have a bank of memories and impressions for Cerdic, when he asked, and she would be truthful. She owed her son that much.

Or maybe this desire to discover her father was simply nosiness? Whimsy? She had little to meddle in here, in provincial Wales. Her hunger had to be sated somehow.

You're a nosy parker, Megan Evens. A natural-born snooper. You root stories out. Like a gourmet foraging for truffles, the deeper it's buried, the harder you'll scratch. At first you may even walk away, but you'll return, guaranteed. She remembered Jack's words.

How she longed to speak with Jack. It was Jack who bridged the two Megans. He was the link to the old Megan, the fearless intrepid correspondent, the cosmopolitan girl who drank neat vodka and talked through the night, putting the world to rights, and Megan the fearful mother, the carer, part-time sub on a provincial rag. She determined to call him from her room. And then she remembered he was in Islamabad, and she hoped that he was sleeping.

She was seventeen again. The lonely girl in the wrong place. The misfit. Too big for Bangor, too insignificant, too ignorant for the world. She knew nothing. But this time she had Cerdic to look out for, and she felt smaller and lonelier than ever.

'You look tired. Let's go to bed. We can form a plan in the morning,' Elizabeth said, rising from her chair. She shuffled over.

Elizabeth felt frail beneath Megan's touch. Megan wanted to squeeze her tight, but she felt her mother's natural resistance, keeping them apart even as they embraced. Elizabeth was brittle, papery, like parchment she could crumble at any moment. A gust of wind, a steel grip and she would flutter through fingers, dust on the air. Megan found it hard to believe that anything this fragile could be anything other than translucent. But Elizabeth was as opaque as ever.

Megan was exhausted: battered by fear of the future, and fear of what the past might hold. She pushed dark, mistrustful thoughts from her mind. She had never doubted her mother's love. She pulled her mother's bones closer.

Chapter Six

'Howdy, Cerdic. How's it going?' the orderly hollered as he walked by pushing the drugs trolley.

'We're good. How are you, Marty?' Megan said, looking up from the game of snakes and ladders. 'And your mum. She feeling better?'

'Not bad. Muddling along,' he said bringing the trolley to an abrupt standstill. 'You in for grub today? I'll have a word with Lottie, see if she can get it to you pronto. It'll still be disgusting but warm at least.'

'No thanks. Quick visit today, thank Christ.'

'Mummy, don't swear,' Cerdic said.

'You tell her, mate. What's it today?' Marty said.

'Scan of some sort or another.' Megan knew the purpose of the scan exactly, but she didn't like to appear like a know-it-all, and she didn't want to dwell. She was fond of Marty and many of the other orderlies. She liked hearing about their lives, their dreams and woes. It helped pass the long hours spent in the county hospital.

Marty leant in, conspiratorially. 'My favourite patient want a chocolate biscuit?'

'Yes! Yes!' shouted Cerdic, throwing his arms above his head.

'Nothing wrong with him today, eh?'

'Not today.'

The professionals poked and prodded, scanned and investigated, checked and double-checked Cerdic, to confirm the consultant's prognosis, and to establish the severity and exact progress of his condition. He was compliant and good natured – all the staff adored him – aided by the fact that he didn't feel in the least bit unwell, the tests were mostly painless and he enjoyed the attention and gifts lavished on him.

Megan insisted upon taking a second blood test. She wanted to believe there had been a mistake, but there was no match. She could not help her son and she felt cheated. She had given him life, she wanted to do so again. It should be her. And unlike Cerdic she found the whole process tiresome, but she was grateful to the medical team for their diligence. And their labours gave Megan a spotlight, practical matters to focus on, enabling her to push emotional encumbrances aside. So busy doing, she had no time to feel.

When she returned to Mr Barnet's office weeks after their initial meeting he was, as before, admiring the view from his expansive window. The hebe's tightly knotted blooms clung on to life, a faded, wounded purple, the St John's Wort was no longer peppered yellow, and though the leaves on the great sycamore at the bottom of the lawn were not yet showing signs of actual decay they were devoid of moisture, brittle-looking and dry.

Megan pulled the door behind her.

'Do you like the autumn, Mrs Evens?'

'It was my favourite season.'

'Why was?'

Mr Barnet swivelled on his chair. He looked genuinely mystified. Megan shrugged as she sank into the chair facing him.

'I love it. The change, the heralding of a period of retreat, hibernation, a restocking, preparing for a rebirth. And the colours are magnificent of course.' He sounded wistful, and reflective, and Megan felt that he might have carried on, lost in his own little reverie had she not pulled the conversation back to professional matters.

'Indeed. Can we talk about Cerdic? What is our next approach? It's Ms Evens by the way.'

He looked put out momentarily and then he recovered himself. The professional, phoney smile emerged, and he picked up a weedy sheaf of paperwork from his desk which he glanced at arbitrarily, before applying his serious mask, and reiterating near enough word for word what he'd said at their first meeting.

'So you see, Mrs Evens, our next line of attack must be to find a close relative who will make a good donor for Cerdic. His father would, naturally, be first choice. You have contacted him?'

Megan had written to Hisham two weeks previously. When she'd heard nothing, she called his boss, explaining that she needed to speak with her former lover (she didn't use those words) on a matter of some urgency. The editor explained that Hisham was on location.

'It's a particularly sensitive story. He may not be able to respond.' His tone was supercilious and condescending.

'Meaning?' Megan said.

'I'm sure he would respond if he could. You mustn't fret.'

'I'm not fretting. I need to speak with him urgently. I do understand. I have worked on similar assignments. I was a foreign correspondent myself.'

'But you're not anymore, are you, Ms ???'

She did not repeat her name. He was pretending to have forgotten it. Of that she was sure.

'The world has changed,' he said. 'I'll pass your message on when I hear from him.'

She felt her mouth dry up as her pulse rate increased. She was a two-bit hack for a provincial news agency. She was a mother with a sick child. She was powerless. She threw her mulmed on the table.

She met the man once. Years ago at a party. Handsome and arrogant, he responded to her beauty in a manner she was accustomed to. And an assumption that she would find him as attractive as he did her. He flirted openly, before collaring her in a badly lit corridor on the way to the toilets. She recognized the glint in his eye as he approached but never thought he would act on it. Though she disguised it well she was surprised when he pushed her against the wall and ran his hand up her thigh, staring brazenly into her eyes. Her rebuke was blunt and left no room for ambiguity. It stunned him into a silent retreat. Weeks later, over a rare restaurant dinner together, Hisham commented that his boss fancied Megan. When she enquired casually why he thought this, Hisham said that he had been so outspoken in his dislike of her that Hisham knew he was jealous.

'What did you do to him, baby? Turn him away? He's not

used to that! He's trying to put me off. He wants you for himself,' he laughed, stuffing a large piece of roast lamb into his mouth. Hisham's perception amused Megan, and she wondered if he had defended her to the man. On balance she thought probably not.

Mr Barnet raised his eyebrows when Megan explained that Cerdic's father's profession meant that he was often out of contact with anyone for weeks at a time. The consultant advised her to try and speak with Hisham as soon as possible.

'Although the progress of the disease is slow at this stage, Mrs Evens, the sooner we can begin treatment, the sooner we will be able to establish whether or not it has any effect on the symptoms. Time isn't really of the essence, but there's no time like the present, so to speak, why put off till tomorrow what you can do today.'

Megan determined to reach Hisham one way or another.

Outside it was muggy. The air was sticky with storm. As always, Megan was dressed in black. She looked like an early morning shadow, long and narrow, and as sweat slipped down her spine and into the top of her knickers she cursed herself for not wearing a t-shirt underneath her light jumper. She brought up Jack's number on her mulmed.

He answered immediately, as she knew he would.

'You okay?'

Before she could reply that she wasn't, he continued, 'In the middle of something, potentially huge. Call you back later.'

'Sure. Talk later.'

A darkening sky crept in from the sea and Megan felt the pull of the tide. She walked down to the coast knowing that to return to work would be futile. She wouldn't be able to give anything her undivided attention until she had spoken with Jack.

Turning to Hisham felt like failure, irrational though she knew this to be under the circumstances. The last time she saw him she had said she would ask him for nothing. She'd gone to tell him about the baby, using precious mileage to talk with him face to face. 'About something important.' One final test. To see if he really cared for her as little as she dreaded. She had phoned ahead with details of when he should expect her.

As she disembarked the train at the Gare du Nord she decided not to walk the short distance to his apartment immediately and took a detour along the banks of the Seine instead. The city seemed quiet, as if in mourning, and its still beauty shimmered with foreboding.

When she approached the tall, dilapidated block that passed as home for Hisham she was over an hour late. She pressed the intercom and endless minutes passed before a husky voice told her to come up. He sounded half asleep, and when she reached the eighth floor, breathless after the steep climb, she found his front door ajar. A muffled giggle snaked down the hall drawing Megan towards the bedroom. A room she and Hisham had made love in once or twice, but in which she had never slept. The heady, musky scent of cheap perfume – or was it sex? – filled her nostrils, and even before she laid eyes on the sluttish, crumpled form in his bed she knew what lay ahead. And she knew it was a calculated, meticulously planned act of betrayal.

Had he known, or suspected, all along what she wanted to ask him? Tell him? She would never know. He knew that by rubbing her nose in his infidelity she would never ask. She was too proud for that. He had other lovers. He never disguised this, but he was discreet and she took precedence over others. She'd been top cat, he'd respected her she thought, but this significant, premeditated 'slip' signalled the end of her supremacy.

'I came to say goodbye,' she'd said.

He turned to the blonde huddled in the duvet and said, 'Get out.' Cruel, uncaring.

'Don't go on my account,' she said to the girl. Then, turning to Hisham, 'I came to ask something of you. For the first time.'

'Then ask.'

'It's too late. I don't blame you. I will never ask you for anything.' And she left. But she had asked: when she emailed him photos of a tiny Cerdic. And she had been rejected. Her and Cerdic.

And now it was her fault that Cerdic was sick. She knew it was absurd, and spiteful, but she wished that it had been Hisham. That he carried the defective murderous genes and not her. Sweat poured from her brow as she marched on, stinging her eyes, and still the veiled sky offered no relief. She thought how cruel nature was.

Time evaporated as she walked. She found herself standing on the beach staring at the murky depths. She was dirty, tarnished, contaminated. Like water in poor countries she held a hidden killer. She looked clean enough, normal, pure even, but too much of her and you could end up on a slab. As an adult she had seen many die, and terrible, terrible suffering. Had her subconscious been talking to her all along? Had she sensed she carried death?

Megan sat on the beach, eyes fixed on the crumbling waves. Her arms rested on her knees and her weary face sat in her upturned, slippery palms. She removed her shoes and desiccated, warm sand trickled through her toes as she flexed them back and forth. It dried her skin, leaving a faint dust in the crook of her toes. Like icing sugar sieved onto sponge. The urge to scoop it up in her palms and rub it into her damp skin was irresistible. She rolled up her jeans and began with her legs. The sand stuck at first, but as she rubbed and rubbed it absorbed her perspiration, she felt the individual grains as they scratched at her skin, and she pressed them into her flesh, harder and harder. Tiny red spots emerged on the white, white skin wrapped round her femurs. Like poisonous, vindictive ant bites they prickled and stung until obscured by scratch lines. If she could have rubbed her insides with sand she would have. The bass ping of the mulmed jolted her into the present. Jack.

'My apologies for earlier, Ms Evens. Always such a pleasure to hear from you. How the devil are you?' She longed to chat, and laugh, shoot the breeze with him. But she knew she could not, so she launched into her request.

'I need a favour. If I call him he won't pick up. At least not the first time. Maybe not even the fourth or fifth time. If your name comes up, he'll pick up.'

'And you're talking of? I don't have my mind reading device in.'

'Hisham. I swore I'd never speak to him again. But now I have to. It's a fucker.' Her voice was sharp and staccato.

'I see.' Jack's response was slow, whispered.

Megan resisted the impulse to scream, 'No you don't. You don't see at all, Jack. How can you? You don't have kids.' Instead she replied calmly, 'Will you call him for me, Jack? I wouldn't ask if I didn't have to. You know that.'

'I know.' Jack's tone was gentle but Megan could hear hesitation swimming underneath. And then she understood.

'Tell me what's going on.'

A crack of thunder obliterated the sound of Jack's voice struggling down the mulmed. Crashing waves obscured his next sentence. The storm was on its way.

'You still there?' Megan shouted.

'Why do you want to contact Hisham?'

'I don't want to. I need to.'

She was on the verge crying, and as she told him the full extent of Cerdic's problems, the tears fell and fell. Her voice cracked and split, her tears mingled with sand, snot and sweat, and at the end she felt empty. There was a long pause before Jack spoke.

'You should have spoken with someone. Shared this. It's a big thing to keep to yourself,' he said.

'I couldn't tell anyone. Not saying it aloud made it less true somehow. Like a dream, nightmare. Mum knows. She's the only one. Apart from you.'

It was Jack's turn to speak. He was precise, deliberate, controlled.

'Hisham went missing in Tajikistan two weeks ago. No one in the Christian media network has heard a peep. We fear another kidnapping, but there's been no contact from any hostage takers. There have been a few small items on the Islamic channels. Hisham is almost one of their own. I imagine you've not been terribly interested in foreign affairs of late.'

It was hard for Megan to take this in and her feelings were so jumbled she thought she might be sick. The pungent tang of seaweed assaulted her nostrils; her lips were dry and salty from tears and coastal air, the sky fractured with another, closer, whip of thunder.

'Is anyone looking for him?'

'The French have people on it but I don't know too much about it. I'll get back to you.'

The rain fell, darkening the sand, and Megan climbed up the beach. By the time she reached the town her clothes were plastered to her skin. She sat on a bench outside the cathedral. Rain massaged her head and back, she lifted her face to the sky, water rolling down her forehead and nose, into her ears, deafening her to the everyday sounds of late afternoon town life. She winced when droplets hit her eyelids, and stuck her tongue out to wash away the taste of salt, as she did as a child. She saw Hisham, bound and gagged, hungry and thirsty, and prayed that he wasn't being tortured. There had been a time when she wished him pain, wanted to hurt him, as he had her. But now the thought of what might be happening to him made her feel sick. He was Cerdic's father; they needed him.

Two days went by before Megan heard from Jack. She resisted the temptation to call him, trusting that he would be doing everything he could, not wanting to badger him unnecessarily. She tuned into European and foreign channels on the mulmed for news of Hisham. Nothing.

She was at home, playing with Cerdic, when there was a loud knock at the door. Elizabeth was in the kitchen preparing the evening meal. The rap punctured the domestic air.

Cerdic screamed, 'Door, door!'

Megan was wary. They received few visitors. She had no close friends other than Ceri, no one on the carer and baby circuit, and no one she would go so far as calling a friend at work. Colleagues, acquaintances, yes. Friends, no. Elizabeth had always kept herself to herself.

Wondering who it could be she struggled to remember if she's ordered another toy lately. Perhaps Elizabeth had bought some garden tools? She'd been complaining about the state of the rake recently. Megan stood, glanced in the mirror above the fireplace, and released her hair from the hastily knotted pony-tail at the nape of her neck. As she strode down the hall she ran her fingers through her locks and flung them over her shoulders, picking a piece of dried fruit from her top before releasing the stiff brass catch. The door swung open to reveal a tired-looking Jack.

Megan stepped back. 'What are you doing here!'

Jack shrugged. 'Good to see you too.'

Difficulties organizing work schedules, child-care and reduced travel allowances meant that it had been six months since they had seen each other in the flesh. Composing herself, Megan resisted the impulse to fling herself at him. Instead, she reached forward and kissed his unshaven cheek, relishing its asperity.

'Good to see you too,' she whispered.

Surprising her once more, Jack embraced her, almost lifting her from the ground. She returned the hug, clinging on a little too long. Jack removed himself from her hold. Placing his hands on her shoulders he straightened his arms and regarded her.

'You're thinner than ever.'

Megan smiled sheepishly. 'Don't be a mum, Jack, it doesn't suit you.' She waved him inside, and he entered the house like a policeman, slowly, imaginary hat off. He followed her into the front room and put his bag on the floor before greeting Cerdic like an old school chum: hand outstretched, waiting for the handshake. Megan grinned wryly, trying to ignore the churning in her gut, and introduced her boy to her friend for the umpteenth time. Cerdic stared upwards with a blank expression and limpid eyes at the tall, dapper stranger. Jack appeared offended that the boy had forgotten him, then as if remembering Cerdic was only four years old he curried favour immediately with the production of a lollipop. Elizabeth fluttered moth-like from the kitchen. She became a girl in Jack's presence and while it usually annoyed Megan this time she found it quaint and amusing. A distraction.

'Jack. How lovely to see you,' Elizabeth said.

'You too, beautiful,' he replied, kissing her on both cheeks.

'Oh you flatterer.'

'Don't fall for it, Mum. He's a rogue,' Megan said.

Elizabeth ignored her and carried on. 'I've some coffee tucked away in the larder, Jack. I know how much you like your little treats.'

'Don't waste luxuries on him, Mum,' Megan tried to joke. 'They cost a fortune. He's the one with the well paid job, not us.'

Jack produced a bottle of Australian wine from his bag and both women gasped.

'You spoil us, Jack,' Elizabeth said, taking the wine and kissing him once more before withdrawing to the kitchen.

'She likes you. She almost flirts when you're around.'

'Someone's got to.'

They locked eyes; silence took the space between them hostage. Cerdic gabbled to himself and several toy superheroes. Megan knew the news wasn't good. She'd known the moment she saw Jack on her doorstep. No one travels to deliver good news. Good news comes on email, via a portable console, or an old-fashioned, handwritten, hand delivered mail, like the odd birthday card. She swept Cerdic up in one clean movement and carried him through to the kitchen with a promise of baked apples and cream after tea if he was a good boy and helped Nana.

'Is he dead?'

The little words ricocheted off the walls, burdened with hope and fear and dread. They could have been Megan's though she couldn't recall thinking or saying them. It must have been her though, it was her voice.

Jack nodded, as if afraid to confirm in words what she already knew. He pulled out a handkerchief from his top pocket and mopped his brow.

'What happened? There's been nothing on the mulmed.'

'The French received a film file yesterday. From Pakistan. Sent direct to the head of international affairs. God knows how it got through. No message, nothing. Footage of a cold-blooded murder. The victim was identified as Hisham.'

'Are they sure? Sometimes these things are faked.'

'There's no faking, Megan. It's made very obvious. The guy who saw it without warning threw up.'

'Why? Why Hisham?'

'Because he sits in both camps. The ultimate traitor. An extremist group. Condemned by Iraq, Iran, Afghanistan, Algeria and so on. He was brave. It was risky. He knew that. He wanted the story. A consummate professional...'

The howl that stole from her body reminded Megan of childbirth: primitive and animal-like. It surprised her that this was her first thought because then she remembered what else it reminded her of: death. So Hisham was dead.

Megan started to tremble. She felt the ground beneath her feet begin to crumble. She sank to the floor, the wooden boards harsh against her bones. Her heart began to flutter, then thump, faster and faster, louder and louder. Surely a heart attack was on its way and if so it would be welcomed, it would be a kind of relief, an escape. Over the past four years Hisham's hold on Megan had relaxed and then, finally, withdrawn altogether. The pain faded, then disappeared. He became what he was: the man who sired her son, a man she no longer knew or cared about. He meant nothing to her.

Until these past weeks. When suddenly the obsession returned. He meant everything. He offered hope for Cerdic. But not any more. The darkness descended.

Chapter Seven

After Jack told Megan that Hisham was dead she howled, then sobbed for a short while. Then she stood, wiped her face, and said, 'He always was such a selfish bastard. He couldn't even stay alive long enough to help his son escape a slow, lingering death. The selfish, selfish bastard. I hate him.' She seemed calm, her tone was cold. Jack had seen people in shock behave like this.

'You don't mean that.'

'I do. He was Cerdic's best chance. He should be here to help if he can. I always knew that I could never rely on him for anything. Even before Cerdic. But I allowed myself to hope this time. How very foolish of me.' She raised her eyebrows as one might at the behaviour of a truculent child, and gestured that they leave the living room.

'You sure you don't want me to get you a drink, Megan? Sit here a while. It's a shock.'

'A blow. A huge blow. But not a shock. Not really. He took too many risks. He said he was like a panther. Well, maybe he used up his nine lives. Let's go have a drink.' She walked to the door and held it open.

After a light supper of cold meats and salad Jack bathed Cerdic while the women cleared up. The boy was relaxed and carefree with him.

Cerdic piled bubble bath foam onto his head creating an enormous wig, the white bubbles contrasting with his dark face. 'Big hair!' he said, and Jack laughed out loud.

'You look like an alien, kiddo.'

'Me from Mars. Hello, earthman,' shouted Cerdic in his Martian voice.

'Greetings, Little Big Hair. You come in peace?'

'No!' Cerdic grabbed his home-made water pistol and fired at Jack.

'We take no prisoners, Big Hair,' and with that Jack took the other pistol and fired back. The boy roared and said, 'No prisoners!'

Afterwards Jack blew bubbles, monsters the boy said, which were popped with repeated slaps, claps and laughter, and they fought again and again with the water pistols.

Megan swung round the bathroom door. 'For Christ's sakes, boys! There's water pouring through the kitchen ceiling. What's going on in here?'

Jack turned and viewed the bathroom. The floor was swimming in soapy water. Dying bubbles clung to the gaps in the floorboards, Jack wasn't sure who was more wet, him or Cerdic. 'Sorry, Mum,' he said.

'Me too,' Cerdic said.

'He's the adult,' she said pointing at Jack, 'it's his responsibility.' She flung a towel at Jack's face, and flounced off.

Jack laid the towel over the floor and began to wipe. 'Mummy sounds like Nana doesn't she?'

'What do you mean?'

'A bossy teacher.'

The boy looked puzzled, and Jack added, 'You're not at school yet, are you Mr Boy? You lucky devil. I'll explain later.'

In the bedroom battered picture books stood side by side with more recent additions. Jack leafed through them as Cerdic lay in his bed, gabbling nonsensical tired-child speak. Some of the books Jack remembered from his own childhood. They predated Megan. So these were Elizabeth's boys' books. He ran his palms across the covers. Ridged with sticky fingerprints, splashed milk. Corners torn, they were yellowed at the edges. He pulled out an especially bashed one and lifted it to his nose. It smelt of innocence and age. Not like the books in his grandfather's study.

The Gruffalo's Child.

'This one?' He showed it to the boy.

'Yeah, yeah!'

Jack enjoyed reading aloud. At school he'd wanted to become an actor, but a popular teacher advised against. It would be a waste of Jack's talents, he'd said. His good brain. He should take control of his own destiny; actors were puppets in the director's hands. Jack wondered if he did control his own destiny. If anyone did.

Cerdic was fast asleep before Jack moved from the bedside. He studied the child. Puffy face, slack jawed, arms outstretched, crucifixion style, Megan said. He looked so peaceful, so at ease with the world. Jack envied him. He went to get his tobacco from his bag.

The spare room was at the top of the house, in the eaves, next to the second bathroom. It was a small, cosy room with bare floorboards, which must have been white when they were first painted decades ago. The bed had a metal frame, cream and chipped with age and use. It was French, Elizabeth had told him, bought in the Dordogne by Elizabeth's mother and father. They'd owned a house there once, a converted barn, lofty and cold aside from in the height of summer. The bed was too short for Jack who could not lie completely flat along its length, but he loved the room, and the house. Cosy and familial. It was so unlike his flat.

Wallpaper decorated with pink roses in full bloom canopied all four walls like a secret bower in midsummer. A careworn wardrobe made from a dark mahogany with metal dropper door handles stood in the corner keeping guard over the room. It emitted a dank, musty aroma as if it had lived too long in a damp basement. In the other corner sat a grandmother clock, with an exquisite painting of a cherub and an old man on its face. It looked like something that had been cut from the roof of the Sistine Chapel.

A telescope pointed at the skylight. This was where Elizabeth came to look at the stars, and the birds. Jack studied a drawing of Megan hanging on the wall.

The curve of her spine. Distinct, unmistakable, even at ten years old. Sketched in charcoal, abstract and stylized it was one of Elizabeth's first and only attempts at life drawing, and though it wasn't good in a conventional way, it was beautiful, mesmerizing. Jack admired Megan's spine. Her long back, the sharp curve before the gentle swell towards her buttocks. The way it arched towards the top of her back, before reaching the elegant neck with the deep, exaggerated nape. A hint of curvature later in life, or perhaps just the natural, almost imperceptible hunch of the very tall wanting to fit in.

He was desperate for a cigarette. He pushed open the sash window that overlooked the garden. It creaked as he did so. The frame was rotten and Jack wondered if he would be able to close it again, it was so stiff and rickety. The scent of the sea drifted in, the salty air exfoliating his mind. He rested his forearms on the windowsill and took out the papers. The first puff was magnificent, it always was, and he relished it. It would not last; it was downhill from then on. By the end of each cigarette he felt sick and repulsed by his own craving. Until the next one.

He watched the oil blue smoke curling into the night air. He blew smoke rings then watched them float on the breeze, dissolving like benign spirits. He twirled the cigarette between his fingers, following the slate path up the garden with his eyes.

'Pssst, psssst. Jack. Got a light?'

He looked down, following the familiar voice, feeling dizzy as he did so. Vertigo. It was a killer. Megan.

Her upturned face and large bare feet smiled at him from the level below. Her toenails were painted a deep red. She was sitting, outside, on the window ledge, legs dangling down the brick wall, fiddling with an unlit cigarette. His stomach turned.

'You ready to catch? I'll drop it, but I can't look, I feel sick just thinking about where you are, Ms Evens.' He held his breath, released the lighter, and breathed again when he heard the clap of metal against palm.

'Thank you kindly, Sir.'

'You're welcome, Miss.'

They finished their smokes in silence, enjoying the company but feeling no need to spoil it with conversation, and waved wordlessly before retiring.

Jack woke to the sound of distant weeping. Or was it music? Muffled sobs and sniffs. The faint scratch of a violin? He thought the crying must be Cerdic, but when he listened harder he recognized it as adult agony.

Aware that this night-time grief was a private affair, he did not want to intrude. Perhaps if he let her know that he was also awake she could come to him if she so desired? He would have to be subtle. He sat up and took a drink of water from the bedside table and once he'd drained the glass he slammed it down on the floor. A sharp thud echoed around the room and he hoped it had travelled downwards. He held his breath and listened for a sign.

Nothing. Silence. Absolute silence. No, he thought he could hear the lap of the distant sea, the squawk of a lone gull. Then again the discomforting sound of silence. It unnerved him, this silence. He was a city boy, and the city was never quiet like this.

He lay back down. It came again. The weeping. A sweep of plaintive strings, slow, then fast and furious, agonized. Jack slipped out of bed, across the room and crept down the first flight of stairs, avoiding the fourth step, which announced any arrival with a loud creak. He hovered outside Megan's room, ear tipped to the pine door, feeling like a burglar, or worse: a stalker. Nothing. Then he heard her breath rise and fall, slow and deep and peaceful. She was asleep, dreaming perhaps. He turned to creep back up the stairs, thinking he'd been hearing things when it came again. Shallow sobs, slightly panicky. Clearer than before.

Cerdic's room was next to Megan's so Jack was sure it wasn't the boy. He tiptoed forward, to the next door, just to be certain. Nothing. The door was ajar and Jack popped his head around. A dim light shaped like the moon, with a large grin and sleepy eyes, threw a cheesy hue over the space. It smelt sweet and sweaty, slightly acrid, with a trace of urine. Cerdic was splayed on the bed, a cream rabbit held by the neck dangling from his left hand, blanket on the floor, a full-looking nappy. Deepest slumber.

There was only one other person it could be. And though he had no idea what drove him on Jack crept down two flights of stairs and followed the fading sobs to the kitchen. He pushed the door ajar and stuck his head around it to find a hunched figure cradling a mug of tea. The scent of rose hip filled the air.

'Elizabeth?'

It was such a dumb thing to say. He felt like an idiot. Of course it was Elizabeth, unless a stranger with an uncanny resemblance to her had broken into Tŷ Mawr. 'Hi.'

She nodded.

'I heard a noise—'

'Did I wake you, Jack? I'm so sorry,' she interrupted, head still down. She seemed utterly crushed. She lifted her head and forced a smile, and Jack edged towards the table. He hadn't meant to come in; it felt so intrusive. Once he had established that the crying must be Elizabeth, he should have turned around, gone back to bed.

Instead he said, 'Are you all right?' Another ridiculous question. The answer was obvious, and Elizabeth would think him a fool for using such a gauche device to enquire about the source of her grief.

She half smiled and said, 'I'm fine, cariad, fine.'

Such pretence struck Jack as absurd, and then he remembered that he had started the charade. He edged closer and went to place a hand on the old woman's curved shoulder, before changing his mind and touching the teapot instead.

'Shall I make more tea? The pot's cold and I could use a drink,' he said.

Elizabeth nodded, and wiped her nose with a handkerchief scrunched in her hands. Jack drifted to the sink, kettle in hand. As he added honey to the cups he glanced at the portable music centre to the left of the bread bin. The first time he visited he had been excited when he saw it. Few people used music centres and discs. He wouldn't have believed that it still worked had he not heard it with his own ears. The sound was poor, tinny. It distorted the songs he loved more than those he disliked it seemed.

There was a CD case on top of it, a recording of a melancholy piece for the cello by a late twentieth century composer. *The Protecting Veil* was one of Elizabeth's favourite pieces of music, and she'd introduced Jack to it the first time he visited her home. She told him it made her cry every time she listened to it. So this was the scratching he'd heard from his bedroom.

He held the case aloft and said, 'Not in the mood for AC/DC then?'

She shrugged, without turning to look at him, and said, 'I can't let Megan see me. She's trying to be strong, she's so strong, that I have to pretend. But I'm not strong like Megan. I'm worried, so worried, about her, about him, about it all.' She twittered on, more to herself than to Jack.

He stared at her profile. When Jack first met Elizabeth she was a long way from his imagined version of her. Jack had pictured an exotic, distant creature, worn by tragedy and loss, indomitable Celtic spirit in tact nevertheless. Megan spoke little of her mother. Elizabeth was the physical opposite of her daughter: short, matronly, frizzy hair, crooked teeth, plump knees and non-existent ankles. She was very Welsh: cosy and slightly stodgy, didactic like a provincial schoolteacher, which was exactly what she had been.

Jack held onto the CD case, enjoying the feel of the plastic, the gentle weight of it, the Byzantine painting of the Virgin on the sleeve. It was concrete, a thing to have and hold. He liked the feeling. And just as the composer tried to penetrate that which was secret and unknowable with his music so Jack wanted to infiltrate the workings of Elizabeth's heart. Of course she was worried about Cerdic. Of course she was worried about Megan. So why did he have the most powerful feeling that something else troubled her more?

Before he met her, he assumed they'd have nothing in common. He thought she would hate him. But he was wrong about that. She didn't hate him and she treated him like a son. He became rather attached to her. They formed a bond independent of Megan, and once, when he was working in the North West Jack visited Tŷ Mawr unaccompanied.

He stared at her hands, still cradling the empty mug of tea, fingernails painted a vibrant blue. Megan had described Elizabeth's hands as extraordinarily beautiful – smooth and white, with nails like seashells – and Jack could see that they must have been lovely once. When he first met Elizabeth she was fundamentally unchanged from the Elizabeth of thirty years earlier, judging by photographs Megan had shown him. So that night it shocked Jack to notice that she had grown old, truly old. She had visibly withered, like a plant deprived of rain, though no amount of water would restore her foliage now. Her hair was thinning, her legs discoloured and misshapen by bulging blue veins that threaded and gathered in great numbers on her calves, her teeth were discoloured, roots exposed by receding gums. Her once beautiful hands were splattered with liver spots. Jack remembered his mother calling them cemetery medallions, the French expression. He remembered his first mother.

If she had survived she would have been in her nineties now. She was old when she had Jack, over forty, even older when his sister came along. Unusual in the early years of the century. But so many of Megan's generation had older mothers, some older than Elizabeth. It seemed that everyone of childbearing age was breeding at that time, or trying to. Those who had chosen to remain childfree before 2015 were encouraged, cajoled, and some would say bullied, to reproduce. There were direct financial incentives, generous ones, and yet the strongest force governing the breeding frenzy was a moral one. To reproduce, to ensure the continuation of the species, to ensure the continuation of a way of life was seen as a civic duty, a moral responsibility. For if society was to continue to support itself, then a new generation had to be forthcoming. For who would drive the wheels of capitalism when the surviving generation were old? Who would look after them when they were infirm? Who would run the country? Farm the fields, drive the buses? Buying in foreign labour from the poorer countries of the world was mooted as an option in some political circles but dispelled hastily. Rampant xenophobia and years spent restricting immigration meant such a policy would be an electoral disaster and no party was prepared to take that risk. No, the West had to breed its own. Mothers as young as sixteen, and as mature as forty-eight littered the birth columns of the 2020s. Women who had six or more children were publicly honoured and sperm donors were assured promotion wherever they worked. Still, it can't have been easy for Elizabeth. In her forties and raising a child alone.

'Is that tea ready?' Elizabeth said, interrupting Jack's thoughts.

Despite the warmth of the night Jack's feet were freezing. He glanced down at them on the terracotta tiles. They were white and bony with tufts of gingery hair sprouting from his toes. His toenails looked yellowy. Suddenly, he felt conscious of his lack of clothing. In his haste to discover the source of the crying he hadn't worn the dressing gown which hung on the back of the bedroom door. It wasn't his. His t-shirt was too short, it exposed his belly button and rounded stomach, and his shorts hung low on his hips. He wrapped himself in his arms and rubbed his biceps. He felt his nipples pushing against the cotton.

'I'm a little underdressed for the occasion,' he said.

'Occasion?'

'Tea with a friend's mother? Bad joke. My apologies.'

The kettle began to wheeze on the range. Jack whipped off the lid before it exhaled a full-blown whistle, glad of something to do. Steam clouded the air, and it was difficult to make out the blue and white teapot. He grabbed a tea towel, took hold of the handle and poured the water over the leaves. A chinking of metal spoon on china teacup broke the silence as Jack stirred and stirred. It was an annoying habit this excessive stirring. He expected Elizabeth to comment on it but she remained silent. He rested the cups on their matching saucers, enjoying the ritual of tea making that he performed only here, and placed Elizabeth's in front of her.

'Here you go.' He remained standing and unsure what to do. He was cold and uncomfortable. Elizabeth had not invited him to stay but neither had she asked him to leave, and the desire to get to the bottom of her grief, find out exactly why she was crying, was too great. He took a noisy sip, savouring the warm sweet liquid, and moved his weight from one foot to the other. He let out an exaggerated, 'Arghhh. Lovely.'

'For goodness sake, Jack, sit down or go back to bed.'

It was the invitation he needed. Ignoring the tone, he sat down on a chair opposite Elizabeth. They continued to drink in silence.

It reminded Jack of duty visits to his grandfather's as a boy. The minutes crawled by. He could read nothing in her demeanour; she was composed once more. Elizabeth poured another cup. She did not pour him one.

Fuck it, he thought. 'Think I'll have another,' he said.

'Would you like a biscuit with that, Jack? They're your favourites. I baked them earlier.' Elizabeth made a stab at normality.

'No thanks. I've reached an age when I need to look after my teeth. And my waistline.' He patted his belly. A coolness washed over Elizabeth again. Realizing his mistake, Jack added, 'They look delicious, mind. Really delicious. A good batch, even by your standards.' This was a lie, and they both knew it. Elizabeth was a terrible baker. He put his hands to his forehead. 'I hope I don't sound ungrateful. It's just... you know.'

Elizabeth smiled and nodded.

Jack could bear it no longer.

'Is there something troubling you, Elizabeth? I know you're worried about Cerdic, Megan.'

'I just wish I could do more, that's all.'

'I'm always here if you need to talk.' As soon as he said it, he knew it was a mistake. It reeked of therapy. She hated all that, Megan said. What had he been thinking? It wasn't only his feet that were frozen. What a twat.

'You sound like a bloody quack! And you're not always here.'

Jack was shocked. He had never heard Elizabeth swear. She looked flustered, her cheeks were highly coloured. He stood up and said, 'I think I'd better go. Goodnight.'

She reached out her hand. He noticed she was trembling.

'Jack, I'm sorry, I didn't mean to snap. You mean well.'

'I don't want to upset you, I want to help.' He turned to leave. 'Jack...'

He turned back. Her thin lips quivered, her face dropped, her eyes were watery. She opened her mouth to speak. Nothing came out.

Yes?' he said.

Her face set again. The mask appeared. 'We all want to help.' Her tone was vehement, conversation closed.

Jack knew when to call it a day. He collected his half full tea and returned to his room. Half an hour later, reading in bed, and close to sleep, he heard the creak of the boards on the mezzanine, the flush of the toilet next to Elizabeth's room.

Chapter Eight

Megan woke to the sound of rain lashing against the window. Clouds had swept in from the Irish Sea during the night. She wondered how long it had been raining, and whether it had woken Jack in the attic with its rooftop window. The rain would sound like hail stones as it would be falling directly, almost vertically, onto the glass. It was one of the few disadvantages of that room. There was no escaping the sound of the rain.

She stretched over the books and newspapers piled on top of her portable mulmed, feeling for the switch on the lamp perched on the bedside table, knocking over a half empty mug of fennel tea in the process. 'Shit,' she said, as the tea dribbled into the carpet. She grabbed a t-shirt from underneath her pillow and swatted at the remaining liquid on the table, brushing it away from the machine. She could not afford a malfunctioning mulmed. The carpet was thoroughly stained, a little tea wouldn't make any difference, though when Megan first moved into the room, Elizabeth's old room, the flooring had been pristine. Megan had removed the heavily patterned wallpaper and painted the walls white only weeks before Cerdic was born, but she stopped short of ripping up the perfectly decent carpet. Elizabeth shrieked that it was dangerous for a woman in her condition to be undertaking such labour, but Megan laughed and said, 'Mother, this is NOT dangerous. Believe me.'

The rain was welcome. Apart from a couple of short lived storms, it had been a dry, humid, mostly overcast, month. Megan thought the clouds must be relieved to unload their cargo, and she sat at her window for a while watching the garden lap up the moisture. On the patio the raindrops bounced on the sandstone slabs turning the soft gold stone a deep mustard. Puddles gathered in the natural dips and curves in the stone, the yellow-green leaves of the robinia tree sparkled despite the lack of sunshine, its flimsy branches bowing to the brown earth with the gathering weight of its foliage. Long grass, beige with age, stooped towards the ground.

There was a knock at her door. 'Morning, Ms Evens. Coffee in bed?' Jack's voice echoed from the landing, then she heard the familiar pitter-patter of Cerdic's feet, and a croaky, 'Hello, Mr Boy. Can I get you some milk?'

Megan hadn't expected Jack to rise before nine. 'You're up early. Did the rain wake you?' she said, leaping back into bed.

'You're kidding. Sleep through anything me. Gunfire, mortar shots, earthquakes.' He would have continued except that a loose, chesty cough broke through his words and forced him to stop.

'But not Welsh rain.' Megan laughed, adding, 'You've got to give up the fags. And come in, I hate talking through walls.'

Jack popped his head round the door, but didn't enter. 'No way. It's my last stand against health fascism. If I choose to risk any number of horrendous, terminal diseases then that is my choice, and my choice alone. I will not be forced to endure years of healthy old age, a bionic body and defunct brain.' And with that he marched off downstairs, Cerdic in tow.

Megan snuggled down into the bed covering her face with the duvet, eyes closed and smiling. It felt good; she hadn't done much smiling lately. She lay still for a few moments. She missed Jack's acerbic, often cruel, humour. In the offices of The North Wales Community Media Group, everyone was friendly, and nice, but there was no one to banter with, to mock the crazy, cruel world.

When Jack knocked on the door again and entered with two mugs of steaming coffee, she was back at the window.

'I'm sorry for just now. How insensitive,' he said.

Megan smiled. 'No need to apologize, Jack. As it happens I agree with the sentiment.' She raised her mug, toast style, and he followed suit.

'To health libertarianism!'

'And to more research into diseases we have no control over,' Jack added.

'Hear, hear.'

Jack pulled up a chair alongside Megan. They drank in silence, both deep in thought. Megan had so many questions.

She broke their reveries. 'Do you believe we should control

hereditary conditions, Jack?'

'How do you mean? So much of what makes us 'us' is heredi-tary, good and bad. My mother's family have a history of osteoporosis. My grandmother had it I've been told, and my own mother was obsessed with bone density scans. She had one annually even as a relatively young woman. Had she survived my sister might well have grown up to be the same way. Who knows? Are you asking if my mother should have had a daughter, knowing this?'

Megan was confused. 'You were young when your mother died. She was quite young herself. Too young for osteoporosis, surely?' she said.

'I'm not talking about my biological parents. I'm talking about Joanne, the woman who raised me, the woman I called Mummy. Who loved me and cared for me. Was always there for me, even when I was a little shit.'

'And I bet that was often!'

He pulled a face and said, 'Now, now.'

'I didn't know you had a sister. Another sister. You never said.'

'Didn't I?'

'What happened?'

'You know I'd already been with one foster family, before the Millingtons.'

'I didn't. But carry on.'

'It took two years before the adoption procedure was com-plete. A few months after it was finalized Joanne discovered she was pregnant. After years and years of trying, and failing, without an apparently solid medical reason, Jo and Tom conceived a child. A daughter.'

'It happens like that a lot.'

He continued, 'They called her Pearl. Ironic really because she was anything but tough. Sickly at birth she spent much of her life in hospital.'

'How awful for you. What happened?'

'She was knocked down on the Archway Road. She was ten,

out of the woods on the whole. We joked that she'd probably grow up to be the healthiest and outlive us all.'

So Jack had lost two siblings. He had never been close to Hermione, his first sister, but Pearl felt like a threat. She said, 'Was she as lovely as her name?'

'I don't know. She was my little sister. I didn't pay her much attention. I think I was jealous of her, all the attention she received, because she was poorly. And perhaps because she was theirs. I wish I had paid her more attention. I'd have liked to know how she might have turned out. Whether we'd have been friends and all that. Met up for an early supper and a show in the West End once in a while. You know the sort of thing.'

'Not really. But I can imagine.'

They continued to stare at the garden. Pools of dirty water gathered on the lawn and in the flowerbeds, the ground so parched and stiff that it was unable to absorb the heavy flow of rain, which showed no signs of abating. The flooding season was fast approaching. Megan wondered why Jack had never spoken of Pearl before. She wanted to know so much more, but didn't want to ask. Not because she feared it would pain Jack, but because he might detect her envy and she didn't like the idea of him thinking badly of her.

'Would you have liked a brother or sister?' Jack said.

'Sharing the attention? No way. Anyway, you're like a brother.' She nudged his shoulder, expecting him to be pleased, but a strange look washed over him, and for a moment Megan thought he looked uncomfortable.

'Not that I could replace your sisters, of course,' she said hurriedly, in the awkward space between them.

'Nothing to replace. Hardly knew them.'

And changing the subject abruptly Jack said, 'I've done some reading round Cerdic's condition. I know that it is most commonly hereditary, and passed down the mother's line.'

'To the boys. Only the boys. Mum had three sons before me.'

'What are you saying?'

'I asked her. If her boys died of plague or AMNA. If they had it.'

'And?'

'They died of plague. She was firm about this. But there's this air of withholding when she talks of that time. Which isn't often. But I feel it. She's always guarded. I know it must be painful, to be reminded of such loss, but… Oh, this is hard to say, but I don't think she's telling the whole story.'

'I've thought the same thing,' he said, uneasily. 'So her boys died of plague. But what if they had AMNA and your mum knew? She feels guilty because she couldn't bring herself to warn you? To bring you such pain? Instead she put her faith in God and she let him decide the outcome.'

Megan glared at him.

'But she loves you, and Cerdic. She would do anything to protect you. She can't have known she was a carrier,' he added.

She leant her forehead against the window pane.

'Why can't she talk of that time?'

Megan spoke slowly and deliberately. 'She lost everything. And you know what, Jack? Whether she knew or not doesn't matter. It won't help Cerdic. I was angry at first. I wanted to blame someone. It would have been easy to blame her. For not warning me. It would have diminished us both,' Megan said.

'Megan, Elizabeth knew.' She turned sharply and looked at him.

'She gambled and the roll of the dice didn't favour her. She feels guilty.' Jack placed his hands around Megan's.

'How can you be so sure?' she spat, withdrawing her hands.

'I can't.'

'Then what are you getting at? If we were at an editorial Max—'

'Julie's home affairs editor now.'

'Julie? Julie Brookings?' Megan thought she'd misheard. But then it made sense. Julie was ambitious, ruthless. She'd sensed it years ago. But that was quick, even for a manipulative little harpy. Megan admitted a grudging respect for the woman – editor at twenty-seven. That was good going by anyone's standards. 'You never said.'

'Didn't I?'

Only later did Megan acknowledge her jealousy. It could have been her making editor. 'Whatever. Julie,' she said the name with emphasis, 'would insist upon facts. Being sure.' She thought what a horrible, unusual, name Julie was.

'I found your mum in the kitchen last night.'

'So? She's insomniac.'

'She was crying. Wouldn't talk to me.'

So it's not just me she won't talk to then, Megan thought. She said, 'She's worried. We all are.'

'It was more than that.'

Megan didn't want to row. 'You're impossible. Facts. More coffee while we've got it?'

They finished the coffee and Jack said no more. As he left she stood, stretched and clicked her knuckles. He reminded her that she would pay for the habit later in life. Megan wondered if Elizabeth had done it. After all she had arthritis now. Perhaps it's hereditary, Megan thought.

As she dressed Jack's words kept coming back to her. His doubt preyed on her mind. She'd thought the same. But if Elizabeth had known about the AMNA and she had told Megan, would she have terminated the pregnancy when she knew her unborn child was male? Definitely not. She had always been a risk taker. Knowing would have altered nothing. And despite her assertion of Elizabeth's innocence Jack's comment echoed round her head. 'Elizabeth knew.'

Chapter Nine

Jack returned to London later that morning. Megan wanted him to stay longer but he wouldn't be persuaded. She was angry with him for deserting her so quickly, though she knew such feelings were irrational. It was good of him to come in the first place.

After he'd gone she entered Cerdic on the European donor database. There were no matching donors currently registered.

'How long does it usually take for donors to come through?' Megan asked the database registrar.

'There's no usually about it. Each and every case is unique. It depends on the condition, the individual concerned. Donors come and go all the time. It's futile to speculate.' He sounded bored.

'There must be some guidelines, averages, that sort of thing.' Megan twisted her ring, feeling impatient.

'Not really.'

'Individual examples?'

'These are by their very nature risky to set any store by. They can raise expectation unjustifiably. Often people become angry and frustrated when they are not as fortunate as others.'

'I'd like a few examples. Please,' Megan said through clenched teeth.

'If you're sure.'

'I am.'

'As you wish. The wait could be as little as a few days, or as long as decades.'

'My son does not have decades.'

'I'm sorry.' He didn't sound it.

She logged off and stared at the wall.

Days passed. She could not eat or sleep. A debilitating sense of anxiety and helplessness rendered her emotionally inert. At home and at work she went through the motions, detached and distant. As if she was reporting on her own life rather than actually living it.

One morning unable to motivate herself to go into work she asked her mother to call in sick on her behalf. She repeated the request the next day. And the next. Finally her boss called her personal mulmed, and she knew she had to speak with him.

'Hey, Meg. How goes it?'

'Not great...' She hated him calling her Meg. She hated the way he affected slang when talking to younger members of his team, like he was trying to be one of them, rather than their boss. But she felt sorry for the man. He was twenty years her senior, lonely, well-meaning but dull. An air of profound disappointment with life oozed from his pores.

'Sorry to hear that,' he said.

She did not respond, waiting for him to fill the silence, which he duly did.

'Look, Meg, this is a bit awkward, but I need to know when you're next in.'

'I'm not sure.'

And without a second thought Megan explained that she needed a sabbatical, an indefinite one. Months, maybe more. It had to start immediately. Either that or she would hand in her notice.

He didn't ask why and she didn't tell him. He was sad to see her go, he said. She was a good sub, but her job-share wanted more hours, and now that Cerdic was growing up he suspected she'd want a more challenging role than he'd ever have on offer. A hint of envy snaked into his voice. If only he knew. Her chest contracted at the mention of Cerdic and she bit back tears.

'Been great working with you, Meg. Good luck.'

'Thanks. I'll need it.'

The decision to resign had not been premeditated. It was instinctive, and she had no idea what she was going to do next. But it was time to be decisive.

She spent the day playing with Cerdic and that night she began to search. Buried in the study on the mezzanine, hoping the cigarette smoke would not filter through to Elizabeth's room she poured over pages on the mulmed. She looked at scientific

112

channels, donor channels, sites for the terminally ill. She bounced from one to the other, without logic or rationale. Just as dawn was breaking she came across a comment on a forum for parents of life-limited children: 'My elderly father wants to donate. It will affect his health – not that good as it is – and it can't extend my son's life, only make him a little more comfortable. Do you think I should let him?' Intrigued, Megan flicked through to the main page.

The front page copy read: 'Special People need Special Help. Despite what the authorities say there are people who need extra support. If you, or your dependent, have any kind of special needs, from physical disabilities, to incurable, life-limiting conditions, you need more than cash. The authorities may think that a compensation package is enough, but we understand that it's not. Emotional and psychological support is vital. And if you need legal advice to claim what is rightfully yours, or need general advocacy, then our team of experts can help with that too.'

The organisation, for 'special' children and their carers ran a network of support groups, one in Chester, just across the border, not far from Bangor. Megan was surprised on two counts: firstly that there were enough 'special' children to warrant the number of groups and secondly, that the consultant at the hospital had made no mention of the organisation.

She clicked onto page two: 'The number of children born with hereditary conditions, disabilities and other imperfections is so low as to be considered insignificant by government. Over the past ten years genetic engineering, abandoned in the second decade of the 21st century, has resurfaced with increased dedication and a massive influx of funding. Once again the ugly desire to build a better, more 'perfect' world has emerged. Prospective parents may not be allowed to select offspring on the basis of looks, intelligence or gender, but the recently introduced Europe-wide screening programme to detect disease and 'abnormalities' is the first step on a slippery slope. Termination may not be compulsory, but the popular mood is such that virtually no one chooses to continue with a pregnancy when the foetus is known to be damaged. What kind of a world are we creating? Where will it stop? And what are the implications for those of us who are 'defective' in some way, or care for someone who is?'

She read on and on, finding comfort in the fact that there were others like her and Cerdic, facing uncertain futures. The support group met every other month and the next meeting was only days away. She emailed to ask if she might attend, hoping she might make some useful contacts at worst. Her mileage allowance was healthy. The positive reply from the group co-ordinator arrived just after lunch.

It was years since Megan had visited Chester and it was as lovely as she remembered with its earth red brickwork and ornate clock on the bridge arching the main thoroughfare. She arrived early and walked the walls that encircled the city before descending to ground level, looking for the café in the remains of the once famous rows: a two-tiered timer-framed medieval shopping arcade in the city centre, originally built in the thirteenth century and rebuilt by the Victorians after it was destroyed in a fire. Once a lucrative tourist attraction the rows had finally been destroyed in 2015. Made almost entirely of wooden beams they were considered a breeding ground and safe haven for all manner of vermin.

Megan wasn't sure what she expected, still less exactly what she was looking for, when she stepped into the back room of the café. In the end she was late, having lost her sense of time as she walked, and all eyes were fixed on her apologetic, awkward figure. The first thing that struck her was that this rag-bag bunch of oddballs was the last thing most people would conjure if asked to imagine someone 'special'.

'Welcome. You must be Megan. I'm John,' said a dark-haired man in a wheelchair, extending a trembling hand. Megan wondered why he was nervous, before realizing that the shaking was involuntary.

'Hello. Nice to meet you,' she said, the lie tripping off her tongue.

There were half a dozen adults, mostly in their thirties like her, who all looked as if they suffered with an affliction of one sort or another. She had expected the adults to be normal; it was the children who needed help? And then she recalled a news story from years ago when she worked at EBC. Adults conceived between 2016 and the early 2020s with varying congenital and hereditary conditions were seeking reparation from government. The story ran for a day or two, the government apologized on behalf of some unscrupulous fertility clinics and smalls sums of money were paid out. The piece was quashed by a senior executive, and then trouble flared up in the Arctic again, and the story was buried, forgotten. It affected so few people.

And here they were: those forgotten people. A woman who appeared to have nothing wrong with her entered the room, offering cakes and weak tea, while people took their place in a small circle. An empty chair sat waiting for Megan.

Then John spoke. 'So, Megan, would you like to tell the group why you're here today?'

'I'm not sure, if I'm honest.'

They all looked at her. 'I was hoping someone might be able to help to my son.'

'What sort of help?' said one.

'Tell us your story,' said another.

And so she did. Afterwards there was a long pause. Finally John spoke.

'You could ask your mother to test. The chances are slim. She's more than likely a carrier. But, there is a chance,' he said.

'But if she does match she will be obliged to donate. And I have to choose between my mother and my son,' Megan said.

The tea woman held out the plate of cakes again. Megan shook her head, her stomach churning. Coming here was not meant to be about debating whether or not Elizabeth should donate. She had wasted her time. 'Do you lobby government? Work with pressure groups? The site mentions advocacy. Have any of you found help outside of Europe? I'll travel. Anything.'

'There is a voluntary legal team which will assess your case to see if you have grounds for compensation.'

'No, that's not what I meant. That's not my problem. I need a donor, fast,' she said.

So there was nothing they could do, well-meaning as they were. She wanted to leave, but it would have been awkward and rude. Drinking her tea she watched and listened. She heard stories of lives ripped apart by disease and discrimination, of quests for justice and understanding. She was reminded of her former work, of the people she interviewed, the little people whose stories she told to an uncaring world, and she felt angry that these people were overlooked. That Cerdic would be overlooked. A faceless name languishing on a database. Waiting. Dying. Rage fluttered in her belly; she thought she might be sick.

'I have to go. I've a train to catch,' she said, rising from her chair.

A bell sounded, and the tea woman leapt to her feet.

'That will be my husband and son. Do say hello before you leave. My son enjoys your weekly blog. Especially your digs at the department of population protection and the peace office.'

'Weekly rant,' Megan said. She was dismissive but flattered, and as she bent to collect her coat from the back of the chair a man pushed a wheelchair into the room. On it sat a boy. Large brown eyes looked into hers. A ventilator covered the lower half of the boy's face, his withered limbs hung from an exhausted frame.

'Duchenne,' the tea woman whispered to Megan, before saying, more loudly, 'Simon, meet Megan Evens. I told you she was coming, didn't I?' She turned to the rest of the group with a knowing wink and announced, 'He never believes anything I say!'

The father helped the boy offer his hand to Megan. It was light in her hand, like air.

'Delighted to meet you, Simon,' she choked. The boy tried to say something. The father said, 'He said "Keep on at those stupid bastards, Miss Evens." '

'I will,' said Megan, and she meant it.

'Will you come again?' John said.

'I don't think so, no,' she said, 'I've too much to do. But thank you. I'll write about your group. I won't let people forget, pretend you don't exist. I wish you well.'

'You too, Megan.'

And she was gone. Outside, rage and fear enveloped her. She saw Cerdic in the boy's eyes, and she felt very, very alone. She needed to walk. She needed to be near water.

The light was fading when Megan reached the river. Dusk. Her favourite time of day. Everything looked better in the dulling light. Worry lines and frown marks faded away. Stains on clothes, chipped paintwork, windowpanes splashed with seagull excrement disappeared. The world with softer edges, fewer flaws. She sat on a bench and watched the water carry a plastic bottle down the rapids and under the shallow arch of the bridge crossing the Dee. The street lamps threw a cheesy haze onto the water's reflection warming the rapidly chilling air. Jetsam and flotsam loitered at the river's bank: broken branches with curling leaves, sticks and weed hovered with the discarded remains of ice cream packaging and aluminium cans. Litter was becoming a problem. Evidence that the human race thought itself infallible once again. When Megan was a child she was told that everywhere used to be dirty, especially the cities. That she was lucky to have been born when cleanliness was valued, that fewer people meant less pollution, less waste.

She recalled a day on the beach at Barmouth. 'Another chance, cariad. We've been given another chance. Thank the Lord, for he is merciful,' Elizabeth had chanted, sweeping her arm across the horizon before kissing Megan hard on the cheek.

With only a handful of threadbare swans pecking away at crumbs on the pavement, and a deserted cruiser named *Diana* bobbing against the jetty for company, Megan surreptitiously lit a cigarette. She could hear the distant sounds of the city under the sloshing of the river against the boat's stern, and then footsteps. She thought about turning, stubbing out her cigarette but didn't. If it was the police she'd be fined for smoking in public regardless. She took another drag, following the amber glow up the stem.

'You got a light?'

A male voice with the soft lilt of a Welsh accent. Megan stretched out her arm, lighter in hand, without looking directly at her fellow smoker, figuring that if he was an officer she may as well provide him with concrete evidence of her crime.

'Ta.'

The click of the flint, a deep, desperate inhalation and thankful exhalation. Not a police officer then, he genuinely needed a light. The lighter was returned with a hesitant, 'You look a bit like someone I went to school with.'

Megan turned to regard the deliverer of such a clumsy chat-up line. An unremarkable man in his mid-thirties, Megan guessed. Medium height and build, dull blondish hair. It was difficult to be precise about his hair colour at sundown. She admired his rebellious, anti-establishment streak.

'It's Meg isn't it? Meg Evens, at least that's what you used to be called,' he said smiling, revealing uncared for teeth.

It was Gareth Williams. The best-looking boy in year eleven at school. Megan struggled to find the gorgeous sixteen-year-old in the dishevelled, slightly shambolic figure before her. She had been in love with him for two years, always from afar, never declared. At least not to him. She confessed her passion to Ceri who, in contrast to Meg, was already well-developed and confident. Ceri dated Gareth's best friend, another desirable boy named Adam, and once asked Gareth to dance with Megan at the end of term disco. He refused.

'I'm still Meg Evens, though most people call me Megan now. It's Gareth Williams isn't it?' she said.

'You remembered. Wow,' he said, visibly flattered. Composing himself he sat down alongside her on the bench and added, 'You've aged well yourself.'

'You've changed. But I've a good memory for faces – it's my business to remember names and faces,' she replied, quashing his nascent arrogance.

'I saw you on the mulmed. In some far off place. We all knew you'd go far. You know, do well. You were different. What a life you've lived. All that travelling,' he sighed.

'Indeed.' She lit another cigarette and stared at the river.

'What are you doing here? Not your usual assignment I shouldn't think.'

'I live here. Well, near. In Wales. I came home.'

'It must seem very dull after all that, you know...'

'Death, destruction? It did take some getting used to. And it can be dull, sometimes. Just like life. It's different that's all. And it's safe.' At least it used to feel safe, she thought. Nothing felt safe anymore.

'Boring, more like. Though less boring now you're here.' He shuffled closer and she thought he might place a hand on her thigh or a similar clumsy and clichéd gesture of seduction. 'Are you still friends with Ceri?'

'Yes. I'll tell her you remembered her, said hello. Are you going to buy me a drink then?' she said, rising. She didn't wait for a reply, she knew he'd follow.

He took her to an authority run pub. She didn't bother asking if he knew of any illegals; she knew he wouldn't. In the toilets Megan phoned Elizabeth claiming to have missed the last train. She would find a hotel, she said, and return first thing in the morning. That Elizabeth wasn't to worry, Cerdic would be fine when he woke up and she wasn't there. He probably wouldn't even notice her absence.

Gareth was polishing off his second, final, pint when she returned to their table. She saw the longing in his eyes, a nervousness, the regret that he turned her down once, that he certainly wouldn't do the same now, that if he made a pass, the tiniest move on her, she would take her revenge for that humiliating rejection a generation ago. He was wrong. She had determined to have him when he sat down beside her at the water's edge. It didn't matter that he was no longer the golden, preening boy, that she didn't find him desirable. She needed to be taken out of herself. To taste something other than pain, something salty, moist, slippery.

The hotel was suitably shabby. A stained carpet and thin towels. Overbearing furniture crammed into every available space, dirty windows. A seedy place for a seedy act. One born of fear and loneliness.

It had been a long time for Megan, and Gareth's clumsiness and initial ineptitude suited her. At daybreak Megan stole out of bed and slipped into her clothes. They felt damp, stiff, as if they belonged to another. She didn't bother to wash. She would feel filthy regardless. As she turned the brass doorknob the bed wheezed, and a hoarse whisper rose from the stinking sheets. She turned to face him and was repelled by his crumpled features and ruffled hair. She was grateful that he didn't state the obvious and merely asked if he might see her again when she was next in town.

'I don't think so.'

'It was good though, wasn't it?' he said.

She looked at him before replying, 'No. It was desperate. Goodbye, Gareth.' Then she dived into the gloomy hall.

The sunlight hurt her eyes as she stepped onto the pavement and she was glad to have a reason to hide behind her sunglasses. The station was busy when she got there. She imagined people were staring, that they knew. Her flesh still rang out, her senses alive, fizzing in the aftermath of energetic physical activity. She wondered if she carried his stale, sour scent on her. She was disgusted with herself for wasting time on cheap sex in cheap hotels when she should be fighting to save Cerdic. She wanted her son to experience the rush of the no-strings encounter, the power of enduring, platonic love, the pleasure of love-making. He must live. She would do whatever it took. And there was something she could do straight away: ask her mother to see the consultant. The group were right. It was a long shot but not impossible. Elizabeth could be a match, and if she wasn't Megan would begin again. Alert and determined, Megan headed home. Today she would ask her mother to see Mr Barnet.

Just in case.

Chapter Ten

Somewhere between Shotton, a lowdown dirty town that had never recovered from the meltdown of manufacturing, and Llandudno Junction Megan called her mother from her mulmed. Elizabeth picked up immediately. She looked happy, the light bounced off her silver hair. She and Cerdic were crossing over onto Anglesey. To explore Red Wharf Bay.

'There won't be too many more days like this Meg before the rain really sets in.'

'It's a lovely idea, Mum,' Megan trilled but her heart sank. They wouldn't return before four o' clock, at the earliest. She would have to wait before asking her mother to see Mr Barnet. Megan would explain to the doctors that her mother had had sons, three sons no less, who escaped the disease. Elizabeth might have some natural immunity, her blood might be good, an antidote to the bad that Megan had unwittingly passed onto her boy. There was a chance. Megan knew that she may be sacrificing her mother for her child, and she knew it to be in the natural order. Always the young first. It was an unwritten law, abided by all but the most selfish and soulless.

It was a beautiful day. The low sun lit the landscape in an amber hue, like honey on Bara Brith. At Bangor station Megan scoured the boards for the next train to Beaumaris. She would head to the island. It would be easy enough to find them. She would not return home first, to change her clothes, wash away the remains of the night.

Cerdic was pushing shells into the turrets of a fairy castle when Megan strode across the sands. Elizabeth recumbent beside the fortress. Seaweed draped across the crumbling drawbridge, seagull feathers swaying from the battlements in the wind. Megan looked across the beach. Sandcastles, stripy windbreaks, flapping kites fighting for freedom from their wiry strings, children running to and from the foaming waves, screaming, ice blue toes impervious to the biting waves, the roaming ice cream van with its tinkling call. It looked much as it did when Megan was a child and when Elizabeth was a child and the children before her.

Megan stepped over writing in the sand. "NERYS WAS HERE". Proof of existence, of counting. No matter that the sea would wash away the evidence, it would be written again. On desks, public toilet walls, carved into tree trunks. She watched a father filming mother and child searching the rock pools for signs of life, nets and buckets in hands. Waving to the camera.

'Hello, it's me, us, here, now, forever.' Proof of life. Megan wondered if the father missed something of that life, with the constant recording of it. The not-experiencing.

Lugubrious thoughts crept into her head. Cerdic would always exist for Megan. But for others? Those who had yet to meet him. Might not meet him. That's why there were images, why the human need to record. Why burial was still more popular than cremation, despite the lack of space and expense. The headstone. Carved names, messages of love and remembrance. The memorial for those lost, the park bench, the planted tree. Cerdic would have his stone. In loving memory to a dearly beloved husband, father, grandfather. A long and normal life.

Megan marched closer.

Cerdic broke the drawbridge when he glimpsed her. He jumped up and down, and fell, before struggling to stand, flinging himself at her. After a cuddle Cerdic returned to his beleaguered castle, busying himself with the task of repairing the battlements. Megan didn't waste any time before posing her request.

She had been thinking, she said, she wanted her mother to see Mr Barnet, to see if there was any chance that Elizabeth could donate. She would not ask if there was an alternative. She had hoped not to have to ask.

'Can we talk about this later, Meg? Now isn't a good time.'

'But there's never a good time, Mum. I've been putting off asking. Cerdic's okay, he's playing. We can talk.'

'We can't,' Elizabeth murmured.

Megan ignored her and carried on. She understood the risks to her mother, the procedures were hard on donors as well as recipients, but if she did match… What a gift to her grandson.

'I love you, Mum. More than everything in world. Everything except Cerdic.'

'Deep inside I knew that it might, one day, come to this. My dreams are peppered with the truth and many mornings I wake to the taste of an unspeakable fear. I've held onto the lie for so long I ache, to let go might be a relief,' Elizabeth said, the words catching in her throat, her voice strange and alien. 'I would help if I could. I would give my life for Cerdic. For you. But I will not match. We do not need to visit Mr Barnet for confirmation of this.'

And Megan knew. The truth transformed the earth beneath her feet to quicksand; she was sinking; she felt she didn't have long before she would disappear altogether. She looked at her mother, hoping she might laugh off her words, explain that Megan had misunderstood. But the earth was pulling Megan down. She was buried to her chest, her arms outstretched.

Elizabeth continued, 'You are my daughter, Meg. In every way imaginable. But I did not give birth to you. You are not of my body. Only my soul.'

And Megan sank, the ground swallowing her entirely, pouring into her. No trace.

Part Two

2015 – 2020

Chapter Eleven

The slow-worm was beautiful. Copper brown and sleek, rare, very much alive.

The slow-worms were dying, or so it seemed to Elizabeth. She had been discarding bodies for weeks. A day earlier she had found four carcasses scattered on the path at the side of the house, buried amongst the drying twigs of the recently pruned hedge. At first Elizabeth thought they were tails only, shed to escape the grip of a predator, but when she looked closer the jet eyes stared back at her, unblinking, the flat tongues dangling from silent mouths.

The worm winked at her. It was coiled into a perfect 's' shape, tucked between pots of apple mint and chives on the dilapidated patio. Dark grey and sprouting weeds the surface might once have been described as crazy paving. It had been there when Andrew and Elizabeth bought the house, a few months before their wedding, and though Elizabeth meant to get someone in to lay a new patio, or some decking – Andrew never showed any inclination towards DIY – work, and children, and other prosaic tasks got in the way. It wasn't perfect but then nothing about the house was, so it fitted in well. She tiptoed to the back door and called for the boys who were playing inside despite the glorious sunshine. The twins were the first to appear, frantic and clumsy. The youngest, Robert, staggered on afterwards. Elizabeth lifted her finger to her lips and pointed at the creature.

'They can move very quickly when they have to boys. This one is a girl. A good sign I think,' she whispered.

'There's another one,' Matthew shouted, pointing to a tub of down-at-heel nasturtiums.

Elizabeth looked up and as she pushed her glasses back to the bridge of her nose she saw a thick scaly snake disappear into the drain. She blinked and it was gone. She closed her eyes to conjure the image, to see if the imprint remained on her retina. It wasn't another slow-worm. Of that she was sure. And when she turned back the worm had slithered away too. Matthew held a stick in his little hands and wore an innocent mask.

The boys played in the garden. The twins kicked a football round the lawn, while the baby mooched in the flowerbeds, miniature shovel and watering can in his mucky hands. Elizabeth watched her children through the kitchen window as she washed the pans that the dishwasher could not hold. She thought she would never tire of watching her boys play. Cleaning up after them was an entirely different matter.

Elizabeth was untidy and the arrival of children compounded her disorder. And no matter how hard she tried she simply couldn't keep on top of the housework. Andrew helped out, but he wasn't a natural housekeeper either. He tidied beautifully but the need to clean, to get down on hands and knees, and scrub, and wipe, and brush, eluded him. So the house was unkempt, and the white walls, white lino and cream carpets only served to remind Elizabeth how low her standards were. With three adventurous boys, a husband and work, it was harder than ever to keep the place clean.

There were brown smudges everywhere. The furnishings, floors and skirting boards were smeared with mud, chocolate, felt pens. In the kitchen, sides of cupboards and the oven dribbled with stains, which mingled with rivers of congealed fat. The boys denied any responsibility for the marks, and no matter how often Elizabeth wiped their hands and reminded them to remove their muddy boots in the lobby, the trails continued to appear, like messages written in invisible ink revealing themselves above the heat of a naked flame.

The first time Elizabeth saw the rat, she saw the tail, and she thought she might have imagined it. The second time she saw the body and she knew she had not. She was curled up on the sofa in the living room, enjoying a battered copy of *Jane Eyre*, the three boys tucked up for the night, Andrew out with crusty university colleagues.

The air was cool for May, and Elizabeth savoured the uncharacteristic chill before the sweaty months to come. She pulled the right sleeve of her grey cardigan down towards her palm and held its bobbled, frayed cuff tight, fiddling with the edging as she read. The cardigan was a favourite. She'd had it since she married, though she only ever wore it at home now, and she felt safe in it, as well as warm.

Natural light was retiring, and Elizabeth knew that she must prise herself off the sofa and turn on the lamp if she was not to damage her already poor eyesight irrevocably. Elizabeth had worn glasses for twenty-seven years, since she was ten years old, and every time she visited the optician her prescription grew stronger. Elizabeth understood all too well the cruel hand Mother Nature dealt some people. As a young woman she persuaded herself that she didn't care about appearances and set about improving her mind, but she was old enough now to recognize that she had, of course, been deluding herself.

These days she took as much care with her appearance as the next woman, though she dealt with the poorest of raw materials. She visited a hairdresser and styled her hair, chose clothes that she felt complemented each other and added embellishment with the odd, subtle piece of jewellery. She was permanently on a diet, though her body remained resolutely solid, if not exactly fat.

She didn't bother much with make-up. She didn't know what to do with most of the products that adorned the vast cosmetics counters of department stores and chemists, and she was too embarrassed to approach the dolls that posed as assistants, with their permanently startled expressions, painted-on eyebrows and immoveable features. They reduced her to a fool with a withering sideways glance and an arched 'Is there anything in particular you're looking for, Madam?' They occupied mainland young and beautiful; Elizabeth was marooned on approaching middle age and plain. She wondered how it could be that a mature woman, with the first strands of grey peeping above the parapet of her scalp did not have the first notion of how to go about making herself up.

She loved nail varnish. The miniature bottles with their elaborate sparkling tops were like precious stones, jewels, all lined up, orderly, conveniently placed testers made applying a sample easy, the colour straightforward to assess. Elizabeth relished the instant transformation, achieved with minimum skill: dab and stroke, dip and brush. No shading, no blending, no matching to eye and skin tone, no areas to avoid, creases to fill. The pitfalls were few, the rewards plenty. Nails were easy, and Elizabeth had an enormous collection of varnishes. Rarely a day went by when she did not have beautifully manicured hands. Ruby reds, purples, turquoise and emerald were her favourites.

Other than Elizabeth's wedding day when Hannah, her mother, had insisted on paying for a professional artist to come to the house and 'do' her, Elizabeth had never worn a full face of make-up. She experimented with lipstick once or twice in the early years of marriage but stopped when Andrew appeared not to like her in it.

'Are you unwell, Izzie? You look a little peculiar,' he'd said over dinner at a fancy restaurant on their first wedding anniversary. Elizabeth was feeling fine and put his comment down to the pearl pink lipstick she was experimenting with. On his fortieth birthday she tried a colourless gloss, little more than a super-shiny Vaseline really, and he'd asked her to take it off.

'It's so distracting, Izzie.'

'In what way distracting?' she said, baffled. When he made no reply she presumed bad, and wiped it off in the bathroom before joining the modest party downstairs.

Her blank face was familiar and safe, and until off guard moments when she caught sight of herself in a reflection or mirror, or a casual remark of Hannah's reminded her of the paucity of her appearance, she spent little time fretting about her looks and remained content enough. Andrew was openly affectionate with her, and their sex life was healthy and, on the whole, satisfying.

The lamp beckoned, she could not make out the words on the page. She turned the open book face down on the cushion next to her and as she struggled to pull one plump leg from underneath the other she saw it in her peripheral vision: a dark shadow running across the wire of Andrew's laptop, which stretched from the coffee table, where he had carelessly left it, to the socket on the far wall. Though irritated by the machine, Elizabeth had left it deliberately; she was tired of clearing up after Andrew and the boys.

She turned and looked directly at the cable. Black and smile shaped, it was perfectly empty. She could have sworn it was a rat. It was too large for a mouse; the tail was scaly, thick, ominous. Rounded, brownish, greasy, the creature moved extremely quickly along the wire, like a circus performer.

She stepped towards the shelf gingerly, taking as few strides as possible, picking her way amongst scattered paper lying on the carpet. She turned on the light and sniffed around the corner of the room, behind the television and the curtains but everything smelt, and looked, normal. She crept into the kitchen, turning on all the lights as she went. She peered around the cooker, checked surfaces for specs of black, droppings, any evidence of rodent activity. Nothing.

And then she saw a smear on the lino by the sink. She had mopped the floor after supper, just a few hours ago. She was certain she had not missed a spec. This was a new smudge, and it troubled her. The boys were in bed. She wore threadbare slippers. Had she been outside in them? She checked the soles for dirt but they were clean. She remembered the thick grey snake slipping down the drain cover. It was no slow-worm.

It took seconds to access the internet from Andrew's laptop. She typed 'pests' into the search engine. Tens of thousands of links. And one word stood out: 'rodents'.

When Andrew returned home it was gone eleven o' clock and Elizabeth was in bed. As she drifted into sleep she heard the whine of the plastic front door. She wondered if he would come straight upstairs or go into the kitchen to make himself a cup of tea and a piece of toast as was his habit after a night out. He would sit in the dining room, smoking a cigarette and listening to music, and then retire to bed. Elizabeth loved the smell of him, slipping into the king-sized bed next to her, fresh tobacco and manliness. She heard the whoosh of water from the kitchen tap and rolled over after making a mental note: tell Andrew about the rat.

*   *   *

Over breakfast, once perfunctory queries about each other's evenings were over, Elizabeth mentioned, in as casual a tone as she could muster, that she thought she had seen a rat in the house.

'A rat? Can you be sure?' Andrew's tone was belligerent. He had a hangover.

'Well, no, but I can't imagine what else it could have been,' Elizabeth was running late, the children weren't yet dressed, and she was determined not to get into an argument.

'A mouse. It would have been a mouse. Poison. That'll kill it. Get some poison.' Andrew slapped the newspaper shut with a flourish and rose from the table. The conversation was over as far as he was concerned.

'Traps would be kinder. And safer for the children,' Elizabeth suggested, unsure if rats deserved compassion.

'Whatever you think, Izzie. Just kill the little bugger.' And with that Andrew disappeared into the study.

Elizabeth glanced at the clock, and leapt from the table. 'Oh God! Look at the time! Boys, boys! Time to get dressed,' she shouted. She was furious. Once again she had allowed herself to assume the role of time-police, child-bully, pulling them from their playing, forcing them to school, even though Andrew was working from home and did not have to get himself ready to go out and face the world.

No answer came from the living room. She clambered up-stairs. 'Boys!' she screeched, sweeping up her two-year-old from the pile of Lego and realizing with horror that he still had last night's nappy on. Another chore before she could get out of the house and on her way to the infant school where she worked.

Andrew's head appeared from behind the study door. 'Must you shout like that, Izzie? You sound like a banshee. You only have to ask for my help.'

'I shouldn't have to ask, Andrew. They're your kids too.' She wanted to slap him.

'You don't have to work, Izzie. If it's all too much...'

She took a deep breath. 'Andrew, I want to work. I like it. I find it fulfilling. I just need a little support from time to time. Boys!' The twins materialized from their bedroom, half dressed and contrite.

'We can't find clean socks, Mam.'

'I'll sort these two out. Where are the socks?' Andrew said.

'Don't worry, I'll do it,' Elizabeth snapped.

'It's difficult to help, because most of the time you won't let me,' said Andrew, exasperated.

'What do you mean? Of course I let you!'

'It's not easy to help, Izzie. You have everything so under control…'

Tears welled in Elizabeth's eyes, she fought them back. Wouldn't do to cry now.

'I'll sort these two. You deal with the baby,' Andrew said, adding a whispered 'Sorry' before charging into the bedroom.

Elizabeth had hoped for some support from her mother. Hannah was fit, healthy, young at heart. And retired. Asking should have been easy. But it wasn't. Elizabeth found it difficult to ask for anything directly, so she rarely did. Petrified of rejection she preferred to eliminate the risk. And Hannah never offered. Anything.

Throughout her life Elizabeth hinted and scrambled for compliments, praise, and help. Hannah rarely took the bait, and often Elizabeth was reduced to the role of beggar. Over lunch one Sunday afternoon Elizabeth mentioned the time another grandmother, a friend of Hannah's, had taken her children away for the weekend.

Hannah laughed, 'Joan Taylor is a very lucky woman. She has so much time on her hands. Why, she doesn't work, she has no hobbies or interests, other than our art class, and I'm sure she only attends for the pub afterwards. Why, she hasn't produced a single painting in over two terms.'

'I know you're busy, Mam. What with all your hobbies. And there's Da too.'

'You're right, Izzie. I really must carve out some time to take the boys on a trip. Of course, the baby would have to stay with you,' she said.

'He is very young. But he's fine at nursery...'

'He's used to it, that's why.'

Elizabeth let the subject drop. After all it was Hannah who was losing out on a rewarding, and special, relationship.

Robert, on the other hand, was a lovely grandfather. At weekends, when the weather was clement and he was free from the day to day responsibility of his post as Head of the School of History at the university, he took the twins walking the hills of Snowdonia, his passion for the mountains as strong as his love of Shakespeare and whisky. In winter time when rain and wind bound them to the home he read myths and legends from the Mabinogion, the logs in the open fire crackling and spitting in time with the boys squeals of delight and wonder.

It was a difficult day at school. The children were always troublesome when the wind blew, though Elizabeth couldn't blame her poor spirits all on them. The rat had unsettled her and she found it difficult to focus. On the way home, before she called at the childminder's, she stopped at a small independent hardware store. Elizabeth had spent most of her lunch break, which was short anyway as she did playground duty for some of it and there was always marking to do, thinking of where she might find mousetraps. Hardware shops, other than a few large chains, were all but extinct, and Elizabeth couldn't imagine herself purchasing a trap at her local supermarket. If the store sold such unpalatable items.

It was only at the end of the day as she rested her head on the steering wheel before turning the key in the ignition that she thought of the ramshackle shop in Upper Bangor. She had seen it many times when collecting Andrew, who didn't drive, from the university, though she had never been in. It was wedged between a trendy café and a tumbledown Chinese restaurant which appeared to be permanently closed for refurbishment.

A bell tinkled as she pushed open the stiff heavy door. The shop was musty, the smell of archaic products, like Swarfega and

Brasso and freshly cut string, rose from the packed shelves. It transported Elizabeth to her childhood. It was the smell of her grandfather's shed. Practical, useful, tinkering. The shop was long and narrow, and chaotic. She wondered how anyone could find anything, and she felt strangely at home. No one appeared from behind the counter at the far end so she wandered down the central aisle studying screws and scrubbing brushes, washing-up bowls and metal house numbers, all sitting in their cardboard boxes. No traps.

Elizabeth jumped when a small man with white hair appeared. He wore a khaki overall, buttoned up at the front, smeared with oil. His face was all but obscured by large tinted glasses. The lenses were as thick as jam jar bottoms, and Elizabeth couldn't make out his eyes.

'Bore da,' a high-pitched voice rang out. The shopkeeper was very still, the calloused fingers of one hand resting against those of the other, as if he were in prayer.

'Good afternoon. I'm looking for traps. Mouse traps. Rat traps, if there is such a thing. Poison?'

He smiled, acknowledging her embarrassment, without making light of it. And then Elizabeth noticed that he was blind. The tell tale angle of the head, slanted to the roof; the immobile irises and expansive whites blurred beneath the thick glass. He didn't carry a stick.

'I've sold out, I have. Traps, poison, the lot. Hard to believe I know. I can hardly believe it myself. I have some on order I do. Be here in a few days I hope. Lots of people waiting. You're not the only one. I'll put you on the list, shall I?'

Elizabeth nodded slowly, and then remembered to speak. 'That would be lovely, diolch.'

The man continued, 'Now would you like traps or poison or both, Madam? I would strongly recommend both I would. Rats are very resilient.'

'Are they?' She paused before stammering, 'How do you know it's rats. Rather than mice?'

'Because I've seen them, I have.'

'Seen them?' She regretted her comment immediately.

'Heard them too, I have.'

Elizabeth knew she should have felt comforted by the knowledge that there were other people, many people from what the shopkeeper said, with a rodent problem. She hadn't been singled out for her slovenliness. She wasn't a slut after all. She wasn't alone. But rather her uneasiness increased.

That night she dreamt of large, yellow teeth, twitching wet noses, and curled pink tails. The teeth were like tombstones, ridged and coated with the debris of decaying food. They chomped and gnashed, looming closer and closer, increasing in number. The sound of the chomping was deafening.

Elizabeth sat bolt upright in bed. She was sweating; her forehead and chest were soaked. She rose and got a drink of water from the bathroom, watching herself in the mirror as she drank. She peeped her head round the door of the baby's room. The smell of milk and sugar filled the air. She crept towards the bed and leant in to her son. He was so still she thought he could be dead. She touched his arm. No movement, but it was warm. She kissed his plump cheek and checked on the twins. All was well.

The headstone teeth dominated her sleep the following night and this time, after she rose and then returned to bed, she found it difficult to get back to sleep. Andrew snored peacefully beside her. She stared at the ceiling, planning the tasks for the day ahead, hoping that the blind man from the hardware shop would telephone. She was on the verge of drifting into unconsciousness when she heard a shuffling from the corner of the room. There it was again. Definite movement, from the wardrobe. As Elizabeth rose to investigate, it came again, followed by a scurrying running the length of the room. The noise wasn't coming from the wardrobe – it was coming from the roof. There was a creature in the roof. And from the sounds of things, it was busy.

They were busy. It was too loud for one.

The animals scampered back along the length of the bedroom, clearly following a set pathway. The sound of their movement mingling with the sound of Andrew's heavy breathing. Elizabeth's stomach turned over.

When Andrew and Elizabeth bought the house there were holes in the roof, and for the first few years, before they gathered the necessary resources and hired a roofer, a dray of squirrels in the loft plagued them. Making it their home, destroying beams and insulation. Keeping them awake at night. Keeping Elizabeth awake. Andrew was one of those fortunate people who could sleep through just about anything. Elizabeth hadn't minded the squirrels too much. She was getting precious little sleep anyway. The twins were tiny and hadn't mastered the art of sleeping for any length of time. No sooner had she fed and changed one of them, returned to her bed and rested her eyes, than the other woke demanding more of the same.

And squirrels didn't seem like vermin. Elizabeth had been dismayed when the roofer employed to block the holes announced that he had called pest control. That the exterminators would come and catch the little devils and destroy them for her. It was illegal to let them go, the roofer reminded her when she looked aghast at his proposition. Elizabeth wanted them evicted from the building they were squatting, not executed by some heartless council thug. As it turned out the squirrels escaped execution by virtue of not being at home when the tiles were replaced, and although Elizabeth found the nest when she searched the roof space later, there were no young slumbering in it.

Edging towards the corner Elizabeth tipped her ears to the ceiling. The creatures stopped moving, as if they knew she was listening, and then the gnawing started. Teeth on wood, grinding, gnashing, gnawing. Busy, busy little rodents. Plotting and planning, fouling and stealing, biting and sullying. Elizabeth leapt back into bed. Drenched in a cold sweat. They would take over. Fecund as germs.

In the morning Elizabeth squeezed her boys extra tight and telephoned the hardware shop, almost begging. There would be traps and poison waiting for her to collect that evening. Elizabeth had ordered both on the basis that if she'd seen one rat there were bound to be more. Now she was sure there were more.

She removed the traps from the paper bag they had been placed in discretely before walking from the car to her front door. She hoped that a neighbour might spot her booty and confess that they too had a problem. No one did.

The traps seemed too small. The boys were fascinated. 'How do they work?' Matthew said, fingers outstretched.

'Don't touch! How can you be so stupid! They're dangerous,' said Elizabeth. She saw the quiver on the boy's lip.

'I hate you!' he screamed as he ran from the room crying.

Later, Elizabeth clambered up the ladder to his bed on the top bunk and placed her hand on his back. 'I'm sorry, Matthew. You're not the stupid one. I am. I just worry about you and your brothers. I have to protect you,' she said.

'From the rats?' he said.

'No, cariad. The traps.'

Afterwards Elizabeth climbed into the loft and laid double the quantity of poison advised on the back of the bottle.

That evening she read the twins *The Pied Piper of Hamelin*. The boys claimed that they would never be so silly as to be tricked by a stranger wearing a red and yellow suit. Elizabeth reminded them of the magical lute, the spellbinding tune, his promises. Her dreams were full of empty, silent towns where no children played in parks, deserted schools dripped with cobwebs, and chocolate rotted on sweet shop shelves.

Chapter Twelve

The dead rat lay on its side in the middle of the kitchen floor, front paws curled to its chest, delicate fingers still and sharp, large grey teeth bared in a death throw of what Elizabeth thought looked like agony. It was a doe. Such an unsuitable name for the female of the species. The word conjured images of young deer, delicate spots on fawn hide, fragile spindle legs, tears and melting hearts. Scattered around the doe's tail were six jelly-bean pink foetuses. Elizabeth retched and staggered to the sink. This was the hardest to clear up. She had found other cadavers and they were much easier to deal with. She pushed on despite the nausea, driven as she was by the need to sweep up the corpses before the fascinated children, who followed her round the house as if she were a magical piper, picked them up themselves. Poison killed five rats the first time. The traps were empty and that night, at Andrew's suggestion, Elizabeth replaced the cheese with chocolate.

Four days later Elizabeth was still finding dead rats in the house. Hands encased in rubber gloves, she picked them up by their tails and marched to the far end of the garden before flinging them into the open grave Andrew had dug. She marvelled at how quickly one adjusts to the most repugnant of tasks if forced to perform it often enough. Twelve brown rats, of varying shapes and sizes, lay stiff and putrefying in the sandy earth. Keen to move away as quickly as possible days earlier, Elizabeth had left the corpses exposed, but it was warm now; Elizabeth detected a faint smell, so she threw spadefuls of earth over the bodies.

The hardware shop looked empty when Elizabeth walked in. She strode down the aisle heading for the counter in front of the key-cutting machinery. At the bench her hand, poised and ready to slap, hovered above the brass hand bell resting on the counter. She resisted the urge to press the bell two or three times in quick succession, and chose instead to press just once, firmly, and study the machinery in front of her while she waited. She felt a presence behind her, like a spectre, and spun round to find herself nose to nose with the shop owner. She fixed on his broken eyes, urging herself to control her repulsion and sadness.

'It's normal to feel disgusted, it is. Don't be ashamed, Mrs Bevan. It's why so many of us wear dark glasses. It's not to protect us, it's to spare you, the sighted. It has nothing to do with protecting our eyes, it doesn't.'

'I'm so sorry, I hope you don't think—' She wondered, briefly, how he'd know it was her, but nothing about this man would have surprised her.

'Please, Mrs Bevan, no need to apologize. No need at all. What can I do for you now?'

'I, I'd—'

'Traps or poison?'

'Poison please. It works so much better than the traps, and it seems less cruel somehow. It can be very messy when a trap catches one, and most of them are empty each morning anyway, and I'm so afraid of the boys catching their fingers in them, they're fascinated...' Her voice faded away, and she felt foolish once more. Another customer entered the shop.

'I'll be with you in a moment, Sir, I will.' The man wandered to the selection of door knockers and number plates.

The shop keeper withdrew behind the counter and returned holding a brown paper bag, the box of poison concealed within. As he passed it to her he took hold of her free hand. Elizabeth felt uncomfortable. She wanted to snatch her hand back, but was afraid of offending him. After all it was only like an extended handshake. She wanted to explain that she was unused to close contact with people other than her immediate family, that such intimacy made her feel vulnerable and exposed. He sensed her resistance and tightened his grip. He ran his thumb along her palm and tipped his head from the ceiling to face her.

'The rats are still coming, Mrs Bevan. Still coming, aren't they?'

Elizabeth nodded and knew that he felt her alarm.

'You have nothing to fear from them. You are safe. Your

140

lifeline is long. Protect the children.'

Forgetting she had mentioned them, she said, 'How do you know I have children? Are they in danger?'

'We are all in danger, Mrs Bevan, all of the time. Go carefully now. God bless.'

Elizabeth snatched her hand away, more forcefully than she intended, and muttered a goodbye as she hurried out of the cloying atmosphere of the shop. She avoided making eye contact with the other customer as she passed. She screwed up her eyes in the glare of the late afternoon sun, and shuddered. This whole rat business was affecting her. Making her nervous, twitchy, tense. She set no store by quacks who believed they could see into the future. But she was reminded of an incident from her childhood.

As a teenager, Elizabeth and some school friends visited a fortune-teller on the pier. It had been a dare, and Elizabeth went in first. In a cramped, brightly coloured hut the gypsy wafted cracked fingers over a dirty glass ball before declaring, in a theatrical whisper, that Elizabeth would find happiness later in life; she would marry a handsome outsider and mother many children, four of her own: three boys and a daughter. All three teens were told variations on a theme. An intelligent, morose child Elizabeth knew that not all of them would be happy, and dismissed the woman as a fraud. But time had proved the fortune-teller correct in at least a few of the details. She wondered if the blind man had a similar gift.

His words hovered around her for the remainder of the day. Once the children were in bed, Andrew and Elizabeth ate a supper of roast lamb and baked vegetables.

'You've not got much on your plate, Izzie,' said Andrew, pouring red wine into Elizabeth's glass.

'That's enough, lovely,' she said, covering the top with her hand. 'You know what I'm like. I'll be light headed, and then I won't sleep.'

'Eat up, and then there'll be something to absorb the alcohol.'

'I have to be careful. You know that,' she said, slapping her thighs.

'I love your legs just the way they are, Izzie.' He raised his glass, and Elizabeth followed suit.

'Cheers.'

She ate while Andrew talked of the rising tension on campus as exam time approached. Her mind was full of greasy fur, scaly tails, shiny cheeks and soothsayers, and absentmindedly she picked at the lamb in the dish in the centre of the table, fat congealing as Andrew talked on. Meals were often like this. He talked and she ate, and finished her plate, then picked at leftovers as he finished his first serving. After the meal, they sat on the sofa together in front of the television, Elizabeth laid her feet on Andrew's lap and he casually rubbed her toes. She was dozing off when an item on the evening news caught her ear. She sat upright.

The presenter spoke of rat infestations reported in scattered pockets of the county. A whey-faced official stressed the importance of not panicking. Rats had always been with us and always would be; the milder winters and hot summers meant that the rat population was on the increase. The council was taking decisive measures to deal with the problem, and there were simple steps that all residents could take to control the spread of vermin and disease.

'There you are, Izzie. If the little buggers haven't gone in a few days, get onto the council. Call in the experts. Let the rat-man sort it out. We pay the buggers enough tax.' His casualness comforted Elizabeth a little, though her heart still felt as if it wanted to escape her chest.

Three weeks passed. A sizzling May turned into sultry June. Elizabeth and the twins were walking in the countryside near Beddgelert. Andrew had taken Robert to a colleague's house for the afternoon. The professor also had young children, and Elizabeth thought it would be an opportunity for Andrew to spend some time with his youngest son.

Even outside of the main holiday periods Beddgelert was a popular spot. Packed with tourists and red-faced hikers with enormous backpacks Elizabeth couldn't wait to get out of the village. Before she could drag the boys away, they made their customary visit to Gelert's grave, to pay homage to the loyal dog, slain by his master, the Prince, who mistakenly assumed Gelert had savaged his infant son when he returned to a blood stained home after a hunting trip. The blood belonged to a wolf that the dog had killed protecting the child, but the body of the wolf was discovered too late to save poor Gelert. The Prince erected a grave in memorial and a town grew up around it. Or so the story went.

At the graveside Matthew said, 'Can we get a dog, Mam?'

'No, my lovely, no.'

'Please, Mam, please,' said Luke.

'But we know who'll end up looking after it don't we, lovey? And it won't be you, or your brother.' She smiled and stroked the boy's head.

'But Maaaaaam…'

It was a familiar conversation. Elizabeth said, 'If you still want a pet when you're older, when you're old enough to care for the animal—'

'Dog,' Luke said.

'Dog then, and don't interrupt, Luke. It's rude. Where was I? Ah yes, when you're old enough to care for the dog I'll reconsider.'

'Promise?' Matthew said.

'Promise.'

'How old will that be?' said Luke, but Elizabeth had moved on to inspect another headstone.

The age at which they might be capable of caring for a dog increased with the passing years. While Elizabeth didn't actively dislike dogs, she would have described herself as more of a cat person, though she didn't much care for cats either. Too unpredictable, too beautiful, too supercilious. Dogs were trustworthy, but stupid. And smelly when old. Cats killed birds, for fun. Vicious little creatures.

Talk of pets over, they headed for the hills, following the icy water of the river, which cut its way noisily through the rock.

After a short while they turned from the main pathway and followed a cormorant that Elizabeth guessed had strayed from the water at Llyn Dinas. They ate a lunch of tuna fish sandwiches, crisps and fruit sat on a charcoal rock jutting from the bruised landscape of gorse and heather.

It was an unpredictable day. One minute the sun bore down on them, making them hot and uncomfortable, the next fleets of cloud blew in from the west, dark shadows sweeping across the forlorn hills, offering welcome respite from the hot sun. On the way back, as they neared a cluster of farm buildings, Matthew shrieked, 'A dog! Look! A dog. It's hurt.'

Elizabeth squinted into the sun, 'Are you sure it's a dog, cariad? It could be any animal, or a sack of rubbish.' She stared at the shadowy shape on the dusty path in front of iron gates.

'It's definitely a dog, Mam.'

They moved closer. Elizabeth heard it before she saw it clearly. She could only just make out the crumpled brown form on the path, but its muffled howling pierced her.

'It's not a dog, boys. It's a fox. A male fox judging by its size.'

'Why's it out now? They only come out at night?' Luke said.

'I don't know, cariad, I don't know.'

The creature lay on its side and barely raised its head as they approached. Its fur was matted and patchy, and the creature scratched weakly at its ears with exhausted hind legs.

Elizabeth motioned for the boys to stay behind. She advanced with a quickening heartbeat. She felt sure that the fox would scarper well before she got too close, though she couldn't be certain, and she knew that wild animals could become aggressive when threatened, or when feeling vulnerable. The howling had stopped, replaced by a low, rasping whimper. Its body shuddered and quivered, spasms waved down its spine, following one after the other in quick succession. It stopped scratching, the action requiring energy the animal no longer possessed. The fox looked at her with pleading amber eyes, tears of blood oozing from the corners and from its ears. If it were a horse, its owner would have shot it. Elizabeth wanted to put it out of its misery but didn't know how. Dried spittle gathered at the corners of its mouth, shot through with traces of blood. Elizabeth was overwhelmed with pity. Cruel, cruel, mother nature. But this was no natural death. The creature continued to gaze at her and many seconds passed before Elizabeth realized that the animal was no more.

'It's dead.'

Everything but the fox had faded, and the sound of Luke's blunt tones returned her to the wider world with a jolt. Luke leant in to poke the fox with a stick collected from the riverbank in Beddgelert.

'What killed it?' Matthew chimed, his golden curls bouncing as he too leant in.

'I'm not sure. I've never seen anything quite like it. It seemed like it was fitting. There's no sign of injury, from a car, or dog, or gun. And it looks too young for it to be old age. At least I think so.'

'Maybe it was poisoned?' Luke chirped.

'Maybe, cariad, maybe.' Elizabeth didn't have a clue what killed the fox, but she knew it was unlike anything she'd seen or heard of. She remembered the rats and a chill washed over her despite the heat.

'Protect the children,' the blind man said.

Matthew and Luke were prodding the carcass, leaning further and further in, fascinated by the gruesome spectacle they had witnessed and death itself. For death was remote, academic to Elizabeth's children. Born long after Andrew's parent's deaths, their other grandparents alive and well, they had no experience of the emotional impact of loss.

Elizabeth grabbed the boys by their t-shirts and dragged them away from the fox, her stomach churning and her mouth dry. As a girl she had watched a cow die from CJD one frosty winter morning. Slipping and sliding in excrement, its bony legs failing to support it, crumbling at the knees. Terrified brown eyes, long startled lashes. She had cried when the farmer came out and shot it. A shocking act, perfunctory in its brutality and mercy.

She wanted to cry now and felt tears threaten. She raised her eyes to the sky, a technique she employed to prevent tears falling too easily, determined not to cry in front of the twins. The fox was nothing to her.

'Let's go, boys. It looks like the storm that's threatened off and on all day is on its way.' She took them by the wrists and dragged them down the lane, taking the direct route back to Beddgelert and the car.

Before they reached their journey's end the storm did indeed arrive. And a strange one it was too. Brief and ineffective. Two shy claps of thunder, no lightning and a torrential downpour, the sun remained shining throughout. Elizabeth asked the boys to look out for a rainbow for one was sure to appear. It never did. Or not that they could see. They sheltered under an oak and watched the raindrops bounce off the cracked earth. When the rain stopped they withdrew from the cover of the tree, and Elizabeth felt a large drop hit the back of her neck and trickle below the collar of her cheap white shirt. A number of droplets may have gathered on a leaf, which bowed under their combined weight at the precise moment Elizabeth walked underneath. It was surprising and welcome on her clammy skin, and she enjoyed it treading a cooling path down her spine.

By the time they arrived home in Bangor the disturbing death of the fox no longer absorbed Elizabeth completely. She turned her attention to other, more mundane, matters. What to cook for tea, preparation for the week ahead at school. As soon as she pushed open the front door the twins rushed into the living room to tell Andrew their macabre news. He blanched as they spoke, smiling uncomfortably before waving Elizabeth into the kitchen.

'Did the boys touch the fox? How close were you to it?' he hissed before she could pull the door to.

Elizabeth shook her head mutely and indicated a distance with her arms.

'Have you not heard the news today? Jesus Christ!'

'Don't take the Lord's name in vain, lovey. You know how I hate it when you do that.'

'For God's sake, Izzie, be quiet. An unknown disease is killing livestock, some wild animals. Not all are affected, some appear to be immune. It lowers their defences, makes them vulnerable to common threats.'

'Like HIV, you mean?' she said.

'Sort of. Higher numbers than usual of badgers are dying from TB, the cows have CJD again, bird flu's on the rise and so on. Not exactly HIV. No one's really sure, useless buggers these officials. There are reports that household pets will be infected.'

Elizabeth stammered, 'Where?'

'Pockets throughout the country. It's not reached Wales yet, but the implication is clear – it will.'

She went to talk but her mouth was dry again.

'No one knows if it can be transmitted to people. Keep the boys away from animals. Culls in the danger zones have already begun. Pets are to be destroyed too.'

Andrew was the colour of semolina. Calm, rational, logical Andrew. Izzie was the hysterical one. He was panic-stricken, and it was this that frightened Elizabeth more than his words.

Dark stains crept from his armpits. A single trickle of sweat meandered down his swarthy cheeks before stalling at the rough of his blue-black stubble. He cut a fine figure, and as Elizabeth took him in she knew she was a lucky woman to have him, to be the keeper of his love.

'What about the rats, Andrew? What are we going to do about the rats?' And she saw the face of the blind man.

'We're going to nuke 'em, Izzie. I have some industrial strength poison, made in the university chemistry department by a colleague. He can't get rid of the buggers either. Totally illegal, but who's going to find out?'

How she loved him.

Chapter Thirteen

The boys sat in the bay window of Tŷ Mawr's front room watching the smoke drifting across the city skyline from the countryside. To Elizabeth it looked like a warning, a message written in suffering across the pure, clean sky. The funeral pyres of thousands of animals filled the air with the sour stench of defeat.

'There's a dragon,' Luke said. 'That cloud looks like a dragon.'

'Does not,' Matthew said.

'Boys, come away from there. Nana's brought the Lego out, look.' Elizabeth took hold of her boys' hands and dragged them away from the window.

Hannah said, 'Oh, I do hate it when you call me Nana. Grandma is so much better.'

'Sorry.'

'And I could do with your help in the kitchen. The boys will be fine by themselves for a moment. Won't you, boys?' Hannah swept out of the living room.

Elizabeth picked up a boxy car made from red and yellow bricks. 'Look at this! You know my brothers, your uncles, played with this when they were little. Maybe they made this car!'

'I made it last time we were here, Mam,' said Matthew.

'Clever boy. Now, I'm going to help Nana. Be good. Don't touch anything you shouldn't. Especially you, cariad.' And she tapped her youngest, Robert, on the chin. 'Mind he doesn't chew the small pieces, Matthew, Luke.'

In the kitchen Hannah, crouched, was bashing around in the cupboards. A batch of home-made beefburgers sat on the chopping board. Elizabeth stared at them nervously.

'What are you looking for, Mam?'

'A frying pan that doesn't stick, and doesn't require two hands to lift.'

'I don't mean to interfere, Mam, but is it wise to be giving the

148

children meat for lunch?'

'Of course it is, Izzie. For Pete's sake! If it's being sold in the supermarkets it must be okay. The government would never allow contaminated cattle to be eaten.' She stood up with a pan in her hand. It looked very well used.

'But isn't it best to be safe? You know how...' Elizabeth caught the expression on her mother's face and her voice trailed away.

'This isn't British. It's from Argentina, the label says, and as far as I know this damned disease hasn't got that far.' She slammed the pan on the workstation and threw in a knob of butter before transferring it to the cooker. Elizabeth's stomach turned over. Like a hound, she could smell blood in the air.

'The rats are everywhere. How are you and Da coping?'

'Like everyone else, with difficulty. The poison doesn't work.'

'Have you tried the latest stuff? The one the council is distributing? I'm waiting for our supply.'

'They appear to have developed a resistance.'

'They're everywhere, Mam.'

'Don't exaggerate.'

'It seems like that to me.' To Elizabeth the danger they presented was almost tangible.

'Look, I blame them for all this too. I really do, Izzie. Filthy creatures.' Hannah picked up a burger and placed it in the pan. The pink of the mince reminded Elizabeth of the rat foetuses, and she gagged.

'Would you like a drink of water, darling? You look a little green,' Hannah said, adding another burger to the frying pan.

'No, thank you, Mam, I'm fine. Really.'

The meat sizzled, Hannah poured herself a glass of wine. 'Everyone's blaming the rats – the government, scientists, experts, whatever they are.'

'Are they? There are so many rumours flying around. I've heard some people say it's come from the food, you know the stuff we feed to livestock, from the air, the water supply,'

Elizabeth said.

'Nonsense! For one thing if it was airborne it would be all over the world, like the common cold, or influenza.'

'I suppose you're right. Andrew says it's our fault though. Humankind's, I mean.'

'Most definitely. He talks such sense, that husband of yours. It's man's fault one way or another. Tampering with the natural laws of the universe, overusing Earth's resources, abusing other living creatures, we've brought this upon ourselves. The warning signs have been there for years. Bird flu, floods, the bees have been disappearing. Oh blast! I've burnt one side.' The beefburgers were indeed black when Hannah turned them over, and Elizabeth was glad. She hoped they were not rare at their centre.

'Andrew says that global warming is responsible for the increase in the rat population. He says they can breed in mild winters. I feel they're at the heart of it, I really do.'

'Izzie, can you throw some salad together rather than standing there doing nothing?' Hannah was perspiring.

'Sorry, Mam, I'm onto it.' She busied herself chopping the lettuces, cucumber and avocados, breathing deeply, filling her nostrils with the scent, and tried to push the rats from her mind. 'I am grateful for you having us today, Mam. I really am. Thank you.'

'You're welcome. I can catch up with the life drawing class next week. Bunch of amateurs. They have no idea at all, most of them. Lay the table will you, darling?' She tipped her head backwards. 'We'll eat in here. Children are so messy.'

Elizabeth took five knives, forks and spoons from the long drawer on the side of the wooden table, enjoying the weight and feel of the smooth bone handles.

Hannah dished up the burgers and said, 'Why did you feel the need to be away today, Izzie? It's not as if the boys have pets. There'd be no men in white suits knocking on your door.'

'But they have friends, Mam. In our street. They'd see the vans, hear the crying, the barking, the screaming as the pets are taken away. They're not daft. They'd feel it as much as if they had pets of their own. I didn't want them to have to go through that.'

Elizabeth was thankful the boys had no pets, though secretly she felt that there was an element of mass hysteria amongst the young. Luke and Matthew cried all the way home one day over the loss of a school friend's Jack Russell. When it was alive they had disliked the beast intensely. In death it was elevated to the status of canine saint. A bad tempered, yappy creature, the ungrateful beast had bitten Luke once. When Elizabeth reminded them of this, and when she dared suggest that the aggressive devil was lucky to have escaped being put down before now, the boys howled even louder.

Hannah removed the pan from the heat and began scraping the bottom. She approached the task with ferocity and said, 'Well, pets are one thing. Wild animals are another altogether. Call the boys, lunch is ready.'

Try as she might Elizabeth could not eat the meat. She left a little of the salad, attempting to cover some of the meat with lettuce leaves, and noted ruefully that she remained a child in her mother's presence, afraid of her wrath if her plate was not cleared. She was surprised that her mother didn't take offence, until she noticed that Hannah's remained untouched too.

The rats kept coming, larger and bolder than before. They slipped out from their usual haunts, brazenly walking across kitchen floors, loitering on street corners, helping themselves to anything awaiting removal and cremation. Or so it seemed to Elizabeth.

The morning baby Robert took ill Elizabeth rose early. It had been another hot and humid night, and he had coughed and coughed. Shortly before dawn Elizabeth gave up on the notion that she might get a couple of hours sleep. She was exhausted, but the twins would rise soon anyway. She crept downstairs to make a drink, leaving the lights off for fear of waking the household. Barefoot and sticky in her long nightgown she tiptoed through the hall towards the kitchen. She heard a ticking. There was no clock in the hall, and the one that hung on the wall above the kitchen door was quartz: accurate and silent. As she came closer she realized that it wasn't a ticking – it was more like the sound of someone eating. She pushed the door ajar and leaned forward. In the gloaming she made out a dark mound, the size of a small dog. Heart racing, feet welded to the hall carpet, she leant in further, flicking the light switch down. And as her eyes adjusted to the glare of the bulb she screamed. For there, in the middle of the kitchen floor was a brown rat, feasting on the carrion of another. Others peered from between the cupboards, the oven, and fridge. A fleshy tail dangled from the sink, like a plug chain, the sound of claws scrabbling on metal mixing with the echo of her cry. Then they were gone.

The baby coughed all day. Elizabeth wiped, and scrubbed, and disinfected every conceivable surface – as she did every day of late, but with added fervour – in between comforting her ailing boy and dealing with the demands of the twins when they returned from school. She called her surgery, asking for Dr Bryant, only to be told by the receptionist that he was just leaving the health centre, on his way to an emergency.

'I'm afraid you'll have to call again in the morning and make an appointment. We do set aside slots for emergency cases,' the receptionist sighed, bored.

'But he's very poorly, and he's only two, a babe really. Please.'

'I'm sorry. There's really nothing we can do. Call back tomorrow and bring him in.'

By evening Robert's temperature was raging, and, afraid he might fit, Andrew insisted that Elizabeth call her mother.

Within fifteen minutes Hannah knocked at the door. Galleon-like she swept into the house and up the stairs to Robert's room. Elizabeth tripped after her, her brain scrambled from sleep deprivation and anxiety.

'Has he taken fluids?'

'I think so, yes.'

'Have you stripped him?'

'Well, he's going hot and cold so…'

'When did you last take his temperature?'

Hannah flung her case onto the floor beside the cot, whipping out a stethoscope and placing it on the child's chest. She lifted her right hand imperiously to quieten Elizabeth who was still listing Robert's symptoms. Only the sound of the child's rasping breath could be heard.

'His lungs are pretty congested. It's a little early to say pneumonia, but we must keep a close eye on him. Have you any infant paracetamol in the house, Izzie?'

'Yes of course, Mam. I've been giving it to him all day.'

'He might need something a little stronger. Any ibuprofen? And get these clothes off him, and an iced flannel for his forehead. Now.'

Elizabeth knew her mother was doing what came naturally, that she was doing her best by Robert, but she resented the distant, arrogant tone Hannah adopted when she was in professional mode. When she was little and ill, with chicken pox and other childhood illnesses, she longed for a mam who wiped her brow, fed her sweeties and let her lie on the sofa all day watching DVDs. Hannah would bark questions at her, stuff her with evil tasting medicine and order bed rest. Hannah had worked as a GP for nearly forty years before retiring. No matter how severe the crisis, she never seemed rocked, unnerved. If she felt it at all she disguised it well. Even when it was her nearest and dearest. She seemed able to detach her emotions from the drama. To see the sick person before her as a patient and not her child, grandchild, lover. Unlike her mother Elizabeth knew she could never stay calm enough to be effective.

Hannah left an hour later promising to call first thing in the morning and with strict instructions that Elizabeth or Andrew must call immediately, no matter what the hour, if Robert's condition worsened.

Another sleepless night. Elizabeth lay on her bed pretending to read, the door ajar, listening to her son's rattling chest. Andrew lay beside her, eyes closed, though she knew he too was awake. The baby slept until midnight, when the fever and coughing took hold once more. Urging Andrew to get some sleep, Elizabeth took Robert downstairs, turning all the lights on, descending the stairs noisily. She did not want to interrupt another rat taking a late supper. She sat on the sofa with the boy in her arms, blowing onto his flushed cheeks from time to time. He fell into a fitful sleep once more and afraid to move him, she turned on the television for company. The news channel filled the screen. A bouncy blonde wearing too much make-up and gaudy jewellery spoke gravely to the sleeping nation.

'Breaking news... Within the past hour there have been reports from a nursing home in Tyneside that three elderly residents have died from an unusual form of pneumonia. The three people, two women and a man, who have, as yet, to be named, were all said to be in good health before the disease struck. The Government is urging calm, but suggests that anyone over sixty-five suffering from a cough or chest infection should visit their GP as soon as possible...'

Elizabeth looked at the face of her youngest boy. He seemed shrunken, taut skin pulled across his formerly chubby cheeks, dark circles round his eyes, lips white and reduced. He opened his eyes and looked at her, and she saw the fox's eyes. The same veiled desperation, resignation – if an infant can feel such a thing – and defeat. She called an ambulance.

Robert Bevan was not the first child to die. He clung on to life for a further two days, during which time there were a dozen reported deaths of elderly people and thirty or so children under five. Elizabeth left her son's hospital bedside – where she had remained near enough constantly since he had been admitted – to get a cup of coffee from the machine at the end of the closed ward when she felt her son's soul departing this world. Years later, when she talked, finally, to a counsellor, she described it like a birth in reverse. An incredible surge of relief, joy even, that no words ever did justice. His suffering was over. Then, a burning, a stinging, a crescendo of pain, an entry into her body, a pulse, two heartbeats, a merging, a fusing, until all she could feel was the steady thump of her own beating heart. She dropped the paper cup of watery brown sludge as she stumbled down the corridor back to Robert's room, slipping on the wet floor as she went. On the way, two members of the medical team joined her, the steady bleeping of the flat-lining monitor increasing in volume as they drew nearer.

There was a mirror on the wall above the hospital bed where her son lay, to create an illusion of space Elizabeth imagined. In it she saw a tired middle-aged woman with scraggy hair and sallow skin. Dark creases swept from the corners of her eyes towards her temples like eyeliner, Cleopatra style. The inner lids were lined with sore red scratch marks. She looked like someone most people would go out of their way to avoid. Her lips were drained of blood, and she was trembling. She tilted her head to the heavens and opened her mouth, wide and gaping and greedy, like a chick in a nest waiting to be fed a half chewed worm from its mother's beak. Elizabeth waited for the scream, but no sound came. All was silent. The woman's mouth stayed open, her eyes bulging and red. Two other women dressed in nurses' uniforms appeared alongside her, their arms touching her shoulders, holding her upright, their mouths moving up and down, up and down, like marionettes in a scene from a movie before the advent of talkies. They led her away.

Hours later, when Elizabeth finally agreed to let the hospital staff remove her baby, Andrew and the twins came for her. She was trapped in a soundless world. She sat on a plastic chair facing the automatic doors in the main reception of the county hospital. Only a respectfully distant security guard for company. Her small overnight bag deflated and battered beside her. She rubbed her left palm with her right thumb. She saw them through the glass first. Andrew, dark and stoic, flanked on either side by a twin, blonde, and pale, and fragile. He bent down to each of them in turn, giving instruction she imagined, asking them to be brave little soldiers. For Mam. As they reached the sensor and the doors

155

slid open Andrew caught Elizabeth's eye. His lips curled in on themselves and she thought he might cry. As they stepped towards her she heard the dull tick of the black and white clock in the reception office. Marking off the disappearing minutes. The shamble of six unhappy feet. A gull squawked in the distance.

Chapter Fourteen

'Please. Please. I'm begging you.' Her voice sounded like someone else's.

Elizabeth felt Andrew's thick arms encircling her like a straight jacket, and she knew she had lost. Her legs gave way; she crashed to the laminate flooring of the hall. The little shoes lined up underneath the radiator faced her; she groaned and curled into herself. The boards were cool against her bare knees and shins; she laid her forehead on the floor. She concentrated on the sound of her blood pumping through her head.

Andrew bent in and whispered, 'There, there, my lovely. There, there.' As if she was a child. She felt the floor shudder beneath her with the thump of the officials' footsteps, like a funeral march. Andrew turned his head and said in a hushed voice, 'The bodies are upstairs. First door on your left.'

'We need to ask a few questions first. Standard procedure.'

'Come through to the kitchen.' He released his hold and rubbed her back.

The boots climbed over her, pulling the door behind them, but try as she might she could not block out the sound of their voices.

'Which one died first?'

'My boy on the top bunk,' Andrew choked.

'The second?'

'Within an hour of Matthew.'

'How long ago did they display symptoms?'

And Elizabeth remembered Luke complaining of a sore chest on the way home from school three days ago. She prepared supper carefully, calmly, and when neither twin ate much she called her mother.

'I can't come out to you, Izzie. We're confined to Tŷ Mawr,' Hannah said. 'Your father is sick.'

'What do you mean confined?' she'd asked, shaking.

'Those households containing contaminated individuals are being asked, wherever possible, not to mix in the community.'

Hannah sounded as if she were reading a government manual. 'You know that.'

'And Da?'

'He's very sick, Izzie. You must prepare yourself.'

'What do you mean?'

'Infected people die swiftly. Within three or four days of the bacilli reaching the lungs.'

'Oh God, Mam…' Elizabeth thought she might lose control of her bowels.

'He's an old man, Izzie—'

'He's not quite sixty-nine—'

'He's had a good life… Take good care of those boys. They are young, they could pull through.'

Remembering, Elizabeth rolled onto her side, cheek resting on the wood, and imagined blood pouring from her temple, through the cracks in the boards and into the sticky, brown earth. Time disappeared. The kitchen door creaked open. Figures stepped over her.

'You're going to have to move, Izzie. I'm so sorry, my darling. So sorry,' Andrew said.

But she could not. 'No, no, no, no no,' a strange voice moaned. And then she saw them, coming down the stairs. White suits, masked faces, gloved hands. Brown sacks slung over their shoulders like bags of cement dust. Andrew took hold of her ankles and dragged her, slowly, gently, across the floor towards the kitchen. She lifted her head and watched, paralysed by grief. Her boys. Her beautiful twins. The door banged shut. Gone.

She closed her eyes and lay very still. When Robert died friends and neighbours came to pay their respects, offer their condolences, desperately trying to conceal the secret gratitude that it was her, Elizabeth Bevan, who had lost her baby and not them. But now she had seen the suits many times. And so had others. From the front room the Bevans had pushed bamboo blinds aside and watched them claim the dead from the street. Day after day.

She opened her eyes again. Andrew stood in the hall wiping

his brow, looking lost, unsure what to do next.

'Why us, Andrew? Why us?'

'Everyone has lost someone, Izzie.'

'Can this be true?'

'Yes. A parent, a grandparent, a child.'

'But so many, Andrew? What have we done to deserve this? We've lost everyone.'

An unexpected, urgent desire to atone pushed Elizabeth back onto her knees and she sat upright, as if she were praying, asking for forgiveness. She said, 'I did a terrible thing. Last year. I wanted to tell you, but I couldn't. It was so wicked, and now we've lost them all. Our lovely children. All gone. I am being punished.' She held her arms outwards, beseeching, and he crouched and took hold of her hands.

'Nothing anyone could have done would have changed any-thing. We did our best for the boys. Do not torment yourself, Izzie. You're a good woman. Nothing will change that.'

'I am not. I...'

He covered her mouth with his hand. It smelt of disinfectant.

'We've lost everyone.'

'We have each other,' he said, and then he kissed her fingers.

She noticed that her fingernails were split, purple varnish almost gone, chipped away to form small islands of colour on her neglected nails. She could not remember the last time she had brushed her hair, and thought it strange that she could think of something so unimportant at a time like this.

The weeks rolled on. They watched the news. More and more people died. The cities were worst affected, and those who could leave did. Initially some even tried to escape to mainland Europe, but within days the ports were closed. And still it did not stop it. The plague crawled across western Europe: Belgium, France, Italy, Germany. Andrew and Elizabeth's detention period came to an end. Other than wandering around their small garden neither Elizabeth nor Andrew had been outside for almost twenty-one days.

'I'll go into town tomorrow,' Elizabeth said that evening as they sat in front of the television eating plain fried rice. They had eaten nothing but rice and beans for five days. Hannah had dropped food parcels on their doorstep for a while, but then the buses had stopped running and the walk from Tŷ Mawr was too much for her.

'Shall I come too?' Andrew said.

'No need. You get on with things here. You may even be useful at the university, if you feel like getting out?'

'I called yesterday. There are some members of staff in, and a handful of students, mostly mature. The majority have stayed at home, with family, others…'

'You might want to catch up? I'll go and get the shopping,' Elizabeth said decisively.

'I'm happy to come too, Izzie. If you need me.'

'I'll be fine, Andrew. Please.'

It was October and the air was cold and mean. Before leaving for town Elizabeth wrapped a black scarf around her head and neck. Her feet were unsteady on the dew damp tarmac. It was early. The streets were quiet. It reminded Elizabeth of walks on Christmas Day, except that the two people she did pass didn't smile and nod and say 'Good morning!' They hung their heads in shame and shuffled by. Apologizing for existing. As if saying, 'I'm so sorry it's me, living and breathing, and not your son, your father, your brother.' They were like ghosts. She longed for the purr of car engines, the prattle of children. She heard the rustle of plastic bags floating on the wind, dried out leaves scurrying across concrete, the horribly familiar scratching of rats round bins. She could hear the disease whispering on the wind, 'Gonna get ya, gonna get ya,' like the monster under the bed in children's stories. She hoped that it would get her. She felt the desire to tear off her scarf, lift her head to the sky and yell, 'I'm all yours! Take me!'

Houses were boarded up with metal grids, pieces of wood, and Elizabeth realized with horror that these were places that people had abandoned, or worse, where everyone had perished.

The gates of other homes were taped over with yellow plastic. Diseased homes, the luminous strips warning people not to enter, to avoid the modern day lepers.

As she turned into the high street she buried her face in her neck and almost bumped into a soldier standing on the corner. She saw his rifle first. Slung across his chest like a sash, gripped at the barrel and handle with either hand. His grip so hard that his knuckles were white. She screamed, her cries echoing up the street. He jumped, straightening himself, attempting to regain his composure. She stared at him and said, 'Sorry.'

He nodded. She noticed his pimples, livid purple-red spots, green pus balls at their tips. Eyes black with dilated pupils. He looked scared and so very, very young. His gun was almost as large as he was.

Elizabeth moved on. She noticed the doors with paper sheets pinned to them: confinement notices, the drawn curtains and overflowing rubbish bins. The lower end of the street was more residential, with only a handful of shops, quirky types like the vintage record store, which still sold vinyl, and a number of charity shops. She passed no one.

As she neared the busier section, where the market was held on Saturdays and Wednesdays, she saw another soldier, standing outside the bank. A window was smashed and the cash machine had been ripped from its brick body, the plastic arteries dangling from the black hole. The grocery store next door had been looted, the shelves empty and bare. As had the chemist. She stopped and looked across the street. The electrical store had been burgled too, and she wondered what sort of people wanted a new television or fridge at a time like this. She had seen similar images on the news, but had not thought it possible that such a thing could happen here, in Bangor, the place where she grew up, knew people, lived. It happened in far away, violent places like London and Paris.

'I need to buy food. We have nothing,' she said to the soldier.

He looked surprised to be spoken to, and clutched his rifle harder. 'Try the supermarkets. Some deliveries are getting through. They're guarded,' he said.

'On the outskirts of town?'

'Yes. There's nothing here, Madam.'

She walked on. As she turned out of the high street she saw the cathedral, with its soot blackened stones. She approached the entrance and took hold of the heavy metal ring and twisted it. The door did not give; even this house of God was all shut up.

She trudged through the city centre to the supermarket. She longed for the sound of cars. She passed the cemetery where gravediggers slaved, a lone policeman walking his beat. A couple of white vans sped past her on the empty roads.

The supermarket was open, guarded by a handful of armed soldiers. She did not baulk at the sight of their guns this time. The shelves weren't full, but there was plenty of food and more people than she had seen in weeks milling around. One woman was rushing down the cereal aisle, piling her trolley high, in a frenzied, irrational desperation. Elizabeth watched, impassive, as a soldier marched over to her and ordered her to empty her trolley.

'Your vouchers, please,' he said.

The woman handed over a torn ticket.

'This is out of date. It is worthless,' he said. She pulled another from her pocket and showed it to him. He shook his head and said, 'Empty your pockets, now.'

Bundles of vouchers appeared from her coat. 'Where did you get these?' he shouted, and by now a small crowd had gathered. Elizabeth looked at her food voucher and scurried to the fruit and vegetable area. She didn't want to witness another's pain, she had enough of her own. There was little in the way of fresh produce, but she came away with a basket of goods that would last her and Andrew a number of days, and from which she could create a feast that would seem positively gourmet-like after the sustenance level eating they'd suffered of late.

As she headed home, weary yet pleased with her catch, she passed a lone woman at a temporary bus stop on the other side of the road. The woman was sat on the kerb, knees pulled up to her chest, arms resting on her knees, her chin on her arms, eyes staring blankly ahead. She wore a padded nylon coat, thick tights, wrinkled at the ankles, and pale blue trainers with chunky white soles. She could have been there for hours and hours. Days. She looked so peculiar. She could have been a teenager, but for the craggy face, cheeks scored with hundreds of tiny criss-cross marks, souvenirs of experiences she might rather not have had, immobile, set in a cast of sadness. She must have been in her seventies. A woman out of time. A woman who no longer belonged, waiting for a bus that might never arrive. Elizabeth wondered if that's how she would pass her old age: alone, forgotten, with no children, no sons, to care for her and Andrew. Elizabeth gazed at her, aching for contact but the woman didn't acknowledge her presence.

She walked on, taking an unfamiliar route to break up the monotony of her journey. In a modest yet respectable residential district she came across a chapel. The plain walls were painted a primrose yellow, the windows framed in a faded white. It felt like the first sign of spring in the bleakest of winters. She had never visited this particular house of God before, and doubted that the doors would open, but she found herself carried, as if by unseen force, down the path. She took the bronze door ring in her clenched fist, and turned it. She heard the click of the latch, and felt movement. The door eased open and as she stepped inside a sea of grey faces turned to look at her. Pews were full of people, but what surprised her most was the smell. The chapel didn't smell like a church. There was no musty dampness, no rotten, waxy wood, no cold stone, bitter incense. Instead the smell of life: sweat and breath and farts and heat filled her nostrils. A minister wandered over, dipped his hands in the font, touched Elizabeth's forehead and invited her to sit down and join his congregation in prayer. For deliverance. Elizabeth wanted to cry – for her boys, her father, her brothers, but all she could think of as she sat on the hard wooden pew was the old woman at the bus stop. Years on, she would think of her from time to time and wonder if she survived.

When Elizabeth returned home there was a heaviness in her bones that made her want to weep. Her hips and knees throbbed, she could almost smell the liquid building up in her sinuses. When she bent to place the bags of shopping on the doorstep, she felt catarrh rushing to the front of her head. The weight of it almost pulled her over and she thought she might vomit. Her chest felt scratchy and frail. The belly-ache of hunger had disappeared. She took to her bed.

The aching intensified during the night and by morning Elizabeth was feverish. Andrew sat at her bedside, holding a damp flannel to her forehead.

'You must promise me you will remarry,' she said.

'I'm not going to remarry, Izzie, because you're not going to die. You're going to get through this.'

'It would be a testament to our love, to faith in the sanctity and preciousness of marriage.'

'Don't talk like this, Izzie.'

'We were a success, weren't we? Our union was good?'

'Of course it is.' He removed the flannel and his head fell onto the sheet beside her.

'Andrew, I need to pee.' He sat up and took the bedpan from beside him before sliding it between the sheets, taking her under the shoulders and lifting her to a half sitting position. He kissed her ear as she urinated, their tears mingling on their cheeks.

'You could have more children...'

'Izzie, no.'

'We might have done, mightn't we?' She forced her eyes open. The room span and then, slowly, Andrew came into focus. There were dark circles round his eyes, but he was as handsome and powerful as ever. She smiled, and heard him say, 'Live, Izzie, live. Please,' before the heat took her once more.

The long grass brushed against her sun-browned calves as she skipped across the orchard towards the picnic. She could see the pink of her mother's blouse and broke into a gallop, but the faster she ran the smaller Hannah became, until she disappeared altogether. Breathless and confused Elizabeth moved between the apple trees, searching. She was frightened now, alone with dusk fast approaching. Abandoned. Then a figure peeped from behind a damson bush. A flash of golden hair and skinny limbs. A cry, 'Mummmmeeee!' Luke. Or was it Matthew? She looked down at her body. All grown up. Soft and pillowy around the breasts and stomach. On the floor lay a tiny sock: Robert's. She touched the cross at her neck and smiled. So this was heaven. A place of dreams. She was dead and she thanked God for his mercy. With open arms she raced towards her boys. 'Where's Daddy?' they cried, and Elizabeth heard herself saying, 'He's coming. Don't worry.' The children were hot and sticky, their heat pouring into her. Sweat gathered on her brow and ran into her eyes, stinging, blinding her. The weight in her arms lessened and she clutched harder and harder, pulling the boys closer. But they were disappearing, fading away, like sea mist. And the more insubstantial they became the more real the world around her felt. The fever receded.

She came round to the sound of a strange drilling. Opening her eyes the familiarity of the room surprised her. Then she remembered the woodpecker the twins listened out for, and realized that she had survived. She didn't understand why God should spare her, and not her boys. She pulled at the silver cross, wondering for what purpose He allowed her to live? The house was quiet.

The phone rang and she wondered if she had the strength to get out of bed and answer it. Andrew will get it, she thought, but it continued to ring. The answer machine clicked on. Andrew's bass tones rose through the floorboards.

'I'm sorry the Bevan family are not here to take your call. Please leave a message and one of us will get back to you, though it may take Robert a few years! If it's urgent you can contact me, Andrew, on...'

She listened to the end of the message, the annoying beep, and then she heard her mother's distinctive, crisp tone. Hannah still lived; her delirium had not been prophetic.

'It's mother. I've had a nasty bout of 'flu, thought it was...

I'm up and about again now. Not heard from you for days. Call me.' She sounded cross. She was. She'd called herself 'mother'.

Elizabeth dragged herself up. The air was fetid, the bed sheets stained, an unemptied bed pan sat on the rug. She had no idea how long she had been unconscious. It was daylight. She looked at the clock. Two thirty. Her legs shook as she crossed the room and she leant against the dressing table, steadying herself, before opening the door and heading towards the stairs.

A whiff of stale urine followed her down before turning into something she almost recognized but couldn't quite put her finger on. She wandered into the kitchen. A plate of pasta covered in a cream sauce with a thick skin sat on the chopping board next to a glass of water. Autumn sunlight poured through the window highlighting a film of dust on the surfaces. Elizabeth could smell sour milk.

The living room looked as it did most mornings: the coffee table clear, cushions plumped, curtains drawn. The house seemed empty, but she could feel a presence. She went back upstairs, hesitating outside Robert's room, before taking a deep breath and pushing open the door to the twins' room. Toys dotted the carpet. She was puzzled, she was certain she had cleared them away when the boys took ill. Then she saw Andrew's broad back on the bottom bunk, Luke's bed. His legs were curled and she could see the ears of an old teddy peeping out above his shoulders.

'Andrew?'

She walked to the bed, heart pounding, and as she reached to touch her husband's shoulder she caught sight of the purple blush on his neck. She shook him. His body flopped over, black-green pustules glared at her, furious and leaking, his tongue protruding and black, his eyes bulging. Screaming she covered her face, pushing her clenched fists into her eye sockets, harder and harder, as if by pressing her eyes out she might push from her mind the image of Andrew's grotesque death-mask. Eventually, she gave up and, shaking, she ran her fingers over the thin, baggy skin of Andrew's eyelids, closing his empty, wracked face. A large part of her shut down. She believed it would never be reopened. Like an old slate mine. She had thought that losing her sons was the worse thing that could happen. But she had been wrong.

A vaccine was developed, with help from people like Elizabeth, those rare types with natural immunity to the bacilli. Winter came and the disease disappeared, along with the rats. But almost half of the city's population had perished, mirroring the rest of the country. Britain was no longer an overcrowded island. The young and the old, the brightest and best. To Elizabeth it seemed that the meek really would inherit the earth.

The night was overcast and mild for the end of December. No stars glittered in the heavens. Hannah and Elizabeth walked along the main road towards the city centre. Others shuffled by, heading in the same direction, but no one spoke. It felt like a pilgrimage.

Elizabeth had not wanted to come out, but Hannah was persuasive. Elizabeth had ignored Christmas altogether, taken to her bed and slept the days away. For the first time in decades she did not attend the Christmas Eve midnight mass at the cathedral. Instead she offered a quiet prayer, begging God that all the love that had once been inside her should not turn to poison. She had warned Hannah to stay away. But around nine on New Year's Eve there was an insistent rap at her door: Hannah, bearing food and a small gift. She could not turn her mother away.

After a supper that Elizabeth didn't think she'd be able to eat, but did, Hannah pushed a gold box across the table. 'For your birthday. It's a bit early…' The box contained an emerald ring that had once belonged to Hannah's mother and that Hannah still wore occasionally.

'I should have given it to you ages ago. But I loved it so much, I couldn't bear to part with it,' Hannah said, only half apologetic.

'Why now?'

'I'm not sure. Because you're the future.'

At the word future, a bitter laugh escaped from Elizabeth's burning throat. She could see no future. Only cowardice, and fear of God's wrath, prevented her from taking her own life.

'I need some air,' she said.

So they walked, and as the midnight hour approached Hannah insisted they join other survivors at the cathedral. Elizabeth did not have the energy to fight. Outside, a crowd held torches. Elizabeth pushed her way through the throng; she wanted to be inside the church, but before she reached the doors a young woman, maybe twenty-one or two, barred her way and told her sharply that it was full. Had been for hours. So Elizabeth and Hannah stood on the muddy earth and listened to the sounds of the organ filtering through the stones, the dull hum of people singing. Outside, some joined in, their voices thin and pathetic in the vastness of the night. At midnight the bells rang out into the hollow air. There was no cheering, no firework display, no kissing and hugging. At the first stroke Hannah took hold of Elizabeth's hand and said, 'We're the only Evens left now.'

Chapter Fifteen

Elizabeth stared out of the window at the conifers that dominated the far side of Hannah's garden. They were threadbare and ragged, dark old bears of trees, which ruined the grass with their fallen foliage, but nevertheless provided welcome shade during the hot, dry months. A great tit flew across the window, landed on the low wall fencing the patio, and surveyed the scene before speeding over to the bird table where a chaffinch pecked at some meagre offerings. The blush of the chaffinch's breast quivered before it fled as the tit bullied its way to a free meal.

Energetic and acrobatic, the tit highlighted Elizabeth's inertia, and she wished that she could soar over the gardens, the rooftops too, to a woodland where sunlight flittered through golden leaves, dappling the cool mossy earth of a coppice floor. She would forage amongst brittle brown leaves, hiding from human eyes.

After everyone died Elizabeth started watching the birds. She had so much time, without the cooking and cleaning, and caring and loving, the living. She took compassionate leave from work; there were few pupils anyway, and extended it and extended it. When she did, finally, hand in her resignation her post had long since disappeared. Fewer children meant fewer teachers.

She'd been interested in birds before, in a casual, non-committal kind of way, but now they fascinated her, these creatures with the power of flight, and watching them helped pass the time. They were so free, so fast. So close to heaven. Bird-watching became a passion, and Elizabeth smiled to think she had become the sort of person that she might have mocked in her other life.

Two years had gone by and still Elizabeth wanted to hide from the world, and she would have hidden more often had she been able to bear the silence. She wondered how noisy it was up there in the big blue sky.

Afterwards, the world was a quieter place. And when so many disappeared, never to return, it was reduced. As if an unseen hand had turned the volume button down a number of notches. And it was unnerving, this hush, this muffled, sighing world. Shop doors stayed shut, buses didn't run to schedule, the air echoed with the pathetic sounds of rustling: uncollected rubbish, yoghurt cartons, plastic bags, drifting along the near deserted streets.

There were those who said that the plague offered Europe a second chance, a way to begin again. A modern day flood. To get it right. But the uncomfortable truth was that a strain of plague bacilli resistant to all medicinal and control measures had been developed by the US army for bacteriological warfare; it had escaped via a number of rats from a British laboratory. Common belief held that terrorists were responsible for the escape, but nothing was proved.

There was a return to the old beliefs. The plague as punishment for sins committed: the damage inflicted on mother earth for profit and greed. Elizabeth saw it as retribution, and though her faith had been shaken she held on as the shipwrecked cling to pieces of driftwood. She marvelled at her mother's resilience, and in bitter moments raged at a God who could take the lives of her children and spare a selfish old woman.

Elizabeth turned away from the garden and leant against the sink, facing her mother who was sitting at the table, pouring tea and jabbering.

'I made some biscuits too. I know how you like them,' Hannah said.

'Too much. I'm getting fatter and fatter,' Elizabeth replied, helping herself.

'You've always been rounded, darling. I can't imagine you any other way, but you do need to watch it you know.'

'Thanks a bunch. Anyway, what's the point?'

'There's always a point, Izzie. It's about self respect. I can't imagine leaving the house without a little mascara and brushing my hair. It's the same with weight. You can't let yourself go. And there's your health to consider. Obesity is very serious.'

'So you're saying I'm obese?' Elizabeth dropped her second biscuit back on the tray.

'I'm saying that you need to take care.'

'Then why the bloody hell did you make me biscuits?'

Hannah's face dropped and Elizabeth felt victorious. 'Let's not quarrel, Izzie. I care for you, and it's a way of showing you that.'

'It's your fault I'm fat,' Elizabeth said, without rancour.

'Nonsense. But I won't make you biscuits in future.' Her mother smiled, and Elizabeth watched the skin beneath Hannah's chin folding in on itself, pressing down onto her neck. She regarded the face before her and marvelled that something so familiar to her was such an oddity to others. For, at almost seventy, Hannah was a rare sight.

The most vulnerable in society, the old and the young had near enough been wiped out. Nurseries and care homes closed. Parks and playgrounds stood empty. Squatters moved into deserted houses. Adult survivors took new jobs, eager to slip into the shoes of the recently departed. Others struggled to adjust to this strange world, find their place in it. It looked so much like the one they had always known, and yet it was so different. Like an egg with the yolk sucked out, devoid of the querulous prattling of children, the stories of days gone by passed on by the old.

Out and about in the town Elizabeth would catch herself staring at the empty spaces where familiar faces and figures should have been. The lollipop lady on the corner of the main road opposite the twins' school, the homeless guy collecting pennies for lager on the bench in front of the cathedral, Mrs Jones at the post office counter with her nicotine stained fingers and chipped nails.

The words 'dating agency' broke Elizabeth's thoughts. 'What?' she said.

'There are so many people joining dating agencies. More than ever before,' Hannah repeated.

She was back in the kitchen at Tŷ Mawr. She wondered how much of her mother's conversation she had missed. Not that it would matter. Hannah appeared not to notice, or care, if Elizabeth listened to her ramblings. Hannah thought out loud, following a pattern of debating the pros and cons of various plans, prior to settling on an amicable outcome, which seemed to pay no heed to anything that any listener may have contributed.

Over her lifetime, Elizabeth had learnt to recognize when Hannah invited genuine debate, and when she did not, to nod or grunt in the affirmative at appropriate moments, to give the impression of someone who was listening, when in actual fact she was planning next week's lessons or working out what to cook for supper. Her mother's musings did not covet a challenge, but the word 'dating' brought Elizabeth careering back into the stuffy kitchen, and demanded a response, even an uninvited one.

'Who's joined a dating agency?' Elizabeth asked. She did her best to sound nonchalant, but she harboured a nagging fear that the person in question was Hannah.

'Me, darling. I signed up last week, and guess what?' Hannah smiled.

Dumbstruck Elizabeth could only shrug; she had guessed what was coming next.

Hannah peered at her over glasses that had slipped from the bridge of her nose as if to say, 'Go on. Guess. I command you to.'

Hannah was an attractive woman, and from a distance looked considerably younger than her years. Of medium height and build, she maintained herself well. Her hair, though not completely devoid of grey, was still dark, aided by generous helpings of dye, and thanks to an investment in porcelain veneers in her early sixties, her teeth were straight and white.

'I couldn't possibly,' said Elizabeth, resigned.

'I have three interested gentlemen already. And all are younger than me,' Hannah chirped. She smoothed the front of her fitted top, placed her hands on her hips, and gave a little wiggle.

'You have got to be kidding.' Elizabeth thought she might cry. She picked up a biscuit, and took a large bite.

'It's true, Izzie. They're all younger than me, and I didn't even fib about my age, though I was sorely tempted I can tell you.'

'Not that they're younger than you. You have novelty appeal

if nothing else, Mam.' Hannah winced at Elizabeth's words. Ignoring her mother's hurt Elizabeth continued, 'I can't believe you've signed up to a dating agency.' Elizabeth couldn't look her mother in the eye.

Hannah blanched, sipped her black, sugarless coffee, composing herself, and then sat back.

'It's the photograph I think. It's a very good one of me. The one your father took in Naples, in my purple smock, with the dusky pink scarf. You can just about make out Vesuvius in the background.'

'That photograph is ten years old,' Elizabeth choked, reaching for yet another biscuit. A decade ago, when she had Andrew, tiny twins, the baby still to come. She longed to hold them, to smell them. She closed her eyes and tried to conjure them. It was difficult. She longed to feel that they were real. That she had existed like that once. Happy, contented, normal. Ten years. It felt like a lifetime ago. Someone else's life. 'Da loved that photograph. Loved you, the time you had there,' she said after a while.

Robert had loved it so much he'd it blown up and mounted in a gilt-edged frame. It sat on the mantelpiece above the fireplace, between the herd of ornamental elephants, carved from ivory in the days before people knew better. They were an heirloom of Robert's, bequeathed to him by his grandfather who had acquired them in India during the Second World War. The elephants were of little material value but Elizabeth's father had treasured them, as she did, and it was a sign of how much he loved the photograph that he placed it alongside them. He had said they should stand alone. Giving that particular photograph to the dating agency felt like a double betrayal to Elizabeth.

'I loved it too. It's why I chose it,' Hannah said. 'I do hope they take me somewhere special. A trip to London! We could take in an exhibition. I've not been to London in years. I'll need some new clothes to wear.' She rambled on but Elizabeth wasn't listening, or even pretending to. She thought of her father. Dear, dear Robert. How she adored him. Stout, fiercely intelligent, a passionate and hard-working man. The best father any little girl could wish for. His only daughter, Elizabeth was a favourite and his love for her sang through the family. It filled every nook and cranny of their dark, gloomy house, and after she left home and married Andrew whenever she was feeling in need of unconditional, all-embracing love Elizabeth turned to her father.

What her mother was doing was unspeakable. Elizabeth said, 'How can you think of trying to replace him? It's only been two years.'

'I'm not trying to replace your father, Izzie. Don't be ridiculous!' Hannah started to crash around the kitchen, banging pots and pans and cupboard doors. 'And two years is a long time to be alone. I don't know how long I have, Izzie. I'm not as young as you. Time accelerates when you're my age.'

Elizabeth was surprised at her mother's rare candour about her age, but remained silent. Hannah continued, 'We have to try and return to normal. Lots of people are building new futures, finding love, having babies, the authorities are encouraging it.'

'The world's gone crazy.'

'People are just getting on with life.' Hannah threw a few mouldy looking potatoes into the pan and turned on the tap, her back to Elizabeth.

'I'm getting on with life. I'm here, aren't I?'

Hannah spun round. 'Oh, Izzie. You're not exactly living, are you? Not really.'

'And you think gadding about, meeting men on the internet is living? Do me favour, mother!'

Hannah dropped the pan, water spilt everywhere, the potatoes rolled across the floor. 'Oh, for Heaven's sake!'

Elizabeth went to get a cloth.

Hannah barked, 'Leave it!' and threw a tea towel on the floor and started wiping it with her foot. 'Do you think it's easy for anyone? Everyone lost someone, Izzie. You don't have a monopoly on grief. Moping around will not bring anyone back. Not Andrew, not the twins, not Robert. Stop being so self-indulgent.' She knelt on the floor and wiped the tiles furiously.

'It's too early for me. I'm not ready, Mam. Let me help.'

'I'm fine.' Hannah wrung out the cloth and bent down again. 'Look, Izzie, moving on doesn't mean ignoring the past, pretending it never happened.'

'I know. I just can't forget, that's all.' She felt the urge to cry.

'Nor can I. I never will,' said Hannah, standing, the soaking cloth dripping by her side.

'Mam, I'm sorry. It's a great idea. If you need to get out and meet people, then you should.' Elizabeth leant across, helping herself to a handful of the sunflower seeds that sat in a hand decorated bowl in the middle of the table. They were less fattening than the biscuits, but they tasted dry and stale, and scratched the roof of her mouth. Elizabeth decided that this dating game was a caprice of Hannah's. Eventually it would be abandoned, like so many of Hannah's plans, and she consoled herself that older men, even those ten years younger than her mother, were rare and Hannah was unlikely to settle down with anyone.

'Oh, do you really think so? I know how you adored your father so. Lovely, lovely, Robert.' She sat at the table once more, plucked a grape from a bunch on the table next to the biscuits and seeds and popped it into her mouth. 'You really should get out more yourself, darling,' said Hannah, picking grape seeds from between her teeth.

'No,' Elizabeth said, bending down to pick up the potatoes, which were still scattered on the floor, but Hannah wasn't listening.

'There are lots of ways to meet new people, you know. Join some clubs, you used to love dancing.'

And Elizabeth felt herself gliding across the parquet floor of the university hall, Andrew's firm hand on her waist, steering her, guiding her, protecting her. She hadn't had such a powerful recall in months, and Elizabeth relished the pain. Like scratching off a scab before the wound has healed.

'I bumped into Morgana Williams the other day. Remember her? She was in your year at school. She's had another baby. I thought she was just looking after it, but it turns out it's hers. She was so proud. Gorgeous creature. Big blue eyes and fat cheeks.

She even let me have a cuddle. Everyone was staring.' Hannah sounded wistful.

Elizabeth's cheeks burned at the mention of a baby. Guilt and grief were killing her. She raised her eyes to the ceiling as the nothingness descended once more.

Chapter Sixteen

'How's your love life, darling?' Hannah's words struggled through the biting wind. 'You really must get out more. And I don't mean with the teachers. Those women, old maids the lot of them. You'll never catch a chap that way.'

Elizabeth's ears were stinging; she wished she had brought a hat. The wind drove a sharp pain through her head, and though she heard her mother's question she chose to ignore it.

Instead she looked out over the raging sea from the cliff top path, watching the waves throw their foaming surf at the beach over and over again. She loved weather like this. Wild, unpredictable, dangerous. She thought she might like to be in the grip of forces beyond her control. She watched the gulls sitting on the swell, rising and falling, at ease with nature, not fighting against it. It was mid-afternoon mid-winter and the light was fading, turning the sky and sea a shimmering dulled bronze. The rocks cradling the cove below grew darker and more ominous, lone trees, their bare branches bent over by the prevailing winds, highlighted against the brooding sky. Soon they would dominate the landscape with their spiky presence.

Elizabeth stood still, her calves throbbing. They had walked miles and Elizabeth, overweight and unused to hiking, was thankful to the retiring sun. It would bring their journey to an end.

The walk had been Hannah's idea. A keen rambler she had persuaded Elizabeth to join her on a walk on Anglesey, as a way to spend uninterrupted time together. There were so many distractions when Elizabeth visited Tŷ Mawr. So much to clean, to repair. A never-ending task. And Elizabeth had always liked to keep busy, more so than ever when she visited her mam these days. She felt agitated, uneasy, if she sat still for a moment or two. Keeping busy conveniently got in the way of talking.

'We can talk. Have lunch in a pub en route. I simply won't take no for an answer, Izzie.'

Hannah had done most of the talking. Elizabeth was too busy

trying to keep up with her mother's long, purposeful strides. It was hard to believe that they were a similar height, let alone a generation apart. Hannah trekked like a soldier, chest out, chin forward, arms swinging, punching the air out of her way as she marched onwards. Elizabeth lumbered along behind her, breathless and aching less than two miles in. She didn't have the energy to chat, much less the desire.

Lately, she didn't know what to say to her mother. It was as if their roles had been reversed, and they had been pushed back in time. One minute Hannah the recalcitrant teenage daughter, Elizabeth the despairing mother, the next Hannah delirious and starry-eyed, Elizabeth a nagging killjoy.

'You really should, darling. It'd do you the world of good.'

Elizabeth jumped as Hannah touched her shoulder.

'Do what? What would do me the world of good?' Elizabeth snapped. Hannah looked taken aback. 'Sorry. I'm sorry, Mam. What would do me good?'

Hannah looked ahead then said, 'Isn't it gorgeous? I love it here. So beautiful. As it ever was. Nothing has changed.'

'But everything has changed. You can't deny it.' Elizabeth turned to face the older woman as she spoke, her expression softening at the sight of her mother's rheumy eyes.

'I'm not trying to deny it, Izzie. I'm trying to move on. I am moving on, and you should too.'

'It's not that easy for me, Mam. I can't explain. We're different, that's all.'

Elizabeth wasn't sure she wanted to move on. She didn't deserve to. She stepped forward, towards the edge of the cliff.

'Be careful, Izzie!'

She glanced down to the beach. Such a long way. So much air between here and there. She lifted her head and looked at the horizon. Ever since she could remember Elizabeth had been fascinated by, and terrified of, heights. Not because she feared she might fall, but because she feared that she might fly. Or try to. Test her overwhelming instinct when looking down from a great height that she could fly, if only she had the courage to let herself go, she would soar, float on the breeze like a glider, a sparrow hawk or eagle.

'Izzie! Come away from the edge. You scare me when you do that.'

Elizabeth pulled away from temptation and walked back to her mother. It would have been so easy to push off, to fall and fall and fall. Into a heavenly nothingness. Better than this earthbound emptiness. She still contemplated suicide. When chopping vegetables with the heavy knife given to her and Andrew as a wedding present, as she reached for drugs when a migraine threatened. It would be so easy to take too many, she had amassed many boxes. Slyly slipping into different chemists and supermarkets, buying the maximum allocation in each outfit, daring herself. But suicide was a sin, her faith prevented her from taking that road, and so Elizabeth waited patiently for the day when she could be reunited with her family once again.

'It's getting dark. We really should head back,' Hannah said as she consulted her map. 'We can follow the coastal path for a while before turning inland and cutting across. We'll save our feet and we'll be back in no time. I have a torch if it gets too dark.'

'Wouldn't it be better to go along the main roads? Where there are lights and signposts. We might even pick up a bus, if we're lucky.'

'Don't be silly. It will take less than a couple of hours across country if we put our backs into it.' Hannah was determined and Elizabeth knew it would be futile to persist. She picked up her rucksack and slung it onto her back. She couldn't be more exhausted, so what difference another few miles?

It was difficult walking the narrow path in the dimming light. Elizabeth fell in a few paces behind Hannah and kept her eyes on the sandy black soil. She could smell the seaweed in the air, feel the salt clinging to her face, hair and clothes, her glasses, obscuring her vision further. She could hear the steady pounding of weary feet on the freezing earth. Hannah was quiet and Elizabeth wondered if she too was starting to feel the effects of a day's exercise. A heavy silence hovered between them. So much had gone unsaid. Not just this day, but all the days since then and now, when the last of the Evens died. But to vocalize her pain, her anger, the unspeakable, cruel truth, was unthinkable. But it was there. This unsaid vicious truth. They both knew it. Best left alone. And yet every now and again Elizabeth felt a nagging drag, to throw caution to the wind, and shout and scream.

Elizabeth knew her mother was trying to tell her something. The walk was an attempt to create intimacy away from the mundane and the domestic. Elizabeth had been deflecting Hannah's purpose all day, but she was tired now, she was less sharp, and she feared she could be caught unawares. It was why she longed for the day to draw to a close as quickly as possible.

A stile loomed ahead. As she fiddled with the gate lock, Hannah turned to Elizabeth. There was no escape.

'Have you thought any more about dating, Elizabeth? You really should. You are not unattractive. There's no reason why you couldn't meet someone. Be happy again.'

'Dating? Isn't that something teenagers do? And no mother, I haven't. Not since you asked me last. It's only been a few years.'

'Longer. Four. I read somewhere that it takes most people two years,' Hannah said.

'Evidently, I'm not most people. And I couldn't meet anyone because I don't want to. I love Andrew.' Elizabeth was grateful that the dark coated Hannah, covering her face like a balaclava. She could not make out her mother's features, and therefore figured that Hannah couldn't see the guilt in her eyes.

'And I love your father. I always will, but that doesn't mean I can't love someone else too,' Hannah shouted.

'So you love him? Owen.' Elizabeth heard the scorn in her voice.

'Yes, I love him. He's a good man.'

'Is that the best you can come up with?'

When Hannah first introduced Owen he had surprised and charmed Elizabeth. She had expected a poor imitation of her father. But Owen was very different from Robert. Tall and lean with a high forehead and piercing blue eyes. Though not large, his nose and chin leant towards each other in such a way that it left the impression that one day, when teeth had fallen away from gums, the two extremities might touch during a smile or grimace. He reminded Elizabeth of an illustration of the Pied Piper on the cover of a book of her boys'.

Erudite, polite and cultured he was born and raised in London, where he spent much of his adult life. Like Hannah he was not native to North Wales and Elizabeth wondered if her mother was attracted to him because he reminded her of a time when she was young and carefree, the capital and its many delights at her disposal. A time that preceded Wales, and Robert and children, and responsibility and pain. Despite herself Elizabeth warmed to him.

It was a few short months before Elizabeth realized it was all a sham, a façade. As he established himself in Hannah's affections, winding himself round her heart like bindweed until she could no longer see with any clarity, until she could not extricate herself without fatal injury, total humiliation, the real Owen slithered out.

'Of course the garden here at Tŷ Mawr is delightful, but it pales before the grounds of my Oxfordshire house. I really must show you some photos one day, Izzie,' he'd said one evening as the three of them sat in the kitchen admiring the autumnal colours splashed across the garden.

'That would be nice. I'd love to see the house too. Your son lives there now, with his wife, doesn't he?' Elizabeth said.

'Ah yes, The Birchlings. Eighteenth century, you know. Wonderful dimensions, so wide, spacious, light. Quite the opposite of this old place.'

'It's a wonder you can bear to stay away so long,' Elizabeth replied coldly.

'Owen is planning to go and visit soon,' Hannah said.

'You could take Mam,' said Elizabeth, knowing full well that he wouldn't fork out for such an expensive trip.

'It's finding the time, Iz dear, finding the time,' he said.

'You're both retired. You should go. A holiday would do you good. I could take care of this place, Mam.'

'We'll see, we'll see,' Hannah said hastily. 'How about a brandy? They'll go with the snaps you made, Izzie.'

'Bloody good idea, H. Get the finest stuff you've got.'

He was as sweet, and seductive, and as bad for anyone as hard candy. Too much Owen made people ill. Except that Hannah couldn't see it.

'These really are fabulous snaps, Iz. How can you afford the sugar?' he said.

Elizabeth didn't answer.

'She's an incredible woman, your mother,' he said, trying again.

'Isn't she?'

'You take after her, I can see that.'

Elizabeth turned up the corners of her mouth, then made her excuses and left.

As Elizabeth distanced herself and made her feelings clear, Hannah grew more and more protective of 'her Owen'. His presence at Tŷ Mawr became ever stronger. He was there all the time, certainly whenever Elizabeth visited. Always leaning against the mantelpiece, contemplating the room, stroking his stomach, like a fat man might. Dining chairs splayed across the room, a cigar stub in an ashtray on the living room coffee table, he left his mark in every room. Elizabeth tucked chairs back under tables, emptied stinking ashtrays – her father had despised smoking – but Owen's spirit pervaded the house, threatening to obscure that of her father. Owen was always fawning over Hannah, treating her like a child, a plaything. Elizabeth wondered what he was after.

And she loathed the way her mother behaved when he was around. And even when he wasn't around his influence on Hannah was apparent. She was coquettish, dumb, and sexual. Her constant innuendo about their sex life made Elizabeth want to vomit, and she didn't bother to conceal her disgust. Hannah giggled like a schoolgirl at Owen's vulgar jokes, played stupid when he paraded his intellectual prowess, which Elizabeth thought was weak, and excused his arrogance and bragging.

'That's the trouble with this bloody government. Spineless, elected by a bunch of superstitious nincompoops who know nothing. Too young to remember anything. The greens have been blathering about environmental catastrophe for decades. And until the Chinese get off their arses and do something about it, why should we suffer? Fewer of us to do any damage now anyway.'

He was at the brandy again, and when Elizabeth was sent to the cellar to collect another bottle she noted there was only one bottle left. Prior to Owen's arrival in Hannah's life, there had been quite a collection. Rare vintages gathered carefully over the years by Robert.

'You have to agree that the weather has been odd, extreme in some cases, for years. Sea levels are rising, there's more flooding, drought and violent storms. The damage has already been done, and it'll take decades before any decline slows. We still need to change our ways, especially as government is encouraging us to rebuild the population as soon as possible. Wouldn't you agree, Mam?' Elizabeth said.

'Oh, I know very little about politics, Izzie,' Hannah said, twirling round before addressing Owen, 'Now darling, what do you think of my dress? It's new. At least it's new to me. I haven't had anything brand new in simply ages!'

'Simply divine, H. You look gorgeous.'

'And my hair? Do you like it? It took forever at the hairdresser's. Hours,' Hannah said.

'You always look lovely, my dear,' he said, kissing Hannah on the cheek, and Elizabeth was piqued that he clearly meant it.

'The hairdresser must have been very grateful for the business,' interrupted Elizabeth.

'What do you mean, Izzie?' Hannah said.

'Well, I'm guessing that there aren't too many people who have the time to spend hours at the beauty salon, when there are vegetables to be grown and cooked, children to care for, a devastated country to rebuild.' Elizabeth wanted to scream at her mother, berate her for throwing away her intellect, her skills, but mostly for cheapening the life she had with Robert.

'Nothing wrong with your mother treating herself from time to time, Iz,' Owen said, and momentarily Elizabeth felt guilty for her churlishness. Why shouldn't her mother enjoy herself?

Three weeks before their coastal walk Elizabeth had called on her mother uninvited. She did this less and less of late. But she was going shopping, and she was feeling charitable, and thought she could pick up some goods for her mother. Hannah had not been well. A potent strain of flu kept her bedridden for two weeks and housebound for a further seven days. Owen's car was visible in the driveway and out of respect for their privacy, and a private dread of what she might walk into, Elizabeth knocked rather than using her key.

When the heavy front door of Tŷ Mawr swung open Elizabeth was dismayed to be greeted by Owen. He smiled, but he did not invite her in.

'Is Mam at home?' she said.

'She's popped out to the shops. I've no idea how long she'll be,' he replied, picking some dirt from underneath a fingernail.

'Is she quite well enough for that? She's been very poorly, and it's quite a walk.'

'She's quite well. She's a remarkably fit woman, for her age. And you know what she's like. Once she gets an idea into her head there's no stopping her.'

'I'm sure she would have listened to you, Owen. Had you insisted.'

His mouth moved to form a facsimile of a smile, but his eyes were steel. For a moment Elizabeth thought he might slap her. Instead he craned forward and said, 'I love your mother. I really do. And she loves me. And nothing that a sad, vindictive, little bitch can do or say will get in the way of our happiness. So you'd better get used to me, Iz. I'm here for the long haul.'

'Elizabeth to you. Tell Mam I called.' Elizabeth turned and strode down the path. In her haste she collided with a stray branch of the large holly which dominated the front garden. The leaves scratched her cheek, she flinched and brushed the branch aside, hoping that Owen had not noticed the double insult, that he could not see how upset and shocked she was. Two mugs of strong coffee later she dried her tears, bathed her cuts, and was glad that their mutual dislike and mistrust was out in the open. They would tolerate each other, be civil, for Hannah's sake, but the pretence of fondness had been dispensed with. Elizabeth was relieved.

'We'll have to climb over. I can't unlock the gate.' Elizabeth stepped in front of Hannah and clambered onto the stile. It was slippery with mud and dew. She turned to offer Hannah her hand, but Hannah waved her away and slid over.

A soft light flooded the field as clouds passed over the moon, revealing it to be fat and full. The edges dazzling in their sharpness. A few cows loitered at the far end of the field and Elizabeth wondered why the farmer hadn't taken such precious creatures indoors. Providers of milk and calves, they deserved to be cared for. Sheltered from the elements, and the long dark nights. As she surveyed the scene and took in its austere beauty a firm hand gripped her wrist and spun her round. She faced her mother, and this time she could see her face. Cheeks rosy and shiny teeth gleaming in the moonlight. Elizabeth had to admit that Hannah was glowing.

'I love Owen. I am sorry that it pains you, but I do. Our feelings are real, and strong, and wonderful. Please be happy for me, Izzie.'

'Is this what you wanted to tell me? That you love him. Fine, I'm happy for you, Mam. Let's go home.' Elizabeth went to trudge on, but Hannah tightened her grip. Elizabeth struggled for a way to prevent her mother from ploughing on. Hannah was about to announce something big, and horrible, and she couldn't bear it. She had no strength left, she was too tired for this.

Words leapt from Hannah's mouth. 'Tŷ Mawr is so big isn't it, Izzie? Too big for me.'

'What are you saying, Mam? It's always been too big. It was too big when the six of us lived there.'

'Do you think so? It was so full of laughter, children's joy, and tears, short lived and simple to wipe away. It never felt too big. Not to me. Not then,' Hannah replied, wistful.

Tŷ Mawr. The house Elizabeth grew up in. The big grey house with arched windows in square bays, turreted attic rooms, and secret places. The house with a shabby, intricately patterned staircase carpet that shifted and slipped when trodden upon. The creaking second stair on the mezzanine, just before the bathroom with its draughty window. The frost on the inside of bedroom windows, exquisite, dazzling, created by a master craftsman, woman, Mother Nature.

A gust of sharp, evening wind rattled across the field and through Elizabeth's coat, hinting at the frost to come. She shivered. She was surprised to hear Hannah mention the past. She rarely spoke of her dead children, grandchildren, or husband. Of late Elizabeth longed to share her memories, the joy she once knew, with her mother, but if she tried to raise the past Hannah would cut her dead. At first Elizabeth thought her mother found it too painful. After all she had never been one to dwell.

Elizabeth understood that her mother found her past difficult to think of, her childhood had been lonely, love noticeable only by its absence, but to blank out her more recent past, when she had a loving family, was incomprehensible to Elizabeth. Lately, Elizabeth suspected that Hannah had never really cared for anyone but herself, that her mother didn't have the capacity for true love. Robert had always loved Hannah more than she did him. It was obvious to everyone, even her children, but now Elizabeth wondered if Hannah's whole life had been a quest for diversion from the emptiness of her soul. Hannah was the glittering centre of her own universe, and Owen one of her planets, a devoted satellite that shone a flattering light on her hollow surface. Perhaps her mother was to be envied, perhaps humankind is fundamentally self-centred? Had she always been this way? Elizabeth couldn't remember.

Elizabeth shivered again. Hannah released her grip.

'Let's keep going, Mam, it's getting late and we've still a way to go.'

They trundled on through the field, both deep in thought, the watchful eyes of the cows following them. They were a mystery to each other still.

Who are you? Elizabeth wondered as she passed her mother's upright figure in the moonlit field. She walked on, sweating again despite the chill, the silence between them threatening to engulf her once more. She craved release. She could not stand it a moment longer. She stopped and turned to her mother.

'Out with it, Mam. What is it you want to tell me?'

Hannah was visibly shocked. She hesitated, wiped her brow, and giggled. A nervous laugh. A cough.

'Owen and I have been talking and we want to cement our love, mark it with something special.'

Elizabeth's worst nightmare was about to come true. 'You have got to be kidding, Mother. A wedding! You want to get married! I suppose you want to wear white, have confetti thrown in your hair, be carried over a threshold like some twenty year old. It's preposterous, ridiculous, obscene.' She was on the brink of tears, the words burning her throat, frying her brain, searing into her chest. She was quaking, a dormant volcano about to erupt. The mixture of pain and rage and dread was too much.

'It's just wrong, Mam. Plain wrong.' She was shrieking, her arms flaying, like a pre-school child having a tantrum. She was glad they were in the middle of a field with the only audience a group of bemused dairy cows.

'No, not a wedding. We don't want to get married,' Hannah stuttered. 'It's just that the house is too big. Too big for one. I need someone to care for me, to be there for me.'

'What then, what?' Elizabeth wailed like a banshee.

'I've asked Owen to move into Tŷ Mawr.' Hannah made as if to continue but stopped herself.

Elizabeth knew that at best her mother was withholding information, at worst lying, but felt that this was her chance, that she, Elizabeth, had the upper hand. Hannah was on the retreat, and Elizabeth determined to use her advantage.

'Are you asking my permission? Because that's what it feels like, Mam.' Elizabeth stared at her mother.

'I wanted you to know, that's all. Be happy for me, Izzie,' she sighed.

Elizabeth wondered why Hannah had stopped short of divulging her real purpose. There was more. Elizabeth knew it. But what? What was her mother up to?

Hannah looked sheepish beneath Elizabeth's harsh, unapologetic glower. Small, like the novice actress unexpectedly caught in the glare of the super trooper light at audition, unable to see her interrogators, unsure how to proceed.

What did Hannah mean by something special? Co-habiting was quotidian, unromantic. She would never consider it special. Unless she really had changed beyond all recognition, and Elizabeth had failed to notice.

'To co-habit, nothing else. No ceremony, no party, no announcement, nothing,' Elizabeth said.

'Nothing.'

'Promise?'

'I promise, Izzie. No wedding bells. No party. There's no one to invite anyway.' It was a feeble attempt to lighten the atmosphere with humour.

Elizabeth feigned a poor imitation of a laugh and replied, 'Indeed. There's no one at all.' A lugubrious smile fixed on her drenched face, she turned to leave the field, and jumped. A solitary cow stood before her, rooting her with its gaze. Elizabeth stared back and thought she saw the reflection of a mad woman in those bovine brown eyes.

Chapter Seventeen

The reception area outside the school office was extremely hot. Wall to wall windows, a pitched glass roof, no blinds or curtains, it could have been a greenhouse. Enormous palms sat inside the main doors – also glass – their spiky, brown edged leaves drooping over the side table and chairs, jabbing at unsuspecting visitors as they went to sit. The leaves offered some respite from the relentless sun, and so Elizabeth curled herself onto a seat underneath one.

She was sweating, moisture gathering under her arms, seeping into the fibres of the once crisp cotton of her blouse. The excessive perspiring could have been thanks to the heat, but Elizabeth was nervous. Her stomach churned, her throat tightened, her mouth was dry as chalk, no matter how much she drank from the bottle on her lap. The water was tepid despite having been out of her fridge for only half an hour. It tasted metallic and coated her mouth with a soapy, manufactured film. The label claimed it was fresh from the springs of mid-Wales, but Elizabeth didn't believe a word of it. What was taking them so long? She fought her irascibility.

She took out her notebook, the one she usually kept for shopping lists, and checked her notes.

Things to remember:
Smile – not excessively.
Speak slowly and clearly. Do not mumble.
Do NOT apologize.
Be positive.
Demonstrate your knowledge and experience.
Do not eat biscuits if offered.
Ask questions.

'Miss Evens, Mr Cardew is ready to see you now. Please go through,' the bursar said, smiling, as she poked through the glass hatch from the office to reception, her cheeks glistening in the sunlight.

189

The interview went well, and despite her nervousness and the enervating heat, Elizabeth might even have described her performance as sparkling. Confident that she stood a better than average chance of being offered the job – a full-time permanent position at a respected state school – Elizabeth decided to walk home. She recorded the time it took, and next to the minutes wrote: 'very hot – leisurely amble'. The head had said he would make a decision before the day was out.

It was a breakthrough, applying for the job. To open herself to the possibility of being surrounded by children. Elizabeth was finally tired of mundane part-time jobs. She had too much time to fill, too much time to think, to remember, to dwell. And now that Owen had moved in she wasn't so welcome at Tŷ Mawr. Not that she wanted to spend any more time than she had to in the odious Owen's presence. He filled her with repugnance – the feeling was getting worse rather than better with time – and she was irritated beyond belief by her mother's increasingly silly behaviour. She needed to work, she wanted to work. Her profession, her vocation. It was selfish not to use her skills; she had been a good teacher. Children needed her.

To get the job would be remarkable. Teaching posts were difficult to come by, average class sizes were well below twenty pupils, and this was when children of different ages were bundled together. Optimistic for the first time in months Elizabeth strode, her head up, eyes shining, all the way home. As she went to retrieve her keys from the bottom of her new handbag – she had bought it as a good luck present – she felt a familiar heaviness in her chest. She had no one to share her news, and hopes, with. No one to dissect the interview with, moment by moment. To analyse every response of the phlegmatic, stodgy head. Determined to stave off the advancing melancholy, the familiar dull loneliness, Elizabeth threw her keys back into the bag, turned around and headed to the bus stop.

'Hello! Helloooo! Mam, are you there?' Elizabeth shouted through the letterbox of Tŷ Mawr. She'd knocked five times, slamming the brass lion head against the door with increasing force. She could hear music drifting through the open windows upstairs. It was Arvo Pärt's *Tabula Rasa*, a composition Owen detested. Hannah was home alone. Luck was on Elizabeth's side. It felt good. Another omen, perhaps.

Exhausted and sweating, Elizabeth leant against the door. The wood felt warm, stirring beneath her flesh. Suddenly she remembered that her mam had been off colour a few weeks ago. She'd felt faint, looked green hued, especially in the mornings. Perhaps the bug had returned, perhaps she'd had a fall. Perhaps she was lying at the bottom of the steep, narrow stairs, a trickle of blood oozing from her brow. Hannah was all she had. Out came the key to Tŷ Mawr, and relief that she hadn't thrown it away despite the impulse to do so on many occasions.

The ground level was empty, the only sign of life the stereo in the dining room, the volume turned to full blast. In other circumstances Elizabeth would have sneered at her mother's poor hearing, relishing the opportunity to remind Hannah of her age, her failing senses. With a strength garnered from terror Elizabeth raced up the stairs.

The rooms on the mezzanine were also empty. She had glanced out of the study window, which overlooked the back garden, for sight of her mother, and found none. Through the next two floors – nothing. The bathroom and the guest room at the top of the house were the only rooms Elizabeth hadn't searched. She raced up the last, shortest flight of stairs, pushed open the white door and saw nothing but paper roses. She flung open the dark pine door. The ceramic handle slippery and moist in her grip. Elizabeth stopped dead in her tracks. Hannah was lying in the iron tub, head underwater, eyes fixed on the ceiling. The water was clear and foam free. She pulled herself up when she saw her daughter.

'God. Sorry. Sorry, Mam. I'm so sorry.' Elizabeth was already pulling the door closed, backing out, as she spoke. 'I thought something might have happened. You didn't answer the door. I wasn't thinking. I was frightened. So sorry.'

Unsure what to do next, Elizabeth loitered on the landing. She leant against the wood chip covered wall, panting heavily. She hadn't seen her mother naked since she was a girl, and she was as mortified as she had been then.

The wall outside the bathroom felt cool. She could hear her mother splashing around, washing presumably. Her mind raced. Elizabeth closed her eyes and her mother's naked form flashed before her, uninvited, the bath water lending her pink skin a rippling, bluish hue. Making her appear vulnerable, nymph-like, not of this world. She saw her mother's cracked hands, shot through with purple-blue veins, ridged nails yellowed and horny. The skin on her shins fragile and translucent, like paper left out in the mid-day sun. The swell of her belly, the pendulous white breasts floating like lilies on the water's surface. The dark nipples. Try as she might to push the image of her unclothed mother from her mind, Elizabeth could not, and she kept coming back to the strangeness of the body she had seen.

Elizabeth had seen few older people without their clothes. Naturists aside, the parading of flesh was pursued almost exclusively by the young. Energetic grandparents who spent the winter months on the continent might wear shorts and sandals, their wasted, droopy flesh around the knees and thighs an uncomfortable reminder of the cruelty of time. But that was unusual before 2015 and now older people were near enough non-existent. Society waited anxiously for the generation down to grow old, those that were middle-aged, but they were showing signs of resistance. Ageing had never been fashionable, and most survivors born in the 1960s and 70s were reluctant to embrace it.

There was something decidedly odd about Hannah's body. It didn't fit somehow and Elizabeth wondered if her mother had had more work done on her last excursion to Eastern Europe than she had admitted to. Hannah had confessed to a face-lift, but perhaps she'd been too ashamed to admit to some bodywork as well. And while the benefits of her face-lift weren't immediately obvious on her return Elizabeth had to concede that lately her mother had looked radiant.

Elizabeth heard her mother clambering from the tub. She imagined her reaching for the towels on the freestanding rail. Wrapping the soft cotton around her wrinkled skin.

'Would you like a cup of tea, Mam?' Elizabeth asked, desperate to busy herself, to push the images from her mind.

'That would be lovely. I'll be done in a minute.' There was a muffled glee in Hannah's tone, like she was bursting. A girl with a secret to share.

Elizabeth flung off her heeled shoes, picked them up and padded downstairs. She walked across the kitchen floor, the stone tiles cooling and comforting her swollen feet. Rays of sunlight beamed in through the window illuminating the dust on the air. The orchestra scratched on and she didn't hear her mother until she was almost beside her at the sink. Elizabeth jumped.

'Sorry, darling. That's twice I've startled you today!'

'Oh, don't worry, Mam. It's me. I was miles away.'

Elizabeth reached into the cupboard above the kettle for the teapot and nettle leaves, avoiding her mother's gaze. 'I'm sorry I burst in like that. I thought something might have happened. The music was so loud, I didn't hear you. I panicked. As usual.'

'You were bound to find out sooner or later, Izzie. Owen and I were waiting for the right moment. We thought it best to wait, until we were sure it was all okay, and then somehow the moment never came. I was worried you might take it badly.'

Elizabeth stopped pouring hot water into the teapot, before turning and staring blankly at her mother. Hannah's hair was wrapped in a towel, grey tufts peeking at the temples, her pink cheeks shone. Elizabeth could see purple veins threading across her cheekbone. She was wearing Owen's bathrobe, one liver-spotted hand resting on her belly, the other touching her cheek in a manner that was both affected and coy.

'Take what badly? Are you ill?' Elizabeth gripped the draining board.

'Good heavens, no! Surely you can guess, Izzie? I've been very tired lately. You've caught me undressed. Isn't it obvious?'

'You're talking in riddles, Mam. What do you mean?'

shrieked Elizabeth, panic rising. As she spoke Elizabeth became aware that Hannah was stroking her stomach. Her distended stomach.

'Oh sweet Jesus. Cancer? You have a tumour?'

Hannah laughed, 'Good God, Izzie, no. But I do have something growing inside. Something special. A miracle.'

'Stop talking in riddles. What do you mean?' Elizabeth was shouting now.

'I'm having a baby, Izzie. Owen and I are having a baby. To celebrate our love.'

Hannah was flushed and smiling. Elizabeth gawped at the old woman rubbing her belly before her. She felt liquid rise in her mouth. Her stomach lurched as she choked, 'You could have bought each other a ring, to celebrate your love. Isn't that what other people do?'

There was a pause as the two women regarded each other, like strangers meeting for the first time.

'I think I'm going to be sick,' Elizabeth said, before turning to the sink and retching.

The pier was almost deserted. Elizabeth sat on a bench, the paintwork chipped and flaking, the hard slats pressing into her flesh. Her mouth acidic and stale from vomiting. She removed the bottled water from her new handbag, and sipped the last of it. She stared across the water. The sea was still, even the gulls were quiet. A black guillemot skimmed the water's surface, fast and low, and came to land in the boulders on the rocky shore. Elizabeth watched the familiar black and white plumage. They were common across the water on Anglesey but it was unusual for them to nest here on the mainland. Suddenly Elizabeth saw the scarlet of the bird's mouth. Its beak was wide open, revealing the hallmark red. It was threatening a potential intruder, its high-pitched whining filling the coastline.

Elizabeth longed to howl at the sky. She had bolted from Tŷ Mawr without another word, afraid that if she spoke her words would damage them both forever. Her rage was as distinctive and alarming as the guillemot's. How could Hannah be so selfish? So misguided? So cruel? Elizabeth would like to have blamed Owen. To claim that he had brain washed Hannah, filled her head with dangerous nonsense, but she knew in her heart that this was Hannah's work; it shone with her mother's self-delusion, her misguided romanticism. Owen was a pompous, vicious prig, but he was a profoundly selfish man, and for one so apparently wealthy, astonishingly mean. He would resent another pull on Hannah's affections and his purse strings. No, Elizabeth was sure that this was her mother's doing.

She remembered a holiday taken earlier in the year. Where did her mother and Owen go? It was Eastern Europe – an unusual choice, especially for an elderly British couple with precious few travel miles. The weather was far less clement than in the UK in January. The temperatures were unforgiving, the economy unstable, and the food terrible. When Elizabeth tentatively questioned their choice over tea one afternoon Hannah finally, and guiltily, admitted that she was visiting a medical establishment while she was there. Elizabeth had never approved of plastic surgery. It appalled her that trained professionals could waste their skill and talent pandering to the whims and indulgences of the vain and wealthy. Hannah had talked about cosmetic surgery for years, and Elizabeth assumed that she was looking into a face-lift.

'Just to check it out. Their reputation is unsurpassed.'

She had been deceived. The trip had not been to buy a new face. It had been a quest to buy a baby. She should have suspected. Her mother had dropped hints, but the deaf can't hear, Elizabeth thought ruefully.

The trade in babies, foetuses, and fertility treatments was booming. Those who couldn't reproduce naturally were encouraged to seek alternative methods, and countries unaffected by the plague with flimsy legislation were most popular. Babies were bought, surrogates hired, eggs auctioned and sold to the highest bidder like pieces of bone china, but still Elizabeth found it difficult to comprehend the doctor who would treat a seventy-three-year-old, when younger, healthier couples were turned away.

A young woman approached pushing a pram. The wheels rattled on the planks.

'Excuse me. Would you mind watching the baby? I need to use the bathroom, and the pram won't fit through the doors.'

Elizabeth nodded, and followed the woman's hasty steps to the pavilion in the middle of the pier. She must have been all of twenty-one, twenty-two maybe. A gurgling sound rose from the pram. Elizabeth peered in. The child was six months or so, with a shock of blonde hair. It smiled and flung out its arms as Elizabeth said, 'Bore da, cariad. What's your name then?'

It was so innocent, so trusting. She ached to pick it up, to place it on her chest, to smell the top of its head. She held out a finger and the child grasped it quickly and firmly. Such reflexes, such strength. For a moment, just a moment, it occurred to Elizabeth how easy it would be to take the child. She looked around, there was no one about. She leaned in. The baby clung on, she began to prise its fingers off her. Her hand brushed his cheek and memories leapt out at her. She remembered the joy, then the pain. She could not inflict that upon another mother. When the mother returned moments later, breathless and thankful, Elizabeth was crying.

Walking home, Elizabeth's head hurt from pent up anger and the questions that crowded her brain. A migraine threatened. She had no idea how she would react when she saw her mother, but she knew that she would find no relief until she spoke with her.

Hannah was dressed and made-up when Elizabeth returned to Tŷ Mawr. She wore a patterned smock over loose trousers, her shoulder length hair wrapped into a neat French pleat. Despite her foundation and powder Elizabeth could see that her mother was pale. Hannah gestured to the living room, a place commonly reserved for guests, and this unnerved Elizabeth momentarily. The family had always gathered in the kitchen. She did not offer Elizabeth a drink. Neither woman took a seat.

Hannah spoke in the measured tones of one who has spent time practising what to say.

'You may disapprove, Izzie, but you cannot undo what has been done. What has happened. I am sorry that you lost your children, your husband, that you cannot move on, but you cannot expect others to remain as you do, welded to the past. I am going to have a baby. You will have a brother or sister. You'll get used to the idea.'

'How? How have you done this? How is it possible? How is it that a woman two decades out of menopause can carry a child? The conception I can guess. A donor egg, obviously. How much did you pay? Then, a test tube. The semen? Owen's, maybe, but he's old. Perhaps you bought that too. How will you give birth? A caesarean? How will you raise the child? Where will you get the energy? Will you take pills for that too? What happens when you die, because die you will. You cannot turn back time indefinitely. It's unnatural, it's unethical, immoral. It's wrong.'

Exhausted Elizabeth sat back on the sofa, stunned at the speed and vehemence of her delivery.

Silence. Then she spoke again, softer this time, still shaking. 'Why, Mam, why? You have everything you could possibly want, especially now that you have Owen.'

Hannah remained standing. She took a deep breath and replied, 'I want a child.'

'You have a child, Mam. Me. I'm still here,' Elizabeth retorted.

'For Owen and me. To cement our love.'

Hannah's comment blew out the hurt and ignited Elizabeth's anger once more. 'And what about the child? This isn't just about you, Owen, your love. This is a life. You have a responsibility towards it.'

Cradling the slight curve of her belly Hannah replied, 'For God's sake, Izzie, you think I don't know that? This child will be loved and cared for. Well cared for. Who can say what the future will bring? Teenage parents know as much or as little as Owen and me. We are fit, healthy, financially secure. We may live for another twenty-five years, or we may die tomorrow. And that is the same for all parents, no matter what their age. You think that because we have the knowledge it doesn't give us a right to use it, to explore it for our own ends? Where do you draw the line, Izzie? Do we stop using drugs to cure diseases that kill, because death is natural? Is it unethical, immoral, to help people get what they want? Make them happy, complete?'

'Children are no more a right than happiness. And helping a childless couple conceive is entirely different to an old woman buying a baby to fulfil her preposterous notion of what love means! You may even be denying a younger woman her chance. Human eggs are not in limitless supply. You disgust me.' As soon as she had said it Elizabeth regretted her final comment. She hung her head in shame.

Hannah replied in a hoarse, choked whisper, 'And to think I considered asking you for one of your eggs, so that it would belong to you too.'

Elizabeth lifted her head again, it felt like steel. She would have a migraine later. 'But that's just it. A child doesn't belong to you or me or anyone. It is not a piece of furniture. A child is a gift. From God, the universe. To be treasured.'

The muffled tones of Elizabeth's mobile trilled from inside her handbag.

'You can see yourself out.' Hannah held open the door and gestured to the hall.

Desperate to avoid her mother's gaze and busy herself Elizabeth bent to look in her handbag. She dug out the phone and walked to the front door, shaking with anger, hunger, and fear. The screen brought up a number she vaguely recognized. Without thinking, as if in a trance, Elizabeth hit the answer button and lifted the mobile to her ear.

'Elizabeth. Elizabeth Evens?'

'Speaking.' The voice was not familiar but she had heard it before. Where?

'Jonathan Cardew, here.'

'Jonathan Cardew?' Elizabeth stuttered, attempting to cross

the road, narrowly avoiding a cyclist. The rider shook his head and shouted an obscenity at her.

'From St David's on the Hill Primary School. I'm calling to say...'

Still trembling from the altercation with the bike and the argument with her mother Elizabeth's mind was elsewhere. She anticipated the standard, 'the calibre of applicants was extremely high, and while I was most impressed with your resume and experience I'm afraid that on this occasion I am unable to offer you the position...' Seconds later, when she realized that Jonathan Cardew was waiting for a response, she understood that she hadn't listened to a word he had said.

'Oh. Well, thank you for calling. For letting me know.'

There was a long pause.

'Do you wish to accept the post, Miss Evens, or would you like some time to consider my offer?' He sounded surprised, and with this uncharacteristic display of emotion Elizabeth realized what he was saying.

'You're offering me the job? That's wonderful. I can hardly believe it. I was expecting a no. But yes, yes. I'd very much like to work at your school. Thank you. Diolch.'

The head rambled on for some minutes, and Elizabeth said the right things but she didn't feel anything. She knew she should feel pleased. Happy, even. But she felt neither surprise nor joy.

Ten days passed without a word from Hannah. Elizabeth picked up the phone several times, only to stop dialling half way through. What would she say? How could she begin to make amends? She was angry still, and hurt. And she believed that she was right, and Hannah was wrong. But Hannah was her mother, and love, and blood, runs deep. Besides, she was genuinely concerned for her health. Owen was idle. Hannah ran around after him like a skivvy, and even in her delicate state he had not altered his behaviour. If anything he demanded more of Hannah. Anyone would think that he was the one carrying a child.

Elizabeth knew that as time passed it would become harder,

not easier, to make up. To forgive cruel words spoken in anger, if not forget them. She had a tendency to allow disagreements to fester, but she knew that an unattended wound soon becomes septic. The morning she received the official letter from the school, offering her a post starting in the autumn term, Elizabeth determined to call her mother. She could use the news as an example that she was, contrary to Hannah's beliefs, moving on, and that she would move on regarding Hannah's pregnancy. She may disagree with the ethics, but what was done, was done. And there was another life to consider.

As she pottered in the kitchen, preparing a coffee and what she would say to her mam, and, much more disconcerting, what she would say if Owen answered, her phone rang. Elizabeth shuffled into the hall and picked up. It was Hannah, and she was bawling, breathless and gasping for air on every word. Elizabeth only just made out what she said.

'Owen is dead.'

Elizabeth shot round to her mother's. They greeted each other with a long embrace.

There had been an accident, the night before. There was no wine in the fridge to accompany supper. Though there was plenty of Chablis in the cellar, Owen insisted on a Chardonnay. Hannah was exhausted, and refused to go out for a wine that she couldn't herself enjoy. Owen went reluctantly, grumbling about Hannah's forgetfulness as he slammed the door. He lost control of the car on the sharp bend on the brow of the hill, skidding into the oncoming lane. He collided head on with a lorry. The driver was shaken but unharmed, and it was he who called the ambulance. Owen was dead on arrival at the county hospital. Hannah had identified the body, and been treated for shock before being sent on her way. She sat up all night, unsure what to do. She wasn't next of kin, they hadn't married – she had no rights. Owen's family in Oxfordshire had been called. A son and his wife.

'Oh, Izzie, the last words we said to each other were unkind. What am I going to do? What will I do without him? Who will take care of me now?' Hannah wailed.

Elizabeth wrapped her thick arms around her mother. Everything was forgiven.

'I'll take care of you, Mam. It'll be all right. We'll be all right. The three of us.'

Hannah smiled, and took Elizabeth's hands and kissed them, long and hard.

Owen's son and his wife arrived, unannounced, at Tŷ Mawr three days later. It was the first time that Hannah had met them. She offered her condolences through her own snivels, though they didn't return the sentiment. He was tall and erect, like a pillar, with a twitch in his left eye. She too was long and lean, sharp and pointed, with a small head, like a compass. Elizabeth thought the woman could inflict some damage.

Elizabeth disliked them both. Supercilious and callous they had come to collect Owen's personal effects, seemingly unconcerned that Hannah might have a claim to some of them. And not only did Elizabeth dislike them, she mistrusted them. Hannah offered them tea, or something stronger should they require it, but this was refused with a curt, 'We return to Oxfordshire this evening. By car.'

In the master bedroom Owen's clothes were tossed out of the wardrobe into a pile earmarked for charity. Elizabeth and Hannah watched from the doorway, and only intervened when the wife removed a pair of silver cufflinks moulded in the shape of a crescent moon from a shirt and went to put them in the box destined for the boot of their car.

'Would you mind if I kept those? I bought them for Owen. For his last birthday. He loved them so much.' Hannah could barely talk for weeping.

'So they're his property, are they not?' said the wife.

'Dearest, it's only a pair of cufflinks. Let her keep them.'

As Hannah snivelled her thanks it was all Elizabeth could do to stop herself from walking over and slapping the woman across the face. She thought this couple would stop at nothing to get something they wanted. Grateful for any small kindness Hannah began to chatter.

'Oxfordshire is a lovely part of the country, isn't it?'

'It is,' the son replied.

'My father went to Oxford, Corpus Christi. Of course I grew up in London, in Chelsea, like your father. Did you live up there?'

'For a while,' he said.

'Whereabouts?'

'Do we want this?' The wife cut right through their one-sided conversation, holding aloft a suit. It was cut from a heavy wool by a Saville Row tailor, at a time when winters were commonly cold.

'I don't think so, dearest. Putney.'

'Sorry?' Hannah said.

'Putney. We lived in Putney,' he said.

'By the river. How lovely.' Hannah paused and smiled, before continuing, 'Was your journey awfully long? Are you staying a while here in Wales?'

The wife cut in again. 'We're returning this evening.'

'Oh, yes. How forgetful of me.'

Elizabeth could bear it no longer and was about to steer her mother away when Hannah said, 'Do you have children?'

The wife blanched, and the son's mean features tightened, a resentful, blaming little wince. 'We don't. Not yet. But we will.'

And Elizabeth saw their Achilles heel. For all their worldliness, their sophistication, and arrogance, they couldn't have children. She saw it in the apologetic, defensive twitch in the wife's eyes, the angry flinch of the man's upper lip, the revealing reply. And she was afraid for Hannah, for her unborn child. Owen could be the child's father, assuming his sperm was used, and though Hannah had not confirmed this Elizabeth feared any challenge. She couldn't bear the thought of how humiliating paternity tests and the like would be for her mam. Hannah was little more than a surrogate, and while UK legislation still favoured the surrogate over the biological parents, it was being challenged in the courts. There was every reason to suppose it was possible that the UK might follow the American example. And Elizabeth knew that this greedy, hard-hearted couple would stop at nothing to get something they coveted. Elizabeth was sure of it.

She dragged her mother downstairs.

'Do they know about the baby?'

'Who?' Grief had turned Hannah's usually sharp mind to blancmange.

'Who do you think? Those two.' She pointed at the ceiling.

'No one knows. Only you. Owen insisted we keep it quiet. Said the press would hound us, turn us into a freak show.'

'He had a point.'

Hannah stared at Elizabeth blankly. Elizabeth blushed with shame. 'Had he changed his will? To accommodate the child? You? Why else would those two hate you so much, Mam?'

'Do they hate me? Grief does terrible things to people, Izzie.'

'And some people are plain terrible.' Elizabeth gripped her mother's shoulders. 'Mam, had Owen altered his will, to favour you or the child?'

'No.'

'You're sure?'

'I'm sure there's no mention of the baby. I am the main bene-factor, though he's not as wealthy as you might think. He has very little, actually.'

When Hannah realized she had talked of Owen in the present tense she began to weep again.

Elizabeth wiped her mother's cheeks and said, 'They must never know about the child. No one must know, not until it's born. And even then you must be careful. Do you understand me, Mam? We will raise your baby. No one else,' Elizabeth said firmly.

Owen's son and daughter-in-law left within an hour. They said that Owen would be buried in a family vault in Oxford, and by way of a half-hearted apology they promised to send Hannah an invitation to the memorial service. They were thanked politely by Hannah – Elizabeth remained silent and stern – and when Hannah waved them off on the doorstep Elizabeth knew it was the very last time her mother would set eyes on either of them.

Two days later Elizabeth typed her reply to Jonathan Cardew, explaining that it was with great regret that she declined his invitation to take up post at St David's School. Unexpected family commitments had made it impossible for her to commit to a full-time position. She was sorry that she was unable to become part of his team, but family had to take precedence. She hand delivered the letter, taking a slow walk back along the route that only weeks ago held such promise.

Chapter Eighteen

The paper roses on the bedroom walls danced as if caught on a summer breeze, the floorboards waved towards the door, and as Elizabeth opened her eyes and the dream faded to white the trembling in the pit of her stomach intensified. For a long moment Elizabeth questioned if she wasn't still in the depths of sleep. And then, she heard them: the birds. They were agitated and alarmed. Calling at the tops of their voices. The air was dense, and even before her eyes adjusted to the dark, and she made out the hands on the cantankerous grandmother clock sat in the corner of the room, Elizabeth knew it was the middle of the night. There was a dead centre feel to the air.

She stepped out of bed and felt her way to the window. The wood was warm against the soles of her feet. She drew back the dusky, wine velvet curtains, and wiped her hands against her nightgown. The curtains were old and rotten, like everything else in the guest room, and she felt sullied when the room's fetid air touched her flesh. She had been living at Tŷ Mawr a month, and no amount of cleaning and airing could remove the stench of decay. When she complained Hannah said that it was Elizabeth's paranoia.

Elizabeth had longed to leave her house, the ordinary, boxy semi-detached, where she once had a husband, a family, a happy, contented life. It belonged to a woman who no longer existed. And she needed company; she feared she might drown in all the empty space. The silence. But she couldn't let go, and there wasn't a solid reason to leave. When Hannah asked her to come back to Tŷ Mawr, to help, it gave Elizabeth the push she needed, but there was even more space to fill in the big dark house.

Outside all was calm. The birds had stopped calling and there was no evidence that anything out of the ordinary had happened. Elizabeth believed she may have imagined it. Despite the full moon it was difficult to make out detail in the garden, but all seemed normal. Elizabeth turned and swept her hand across the left hand wall, it felt parched and dusty, but solid. No sign of the movement moments before.

Elizabeth shuddered. She thought it was a reaction to having touched the crumbling wallpaper until she realized that the trembling in her stomach remained. She felt sick, and she knew why.

'I have to get out of here,' she said, aloud. She rubbed her fingers against her thumb, wiped her hands against her nightdress, desperately trying to rid herself of the walls.

Her suitcase lay underneath the wardrobe, swathed in grime. She hadn't got round to storing it in the loft as suggested, perhaps sensing a premonition that she wouldn't be staying long, or perhaps because it comforted her, seeing it when she lay in bed at night. A symbol that she was a visitor here, not a prisoner, that she was free to leave whenever she choose, though in her heart Elizabeth knew it could never be that simple.

A puff of dust billowed up as she dragged the case from its resting place. She flung the lid open to greet yet more dust, coughed, and then realized that she would need light to pack. She crossed to the switch. Seconds passed as the energy saving bulb warmed up, bathing the room in an amber glow, like cloud passing over the sun, a slow unfolding of light. Elizabeth pushed her case away from the front of the wardrobe and flung open the double doors. A gentle creak hovered on the air and then landed, like a bee on a flower, a faint residual hum.

Elizabeth studied the pathetic selection of cloth hanging in front of her. A couple of black skirts, mid-calf in length, a pair of black trousers, wide-legged and elasticated at the waist. A ragged patchwork jacket in hues of violent, primrose, and jade. Three white shirts, one pair of loafers and a pair of heeled black court shoes. She dumped them into the case, hangers and all.

Next Elizabeth turned on the dressing table. She yanked out the middle drawer and tipped the contents into the bag. Turtle neck jumpers in varying shades of brown and purple tumbled down, along with a few t-shirts and a dark blue cardigan with brass buttons. She grabbed the metal teardrop handle of the bottom drawer before remembering that it was empty. Elizabeth owned few clothes. The two smaller top drawers contained an unappetizing assortment of waist high white knickers, thick strapped bras and flesh coloured support tights.

The clothes formed a mound in the bottom of the case. Elizabeth plunged in, shuffling fabric, evening the spread, as she would a crumble topping over stewed rhubarb or plum, and as she did so her right hand stumbled upon a book. The leather cover was white, the pages sepia at the edges. It was the bible she carried on her wedding day, the one she kept with the clothing she wore next to her skin. Elizabeth stopped and stroked the cover, the golden cross winked at her in the light. She turned it over in her hands and flipped the pages, from back to front. Dried flowers, poppies and rose petals, peeped out from their resting places between the pages. It was a book of pressed memories. She read the inscription on the inside front cover, the elaborate handwriting in dark blue ink scratched at her heart. It was a hand full of hope, joy, and expectation.

To my darling Izzie. Love is forever. Andrew

The clouds were heavy and slate grey the day she married Andrew. They loitered over the depths of the Menai Straights, bore down on Anglesey, and covered Bangor in a film of dampness more apt for a February afternoon than a June morning. Elizabeth barely noticed. She stood in front of the Victorian mirror in her bedroom at Tŷ Mawr and smoothed the satin of her gown with her palms. Cream turning to ivory in the tepid light, the dress shone softly, adding warm hues to Elizabeth's already glowing complexion. At twenty-eight Elizabeth was to shed a skin: that of single woman. She would turn her back on Izzie Evens, spinster, unadmired and unnoticed girl. She would be introduced as Elizabeth Bevan, wife of Andrew Bevan, Doctor of Biology, Bangor University.

Andrew had given her the bible as a pre-wedding gift declaring it could be her 'something new' and from the moment she removed it from the red velvet-lined box Elizabeth loved it. She liked to stroke the jacket, press the cross into the pad of her index finger. She lifted the open book to her face and inhaled the scent of the freshly inked pages. It was minutes before she read some of its pages, at random, with deepening awe. The pages were as fine as tracing paper, containing messages as delicate and revealing. They screamed, 'Treat me with respect,' and Elizabeth knew that she would always do just that. She didn't carry flowers in her hands as she floated up the aisle, she held the little white book and she felt love and comfort pouring through the pages, through the leather, through the seams and into her soul.

Up to this point Elizabeth had not been a religious person, and though she knew Andrew was a believer, he was not evangelical, he did not push his views on her or even encourage her to take an interest in any way. The small act of presenting her with the bible was to change her life as significantly as marriage itself. From that day on Elizabeth was a different woman.

In the bedroom, the air grew warmer around her as she remembered the next time she held the bible in church. It brought her out in a cold sweat. She was burying the first of her children. Like all victims, Robert was buried quickly to avoid the spread of disease. His was a traditional funeral, with flowers, and mourners and pallbearers. He was lucky. Within weeks the pestilence was claiming the lives of so many that few went to their final resting place with the pomp and ceremony of a service. By dying early Robert avoided the mass graves and Elizabeth was grateful that he was laid out in a plot of his own, with a simple but dignified headstone. It had cost her and Andrew dear. The twins, Matthew and Luke, were not so fortunate. By then, even the mass graves were full. They were cremated, without ceremony, along with hundreds of others that day. As was Andrew when his time came. No relatives were permitted during such cremations, and on these days Elizabeth had sat at her bedroom window staring at the sky for hours, wondering which curl of smoke was Matthew, Luke or Andrew, which gull or kittiwake or guillemot flew by with a waft of her loved ones on their wings.

Until Hannah told her the news of her impending motherhood,

Elizabeth tried not to ponder her former life: her husband, children, promising career. It was too painful. She got on with a survivors half-life. Back to being single, childless. She reverted to her maiden name, Evens. She was offered counselling to combat the guilt the authorities assumed she must feel, but she refused. Elizabeth did not feel guilty for surviving, she understood that it was God's decision and he must have had his reasons for taking her precious sons and husband. Occasionally, she allowed herself to feel angry, and envious of those whose loved ones were not claimed, knowing that He would understand and forgive her this occasional weakness of spirit.

But here, in this room full of memories, with its vista to the heavens, on a midsummer's night, holding the precious book, Elizabeth's mind wandered back. Sweat trickled down her spine, her chest tightened, her stomach swam as she remembered. The boys running on the beach at Harlech, through the dunes at Shell Island, crabbing in Barmouth harbour, leaving school with their lunch boxes and book bags. The memories flooded in and Elizabeth thought she might drown. The scent of the newborn, the tiny hands, vice-like grasps, cherry red mouths and soft, soft tummies. So new, so fresh, so hopeful. So needy.

Elizabeth returned with a thud. She dived into the suitcase and hurled her possessions across the room.

'She will need me. The baby will need me,' she screamed, and she started to cry.

It was nearly five am before Elizabeth fell into a fitful sleep. She woke at eight to the salty tang of bacon. Hannah was hunched over the stove when Elizabeth walked into the kitchen, sandy eyed and crabby.

'Morning, darling. You've slept late. Not often I'm up before you,' Hannah trilled.

'I think I'll move out of the guest room, Mam.'

'Good idea,' Hannah said.

'I had trouble sleeping last night. I hope I didn't wake you.'

'Not me, darling. Says on the news there was an earthquake last night. A minor one of course but the aftershock measured 3.2, so not bad for Wales! Slept right through it I did!'

'And a baby's cry will wake you? Thank God I'm here, Mother! Thank God I'm here.' Elizabeth snatched the remote control from the table and turned up the volume. A reporter was interviewing a young man from Caernarfon who had been woken by the tremor.

'And the strangest thing was that all the birds started calling.'

Elizabeth walked out of the kitchen.

Chapter Nineteen

The row that followed was brief and vicious. Hannah shouted and screamed, raging at her daughter's jealousy and cold, resentful nature.

Elizabeth remained controlled, she felt the blood draining from her face, she dropped her voice to a quiet monotone. She channelled her mother's anger like a lightening rod, rendering it harmless, but as Hannah stormed from the kitchen she threw her parting shot.

'Do not punish me because of your guilt!'

Elizabeth's lips were dry. 'What did you say?'

'I know you feel guilty, Elizabeth. All those "What ifs" cling to you like dirt. What if I'd kept the child. What if it'd survived. It's not too late for…' Elizabeth left.

Her mother's comment cleaved Elizabeth in two. When she slammed the front door behind her Elizabeth thought she might never be able to see her mother again, for were she to see Hannah she just might hit her. What she had said was unforgivable. And so true it hurt like a knife wound.

Elizabeth staggered down the rise, thinking it strange that she should notice the smells of a summer's morning, the shaving foam clouds splattering the sky, the sticky air brushing her cheeks. She noticed that she wasn't crying and felt that she should be. She was empty.

The streets were quiet, more so than usual, and Elizabeth was grateful. She did not want to bump into anyone she knew, even vaguely. She feared she would appear like someone whose soul had been abducted by aliens, like the hapless victims in the corny old films she loved so much. She found herself drifting towards the city centre, and was powerless to stop herself, though she knew it would be dangerous. She felt an invisible pull, a guiding force. Later, she would think that the Lord did move in mysterious ways indeed. It was market day.

The market was a shadow of its former self. A few stalls lined the high street with a meagre selection of produce. There were mostly salad vegetables and fruit on sale. One stall was decorated across the top with freshly slaughtered poultry. Blood dribbled from the birds' headless torsos down the awning poles of the cart. A small crowd huddled round the vendor, calling and jostling for attention. The vendor was selling the birds and trays of white, beige and dark brown eggs to the highest bidders. The eggs were still covered in feathers, faeces, and other bird discharge. Elizabeth had never liked egg. The yolk was too yellow, vibrant, lively. The white a colourless amniotic fluid, slippery and tasteless. The chickens, at least that's what Elizabeth assumed the carcasses were, looked scrawny and diseased, but this wasn't deterring the eager crowd. Meat was rare, disease had annihilated much of the livestock population, which had not yet replenished, and trade between plague affected and non-affected countries had not resumed fully. Most people were wary of meat, though none present seemed to be heeding such warnings. Elizabeth looked on, fascinated.

She skulked by the stalls, glancing up on occasion to check for familiar faces and the general direction she was heading in. As she approached the middle section of stalls she saw the dirty green of a municipal bus pulling into a stop just beyond the market borders. A woman stumbled off, pulling a battered shopping trolley behind her. A younger woman with a buggy followed, reprimanding her charge as she bounced the pushchair down the steps. A shock of blonde hair jumped up at every jolt. Hannah no longer drove, and Elizabeth's stomach lurched at the thought of her mother struggling with a pram and public trans-port. She caught sight of the third passenger disembarking. She looked again. A man in a blue suit, fifty-something judging by his greying hair and general demeanour, carrying a distinctive leather briefcase. Brown, faded and cracked at the edges, a large brass buckle dulled with use and age, it was a kind that wasn't seen any more, and hadn't been for years. It looked like an old doctor's case. Surely there couldn't be too many of this type around?

The case transported Elizabeth back to a discreet clinic with mint green walls, and a young receptionist with bright red talons and matching lipstick, a thin voice and no sensitivity. While Elizabeth sat on a cold plastic chair, the receptionist jabbered on the phone.

'I can't wait to see the little darling. Don't you just love their tiny toes and fingers?'

The man carrying the case was disturbingly familiar. Elizabeth watched as he moved from the bus to the pavement. The gait was unmistakable. She remembered him shuffling across the consultation room as she lay on the bed, the paper towels crackling beneath her bare bottom as she tugged at her knickers, pulling them across her knees, down past her shins, and dropping them onto the tiled floor. He made small talk as he scrubbed his hands, never meeting her gaze. And Elizabeth wondered why medics did this: scoured their hands in liquid carbolic only to encase them in soft, cold latex. The persistent tick-tocking of the clock clutching the wall, the leather case resting against the desk, the quiet thwack of the rubber gloves, the chilly hand pressing on her stomach, a little too hard, but how could she complain? She deserved to suffer.

Elizabeth felt her knees buckle, the taste of vomit coated her mouth. She swallowed the sour liquid back and clutched a lamppost, gulping in the morning air.

For the abortion itself she had insisted upon a general anaesthetic. She paid extra, for the deviation from what was usual – a local would have been sufficient, she was only fourteen weeks pregnant. But she did not want to be present when it was done. She did not want to remember. But her recovery time was longer. She couldn't do it alone, otherwise Andrew would have suspected something, thought she was ill and asked all manner of awkward questions.

Hannah had been a willing accomplice. Elizabeth would have preferred her friend Jane's help, they had trained together and remained close, but Jane was working overseas, teaching AIDS orphans in Malawi, and Elizabeth had no one else she could call close outside of her immediate family, so that was that. Hannah had been a stalwart, but Elizabeth felt uneasy and harboured treacherous suspicions that one day her mother would use this secret against her. She hadn't been wrong.

The sun disappeared behind a large cirrus, gulls squawked overhead and Elizabeth felt her legs move forward, though she couldn't remember making the decision to walk. Her limbs gained pace, and she ran through the market, towards the doctor, shouting, as he ambled up the road.

There was a moment of doubt, a flicker of uncertainty, when he turned to face Elizabeth. Was it him after all? This shabby, fragile man with washed out eyes and waxy skin? He had been detached, arrogant, he barely made eye contact then, surrounded as he was by an air of professional invincibility.

'Do I know you?'

There it was. The voice. Quiet, clipped, devoid of musicality. Not at all Welsh. Unmistakable.

Elizabeth stared, beseeching. She had not been a sickly woman, she was rarely ill, and neither were the boys before the plague took hold, so her visits to the clinic were sporadic and short, but this man had been her doctor for two years before she moved practice. After she lost her boys. How could he not remember her? He might even know her mother or have known her. His lack of recognition wrong footed Elizabeth and she was affronted. He must know her. He was pretending not to. To spare any embarrassment.

'Are you all right? Do you feel unwell?' He stood before her, brows creased.

'It's okay. I forgive you,' Elizabeth said, reaching out with her hand.

He leant back, as if from a leper, stuttering, 'Sorry?'

The icy tone again. The stammer. Elizabeth's cheeks blazed, her ears burnt. The gulls screamed.

'You don't remember me? My boys?'

He shook his head, slowly, uncomprehending.

'You know I lost my boys. All of them. My three lovely boys. My babies.' Her eyes began to sting.

214

'I'm sorry for your loss. Many of us lost someone dear.' He checked his watch. 'I have to go, I have a meeting to attend.'

The formality.

Her head swam, her pulse raced and she was dragged back into the sea of resentment and silent fury. Thrashing around, drowning, she grasped for a life belt, but none were offered.

'I was a patient of yours. So were my babies. You couldn't help them. When I came to you, you told me there was nothing you could do. You abandoned us.' She was losing control. She heard her voice rising, crackling, the anger flickering and spitting like a fire fed damp logs.

The doctor turned and began to walk away. Elizabeth leapt in front of him and grabbed his forearm and held on fast. He blanched but didn't try to free himself.

'How could you forget? You said you were sorry. I cried at your desk. I reminded you what we did,' she said.

'What we did?' He sounded confused, he looked frightened.

'Oh, it wasn't illegal then. But we shouldn't have done it. You shouldn't have let me do it. You helped me. You should have talked me out of it. You are a saver of life, not a destroyer. You made a pledge. An oath. Hippocratic, isn't it?' She saw herself as he must see her: demented, pitiful.

She was sobbing now, huge convulsive sobs. Her knees gave way and she crumpled to the ground, the concrete hard, and warm and dusty. He bent in to her, placed his arm on her shoulder.

'Have I really changed so much?' she said.

'No, not so much. I remember you now. I have tried to forget those I couldn't help, but it's not easy. I'm haunted by the living and the dead.' His head hung, limp.

'I wasn't the only one?'

He kneeled, resting on his haunches, and said, 'I see those I prescribed birth control pills for years, desperately trying to conceive. But it's too late. I see women like you, married with children, desperate to get their lives back on track. Babies were expensive, marriage wreckers, career halters. Young girls, caught short, fathers nowhere to be seen. I helped them all. I thought I was doing the right thing.' He faltered, took a handkerchief from the breast pocket of his frayed suit and dabbed his nose with it. There was a fey quality to him, effeminate almost.

'Excuse me, I have a cold,' he said. The merest suggestion of a smile crossed his lips. 'How could we have thought we would beat it? The common cold still has us utterly baffled.' He offered her his handkerchief, as if unawares that he had used it himself.

Elizabeth stopped crying and observed the doctor closely. Though she had tried to forget it, she remembered his name: Bryant. Dr Bryant. He wasn't a bad man after all. He did what he thought was right. She had been grateful once upon a time. He didn't have to authorize her termination. She was healthy, the family were prosperous. There was no medical reason why Elizabeth should not have another child. She hadn't wanted one. Her family was complete. Another would have got in the way. She had sinned and she had been punished for her transgression.

Her throat tightened once more. She would do anything to turn back time, to face that difficult crossroads again and take the other road. It might not have changed anything. She might still be alone. Disease might have claimed the girl too. After all, she would have been less than twelve months old and amongst the most vulnerable when the virus hit Welsh shores. She couldn't explain why but she always thought of the baby as a daughter. She shuddered, then replied, 'What must we look like? Two old tramps sitting on the pavement, snivelling.'

'You are not old, Mrs... Forgive me, I cannot recall your name.'

'Evens. Miss Evens. You knew me as Bevan – I use my maiden name now.'

'We cannot erase the past Miss Evens. It makes us who we are, for better or worse.'

Elizabeth shuddered.

'Forgive me. That was very rude of me. What I meant was – you're still young. There's time for you.' He stood up and offered her his hand.

Elizabeth took it, surprised by the strength of his grip. 'You are not the only person saying that to me Dr Bryant. My mother constantly reminds me to move on. "Get a life," she says. Like a teenager from a TV show.'

'But of course! You are Dr Evens' daughter. It was this likeness that confused me earlier. Your mother survived? Extraordinary. Marvellous. How is she?'

'Fine, fine. Very well.' Elizabeth brushed grit from the cracked, uncared-for concrete from her knees, not daring to meet his eyes for fear he may discern the lie in her reply.

'Let me take you home. Where do you live?' he said.

'You have an appointment.'

'That was a lie.'

Elizabeth feared he might enquire further about her mother. Might expect to be invited in once they reached Tŷ Mawr. She knew she should refuse his offer to escort her home, but a recklessness took hold. She liked his face, the feel of his hand encasing hers. 'It's a long walk. I often take the bus,' she said.

'Whichever you prefer.'

Elizabeth preferred to walk. It was a long time since she had enjoyed the company of a man and Dr Bryant seemed in no hurry. He said he was in need of some light exercise. Still feeling shaky she linked her arm in his offered elbow, thankful for his old-fashioned chivalry. Their pace was leisurely and despite the unusual circumstances, or perhaps because of them, they both felt remarkably at ease in each other's company. Elizabeth found herself confiding in him, in a way that she might have done years ago had their doctor/patient relationship been different.

After walking for over fifteen minutes they neared the city boundaries and Elizabeth told Dr Bryant of her mother's situation. She needed to share, the load of the secret was dragging her down, and there was a practical reason for telling him too. Elizabeth spoke of her fears for Hannah, and the child. Of the row that morning. The savage words. He did not judge, condemn, or condone.

'Are you afraid for her, or envious of her?'

'Don't be ridiculous,' Elizabeth laughed.

'You're not too old yourself, Elizabeth. If you wanted another child. You wouldn't even have to have a partner. There are so many options. All government authorized. All with a financial incentive. I arrange them all the time these days.'

'I'm sure you do, but it's not for me. Nothing can replace my boys. Anyway, I'll be too busy helping the old dear.'

He smiled, though Elizabeth wasn't sure if he found her feeble attempt at humour amusing or in poor taste. They were outside the city, Tŷ Mawr wasn't so far away. Elizabeth slowed her pace.

'Are you tired? Your legs are sore?' he said, glancing down as he spoke.

When she fell to the ground Elizabeth had grazed her knees. The dirt and dust and dried blood accentuated the bluish, voluptuous flesh of her legs, her non-existent ankles. Her legs needed a shave. Elizabeth wished she had worn trousers.

'No, no. Do you mind if I go on alone? I'd like to walk alone for a while before I speak with Mam.'

'Not at all. I'm glad you're going to make up with your mother. She will need you. Are you sure you're going to be all right?'

'Yes. Thank you, thank you so much.' She paused. She needed him, but it was more than that. A feeling she barely recognized: yearning. She wanted to see him again. 'We will need a doctor. Someone we can trust. Someone who can keep a secret. Will you help us, Doctor? Please?'

'Call me Chris. I'm not your doctor, and haven't been for years. But I will attend to your mother, her antenatal care, with her consent. Here's my card.' He nodded, smiled, touched his forehead with his index finger, military style, spun on his heels and strode off purposefully.

Elizabeth blushed as she smiled and waved back. She didn't start walking on immediately, but stood and watched as he bounced down the rise, the leather briefcase swinging backwards and forwards, the buckle glinting periodically as the sun caught it in its beams.

Chapter Twenty

As the weeks rolled on after Owen's sudden death, Elizabeth's fear that his son might claim a right to Hannah's child subsided. She even thought it might have been an illogical fear, whipped up by her delicate emotional state. But still they kept their secret.

Women of child-bearing age were encouraged to breed for the health of the nation. Every other woman between twenty and forty-five seemed to be pregnant. On municipal buses people clapped as bottoms lifted from seats when swollen bellies boarded, in shops vitamins and milk were distributed free of charge to expecting mothers, those not visibly pregnant wore badges proclaiming their special status. The barren flashed bitter smiles through jealous teeth. The unwilling, like Elizabeth, feigned congratulations, secretly condemning those who could replace so easily, so quickly.

Occasionally, Hannah expressed a desire to tell the world her news, a quest for celebrity, her vanity and self-obsession surfacing, but Elizabeth talked her out of it. The hounding would be relentless.

Hannah seemed to miss Owen, but not in the desperate, painful way that she had missed Elizabeth's father. Her tears were fierce, but as the summer rolled on increasingly short-lived, and she said having Elizabeth back at Tŷ Mawr made her feel less alone, less old.

Elizabeth knew that ageing terrified Hannah. Much of the time she pretended she was a young mother again, one daughter at home, another child on the way. Elizabeth did her best to humour her, but for Elizabeth the passage of time brought Hannah closer to the grave, as well as a new life. Elizabeth envied her mother her delusions; often she wished she was as close to death as Hannah, and she toyed with the idea of suicide again. But she feared His wrath.

The short warm nights were troubled for Elizabeth. Commonly she woke three, four times. Her dreams vivid. She dreamt of faceless, frightening children, and those she had loved and those she had taught visited her nightmares too. Like Annie Pointer, a stunted, whey-faced girl with red hair and a mouth like a ferret. In a recurring nightmare the twins Matthew and Luke would call to her from a grey playground as she taught eleven-year-olds in a spacious yellow classroom. The door to the classroom was locked and only once the lesson was complete would it open again. The boys appeared small and vulnerable, holding hands, shivering in short trousers, looking up at their mother trapped inside the monolithic building teaching a never-ending lesson. As Elizabeth turned to her pupils, desperate to escape, the children's teeth grew before her eyes, dropping over the bottom lip as the top lip curled and disappeared into the face. Whiskers emerged, tails grew, and then the squeaking began. Elizabeth tried to shake off her visions, acknowledging they were manifestations of her increasing anxiety about Hannah and her baby, but it was hard.

The world spun on, following its timeless course round the sun without regard for Elizabeth's mounting fear. She wished she could stop time. She imagined herself setting up a roadblock across the universal path, the earth rotating on its axis, never moving forward and never moving back. For everything to remain just as it was. But September turned into October, and the weeks rolled on. Halloween was approaching and the gestation period was almost complete. Elizabeth knew that she and Dr Bryant needed to plan the birth carefully. He had raised the matter, in the tactful way he did when discussing Hannah with Elizabeth. They were enjoying a glass of wine.

Staying for a drink or two was a regular feature of his visits these days. He would arrive early evening, once his surgery had closed, check on his patient, and then sit and chat with Elizabeth on the bench at the bottom of the garden. They would listen to the wood pigeons cooing, the evening song of the thrush, the gentle whirring of the lone turbine at the edge of the garden, finding solace in the sounds. The birds did as they had always done, always would do. After the initial report on the mother-to-be's progress, they would talk of life before and since 2015. It seemed like the most natural thing to do with Dr Bryant. Perhaps it was his enduring air of professionalism, the carer, the repairer. Elizabeth had thought him cold and distant years ago, but now she saw that he was a considerate and considered man. He was sincere and trustworthy. It was during one such visit that he asked if he might take her photograph.

'Whatever for?!' Elizabeth had never liked having her photograph taken, it suggested an intimacy that made her uncomfortable.

'Because it is a beautiful evening. Because I am sat here in a delightful garden, with an intelligent and captivating companion. And when I am a decrepit shell of my former, fabulous self,' he laughed, 'I can recall and relive a time of utter bliss. A secret rapture.'

'Well, after that, how can I refuse?'

He took out his phone and stepped back across the lawn.

Elizabeth shifted in her seat, pulled her thick cardigan tight, and smoothed her hair.

'Look at the camera,' he said.

'Shall I smile?'

'Just be yourself.'

Click. It was over.

Elizabeth didn't ask to see the image and he didn't offer. He slid the mobile back into the inside breast pocket of his tweed jacket and returned to the bench.

Lately his visits had increased to once a week and Elizabeth looked forward to them more and more. It was the highlight of her lonely week. She chose wine from the cellar with care, and had taken to buying olives and nuts, if they were available and she could afford them. She wondered if it might be considered forward to invite him to stay for supper, or if this might be compromising his professional relationship with her mother. After all, she could hardly exclude Hannah from the evening meal.

Though it was a mild October the day came when it was no

longer comfortable to sit outside. The turning back of the clocks finally put paid to their garden chats. When Dr Bryant called Elizabeth suggested the front room as an alternative, the kitchen seeming too familiar still. As she entered the lounge a mild anxiety set in. She placed Dr Bryant's glass on the coffee table opposite the sofa, and though it was large Elizabeth could not bring herself to sit next to him, as she had done on the upright garden bench. Outside on the patio the bench was the only seat and there was a purpose to sitting on it together: to view the garden at dusk.

The sofa was expansive and deep, to sink into its voluptuous cushions was the only option, unless you perched on the edge, which Elizabeth knew she could not do with grace or dignity. The alternative was one of three armchairs. They were upholstered in a burgundy leather, dull brass buttons studded along the broad arms. Their shape made it impossible to sit up straight if you were short, and if Elizabeth slid herself up against the back of the chair her feet raised off the floor, and she felt like a child. She considered slipping off her shoes and tucking her legs, as gracefully as she could, underneath her tail, but dismissed it as too young, too casual a pose to strike. She hesitated before the armchair and glanced back at the sofa.

Dr Bryant sensed her unease and gestured to the sofa. 'It will be so much easier to reach your drink if you sit here. I promise I won't bite.'

Elizabeth laughed, relieved that a decision had been made for her, and sat down at the far end. She coughed and turned her body as much as she could to face him. It was odd not to have anything to view, to comment on, other than each other. 'Shall I put some music on?' She went to get up.

'I don't mind the quiet. In fact I enjoy it.'

'Do you like the painting?' she said, gesturing to the Kandinsky print above the fireplace.

'Not really. I have never understood the appeal of most works of art post 1920. I like Holbein, and the pre-Raphaelites. You?'

Elizabeth felt ridiculous and exposed. She had no particular interest in art and so her knowledge was scant. She liked what she liked and that was that.

'Not really. I mean, I don't have a strong opinion about it. Though I do like the pre-Raphaelites, they're so beautiful, especially the women.' She blushed as she spoke.

'Not all the women are beautiful.' He paused. 'Does anyone call you Lizzie?'

'Mam calls me Izzie.' Her colour heightened further.

'May I?'

She dipped her chin twice.

'Izzie it is then. There is a painting, by Millais, *Christ in the House of his Parents*, which was criticized for portraying Mary as ugly, Jesus as an urchin. By Dickens, no less! But I think it is exquisite, and Christ's mother is too. I have a book of his work,' he said.

'I'd like to see it, if I may? Mam is the one who knows about art. She likes to paint. She probably told you. Showed you.'

'She has pointed out a nude in her bedroom. I'll bring the book over next time.'

'Thank you,' said Elizabeth before continuing hesitantly, 'What do you think of her work?'

'It's interesting.' He lowered his voice and leant over. 'It was a little embarrassing looking at the nude, strangely enough, given my line of work, and what I was doing at the time. It was a touch awkward.'

'What happened?'

'Your mother lay on her bed while I prodded her stomach. She giggled, like a schoolgirl, and pointed to the painting. "That was me doctor. Young, and nubile, and slim. See how slim I was. It's a self-portrait. I sat in front of the mirror for hours, examining myself. Almost as you are now!" She laughed again, and glanced at me, heavy lidded. I wondered if she was flirting with me,' he said.

'I'm sure she was, Doctor!' said Elizabeth, annoyed with her mother, and flattered that he'd confided in her in this way.

'It feels very odd, disloyal – talking about your mother like this. I do hope you don't think badly of me.' He looked at his hands.

'Not at all! I could never think badly of you.'

'Then call me Chris.'

'Okay. Chris.' They laughed at her clumsiness, and silence fell once more. Elizabeth stared at the Kandinsky, unsure what to say next. Her stomach turned, aware that she was being watched. She tried to imagine what she might look like to him and hoped that he liked what he saw.

Chris was first to break the silence. 'Tell me, Izzie, what are you passionate about?'

'Me?'

'You.'

Elizabeth's mouth was dry. He leant forward again, and for a second she thought he might try to kiss her. He took an olive. It was green and dripping in oil.

'Food,' she said, 'I'm passionate about food. I'm not much good at cooking, mind you, but I love good food.' Then conscious of her fleshiness she said, 'and music.'

'Do you play anything?'

'Heavens no. I have no talent. But I like to listen, it restores me somehow.'

'You have many talents, Izzie,' he said shyly, wiping the corner of his mouth before taking her hand and squeezing it gently.

Suddenly, Elizabeth felt uncomfortable. 'My mother is okay, isn't she? And the baby?'

'Everything is as it should be,' he said, removing his hand, reverting to doctor again.

'Well, perhaps not as it should be,' she retorted. Elizabeth sounded vindictive, but she couldn't help herself. She blamed nervousness, in this new surrounding with Dr Bryant.

A noise came from the hall, followed by the creak of the broken step into the kitchen. Elizabeth leapt to her feet and said, 'Mam's up, I'll go and check that she's okay.'

Hannah was filling the kettle; Elizabeth bustled over, reaching for the teapot and a mug. 'Not too full, Mam, it's just you. I can do this. You go back to bed.'

'I didn't want to disturb you and Dr Bryant, or should I say Chris.' There was a hint of teasing, delight mingled with mockery, in Hannah's voice; it reminded Elizabeth of when she was a teenager and a spotty boy from her form class called. Elizabeth wondered how long Hannah had been lurking outside the lounge door, eavesdropping. She said nothing.

'I nearly died when I heard voices in the lounge. I was expecting to find you here – it's more intimate somehow.' Hannah lumbered across to the table. 'Don't be churlish, Izzie. I'm pleased for you. The doctor is a nice man, you could do worse. He's not handsome like Andrew was, but you could do much worse. He's kind, honest...'

At the mention of Andrew, Elizabeth was seized by guilt, and a rage directed at her mother. How dare she compare Dr Bryant with Andrew? She hardly knew the man. With shaking hands she offered the mug to Hannah. She wanted to hurt her mother, the way she had been hurt. Her voice trembled as she spoke.

'Would you like me to take this upstairs for you, Mam?'

'No, darling. You get back to your doctor. He'll wonder where you've disappeared to.'

'I'm sure he'll work it out.' And with that Elizabeth turned and left.

It was awkward when she returned to the living room; she hovered, unsure where to sit again, if she should even sit down. It felt like a party when the majority of the guests have left, only stragglers remain, desperate for the evening not to end, unwilling to accept that the fun's over. Her earlier good humour had evaporated.

Dr Bryant coughed and asked if all was well. Elizabeth nodded.

Rising to leave, he said, 'Hannah is very fearful of the operation. She hasn't said it in so many words but I feel it.'

'Why? She was a doctor herself.' She sounded tense.

'It's the idea of a needle entering her spine. And the fact that unless I can persuade another doctor to help us, someone who will keep quiet, you will more than likely be the person helping me to administer the epidural. I'm not an anaesthetist.'

'So, it's because of me. She doesn't trust me. I can understand that. I'm not sure I trust myself,' said Elizabeth.

'She doesn't trust either of us. Not entirely,' he reassured.

'For God's sake she should have thought about all this before she went ahead and got herself pregnant! She has been so irresponsible about all this. It drives me mad.'

'She cannot have known it would end up like this.'

Elizabeth knew Hannah was petrified of the spinal block. She would much rather a general anaesthetic. Elizabeth wondered if they were being overly secretive, after all. Perhaps the publicity wouldn't be so bad, if there was any? Perhaps they should admit Hannah to hospital? Perhaps they were mistaken about Owen's son? Then, she saw the wife's tight face, the son's fish eyes, felt their insensitivity and greed. She shivered.

Gathering his things, Dr Bryant said, 'We must do it soon. It is highly unlikely that Hannah will go full term, and the longer we leave it the riskier it becomes.'

Elizabeth's pulse raced.

He continued, 'We should aim to get the child out in a couple of weeks.'

A wave of dread rushed over Elizabeth; she felt quite faint. She wished with all her heart that she could fast forward time, or stop it altogether.

'I won't tell Mam straight away. I'll give her enough time to prepare, but not so long it drags. I'm not sure she's thought about when it might happen. Let's leave it that way.'

He started towards the door, 'As you wish, Izzie.'

A moan wafted down from above. He stopped dead; Elizabeth stepped into the hall. It was cold and empty. Only the landing light was on. She moved to the bottom of the stairs and looked up towards the mezzanine. In the half light she could see Hannah's stooped figure near the top of the first flight, hands clutching the banister, knuckles white. So she'd been eavesdropping again.

'You okay, Mam?'

Hannah turned and though her face was in shade Elizabeth felt sure she had been crying. 'The baby kicked, that's all. Just letting me know that my body's not my own. Not anymore.'

'I'll be up in a minute.'

After showing the doctor out, Elizabeth headed upstairs. She knocked lightly on the bedroom door and when there was no reply she turned the handle and opened the door. The room was dark.

'Mam? You asleep?'

There was no reply. Elizabeth closed the door and went to clear the wine glasses.

Chapter Twenty-one

The shadows grew and grew, the rats poured from every crevice, snapping and biting, peals of laugher turned to screams, children ran, and jumped, and fell. The teeth sank into peach flesh. Blood poured everywhere. Elizabeth clutched plump hands with dirty fingernails, grasping, slipping, failing. She was too late. Faces elongated, teeth and whiskers grew, a wailing filled the class-room. The walls crept in as the cacophony built. Elizabeth turned away from the children, the beastly creatures, and fixed on the glass jar on top of the bookshelf. It was covered in dust, but she could make out the folded form, squashed into the glass, pre-served in a yellow aspic. A half-formed foetus. Grotesque and mesmerizing. A half-life. Preserved to be observed, studied and discussed. A monster. Forced from the womb into an endless future. As Elizabeth stared at the beast its gigantic head turned, owl-like, to face her and the lipless mouth opened, as if in speech. She pulled away and looked down at the rat-children, their faces metamorphosing into those of the foetus's.

Elizabeth woke with a start. The clock read half past mid-night. It was All Saints' day.

She sat up in bed. The radiator hissed at her. Elizabeth was soaked with sweat and tears. As she gulped water from a glass on the bedside table she heard the yowling. She put the glass down. It came again. Distinct, real, of this world. Throwing the duvet aside she leapt from the bed, tripping over her plaid carpet slippers as she headed towards the door. She grappled with the handle and cursed herself for not oiling it – it was stiff and her clammy palms made opening it difficult. She grabbed her nightdress at the hem, pulled it over her hand and took the brass handle in her grip again. She twisted clockwise, and this time, the door opened. Elizabeth charged along the hall to her mother's bedroom, her stubby feet with their curled toenails clattering on the floorboards as she went.

Hannah was on all fours, head buried in the pillows sitting at the top of the king-sized bed. As Elizabeth burst into the room Hannah lifted her head and grimaced. She brought to mind the family dog of Elizabeth's childhood: a bulldog, solid and constantly dribbling.

'Dear God, I think I'm going to die,' Hannah said.

'Labour?' Elizabeth felt sick.

'I think so. I'm not sure. Izzie, I'm losing blood.'

'We need Dr Bryant. We have to get you to his clinic,' she cried. Elizabeth tried to control the rising panic in her voice. She took a deep breath and said, 'Mam, when did the pain start?' Her voice was strangled.

'I don't know. It woke me up.'

'And how long have you been awake?'

'I'm not sure. Not long?'

'Oh God, Mam.'

Hannah let out a slow rumble, which built like thunder.

'We need to get you to the clinic, now. I'm phoning Dr Bryant. He can meet us there.'

'But will he be ready? It's the middle of the night. Izzie, Izzie. I'm so frightened.' Hannah's eyes were like saucers, brim full of terror and trust, like a child's.

Elizabeth turned on her heels and ran onto the landing. She telephoned Chris, dressed, and marched back into her mother's bedroom. The air was thick. Hannah hadn't moved.

'Get off the bed now.'

Hannah did as she was told and slipped from the bed and staggered round it, her body forming an L-shape. As Elizabeth threw a few items of clothing into a holdall she watched her mother from the corner of her eye. Hannah looked like a crone. You couldn't see the bump, just an old woman in a brushed cotton nightdress, with dyed hair, grey at the roots, swollen ankles and transparent shins decorated with broken veins. She looked as though she might collapse with the effort of living, like a bookshelf straining with the weight of too many hardbacks.

'I can't believe it. The baby isn't due for another five weeks. I just can't believe it.'

'How is this happening, Mother? What is going on? I can't believe that we haven't got anything together. Nothing at all. Unbelievable.'

Elizabeth plunged clothes into the bag. She was swift, efficient, and brutal. She closed her eyes and remembered the children she had laboured for, sweated and pushed, and screamed and trembled. The images rushed in.

The bed shimmered with blood, red-black and sticky. She saw the blur of the powder blue creature that was her last born as he hit the thick white sheets, the purple hole that was his mouth before a wail, the swollen, boxer eyes peaceful in sleep. She smelt his scent: sweet bottle-top milk and talcum powder, and the touch of him: vice-like grip and the soft flesh of thigh, arm and cheek. Later, perched on the stiff ward bed, the shock, the pain, the blood was forgiven as she stared at this life, this terrifying, awe-inspiring life. He was beautiful and alien, and she wondered what he would make of it all, this world, this unasked for gift of life. She would have cried tears of joy, just as everyone said she would, but she had no water to give that evening. Instead she watched and waited for him to wake, wonder struck and fearful. Periodically she brushed his apple cheeks, smelt his brow, checking he was real, no longer trusting to sight alone.

The past engulfed Elizabeth like a fog, her eyes stung. But it was no time for mawkishness. As Elizabeth struggled to find her way back Hannah started hollering again. What began as a strangled moan turned into a primal howl of horror and repulsion. Elizabeth looked up. Hannah was standing, disbelieving, at the foot of the bed, hands clamped to the bedstead. A rusty puddle of liquid at her feet, staining the sheepskin rug.

'My waters are breaking.'

'I can see that, and by the looks of things the baby is in distress.'

'Oh my God, oh my God.'

'Be quiet. Start walking. Focus. Take my arm.'

With one arm supporting her mother, the other clutching the bag Elizabeth manoeuvred Hannah downstairs and out onto the street where the car waited. She was neither graceful nor smooth. The women hobbled and lurched from one key location to another. Elizabeth was thankful for her corpulence; her size gave her a feeling of control, of parity with Hannah, misguided though she knew this to be.

The night air was brisk and offered little solace to Hannah who wore only her nightgown. Hannah's breath spotted the black air, and Elizabeth wished she had grabbed some coats. She opened the car doors, lowered her mother onto the back seat, pushed the key into the ignition and turned. Nothing happened. The engine remained unmoved. Elizabeth prayed to her God. She turned the key once, twice, and the car juddered into action. Elizabeth sped off into the night.

The county hospital loomed in the distance, growing taller with each passing second. Like a glorious cathedral its gleaming towers dominated the skyline like spires, a beautiful beacon, and Elizabeth wished they could stop, that she didn't have to drive on to Chris's clinic on the other side of the city.

He was waiting for them in the doorway with a wheelchair when they pulled into the car park. He was dressed in surgical blue, his salt and pepper hair covered with a cap. Elizabeth leant across and held Hannah's hand. It felt clammy and cold. Her chin rested on her chest.

'Hang on in there, Mam. You can do it. You've done it before. You're good at this,' she said.

Hannah lifted her head and rasped, 'I'm going to die, Izzie. If we can't get this baby out quickly. I can't stand this for much longer. Look after him for me.'

'Don't be ridiculous, Mam. It'll be fine, we're here now.' She gestured to Chris, who was trying to smile, reassuring, and continued, 'Dr Bryant will deliver your baby and then we can go home.' Elizabeth wiped her mother's brow, and whispered another private prayer.

Dr Bryant stumbled around the clinic with a small torch, looking like an intruder, before realizing that he could not sensibly prepare for the trial ahead without light.

'We need to close the blinds before we turn on the lights,' he said. 'It's isolated here but we can't risk the suspicion of an idle passer-by, the lost drunk looking for home, the teenage runaway looking for shelter.'

Alcohol sale restrictions meant street drunkenness was near enough extinct and there were few teenagers. It dawned on Elizabeth how much she missed watching groups of young people hanging out. Their slouching, shy stance, the awkward, sexy clothes, the sense of discovery and ownership. Chris had daughters once: Katy and Regan. He told her they had driven him to distraction when they were alive, but now that they were gone he missed teenagers per se, not only his girls, he said. Elizabeth just missed children.

Chris whisked Hannah through to theatre. It was a room designed for minor surgical procedures, of moderate size, achromatic and cold. A bleak, impersonal space. He helped Hannah onto the plastic bed, which he hastily covered with a sheet and a thin blanket. Gesturing to Elizabeth he began to scrub up. She pulled on surgical trousers and smock, identical to his, and tucked her fine, wavy hair into the cap. She was self-conscious, she lowered her eyes, avoiding his gaze.

'You look magnificent, Izzie: dependable, brave.'

Elizabeth knew what to do. They had spoken of it often enough. And they had been successful at keeping Hannah's pregnancy well hidden. She visited the clinic when absolutely necessary, for scans and such, when Chris required equipment that could not be carried to the house, but no one suspected a thing. Hannah wore loose clothing. She was an old woman. Of course she would have ailments.

As he scrubbed up at the sink he whispered, 'This is not going to be easy, Izzie. She's in a lot of pain, getting the needle in will require a steady hand. Doing it for real will be very different to practising on the doll.'

'For God's sake, why couldn't she hold on for another week? You said thirty-six weeks. Plenty of time you said,' Elizabeth snapped.

'I'm sorry. This shouldn't be happening. Have you been watching her?'

'Of course I bloody well have. But even I can't be there all the time.'

Hannah moaned. Without energy, lethargic and moribund.

'We must attend to her. I'm sorry, Izzie. It's a long time since I performed a caesarean. And we need to work quickly. I have only a small amount of epidural. Let's do it.'

Elizabeth and Dr Bryant made a good team. He was a first-class teacher and she a fine pupil. They administered the spinal block without too much difficulty, and Hannah relaxed once the pain receded.

Elizabeth stayed by her mother's head, holding her hand, stroking it, and talking while Dr Bryant cut into her mother's belly. Mother and daughter were startled at the speed of his work, so busy chatting about the wild weather that they jumped when they heard the angry mewling of a newborn.

Dr Bryant beamed as he held the child aloft, proud as any new father. 'You have a daughter, Hannah. Another beautiful daughter. A sister for you, Izzie!' he said.

The miracle of birth: a new life, the future. It took their breath away.

Elizabeth leapt to her feet, tears welling in her eyes. 'I'll clean her up, clear her passages, check she's okay.'

'And I'll clean you up, Hannah, and then you can hold your baby,' said Dr Bryant.

Dawn approached. Elizabeth looked out of the window. From Chris's clinic on the top of the hill she could just make out the church she used to attend, Norman and squat with its stout bell tower, Welsh flag fluttering in a breeze. She thought she heard the bells chiming, ringing out, a call to worship, or a death knell. Was it Sunday? She couldn't recall the day. It was too early for bell ringing. It was all in her head. She felt leaden, she wanted to cry, but she had no tears. It was different this time. Hannah was silent; she looked like she was sleeping.

Elizabeth sat very still, holding the sleeping baby. Chris was in the bathroom. The ticking of the surgery clock marked the passage of man-made units of time. Elizabeth's heart pumped sadness and joy.

'Izzie?' Dr Bryant was ashen and his hands shook. He had been crying.

Elizabeth looked up, then her eyes locked on the girl in her arms. She was everything now. She stroked the top of the infant's skull, the unexpected, thick tuft of black hair tickled her palms. A pure scent wafted up and she gulped it in. The baby was wrapped in a towel. There was nothing else to cover her. She looked like a doll from a nativity scene, and Elizabeth would not have been surprised if men had walked through the door bearing gifts.

'Izzie? I'm afraid we have to move Hannah's body. The clinic staff will be here soon. There are procedures scheduled. It wouldn't be right to leave her here anyway.'

'Move her where you think best. I can wait in reception. Be gentle with her, Chris. She was a good mother, to me. A good woman,' Elizabeth said. She stood, pulling the child closer to her breast and whispered in her tiny ear. 'It's okay, cariad, you're safe with me, safe with me.'

'I'll phone the morgue. The coroner will have to be called. I'm afraid it will all come out.'

'What about her?' She glanced down and held the baby tighter. 'What will happen to her?'

'I'm not sure, Izzie. I assume Hannah had written a will?'

'Yes. I believe so. Everything to me she said.'

'Her unborn child. Did she entrust the care of her child to you?'

'I don't know. I don't think she'd altered her will in four, maybe five years.' Elizabeth was cooing, barely listening.

'Izzie. This is harsh, but unless there is written evidence to support Hannah's wish that you care for her child, there is a risk that Hannah's baby may be taken into care for a time. You must prepare for this.'

He had her attention at last, and to check that she had heard correctly Elizabeth asked him to repeat what he had said. She listened fully this time.

'Do we have to do it now? Move the body I mean. I think she's going to need feeding soon,' she said, turning to the child once more, 'aren't you, cariad?' Elizabeth lowered her face and touched her nose against the baby's.

'I'm afraid we do, Izzie. The longer we leave it the worse it will look. You can give the child some milk when she wakes. There's some formula in the store cupboard.'

Elizabeth cradled the child to her breast, waiting for the feel of her heartbeat. Two hearts beating together in unison. All she could hear was the tapping of Dr Bryant's shoes against the tiled floor. Stripped of his surgical gown he looked shabby and small.

The room smelt medicinal and clean. Death did not seem to cloak it. Elizabeth walked to the operating table. The body that had been Hannah looked peaceful. 'I hardly recognize her,' she said. 'Do you think me heartless?'

'What do you mean?' His brow was furrowed, his bottom lip shook.

'I do love her. I know that she is gone, but I can't feel it. I feel nothing.'

'Izzie, you've had a terrible shock. It's not uncommon, a reaction like this.' He stepped towards her, hand outstretched.

She turned her back on him and said, 'She was old. She would have died soon anyway. It's not tragic. Not like the others.'

He placed his hand on her shoulder. She smelt the disinfectant on his skin. 'Death is hard to comprehend for the living. Impossible.'

'Perhaps all my tears went years ago. On the others. Maybe I have no grief left.'

'I'll leave you alone for a moment. I'll go and make the call. I have no idea what I'm going to say.'

She spun on her heels. 'No. Stay a moment. I have something to ask you.'

The words slipped out, unplanned. Until now her intention had been invisible even to her. Later she was astonished at her boldness, her coldness, that she thought they could get away with it. She felt the need to perfect and protect, to rewrite a dirty history, and make it pure and clean, like the child in her arms. She said, 'I could keep her.'

Dr Bryant looked alarmed, then his features melted into concern. 'It's not that simple, Izzie.' Stammering hard he tried to move the conversation on to more pressing matters. He touched his forehead and rubbed between his brows with his middle finger. It slipped easily to his hairline.

'Was it the birth... the operation, that killed her?' Elizabeth said.

He stared at her, his eyes widening in horror, and fear.

'I mean, would she have had a heart attack if she hadn't had a baby?' she continued.

He coughed, struggling to keep his composure. Then said, 'Izzie,' before drying up.

'She's old. Was old. She could have died of natural causes,' Elizabeth said.

'I did everything I could to save her, but...' his voice trailed away.

'I know you did, Chris. I don't blame you. I'm saying that maybe it wasn't our fault.' Elizabeth took a deep breath and ploughed on. She had started, and she couldn't stop. 'Chris, we could take Mam back home. No one knows we're here. You could write the death certificate. No need to call a coroner. She's been in your care for some months.'

'What will I say she died of?'

'A heart attack. Isn't that what you said you were treating her for when staff asked? Angina? It's true enough. And why would anyone doubt it?' There was a tremor in Elizabeth's voice. 'You and I are the only people who know the truth. I keep the baby, you keep your job, and Mam's memory isn't dragged through the mud.'

'You keep the baby?' he said, staring at Elizabeth.

'I want you to do something for me.' She smiled, and gazed at the baby who seemed to smile back at her.

He stumbled over the words. 'Something for you?'

'I want you to put my name on the birth certificate.'

'Your name?'

She nodded.

'You're upset, Izzie. You don't know what you're saying.'

'I do.'

'I can't. What you're suggesting is wrong.'

'You must put my name on the birth certificate. After all I will raise her, won't I?' She kissed the child's milky head and continued, 'I will, to all intents and purposes, be her mother.'

'But you're not, Izzie. She is.' His eyes flicked down to the corpse: Hannah.

'She isn't. How could she be? She's ancient. She's dead.' Elizabeth knew she sounded brittle, desperate.

'We both know that your mother used donor eggs, but she carried the child. Her name must appear on the birth certificate.'

'In America the recognized mother is the biological one, not the surrogate.'

'But this is Wales, and under Welsh law...' Chris started to stammer and Elizabeth knew that she could win this argument. She would persuade him. She lowered her voice and spoke carefully.

'I donated the eggs. This child is mine as much as hers. And I am alive. I can care for her. She cannot.' Elizabeth stared at him. His disbelief was palpable. She imagined herself crushing it with her bare hands.

'You never said that the eggs were yours. Until now,' he said, finally.

She said nothing and looked him in the eye. Wavering a moment. Challenging him to doubt her again. How dare he.

'There's no need for this, Izzie. You will almost certainly raise her, as her next of kin, especially if,' he corrected himself, 'as the eggs are yours. Even if there are some legal shenanigans to get through first. I'm sure you will.' His lips were white, his pupils dilated.

Elizabeth smelt victory. Her resolve hardened. Innocent and

pure, she determined that this baby would be untainted by messiness, scandal.

'I'm not sure,' he said, his voice fading away.

'I think you are, Chris. You took one child from me, you won't take this one, will you?'

'You can't mean that, Izzie.'

'I do.'

'You're blackmailing me? I thought you felt something for me. Respect, fondness, love even. Did you plan this all along? Have I really been such a sap? I don't think you're capable of such deceit.' His words were cracking, she saw them tremble.

'In the animal kingdom the female will kill to protect her young,' she said.

'We're not animals, Izzie.'

'We are.' Her betrayal complete. 'Really, it's best for everyone. Especially this little angel.' And as she spoke the child awoke, big bug eyes fixed on her face.

He was trapped, by his loss, his confusion, his fear. Elizabeth witnessed it. Without making eye contact Dr Bryant replied, 'We had better move the body quickly. Your baby will need feeding soon, won't she?'

Elizabeth had never lifted an adult body before and the weight astonished her. Dr Bryant brought her car to the delivery entrance and they were grateful they only had to carry Hannah a few metres. Neither of them spoke. Before she left Elizabeth splashed her face with water in the staff toilet and caught sight of her reflection in the small scratched mirror. She looked exactly the same, but she was a changed woman. She looked back at the room, and was surprised that it showed no signs of the momentous event that took place only hours earlier. It wasn't that Dr Bryant's clean up was so effective, it was that it looked like any other medical room in a medium sized health centre. Elizabeth expected a sign of some sort, a golden glow in the air, proof of something wonderful, and hideous, having taken place.

Dr Bryant stayed at the clinic. He was always one of the first to arrive and it made no sense for him to follow Elizabeth back to Tŷ Mawr, he said. It was light, and though Tŷ Mawr was isolated they could not risk moving Hannah's body again until nightfall.

The baby lay in a cardboard box on the floor of the car, warm and pink. Hannah lay in the boot, grey and stiffening. Elizabeth drove with care, avoiding the main routes across the city, but she did not worry that she might be stopped, that an eager police officer might notice her failing side light and force her to pull over, or that a novice driver might plough into the back of her, exposing her unusual cargo. She knew now why she had been spared, why she had survived the plague. She was the child's protector. A form of transcendence washed through her. Thank you, Lord. Thank you. How could I ever have doubted you?

It was Elizabeth's irrefutable conviction that what she was doing was right, and she knew that she would be defended. Her actions would remain undiscovered.

Part Three

2052 – 2053

Chapter Twenty-two

'Blimey. Just goes to show how little we know people, even those closest to us,' Ceri said. 'I don't know what to say, Meg.'

'Close? We love each other, but there's a distance between us, always has been. It makes a kind of sense now. Why she clammed up, couldn't talk about the past.'

They were sat in a meeting room in the offices of the vineyard where Ceri was marketing director, glasses of tepid water untouched in front of them. After listening to Elizabeth's confession Megan left the beach on Anglesey, kissing her boy hard on the cheek despite his attempts to escape her embrace, before promising to return to Tŷ Mawr in time to say goodnight. On the bus she tried Jack's number but he was unavailable. She felt an overwhelming urge to tell someone, to report this shocking secret. In town she changed buses and put in a call to Ceri. She said only that she needed to talk.

'Listen, I've got a meeting at the end of the day. Get here as quickly as you can and we'll talk in the boardroom. We'll have some privacy there, otherwise all the nosy parkers will be wondering what we're up to, why you've come to see me at work. You know what they're like. Lives so bloody boring they have to get their thrills elsewhere,' Ceri said.

Megan studied her friend's image on the mulmed. She noted the lower than usual plunge of Ceri's shirt, the expensive organic cotton straining from the effort of containing her ample breasts. In an attempt to end on a light-hearted note she said, 'I'd have thought they'd find your cleavage thrilling enough.'

'This is nothing, Meg. You wait till you see the length of my skirt.'

Megan took a sip of the water. The water tasted dusty, as if it had sat on the side table of the meeting room for weeks. She said, 'Maybe that's why I'm so secretive. I've grown up in a clandestine culture.'

'Maybe. But to be honest how much do we really know anyone, Meg? I mean, we choose which facet of our personality, of our inner selves, to display to the world. And it changes depending on the situation and the person we're with. I'm a ferocious witch here, they're all scared of me, but you know I'm a pussy-cat.' Ceri took a drink of water and said, 'Jesus! This is disgusting. Tastes like flood water. I must ask Aggie to check the filter system.'

'I hardly recognized the mother I thought I knew from her story,' Megan said.

'I don't think that's unusual. When I asked Mam about her and Dad, she told me this story about these two kids who met at a festival in the West Country, who took drugs and slept, covered in mud, under the stars. I thought she was making it up it sounded so far removed from the boring old gits that raised me and my brothers.'

Megan laughed and gazed at the water, hoping for a reflection. There was none. 'Grief drove her mad. And envy. I understand why she did what she did, Ceri. What I don't understand is why she couldn't tell me. Especially with all this about Cerdic. She knows what it is to lose a child.'

'Fear. She's afraid of losing you. Everyone she ever loved has been taken from her. And now Cerdic is threatened too,' Ceri said, before bursting into tears. Megan held her friend's hand and wondered why she was comforting, rather than being comforted.

'Go and talk to her,' said Ceri after a while.

'I'm too angry.'

'You have to. For Cerdic. For yourself.'

'It's all so messy. So many lies, so much time has passed.'

'You and your mother are more alike than you think. You're both emotional cowards. You've no fear of danger, war, physical pain and all that. You can talk to perpetrators of genocide, but you can't talk to your own mother.'

Is this true, Megan thought. Perhaps Ceri was right. Megan sought the truth for others, but the truth about herself? Had she always run away from it? 'It's so painful for her to talk about it all, but I need to dig deeper.'

'Treat it like an assignment.' She leaned over and gave Megan a hug. 'I'll bet it's been cathartic for her. It's not healthy, holding stuff in.'

Megan stood and said, 'I'll find the donor, Ceri. I will.' And she went to crack her knuckles then stopped.

Ceri stood and hugged her again. 'Of course you will. Nothing's going to get in your way. It never does, when you go after something.'

Megan didn't go straight home. She sat on the pier watching the waves, the fading sun on the horizon. When she arrived home it was after eight. She studied the hall, the landing, her bedroom afresh and questioned if she had ever belonged here. She lay on the bed staring at the ceiling, listening to Elizabeth tucking Cerdic up for the night. When she heard the patter of Elizabeth's footsteps on the stairs she stole into his room. He sat upright. She placed her index finger to her lips.

'I didn't think you were coming,' he whispered.

'Goodnight angel. I never break my promises.'

'Where have you been, Mummy?'

'With Ceri.'

'Why?'

'To talk.'

'Why?'

'Why, why, why!' She tickled him under the chin. The boy giggled, begged her to stop, and then said, 'Again.' Megan shook her head.

'Mummy, Nana cried after you went today. Why is she sad?'

'Because she wants to help you, and she can't. Like me.' And her eyes filled with tears.

'Don't cry, Mummy. I'm okay,' said the boy.

She walked backwards out of the room, kissing her fingertips and blowing her love to him across the dusky air.

Afterwards Megan had sat on her bed and studied an old photograph of Elizabeth hanging on the bedroom wall, next to the one of Hannah and Robert. She was sat on the banks of Cwm Bychan, near Shell Island, along the coast from Harlech. Back lit by the sun her fine hair formed a halo around her head. On her lap sat a dark-haired, dark-eyed baby, chewing on a wooden teething ring. Elizabeth looked tired but happy. She was bent forward, her face cheek to cheek with the baby's, one arm raised, pointing at the camera. Megan almost could hear her saying 'cheese'.

It was impossible to comprehend, to reset and readjust three decades of relationship, of love, in a few hours. Did it matter that the woman she called 'Mum' was a kind of sister? Of course it mattered.

Megan removed her clothes, ready to shower, and stood in front of the full-length mirror. She studied the woman before her.

A forget-me-not blue hue drenched the limbs. An icy plain of flesh, broken with the jagged ledges of clavicle and ridges of hip. Underneath the full breasts ribs jutted, nipples bloomed like petals.

In the shower Megan soaped and sponged this new person with the familiar body. Afterwards she stood in front of her wardrobe, examining its contents. She longed to wear something different, to reflect the person she had become, except that she didn't know who this person was and what she would wear and anyway the closet was Megan Even's and she wore black. She pulled on straight jeans and a turtleneck fitted jumper. She lifted her hair over her right shoulder and plaited it into one long knot, then ran her fingers through her thick fringe. It needed trimming, her eyebrows were totally obscured and soon her eyes would be too.

She was approaching the mirror for inspection a second time when the glass caught the light, revealing its message of devotion. Greasy fingerprints, kiss marks and nose smears low on the glass, little smudges of love glistened in a yellow haze, reminding Megan who she was.

She never wanted to look at a clean mirror; she swore not to polish the glass. Not until she had found a one hundred per cent foolproof match for Cerdic. She took a deep breath and headed downstairs.

Elizabeth sat in the kitchen. 'Were you ever going to tell me?' Megan asked as she swung the door open wide. Elizabeth cradled a cup of tea, an open bottle of wine and a clean glass sat on the table waiting for Megan. On the surface everything was the same.

Megan stood for a few moments, then took the glass and bottle, and sat down. She had rehearsed the words in her bedroom, checking her tone, watching her expression in the mirror, wanting not to sound angry. It'd come out all wrong. Curt, harsh, resentful.

Presently Elizabeth said, 'I meant to tell you so often. I told myself I would tell you when you were sixteen. But you were so happy that day, so beautiful, so carefree. You made me feel like the best mam in the world and I needed to hold on to that. To believe it. And then I planned to tell you when you left for London. I knew how much I would miss you, that a mother loves her child more than a child loves her mother. That a daughter would write, phone, visit a mother. But a nobody? I couldn't be sure. And when you told me you were to be a mother yourself…

'And often I would say to myself that I was your real mother. After all what is the meaning of the word 'real'? Genuine, sincere, existent? I have always been here for you, Meg. I will always be here for you. I have nurtured you, cared for you, raised you, mothered you. I wish to God that I were your 'real' mother, that I had given birth to you. That you were created from a part of me, because then all our worries would be over. I would help to cure Cerdic and we would all live happily ever after.

'I may not be your real mother, Meg, but you are part of me and I am part of you. Whether you like it or not.'

It was Megan's turn to speak but she didn't know where to begin. Thoughts tumbled round her head and then, like a washing machine opened mid-cycle, they slopped out, heavy, wet, still dirty. 'It's not that I don't love you. I do. It's that I don't know who you are or who I am. The cuckoo in the nest, that's me. All the way home I kept thinking "She is my sister. My sister. Sister." The word felt alien on my tongue. And then upstairs I realized you're not my sister. Hannah used a donor egg. You may have

247

fooled that doctor, but not me. That was a lie.'

'I didn't fool the doctor, not for one moment.' Elizabeth eyes welled with tears at the memory of him. Dr Bryant. Chris. A man who loved her and who she might have loved had things turned out differently. She had seen him only twice since that All Saints' morning almost thirty-two years ago.

The first time: when he came back to help her move the body from the back of the car. Elizabeth never doubted that he would turn up. He brought the death certificate and a notification of Megan's birth on the clinic's headed paper. The column marked 'Father' remained empty. He said that he wasn't sure whether or not to put Owen's name there, but that Elizabeth could choose at the office in city hall when she registered the birth.

She recorded the birth and death on the same day and the registrar had commented how well she looked. 'Glowing,' he said, predictably enough.

The final time Elizabeth saw Chris was at Hannah's funeral. As the red curtains parted and the plain ash coffin glided into the flames Elizabeth felt a presence in the chapel. She turned round to see him standing at the back, head bowed, crossing himself. As there was only the chaplain to witness her unusual actions Elizabeth bolted down the aisle towards Dr Bryant, leaving a sleeping Megan in a pram at the front. As she neared him she realized she didn't know what she wanted to say and came to an abrupt halt.

'Thank you, for coming,' she muttered, feeling foolish and disrespectful, though later she noted that she had stooped so low that another minor misdemeanour could hardly lower his opinion of her. She turned back to say goodbye to her mother only to see closed curtains swaying from side to side. The music tinkled on, a cheap recording, reedy sounding and pathetic. Hannah would have hated it.

'I wanted to say farewell,' he stuttered, cheeks flushed.

'That's nice of you. Mam would have appreciated it.'

'Not to your mother, Izzie, to you. I'm moving away. I think it best, under the circumstances. Don't you?'

Elizabeth's stomach tightened when she heard him call her name. Regret, longing and shame mingling to steal her tongue. She was thankful that the living embodiment of her deceit would not be around to remind her, to torment her, and sad that a true friend would be gone.

'Yes,' she said, head hung low.

'We will be punished, Izzie. You know that, don't you? What goes around comes around. An eye for an eye and all that.' Their eyes met fleetingly, before he turned and headed out of the open doors. She watched him walk through the memorial gardens, his shoulders stooped, hands buried in his pockets, head tilted down against the bitter wind, and she thought how different he looked. Like a stranger.

The kitchen was warm, the wood burning stove at its angriest by this time in the evening. There were beads of sweat on Elizabeth's upper lip. Megan was as cool as ever.

'Where did she get the eggs from, Mum? Where did Hannah get the egg? I have to know, I have to find out. I have to look for her. My birth mother. No, my biological mother. I don't even know what to call her. I don't want to hurt you,' she reached out to touch her mother's hand, but Elizabeth withdrew sharply. Megan continued, 'This is not about you and I. That can wait. You understand why?'

'I understand.'

'You will help me.'

'As much as I can.' Elizabeth pushed her chair from the table, clambering up, moving towards the sink. She began to wash dishes, frantic, carelessly. 'I should have told you as soon as we knew Hisham was dead, but I couldn't find the moment. I prayed for a miracle. I knew how difficult the search would be.'

'You almost told Jack.' It wasn't a question.

'Almost. I didn't ask Mam many questions. I didn't want to know. I resented her. I thought she was wrong. It'll be so hard.'

'I'm a journalist, I seek buried things. I will find the donor.'

Elizabeth tipped her head in silent agreement. Megan wandered to the sink. 'And my father? Owen? If he is my father? Didn't he say anything? Drop any clues.'

'I asked even less of him. I barely spoke to him most of the time. I didn't like him. He wasn't a bad man, not really, it was just that he wasn't my da. I felt he didn't deserve Mam.'

'You sound like a spoilt ten-year-old, not a woman in her late thirties.'

Elizabeth squeezed a cloth out and went to wipe imaginary dirt from the table. 'Forties. I was forty-two.'

Megan slumped against the sink. 'Why didn't you ask questions? Why didn't you donate your eggs? We wouldn't be in this mess if you had.' She marched to the table, sat down, flung her head in her arms and thumped the heels of her palms against her forehead. 'Why, why, why?'

'She did ask me for my eggs. I didn't think she was serious. I didn't even know she'd met someone at the time. She didn't tell me about Owen for many months,' Elizabeth said, sitting down once more. She took a sip of her tea, hands trembling. Her mouth was dry, crusts of saliva gathered in the grooves at the corners of her mouth. She continued, 'I said no, God forgive me. The idea was repugnant to me. My mother giving birth to my child. It was unnatural. She quoted Genesis, Rachel and Bilhah. A distortion of the fable – she never did know her bible.' She rubbed the cross hanging from a chain round her neck between thumb and index finger.

'When you told me about Cerdic I wished I had said yes. But then you wouldn't be you, Meg, and Cerdic wouldn't be Cerdic and neither of you would exist.'

'Everything would be different anyway,' Megan said.

Elizabeth studied her and Megan found such scrutiny uncomfortable.

'You're nothing like Hannah, or Owen, or what I remember of him. I see elements of myself in you, mannerisms, the occasional attitude, the rhythm of your voice. I gave you a life, I shaped you, moulded you. And you created Cerdic and I wouldn't change him.

Who knows how things might have turned out if I'd donated eggs, but you, as you are, would not exist, and how could I regret that? I love you.'

'That photo, the one of Hannah and the strange man. The one you hid away in that box we cleared out. It's Owen isn't it?'

Elizabeth nodded.

'My surrogate mother. My father? Possibly.' Megan was thinking aloud, her mind whirring with a maelstrom of questions. She had to hold fire. The questions were too random, unrelated to what she needed to know now. I must be clear headed, she thought.

'There's so much I want to ask you but that can wait. My priority is to trace the egg donor. There's Owen's son, though he will be old, and the mother's line is closer. A stronger chance for Cerdic.'

Though it was years since Megan had done investigative work it felt like only hours and she relished it. Pushing personal feelings aside, she began as if embarking on an assignment. Distance creation was essential to ensure a clear head. She grabbed her mulmed from her pocket and began to make notes. Elizabeth watched in silence.

Megan drew OWEN and HANNAH in block capitals across the top of the screen, underlining them both. Then Megan placed brackets around Hannah's name followed by an arrow pointing downwards to a large question mark.

She looked up at her mother. 'When did Hannah broach the subject of egg donation?'

'I can't remember. I thought she was joking, that much I do remember.' Elizabeth pulled a face and shuddered.

'Had she already met Owen when she asked?' Megan's fingers hovered above the screen.

'I'm not sure. I certainly didn't know about him then, I'd have guessed what she was up to, I think, if I had.'

'Did you tell her how repulsive you found the idea?'

'I think it may have been obvious.'

'I can imagine.' Megan put the mulmed down, and continued,

'I think your reaction pushed her into keeping the whole business covert.'

'You're blaming me?' Elizabeth's voice shook.

'I'm not blaming you, I'm speculating. Trying to understand Hannah.'

'Well, that might take a while,' Elizabeth said bitterly.

'Had you kept your feelings of disgust to yourself, had you not disapproved of the idea of egg donation she may well have told you.'

'She may not.'

'She knew you disapproved. Perhaps that's why she kept it a secret.'

'If I could turn back the clock, Meg...'

Megan's mind span; she stood, mulmed in hand and paced the kitchen. 'Did Hannah keep a diary? Have you kept it? Are there photographs, postcards?'

'I never throw anything away, unless I have to.'

'No one does, rubbish tax is too high. Show me what you've got.'

'There's a suitcase in the loft.'

'And Owen. I'd like to know more about him. Later when there's time. There must have been some good in him,' Megan said. She doodled, absentmindedly, as she paced, writing her name in rounded letters on the near empty screen.

Elizabeth was ashen. 'Of course there was good in him. There's you.'

'It's a huge assumption to make.'

'What?'

'That Owen was my father. Who knows where the sperm came from, it might not have been Owen's, after all.' Megan looked up. 'Did his son and daughter-in-law take everything of his from Tŷ Mawr?'

'No.' Elizabeth pursed her lips. 'There are photographs on the computer. And I hid an old shoebox of his. It's full of letters and pictures. From his youth, I believe.'

'You sneaky devil.' Megan stopped and looked at her mother.

'Why did you do that?'

'I'm not sure. To spite them I suppose. They were vile. For Mam.' And a smile spread across Elizabeth's pale, crumpled cheeks.

Megan returned the smile. 'It'll be easy to check out the most popular fertility centres in the country around 2019, 2020. They'll be records of patients, consultations and so on. A quick search will throw up some leads.' Megan took hold of the door, ready to go. 'You've got stuff of Hannah's in the loft? Photos on the hard drive in the study? Of Hannah and Owen? They may contain clues.'

'What now? Can't this wait until the morning?'

'The search could take years. Cerdic doesn't have that long. I have to start now.'

'There is something you should know,' said Elizabeth, coming towards her. 'Mam and Owen took a holiday to Eastern Europe, early in the year you were born. I did wonder why they chose such a location, at that time of year, and with all the travel restrictions it can't have been easy. It was even more difficult to travel then than now. Many countries were still reluctant to allow visitors from plague affected countries. They'd have needed doctor's certificates, visas. There'd have been all sorts of administrative hoops to jump through.'

'Not difficult for a former G.P. You think they got the egg there?'

'Hannah didn't confirm or deny it. There was a row. I thought she'd gone for cosmetic surgery, only later I suspected a baby.'

'Can you remember where they went?'

'I'm afraid I can't, it was all so fraught. I'll look at a map. See if any place names jog my memory,' Elizabeth said.

Megan twisted her ring round and round her finger. 'There've been scandals surrounding clinics in Europe. Jack worked on a story once, years ago. Very few questions were asked of donors, huge sums of money exchanged hands, allegedly. The support group I went to – someone there mentioned it. Lax regulations, unethical practices. Children born with deformities, and disease.'

'I can't believe even Mam would take such a risk. She was a doctor.'

'Desperate people do strange things. You said yourself that Hannah went slightly mad. Seems like the whole country went mad to me.' She saw the look on Elizabeth's face and regretted her remark. 'You're right. We can't be sure, and it will be relatively straightforward to check the records here first.'

'I'll show you where her photographs are,' Elizabeth said. 'There's a website she had.'

Megan stepped aside and followed her mother up the stairs to the study.

Elizabeth had not used the room for a while, and Megan saw the shock in her expression. Books tumbled from the shelves, others lay scattered across the floor, open at various pages, scissors, pencils and torn paper were strewn across every conceivable surface. Mould floated on the surface of three half finished mugs of tea and a cereal bowl overflowed with contraband cigarette stubs. Megan had all but given up, treating herself to a single cigarette each evening once Cerdic was in bed, until recently when she had begun smoking again in earnest. She meant to empty the ashtray but never had. The room smelt of incense, tobacco, damp and hard graft.

Elizabeth picked her way through the debris and sat on the office chair, almost falling off when she lent forward to turn on the mulmed. Megan stood and watched over her shoulder. Elizabeth brought up the grid and typed in an address Megan didn't recognize. It was Hannah's photographs and films. Elizabeth stood from the chair, gesturing for Megan to sit.

'I'll bring you a drink. No doubt you'll be burning the midnight oil.'

'No wine. I drink too much.'

'And don't smoke. I thought those days were over.' She touched Megan's shoulder, gave a gentle squeeze and walked out of the room, closing the door behind her.

Megan stared at the screen and began to scroll. Collection after collection rolled before her eyes. The titles of the sets were so personal and obscure that Megan thought they might be coded. They certainly offered few clues to their contents. The first few pages all dated from 2020. Hundreds of pages later they went as far back as 2009. Megan returned to the most recent collections and decided to open the first one.

Taking a deep breath Megan raised her index finger, noticing, as if for the first time, her long fingers, sharp knuckles, and flat, cracked nails. She wondered if she had her mother's hands; they were nothing like Elizabeth's. She tapped the screen twice. She hit the first thumbnail and gasped. The screen was filled with an image of a woman she knew to be Hannah. Hannah stood side on to the camera, her head turned away from the photographer, as if looking over her shoulder at another viewer. Her nudity and pregnant state and age made for an astonishing image. Had Megan not recognized Hannah she would have assumed the picture had been digitally enhanced, meddled with.

It was shocking. Extraordinary. Hannah looked unashamed. Gnarled fingers rested on her swollen belly, her ancient, empty breasts dangled lifelessly on the top of her mound of belly, thread veins wound across her thighs, a tuft of pubic hair, grey and fine, peeked out from between them. There was no bloom, no rosy shine. And there was no indignity either. Hannah looked proud, and there was something else, difficult to define, mercurial and elusive. Hannah was happy, yes, but there was something else. It took Megan a while but at last she identified the aura as contentment and was surprised that it took her so long. She felt certain she hadn't experienced utter contentment for a long time, if ever.

Megan was entranced, she could have looked at the picture for hours. It was voyeuristic and exciting. This was an intensely private photograph, presumably taken by Owen, as a record for just them. Megan felt sure it was never intended for public viewing, so why had Hannah not protected it with a password? Perhaps she wanted it to be discovered. But by who?

In the end she moved on. She had to. There was so much to do. There followed subsequent images of a naked, pregnant Hannah, though none so alarming and captivating as the first.

Skipping through the photographs Megan thought that familiarity may not necessarily breed contempt, but it certainly breeds acceptance, swiftly followed by disinterest. Bored by a naked Hannah, Megan moved onto another set of images. She went further back in time, to what she calculated would have been early days in Hannah and Owen's romance. The couple on the slopes of Snowdon, walking the promenade at Barmouth. They must have asked strangers to take the pictures, delighted individuals who could stare at these rare creatures, old folk, with impunity. They were gazing legitimately.

This time Megan focused on Owen. There were many more images of him than Hannah. The camera must have been Hannah's. She was the biographer of their relationship.

He was not how she'd imagined her father. If he was her father. As a child she had never formulated a firm image of his physical appearance. All she had to go on was the mug shot lodged in the back of the art book in the library. Physically, he was nebulous and indistinct to her then – his imagined personality, decency and specialness were as real and tangible as Elizabeth's. But somehow the elderly man on the screen before her did not equate with her childhood vision. There were areas where Megan's imagination and reality collided: he was tall (she had never entertained the idea that he might not be. She had to get her height from someone and it was not from Elizabeth), and judging by his eyebrows, which remained dark despite a thick head of silver hair, he had been a brunette in his youth. Other than these obvious characteristics Megan could see nothing of herself in the man. She was convinced Owen could not be her father.

She flicked on through the photographs but they offered no clues. Megan wondered what she expected. A photograph of Hannah arm-in-arm with the donor outside a fertility clinic with a large sign, the doctor smiling beside them, brandishing a bubbling test tube? Her instinct told her that Hannah and Owen went abroad. Elizabeth mentioned a holiday. But where on earth to start? At 3.45am Megan asked the mulmed to switch off. There was nothing to be found here. Not this time.

She smoked her last cigarette hanging out of the window, looking at the night sky. Pipistrelle bats flitted before her, birds foraged in the bushes, and she heard the distant hooting of an owl. The cigarette went out yet again. She had rolled the paper too tightly, and held her lighter in her right hand as she smoked. She struck her thumb across the metal flint. Nothing. She tried again. Harder and faster this time. Nothing. There was over half a tab left. She was not going to forego her last smoke. She pulled back into the study and explored the shelves looking for a stray box of matches. Nothing. She pulled out the top drawer of the desk and rummaged around. Buried underneath a camera manual she found some matches. She sank onto the sofa and studied the box as she inhaled deeply. What a marvellous invention these little wooden sticks were. She thought of the women and children who laboured to make them in times gone by, risking disease and even death. She remembered her mother telling her the story of the match girls and their bold stance, and ultimate victory, against their employers, Bryant and May. She loved that story. Bryant. It was a familiar name. Why? Then it came to her: Dr Christopher Bryant. The man that delivered her, the man she had been led to believe was her father. He was the key.

Would he still be alive today? Elizabeth said he was only a handful of years older than her in 2020, though he seemed much older. Elizabeth had also said that she suspected Hannah told him things she didn't or couldn't tell her daughter. After Hannah's death he moved away and Elizabeth had never heard from him again, but if she could find Dr Bryant… He would be a good starting point.

Megan crossed to the window, stubbed out her cigarette on the brickwork, flicked the butt into the air, sat down and turned the mulmed back on. She said, 'Dr Christopher Bryant – find.' Pages of results. Momentarily Megan felt her optimism evaporate. She felt the gargantuan scale of the task before her. She could not do this alone, and though Elizabeth would help, she would be amateurish, and perhaps not entirely reliable. Megan needed the help of a professional.

Chapter Twenty-three

It was two minutes past six. The train stood in the no man's land outside the station. It should have arrived five minutes ago. Despite massive investment in the rail network, trains ran late occasionally. Megan stood, stretched her stiff limbs and, face pushed against the window, peered down the track. The platform was in view. Megan was desperate to disembark; the journey had been uncomfortable. It seemed that the entire population of Wales and the North West were using their travel allowance that day. With no free seats Megan had spent the whole journey sat on her suitcase, outside the toilet, and she was no longer used to roughing it.

She pulled a mirror from her handbag and checked her appearance for the umpteenth time. Dark rings circled her eyes, her face was gaunt and drawn, she hadn't slept in days and she'd lost weight. It was as if she'd had another layer peeled off and was reeling from the exposure. She pinched her cheeks and ran a dampened finger across her brows. She needed to look good; she was going to call in a favour.

Three long minutes later the train slid alongside the platform. People pushed and shoved and when the doors glided apart she virtually fell onto the platform. The smell of human waste dispersed and Megan felt like she could breathe easily once more. Almost.

She saw him before he saw her. Centimetres taller than the average male he loomed into view, neck craning, searching for her amongst the swarm of people. It didn't take him long. He flashed a cheeky grin.

They embraced on the platform. Jack took Megan's suitcase and navigated through the hordes. Outside the station Jack said, 'Where to? Back to my place, dump the luggage and hit the pub? We could get a taxi, I'm feeling reckless.'

Initially, Jack had suggested that Megan stay in a hotel, citing the state of his flat as an excuse. She wasn't keen; she didn't want to be alone. She used to relish her own company, but lately she needed people around.

'But you're immaculate. Your place is like a hotel!' she said.

'I'm not a great sleeper. I'll keep you up.'

'I'm up anyway. We can carry on working.'

She was insistent and he relented soon enough, but she wondered why he didn't want her in his home.

'A taxi. Great. I can't face the tube. I sat outside the toilet for over half that fucking journey. Which blocked half way, or so it smelled.'

'Nice!'

They grumbled light-heartedly about the transport system, the weather, the litter. Anything to keep away from the more serious matter of why Megan was there. It was a conversation for later, over a drink.

The journey from the Euston Road back to Jack's flat in Hampstead was fast. Megan thought how unbearable it must have been decades ago when London regularly came to a complete standstill. Streets gridlocked with sheer volume of traffic. Minutes clocking up to years of lives wasted sitting in queues. She couldn't believe the old photographs, and though she moaned about the transport system, like everyone else, she wholeheartedly agreed with the ban on cars in the major cities, other than for essential services, and she was glad of the controls on travelling.

Hampstead remained unaltered from her earliest memories of it: the picturesque village within the metropolis. As a rookie journalist and a returning foreign correspondent she would walk the heath when she wanted to think, swim in the pools when she wanted to forget and drink in the regulated pubs hidden in the narrow streets behind the main thoroughfare when she longed to rub shoulders with people yet remain alone.

Jack's flat was only seconds from the tube station. A gothic red-bricked tower decorated with an ornate white façade. The tenements had been built by a Victorian philanthropic trust to house the deserving poor. In the 1960s an artistic crowd moved in, and their creativity and energy popularized the area, rendering it too expensive for subsequent generations of artists. Since the 1980s the flats had housed wealthy professionals, though the block's air of shabby chic was never quite dispelled. It suited Jack. He bought the flat at twenty-one when he came into his inheritance and had lived there ever since. Megan loved the romance of the building. Its history.

High ceilings, stripped floorboards, a round bay window in the corner of the living room. It had a faint smell of Tŷ Mawr. The yang to Tŷ Mawr's black yin. And it was very much the bachelor pad: modern, spartan, with little furniture other than the essentials, whitewashed walls. It was as pristine as she was messy, and though she dreamed of a stylish, uncluttered home, she didn't feel entirely comfortable at Jack's place. Not that she'd ever spent much time there. When she lived in London she had been invited in only once, after a party one New Year's Eve. She was so delighted to have an opportunity to celebrate the incoming year with friends and colleagues in her homeland that she made no arrangements for the journey home. At four in the morning, when she'd had enough of the party, there were no cabs available to take her back to Highgate. She thought about walking, but it was unusually cold and Jack insisted that she crashed at his place. She lay underneath a blanket on the sofa in the living room, fully clothed, not daring to sleep for fear he might wake before her and catch her there, exposed, dribbling, moaning in her sleep. She left before he woke on New Year's Day.

Since she'd moved to Wales she had stayed at Jack's a few times. She liked the fact that his apartment was a place to crash, to house a few meagre possessions. It reminded her of her past life, moving from one camp to another with just a rucksack. Even now she collected little in the way of clothes and personal effects. She felt a rush of adrenaline as they climbed the concrete steps to the fifth floor. She still missed her old life from time to time.

As Jack pushed open the heavy wooden door the tang of curry and tobacco hit her. Along with another, muskier, scent that she couldn't quite put her finger on.

'Sorry about the smell. Had a take-away last night. Let's dump your bag in the spare room and head off out. The place is a bit of a tip, Ms Evens. No reflection on you.' He shrugged, and ran his hand through his hair from forehead to crown.

'It's spotless, trust me,' Megan said, looking around for evidence of mess or dirt. There was none, but she noticed the corner of a glossy magazine poking out from underneath the sofa. It didn't look like Jack's usual reading material. She was about to comment on it when Jack clapped his hands together and spoke.

'So. The pub and a couple of government-approved beers? Or an illegal and as much home brewed vodka as we can manage?'

'The pub. Mustn't drink too much. I want to have a clear head tomorrow.'

'Very sensible. Boring, but sensible.'

Before they left Megan nipped to the bathroom. As she washed her hands she noticed a hair grip tucked behind Jack's shaving equipment. Almost without thinking she glanced down at the bin, and there, at the bottom, sat a wipe covered with the unmistakable beige-tinged smears of foundation. She was surprised. Jack always played away from home – for a quick getaway, he'd confided during a drunken evening years ago. She wondered if this woman was special. Not boring or sensible, but reckless and exciting. Was this why he'd not wanted her to stay?

In the warmth and comfort of the bar, drinking weak beer Jack listened as Megan recounted Elizabeth's story. She was calm and detailed.

'You were right after all. Mum concealed the truth.'

'We're both orphans — lost things, raised by loving impostors. We know little of our true history, we are free to invent ourselves, unencumbered by the shackles of the past, we can focus on the future,' he said, flippantly.

'But I need to find out about my history, Jack. Cerdic will die if I don't, and I need your help. You can access so much information, and quickly, under the auspices of EBC.'

'I knew you were after something. I'm in the middle of something big.'

'How big?'

'Cuba. A descendant of Castro, illegitimate of course, has some following, there's talk of revolution again. The US are pooh-poohing it, but my sources say they're nervous.'

'Christ, Jack, that one has come and gone for years. It was around when I was at EBC. Is there any proof? That this man is not just another opportunist looking for fame, to make a buck or two?'

'That's what I intend to find out.'

'You can spare me some time. Run the two projects concurrently.'

'I need a good story. It's been a while for me. There are young guns out to prove themselves. I need to follow this one through, not get diverted.'

'Jack, you're an ideas man. Always have been. Get someone else to do the donkey work. Like I did for you, for years.' She held his gaze. His eyes darkened and he turned away, and took another drink. You might be stubborn Jack North, she thought, but so am I.

'I can give you some desk space. Maybe a researcher for a couple of days.'

'Not good enough. I want you, not one of your lackeys.'

'This is flattering, Ms Evens, but really… You don't need me. You're brilliant.'

'Don't try to charm your way out of this, it won't work on me.' She touched his hand. He jumped. She said, 'Please. Don't make me beg.'

'Couple of days, that's all. I'll say you're working on a piece, as a freelance. I could even get you a fee.' He raised his eyebrows and winked, though there was no smile behind his eyes. 'We'll take the morning. If we can't trace this doctor and get an interview within a couple of days then you really have lost your touch.' He finished his drink.

'Fear not, Mr North.'

'I was kidding. It'll be like getting back on a bike.'

'Who knows we may even find you a story,' she said. She nodded at his drink. 'Another?'

Megan followed Jack across the newsroom floor; it felt strange to be back. Everything looked much as it did when she left, but many of the faces were fresh. Those who knew some broadcasting history recognized her; she noted the respectful nods and outstretched hands, and relished the sense of worth and identity such gestures gave her. Despite everything, she was still Megan Evens: journalist, broadcaster. She took a place at an empty desk opposite Jack; it was as if she'd never been away.

They'd been sat down for less than a minute when a small, suited, figure minced across.

'Megan? Hello. It's been a long time.' Julie Brookings held out a dainty manicured hand.

Her handshake was weak, her fingers icy. 'Easing your way back in are you? Can't be easy after such a long break.'

'Not exactly,' Megan said, unsure if the comment was barbed or meant kindly.

'Well, if you need any help, references, etcetera, don't hesitate to ask,' Julie replied. And in that instance Megan knew that should she ask, which she had no intention of doing anyway – the woman was mistaken, she was not here to revive her career – there would be no help forthcoming from Julie Brookings. Serves me right, I suppose, Megan thought.

'Any news on the Cuba lead?' Julie addressed Jack. He had a peculiar expression on his face.

'No. But that's none of your concern is it?' he said, avoiding Julie's eye.

There was a vaguely familiar tang in the air. And then Megan placed it: it was the musky scent from Jack's flat. Julie's perfume. Was she the woman he allowed into his lair? Was he serious about her? Megan bristled. Julie Brookings didn't suit Jack at all. Megan could hardly believe it.

Julie drifted away after a short, polite but strained, conversation.

After she'd gone Megan said, 'I'd never have had her down as your type.'

'She's not.'

'But you are seeing her.'

He nodded.

'Serious?'

'I'm never serious.'

Megan didn't believe him, but there was too much to do. She dropped the subject. 'To work, Mr North. We've business to attend to. You start with the back up plan – Owen's son.'

He looked relieved. 'What's the surname?'

'Jones.'

'Had to be, didn't it?'

It was straightforward tracing Marc Jones. He divorced in 2024 and emigrated to Australia the following year. He lived in a small township outside Perth.

Jack said, 'Wonder how he swung that. Can't have been easy.'

'Mum said he was slippery. Look, he's a last resort. Old, not definitely related. But good to know where he is, just in case.'

It took longer to trace Dr Christopher Bryant. The Medical Council had been surprisingly forthcoming, but it was a common enough name, and after he left Bangor in 2020 it appeared that he didn't practise medicine again. There were five leads that looked promising: five elderly men who matched the profile, who could be the doctor that had delivered Megan and forged the papers for Elizabeth.

Megan tapped the desk with her ring. Jack glanced up. She said, 'Two of these guys died within the past couple of months.'

'So that leaves us three.'

'One lives in Chester.'

'Too close to the scene of the crime.'

Megan felt he was right. 'So that leaves us with one at a private address in Cambridge, the other is listed as living in a retirement home near Land's End,' she said, 'but I don't think that a man born and raised, and who'd lived most of his life by

264

the sea would choose to be landlocked.'

'How you can be so sure.'

'How come you're so sure about Chester?'

'Just am.'

Megan was irritated by his certainty. Jack was searching through patient records of fertility clinics operating after the plague. Though they both doubted that Hannah and Owen used a British clinic, they were agreed that it would be foolhardy not to double check. He had found nothing. There were thousands of clinics and they were doing a roaring trade at the time; everyone wanted to replace the lost generation, but none appeared to have seen Hannah and Owen.

'How about I ask Mum to take Cerdic on a day trip to Chester? This address is in the city centre. They could pop in on the off-chance, and if he's not at home, there's nothing lost…'

'Do you really think she'd do that?' Jack strolled round and perched on the edge of the desk, one leg on the floor.

'She'd have to, if I asked.' Megan noticed the square line of Jack's jaw, the high cheekbones, the sea blue eyes.

'Would you ask?' he said, 'It would be very painful for her.'

'If I have to.' Her face tightened.

Jack stood. 'Leave Chester for now. We could be in Cambridge in forty-five minutes. We could have the whole thing sewn up in a morning.'

'If it's him. You'll be back to your stupid Castro story soon enough.' She took a slug of her drink. It was cold, the coffee tasted old and burnt; she wanted to spit it out.

'That's not how it is.'

'I think it is.' She turned away from him, and stared at the screen.

'Let's toss a coin. Nation for Cambridge, crest for Land's End. We check one out, if we draw a blank we check the other, and then, if necessary, you go to Chester…' He dug his hands in his pockets and ferreted around.

'I'll call,' she said.

'You got a coin?' he said.

265

She smiled and bent to pick up her bag which she'd slung on the floor when she first sat down.

'There are cloakrooms for bags, Ms Evens.'

She rolled her eyes as she handed him a coin. Up until recently she'd considered herself a lucky person; now she wasn't so sure, and as she watched the silver coin spinning in the air her stomach turned. Jack caught the coin with one deft, swift motion and slapped one hand over the other. She cracked her knuckles and called. He peeled back his fingers theatrically and smirked.

But she'd won the toss.

'So where to exactly?' Jack asked.

'A state run home for the elderly called Eden,' said Megan.

'I'm guessing it'll be no paradise, at least not for our chap. Look, I'll put Cuba aside for another day. We'll leave for Land's End in the morning. No point phoning beforehand to ask for permission to speak with the old boy, only to be turned down by some over protective matron, afraid we might be long lost relatives seeking an inheritance. I'll get an EBC car and travel pass,' Jack said.

Perhaps she was still lucky after all.

Megan had never been to the western tip of the British Isles. As a child it was too far for holidays, it would use up so much of their allowance and Elizabeth always maintained that Wales was the most beautiful place on earth. Megan looked forward to the journey, to discovering another part of the world. She was a born traveller and even before they set out she determined to visit again with Cerdic after all this was over.

'Let's take the coast roads,' she said, 'I'd love to see Dorset and south Devon.'

'It will take us over six hours to get there that way. Cutting across country will save hours, and we may even get to talk to the old man later today. Besides I'm driving, and I don't fancy doing it all day.' He was adamant.

'I'll drive for a while,' she said.

'No thanks.'

'Control freak.' Megan sulked for a while, tired and a little hung over after another night in the pub, followed by a take-away and contraband whisky at Jack's flat. He had so many contacts; he was never without tobacco or liquor, even during the droughts.

She studied the map. There was nothing to look at from the motorway, other than the stiff white forests of wind turbines. She enjoyed their surreal beauty but longed for real trees. Then she realized they would cut through Wiltshire.

'Can we stop at Stonehenge? We could have a picnic. I've never seen it. Please.' She fluttered her eyelashes, mocking the mannerisms of the female staff at EBC when they spoke with Jack.

'Stop that. It doesn't suit you.'

'Please.'

She wondered why he thought it didn't suit her. He liked women, and women liked him. He'd succumbed to the charms of the blatantly coquettish, the exaggerated reflections of woman-hood, the breezy and straightforward. She wondered if Julie was anything like his ex-wife. He'd been married, a long time ago, Megan'd been told by a reporter in Palestine. Jack never spoke of his wife, or even referred to the fact that he had once loved.

And Megan knew he could not be drawn on this matter. A former lover of Jack's, a runner at EBC, had created a scene at a wrap party once. It was alleged that she knew Jack's ex-wife. A group of journalists were discussing the rise of fundamentalism in the regions of north west China.

'They're all Buddhists. It'll blow over, and then you'll have to look for trouble somewhere else.' The girl was drunk.

'Some of us have colleagues there. Stay out of things you know nothing about,' Jack snapped. 'Stick to looking pretty and fetching things.' He raised his glass and sank the whisky.

'That's how you like your women isn't it, Jack? Pretty but dim. We're not all fucked-up blue-stockings...'

His face flared like a beacon; his hands shook; he grabbed her arm and bit his bottom lip. Everyone looked at the floor, said nothing. And though Megan knew Jack abhorred violence she thought he just might hit the silly, ignorant girl. He released his grip and turned, very slowly, and walked out of the room. He didn't return to the party, and Megan never saw the girl at EBC again. Megan never asked Jack about his marriage, or his former wife, and he never raised it.

'As you wish – we'll stop at Stonehenge. Briefly.'

'Why doesn't eyelash fluttering suit me?' she said, after a while.

'Has this been troubling you?'

'Don't make light of it. I'm serious.'

He took his eyes from the road and turned to her and said, 'Because you are far too clever for such nonsense.'

'Look where you're going,' she said, embarrassed by the compliment.

She wondered if his wife was clever, and if she ever fluttered her eyelashes, like Julie did. She'd tried to look his wife up once, on the grid. Megan knew only that her name was Eleanor, and that she was a geologist. The search for Eleanor North was fruitless. Thousands of them, none plausible. Megan figured that she would more than likely have reverted to her maiden name anyway and gave up.

'Have you been there?' she said, changing the subject.

'Where?'

'Stonehenge!'

'Once, as a boy. With my father. We only went because he had an important friend from Africa staying that summer. He was American, the friend, and was obsessed with how old England was. So we went. The whole family, hauled there one hot July day. I expected to feel the magic and was disappointed when we couldn't get close enough to touch the stones. I wanted to see monkey-man howling to the sky, falling to his hairy knees as the sun rose over the plains.' Jack laughed.

'You sound unimpressed. I can't wait,' Megan replied, and she meant it.

As they rode the rise and swell of the single lane road that loped across the plains Megan was struck by the grandeur of the landscape. It was a complete contrast to Wales but equally awe-inspiring.

As they reached the brow of a hill Jack said, 'Look to your right. You'll see it. Now.'

And there they were. The pile of grey stones. Humankind and nature. They looked so small, so insignificant against the splendour of the plains.

Cornwall was ragged and bleak, and less prosperous than Megan imagined. Like Wales the architecture was delicate, low and unambitious. It didn't attempt to compete with the landscape, and Megan felt at home there. As they approached the outskirts of Land's End Megan saw a large sign, *Eden, first right*. Jack pulled off the main road and followed the track up a slight incline to a stodgy building with small leaded windows. An expanse of bowling green perfect grass spread before it. It could have been a prison except for a terrace, with benches and chairs and large rainbow coloured umbrellas, incongruous against the incarcerating stone.

The reception area was empty. It was dark and smelt of wax. Oak wood panelling clad the walls, threadbare rugs were scattered on the floorboards. They looked Eastern, though Megan thought they couldn't be the genuine articles. The place was trying too hard to look opulent, it didn't feel as if it had had serious money spent on it despite initial appearances. Gilt framed oil portraits of dour-looking individuals adorned the walls on the landing at the top of a wide staircase. The silence was broken by the steady ticking of an ornate grandfather clock. Time ticking away, relentlessly, waiting for nothing or no one. It was a place for waiting. Scratching off the days on the cell walls. The clock struck three-thirty.

Megan said slyly, 'Perhaps the inmates are napping after lunch?'

'Not sure that the management would appreciate you referring to their guests like that,' Jack commented, as he hit the brass bell on the desk. Mirroring the gulf between appearance and reality of the hall, it gave out a feeble, apologetic ring and Megan called,

'Helloooo!' before whispering to Jack, 'It's all very dated here isn't it? I didn't think anyone used bells like this, and what happened to security? Anyone can walk in — the doors aren't even locked, let alone have security codes! It feels like we've stepped back in time.'

'Despite what you might think, Ms Evens, it's not a prison. And perhaps this,' he swept his arm over the hall, 'is to remind the guests of their youth. Make them feel good about life. Optimistic, as if there's everything to live for.'

They waited a few minutes before Jack rang the bell again. As the echoes of the last ting reverberated across the hall, the ticking of the clock mingled with the clicking of footsteps. A strikingly plain, tall woman approached them. She wore a yellow uniform and sensible brogues on flipper-large feet. She came to a standstill directly in front of them and looked at her watch before addressing them. Thread veins slipped across her dry cheeks, her eyebrows met in the middle and downy hair trailed from her temples to her jaw. Her name badge might just as well have read 'Spinster'. And she was clearly in a hurry.

'And how may I be of assistance?'

Before they'd got out of the car, they'd agreed that Jack would do the talking.

'Good afternoon,' he said and smiled, though she did not return his warmth. Jack continued, 'We're friends of a resident, and we're holidaying nearby. We were driving back from Mevagessey and we thought we'd pop in on the off chance...'

'Visiting hours are over, I'm afraid.' She looked at her wrist again, and Megan noted that she didn't look sorry in the slightest.

'I do appreciate that, but it would be lovely to say hello to the old boy. If only for a few minutes.'

The nurse wasn't going to budge. 'You'll have to book an appointment. Visitors are admitted daily between ten and noon, and one and three in the afternoon, with an evening slot between six and eight pm at weekends.' A thin smile forced its way across her cheeks; she gestured to the door and took a step forward.

'We're due to travel home tomorrow. It might be our last

chance,' said Jack, stepping sideways to block her path.

'There's nothing I can do about that. I'm sorry. Now, if you please.' She pointed at the door and stepped forward again. From where Megan stood Jack and the nurse looked as if they were nose to nose, like opponents in a wrestling ring.

Megan took hold of Jack's arm and pulled him towards her. The nurse went to say 'Good d...' but was interrupted by the purr of a mulmed. She pulled it from the generous pockets on the front of her uniform. The mulmed was purple splashed with magenta stars. She turned her back on Megan and Jack, who looked at each other with raised eyebrows, and said hurriedly, 'One moment, David,' before turning to face them once more, her jaw set. 'Good day, Sir, Madam. Come back in the morning and I'll see what I can do.' Megan wondered if the caller was a friend, a lover, or a son.

As they made their way to the double doors, Jack leant in and whispered, 'Nothing. That's what that bitch'll do. Absolutely nothing. Do you think she could smell a rat?'

'Ssshhh.' Meg stopped, glaring at Jack, brows furrowed. Then she dropped her unzipped bag; lip gloss, sunglasses, id card and other items spilt on to the shiny floor. She bent to retrieve them and Jack crouched down to help. She mouthed, 'Listen.'

'I'll be there in half an hour, tops. I'll come straight over, I won't even change...'

'She's going,' Jack mouthed. Megan nodded, and asked Jack to wait. She stood and approached the nurse who was closing the conversation on the mulmed.

'Would you mind if I use the toilet?' Megan said.

The nurse twitched irritably and then said, 'There's a visitor's lavatory over there, on your right. We don't usually...'

'Please. There's nowhere for miles.'

The nurse nodded, glanced over at the grandfather clock. Megan turned to Jack and said, 'Wait in the car, darling. I'll be with you in a moment,' then strode over to the bathroom. As she closed the door she saw the yellow of the nurse's uniform disappearing up the stairs.

It was a spacious, windowless room with a handrail next to a high toilet. Megan detected a trace of freshener in the stale air. An ancient can with rust round the nozzle sat on the cistern. The daffodil yellow and orange lettering read 'Spring Bouquet'; it made Megan feel sick. As she pulled out her mulmed, she heard the clacking of footsteps outside. She called up Jack and pressed the modesty button at the same time. A ghastly tune fluttered round the room.

She whispered into the handset, 'Jack, look out for Ms Pink Stars leaving. Let me know when you see her go. And don't let her see you.'

'Okay, okay. Granny, eggs. I've been doing this a lot longer than you. And what the bloody hell is that racket?'

'The modesty stuff. Music. Who'd have thought they'd install that in an old folk's home? This place feels like it should have a sign at the front: Leave dignity here. Collect on exit.'

'Now, now. You'll be old one day... Oh, here she comes. On a bike, pedalling fast. She really is in a hurry. I wonder if the mysterious David is a lover and she's off for some...'

'Jack. Listen. I'm going to get into this Bryant's room. Find out if he's the one.'

'You can't do that.'

'I can. I'll get his room number from the mulmed in reception, I'll—'

'He might have a heart attack or something, press an alarm button, if you just walk into his room unannounced...'

Megan heard footsteps again. Squeaky shoes. She turned off the modesty music and pressed her ear to the door. Voices. 'Another nurse has just come on duty,' she whispered.

'Let's try again. This one might be willing to bend the rules,' Jack said.

'They're probably all the same, aren't they?'

'It's worth a shot. We could at least get his room number so that you don't have to try and hack into the system before breaking into the old boy's pad.'

'Okay. I'll have to wait till it's clear before I can get out of this toilet.'

'I'll alert you once I'm in reception, and you can slip out. Let's hope the desk isn't manned.'

Ten minutes later they stood in the empty reception once more. Jack rang the bell. And then again. At last, a plump, middle-aged blonde woman in uniform made her way steadily across the space, shoes squeaking all the while, a broad smile fixed on her round face. Megan thought she looked like a banana.

'Good afternoon,' she said.

'Hello,' replied Megan and Jack in unison.

'I am so sorry to keep you. I wasn't expecting anyone. You see, we don't admit visitors at this time of day, unless by prior arrangement that is, and as far as I'm aware we're not expecting anyone today, I've only just come on duty so I'll need to check the diary,' said the nurse. Her voice was warm, her tone friendly. She reminded Megan of her mother. She detected a trace of a Welsh accent.

Jack said, 'You're quite right, we're not expected. We only dropped in on a whim. On the off chance... You see we're holidaying in the area, and an old friend of my father's, Christopher Bryant, Dr? Bryant, resides here I believe, and we thought it would be lovely to pop in and say hello. They went to medical school together. He did say if we were in the area...' Jack faltered, another nurse was not responding to his charm.

Megan jumped in, noting the nurse's nametag before she spoke. 'We've travelled a long way, Miss Jones. From Wales. It would be lovely to spend a short while with him. If it's not too inconvenient.'

'From Wales you say?' The nurse's interest was piqued.

'Yes, from Bangor. Where are you from, Miss Jones?'

'Neffyn. Just down the road from you. How I miss the mountains.' She looked up at Megan as she spoke, the craggy peaks in her eyes.

'Do you get to go back much?' Jack interjected.

'Not often, no. Too many miles, and my mother lives here now,' she said, pointing upstairs.

'We may not get another opportunity for many years... What

with travel allowances looking set to be reduced again. It would be so nice to say hello for Jack's dad. He's eighty-four you know. He'd be so grateful, and Dr Bryant might enjoy hearing news.' Megan's accent grew stronger with every word.

'I don't suppose it would do any harm, would it? And it is such a long way from home.' Miss Jones nodded her as she spoke, her yellow curls bouncing in the dull light. 'You mustn't stay long. He's not a well man. But I'm sure you know that.' She looked at Jack, and said, 'From your father.'

He nodded in agreement and Megan said, 'Such a shame. We won't outstay our welcome, Miss Jones.'

They followed her up the stairs, their footsteps combining to fill the hall with the sound of clattering. Jack mouthed at Megan, 'You were brilliant!'

'I know.' Megan mouthed back, 'You were shit. What happened to your legendary skills of persuasion?'

'She must be gay,' he mouthed, and Megan rolled her eyes.

'Is he getting worse?' Jack asked, as they followed Miss Jones down another long door-lined corridor. Megan felt like Alice chasing the White Rabbit. Then she heard the sound of mulmeds. So there were people here after all.

'The nightmares are. His physical health isn't too bad really. He's a troubled man, Mr ?'

'Grainger. William Grainger. My father is Nicholas, Nicholas Grainger,' said Jack.

'Here we are. You wait outside. Let me speak with him first.' And she closed the door behind her.

Megan and Jack stared at each other, straight faced. Megan had her fingers crossed behind her back. They were banking on Bryant not having heard news of his university contemporary's death earlier in the year.

Jack whispered, 'Nice touch, using the Welsh connection.'

'The Welsh are proud of their ancestry, we stick together.'

'Except you're probably not Welsh, are you?'

'I am. It's part of me. I'm as Welsh as daffodils and...'

The door opened and the nurse appeared. 'He'll see you now.

He's a little confused. Says he wasn't close to Mr Grainger. He doesn't get many visitors. You've intrigued him! Don't forget, not too long.' And with a smile and a nod Miss Jones stepped into the corridor and held the door ajar.

The room was hot and stuffy. In front of an enormous mulmed screen sat a high-backed blue armchair. A synthetic flora aroma fought against the stink of stale cabbage. From her vantage point Megan could see a pair of fleece-lined slippers and pyjama-clad legs poking out from the chair. Swollen veins laced across a trowel of a hand resting on the arm, a shock of fine white hair peeped from behind the back. Like a fledgling.

Megan shouted above the sound of the mulmed, the volume so high she assumed the old man must be deaf, 'Hello. Dr Bryant? Hello?'

The hand picked up the remote and the mulmed was silenced. 'There's no need to shout. I'm not deaf,' replied an authoritative, clear voice. The man turned to face his uninvited guests.

'Sister said you're the offspring of a university colleague of mine.' He regarded them closely as he spoke, watery eyes glaring from a remarkably smooth, transparent skinned face. A blue vein ran down his high forehead, throbbing to the rhythm of his heart. His gaze was direct, searching. Neither Jack nor Megan spoke.

For a moment Megan was stricken with guilt. The man was old, in poor mental health the nurse said. They had deceived him. Megan imagined them revealing their true purpose, Dr Bryant clutching his chest, dying of a heart attack. Shock. Yet there was something in the doctor's countenance that made her doubt he was at death's door. If she was honest, the man barely looked surprised to see them.

He looked directly at Jack. 'Grainger, Sister said? Nicholas Grainger?'

Jack hesitated before replying. Megan had the distinct impression that the old bugger was toying with him.

'Yes. He's my father.'

'How is he?'

'Fine.'

'For someone who's been dead six months,' the doctor replied dryly.

Jack bit his lip and ran his fingers through his hair. It was hot; Megan could feel the sweat gathering in the small of her back. The old man raised his brows and turned to her.

Megan felt his eyes boring into her, and though she longed to turn away she didn't dare.

'I'm sorry we lied to you. We mean no harm. We need your help. It's a matter of life or death. Please hear me out,' said Megan finally.

Chris Bryant smiled and said, 'You did not deceive me. I knew you were not who you claimed and I let the nurse show you in.'

Megan's brow furrowed. She couldn't read him; it unsettled her. She kept her eyes on his.

'I have been waiting for you for years. I knew you would come, one day. I have dreamt about this moment. Many, many times, but the dreams have been more persistent of late.' He sighed, resigned, a little relieved, Megan thought.

'You know who I am?' Megan stepped forward.

'I'm as sure as anyone can be about someone they have not seen in over thirty years, especially when that someone was an angry newborn.' He leant to one side and scrabbled amongst the books and pill bottles and tissues on the table next to his chair. He took an envelope from the back of a bible at the bottom of the pile and pulled out a photograph. He handed it to Megan.

'It's Mum. Elizabeth.'

'Izzie.' He sounded wistful.

'She looks so young. Bashful. No, flirtatious. This is Tŷ Mawr?'

'Yes.'

'So it is you. The doctor who delivered me. Dr Christopher Bryant. I didn't dare hope we'd find you.'

'Tell me, what is your name? Your Christian name.'

Megan pulled up a stool and sat opposite the doctor. She turned her ring and whispered her name.

'It suits you.' He removed his glasses and examined her closely. 'You want to know why, I suppose?'

'I'm not asking you to explain yourself, justify your actions,' Megan said.

She gave Dr Bryant a potted version of her life story. She was detached, verging on the indifferent, as if she was reporting someone else's story. Until she spoke of Cerdic, when her head and her heart fused. Until Cerdic came into her story, it sounded pathetic. The chasm between her dreams and her reality as wide as the world. She didn't solve problems or make things better. She told the world about them, and then walked away, ready to report on the next.

He asked if she had been a happy child, and she replied that she had. There were the usual childish dilemmas and squabbles, but yes, she had a good upbringing, she could not have wished for a finer mother. He enquired after Izzie, as he called her mother, and Megan thought she detected regret when he uttered her mother's name.

'But I'm not here to ask why you did what you did. You did what you thought was best at the time. Elizabeth too. I'm here because of Cerdic. None of us can change the past, but we have the power to alter the future. To save Cerdic. But I need to understand the past to do this. I need to know what you knew about the donor. Where did Hannah get the egg? Where was she treated? Is there anything you can remember that might help me, help Cerdic?' Megan pulled her mulmed from her bag and pulled up an image taken on the beach at Harlech: Cerdic buried to the neck in sand. A laughing head amongst a row of sandcastles. He looked beautiful, pure, crazy. She held it up.

Bryant took the handset and said, 'He doesn't look much like you.' Then he turned to Jack who was trying to blend in with the wallpaper. 'Do you have children too Mr ?'

Jack jumped. 'North. Jack North. No. Like kids, couldn't eat a whole one,' he said.

Megan wondered if Jack wanted children. He never spoke of it, but he rarely spoke of personal matters like that. She wondered if he'd end his days like this: a lonely old man with only his memories for comfort, or torment. If she might. Her stomach lurched.

'They enrich us, Mr North. Give us purpose. Like love,' he said.

'Can we go back to when Hannah was still alive?' Jack said.

He sounded rude but Megan took the opportunity to push on, aware that Miss Jones would be knocking on the door all too soon. 'Was there anything Hannah said that might lead us to her egg donor. Anything?'

Bryant closed his eyes, fingers tapping on the arm rest. Megan couldn't tell if this was involuntary or not. A nervous habit or tic. A sign of concentration.

'There was nothing she said directly. And it would have been improper to ask outright, you understand. But I think she travelled abroad,' he said.

'What makes you think this?' Jack interjected.

'The West was devastated by the plague. The major concern of government was to rebuild the population as quickly and effectively as possible. The supremacy of the West depended upon it. Economic, ideological.' He paused.

'I understand people wanted to rebuild, replace their lost children,' Megan said.

'Having children was seen as a kind of civic duty, a measure of one's patriotism. But not for those outside their reproductive years,' Jack interrupted again, before sinking back after a sharp look from Megan begging his patience.

Of course, they knew the background, but Dr Bryant didn't know this and she didn't want to appear rude, unlike Jack it seemed. But she wished Bryant would hurry. They didn't have long.

The old man coughed and said, 'Infertility had been rising sharply before 2015. In the 80s, when I was very young,' he sighed, 'there was a sharp drop off in the birth rate. Feminism, women waiting until they were in their thirties and forties before having children. Infertility levels were high in both the male and female populations.'

'But legislation prohibited direct financial transactions in eggs and sperm in the late twentieth and early twenty-first century?' Megan had read about this.

'Oh yes. There was a severe shortage of both. People travelled to America, Europe and India to buy and sell eggs. Later, the number of people trying to conceive was unprecedented. There were difficulties, no clear explanations. Pressure, stress, I think. What had been done in food production, what had been poured into the water supply. All in the name of profit. Progress, so called. We were greedy, stupid, and selfish. When will we ever learn...'

He stuttered, rubbed his thumb across his finger tips, lost in his own world, the way elderly people often are when recounting stories from the past.

At least ten minutes had passed. Megan needed to hurry him. 'Dr Bryant?'

He coughed, then continued, 'Fertility clinics and centres were packed with couples desperate to conceive. Younger, more fecund, women were encouraged to donate eggs in return for financial rewards, others donated for cut price IVF, but the truth was that there simply weren't enough eggs to go around. Women guarded them. They were an almost priceless commodity.'

'Dr Bryant. Tell us about Hannah. We know all this,' Jack said.

Megan could hear the frustration in Jack's voice, but she did not want the old man to clam up. She reached out and touched his hand. It felt paper dry, but strong, more solid than she imagined.

'A legitimate fertility clinic would not treat a woman in her seventies when there were so many other, more suitable, women desperate for children. The ethics, and morals, surrounding reproduction had lagged way behind the science for decades, but I do not believe a self-respecting doctor would have treated Hannah.'

'But you can't know that for sure, Dr Bryant. This is conjecture,' said Jack.

Megan scowled at him, but the doctor replied, 'You are right, I cannot be sure. But it is legitimacy that is the key. Stories sprang up of couples travelling to poorer nations, where the plague had barely touched, which welcomed the extra revenue that such a trade afforded. Ethics are a luxury, wouldn't you agree? When you are poor. Why not sell your child to a wealthy Western couple? Why not sell your eggs? Or your sperm. You don't want any more children. You have too many already.'

'You're saying Hannah went abroad?' Jack said.

Bryant ignored him. 'The countries in the eastern most corners of Europe were very popular. The peoples there are Caucasian. Easier to pretend the child is yours. Foreign governments tried to block this trade, but the black market was rife, and it was difficult to police.'

'She went to Eastern Europe?' Megan said, heart pounding. This tallied with Elizabeth's memories. They were getting somewhere. Finally. She dreaded the sound of the door and the nurse returning. They needed more from him.

'During my visits to Tŷ Mawr, to monitor Hannah's pregnancy, she often spoke fondly of a trip she made to Romania. She even showed me the photographs.'

'This is where she found her donor?' Megan was excited. 'Can you remember where in Romania?'

He named the place. 'I remember the photographs, such a beautiful city. I cannot be sure this is where they had treatment, of course. And even if I am right, it will be difficult. Many of these places were unregulated, operating on the fringes of the law. Record keeping would have been extremely poor, possibly non-existent for such practices.'

A door slammed in the distance. Megan jumped and glanced at Jack who jerked his head at the door. 'Dr Bryant? We have to go now. Your nurse is coming. Thank you. This is very helpful,' she said.

'I wish you luck, Megan Evens, and I am very glad to have met you. I beg your forgiveness, but I was in love with Izzie. I would have done anything for her.' He hung his head then said,

'How is she?'

'She's fine, thank you.'

Megan wondered if this was how she might be one day. Stumbling over memories of missed opportunities and love lost. It was a depressing thought. He looked exhausted, drained from the dredging up of the past. Megan stood up and offered her hand. As he shook it, she leant forward and kissed him on the cheek. There were tears in his eyes.

'She loved you. It's just that she couldn't see it at the time,' she said.

'She loved you more.' He studied her face. 'Quite right too.'

They walked down the staircase in silence. Outside Jack said, 'To Romania then, Ms Evens?'

'What about Cuba? Your budding revolutionary?'

'It can wait. Your hunch may be right. There's more than one story here. Remember the "Bad Eggs" scandal? Some years back. It was buried.'

'Yeah. And last year the Romanian Government made a pledge to help people trace their origins. I thought it was window dressing…'

'It probably was. I think it's time to resurrect this story. Create a stink.' He smirked at his own poor pun. 'I have some contacts there.'

'Stop it.' But she smiled. 'To Romania then, Mr North.'

Chapter Twenty-four

'Legend says that the lost children of Hamelin emerged from the cave into central Transylvania,' said Jack.

'Really? I had no idea.' Megan was tired. It had been a difficult journey from Bucharest.

'We're in Pied Piper land. Feels like a good omen,' he said.

'I hope you're right.'

'That was one of my favourite stories as a kid. What was your favourite story?'

'You wouldn't believe me if I told you,' she said.

'Try me,' he said.

They were sat in a bar. An unrestricted pub, like those back home from days gone by, where beer and spirits flowed freely provided you had the cash. Minutes earlier they had stood in the main square of the medieval city consulting a frayed, badly drawn map. In the distance the peaks of a mountain range glistened with snow, despite the absence of sunshine. Dark blue clouds lingered against a grey sky; cold inched up from the cobbled pavement through the soles of their boots, snapping at their tired feet. Spiky buildings with steep red-tiled roofs leant in towards the square. A smudged cathedral dominated the scene, its fearsome gargoyles screaming out at the world from their rooftop homes. Megan felt small and insignificant.

They had arrived by train less than an hour ago. It was mid-afternoon and the light was disappearing. A battered taxi had taken them to their hotel, where they checked in and dumped their luggage before heading straight out.

It was a beautiful city. As mysterious and surprising as Venice, as mystical as Istanbul. Megan recognized the spires and golden domes from Hannah's photographs. Pictures of Hannah and Owen standing in this square, wrapped in scarves and large fur hats, red noses and cheeks, smiling, happy and hopeful.

Bryant's intuition was correct. Jack and Megan felt it. When they returned from Cornwall Megan went back to the site where

Hannah kept her memories and trawled through the sets carefully. There was a handful of images of what to the unsuspecting eye looked like a holiday, but they were enough. One at the airport. With the plane in the distance, a down-at-heel Boeing with 'Transylvanian Air' scratched across the tail wing in chipped blue paint. Another of them sitting on a bench at a river's edge, spires shining gold against the white of the mountain slopes. An imposing gothic church. Spiky and foreboding, thrilling and terrifying. A delicious cocktail of East and West. Owen and Hannah in the square, fountains foaming behind them, fairy lights twinkling from the lampposts. Bleak mid-winter, January possibly, maybe February, shabby Christmas decorations flickering in the background, awaiting dismantling.

Back at EBC Jack had located four fertility clinics in the Romanian city named by Chris Bryant. Forty years ago there were no less than a dozen doing business. Those remaining had branched out, offering all manner of cosmetic procedures as well as fertility treatments. Megan had spoken again with Elizabeth, and it all fitted. Hannah and Owen travelled to Romania, nine or ten months before Megan was born.

'Go on, try me. Your favourite story,' Jack repeated. She remained silent, staring at her drink. Jack sipped the amber liquid in front of him. The bar was warm and welcoming, as was the brandy. They had stepped inside looking for directions having abandoned the map. A log fire roared in the corner, the smell of wood smoke filled the air, and it was enough to persuade them to stop a while.

She didn't answer him. Her mind was elsewhere. Instead she said, 'I wanted to ask Mum about Hannah. You know, more than the basic factual stuff, to get a feel for her. I wanted to connect in some way. Or perhaps it was something about it being Christmas, that looking back thing. I'd had too much to drink. In the end I didn't. I was afraid of hurting her feelings. Stupid huh?' she said.

'I rarely spoke of my mother and father with the Millingtons, even though they repeated often enough that it was perfectly natural to ask questions. But it felt wrong. And I wasn't that interested.'

'Did you ever try?'

'Yes, once, but I simply couldn't get the words out. They lodged somewhere around my tonsils, poisoning them.' Megan laughed. 'I was forever contracting tonsillitis. At lower school my attendance record was appalling. In the end the tonsils were whipped out when I was seventeen and studying to go to university. Nothing was to come in the way of my getting to Oxford. And certainly not a couple of useless glands.'

Megan laughed. They finished the brandy and ordered a second drink. Megan took a sip of colourless liquid, a local aperitif recommended by the barman, a giant of a man with a potato shaped face and no teeth. The aperitif was thick and sticky and sweet. She rolled it round her mouth, letting it cling to her teeth, tongue and roof, then she swallowed. It nearly took her head off. She couldn't drink the way that she used to, before she had Cerdic. She began to cough, loudly, and when Jack started, unhelpfully, thumping her back, the locals, who had hitherto paid little attention to the strangers sitting by the fire, turned and began to smile and gesture to the drink. The ogre behind the bar grinned a gummy smile then nodded gravely, as if to say, 'I warned you.'

When she had regained her composure Megan smiled back, blew an imaginary flame from her lips, waving her hand in front of her mouth, and then swallowed the remainder of the lethal brew in one gulp. She thought she might regret it later and didn't care.

Jack finished his drink then said, 'Go on. Your favourite story.'

'That's hard. Elizabeth told so many. She was great like that. Said she got it from her father, Robert.'

'Welsh tales then?'

'Mostly. From the Mabinogion. I loved Rhiannon's tale.' She stopped. He looked at her and nodded, as if to say, 'Go on then.'

'She was a beautiful lady...'

'Aren't they always?' he interrupted.

Megan ignored him and carried on. 'Dressed in gold and riding a white stallion, she was spotted by Pwyll, Lord of Gwynedd and King of the Other World. He fell instantly in love. They married, eventually, and Rhiannon gave birth to a son. One night while she slept, exhausted like all new mothers, her child was stolen and her jealous handmaids slaughtered a new born pup and smeared Rhiannon's face and clothes in the dog's blood, then claimed she had murdered her own child. As punishment she was placed in a mounting block in the city square each evening and forced to tell her story to passers-by. But her boy was not dead. He was raised by a surrogate, a loving mother and father...'

Jack raised his eyebrows and whistled. 'Elizabeth told you this?'

'I said you wouldn't believe me.'

'What happened?'

'After many years, the boy, Pryden, was returned. Rhiannon was forgiven, and they all lived happily ever after, or something like that. I can't remember the exact ending.'

'Wow,' Jack said. They looked at each other, and laughed. Then Jack said, 'So which clinic do we start with? Any preference?'

'The three that have been going for the longest. One of them is quite new, so Hannah can't have gone there. The problems will start if we find nothing at those three.'

'Let's stay positive, Ms Evens.'

'But they could have gone to one of the clinics that folded after the boom years. I wonder what's happened to the records?'

'If that's the case it'd be easier to trace staff and go from there. We could gather information anecdotally, but let's not leap ahead. If we're lucky they'll have been treated at one of these.' He pointed at three crosses marked in red on the map.

'You're right. Stay positive. Whichever is closest is the one we'll approach first. Another drink before we head off?' She was enjoying the warmth from the fire and the drink in her belly.

'God yes,' Jack replied.

'Come on then, you're buying.'

Clinik Stamenov was the oldest and most prosperous clinic in the city, set on a hill in the new town outside the walls. The receptionist spoke no English, and after a short ping-pong match firing languages at each other it seemed that both the receptionist and Jack spoke some Spanish. He explained that they were British journalists making a programme about people searching for their birth mothers in the light of recent scandals and admissions by former doctors working at clinics like this and the Romanian administration's public promise to help people trace their origins. They were researching both sides of the story. The programme would be balanced and fair, he said.

Both Megan and Jack knew that a commitment from government would not be enough for some centres to co-operate and figured that the carrot of positive publicity might be enough to tip the balance. They did not have the time to fight through reams of red tape, waiting for official paperwork which could take months, even years, by which time it could be too late for Cerdic.

Gleaning enough from Jack's explanation the receptionist called her superior: a good-looking woman in her mid-fifties with a colourful hijab wrapped round her head. She did not speak Spanish, or Mandarin, or Italian, or French or any of the half dozen or so languages Jack had a working knowledge of.

Noting the hijab Megan said, 'Arabic?'

The woman nodded, and Megan gave a silent prayer to Hisham. She repeated their cover story. Stiffening before their eyes the woman explained that this particular clinic had always worked within the law and firm ethical guidelines. She held her hands clasped in front of her, resting on the desk.

'But how can you be so sure, Madam? You are far too young to recall the heyday of fertility treatments,' said Megan.

The woman touched the tip of the hijab resting half way down her forehead with a slim finger. Her kohl-rimmed eyes softened, and she said, 'I will speak with our director, but you understand that I cannot make any promises.'

'Perfectly,' Megan said.

'You flatterer,' said Jack, as the woman disappeared from reception.

'I learnt from a master,' she replied.

Presently the director appeared. He was a tanned, grey-haired man who despite a rather heavy-handed face-lift had evidently been extremely handsome when younger. He carried a little excess weight on his athletic frame. Like a pigeon wooing a mate he swelled at the sight of Megan, puffing up his feathers. She was glad she had chosen to wear make-up and had left her hair loose. She regretted her bulky jumper; her breasts were barely noticeable.

The director spoke perfect English. He ushered them through to his office, the fabric of his trousers noisy as his heavy thighs rubbed against each other with every stride, his heels clicking on the polished tiles. Megan noticed the seam across his ample buttocks straining; the stitching was discernible.

He was suspicious and guarded, but the promise of coverage for him personally, with plenty of interview footage and vox pops was enough to sway him in the end. Pandering to his vanity and greed sealed the deal. He would be portrayed as a vehement opponent of the clandestine, possibly illegal, nature of the former trade in human life. A civic minded fellow who would do everything in his power to help individuals discover their roots. The hint of increased traffic to the clinic from the UK as a result of such coverage undoubtedly helped their cause.

It was late when Megan and Jack returned to the hotel. But they had guaranteed access to the clinic's records, staff and former employees. They planned to start in the morning.

After days of relentless research, digging through notes, emails, and medical cards, translating what they could with the help of the mulmed's crude but instant translation service, the only thing that was apparent was that between 2016 and 2021

Clinik Stamenov had treated and impregnated far more women than they had egg donors. Unless donors were offering handfuls of eggs the figures didn't add up.

Initially, Megan and Jack agreed that the clinic might have treated women who had plenty of their own eggs, who suffered from problems like blocked fallopian tubes, but when the same pattern emerged from the other clinics they visited Jack and Megan knew they were onto something. It hadn't been difficult gaining access to the records of the other centres. They were competitors and agreement from one led to agreement from all. They all wanted a presence in the 'film'.

Megan was excited for the first time since their arrival in Romania. She was no closer to tracing Hannah's donor, her biological mother, and potential saviour to Cerdic, but she could smell a story and like a hound on a trail she couldn't stop. Jack was right – there was more than one story to be uncovered.

But days went by and still they found nothing. As Bryant had warned, records were incomplete, damaged and missing altogether. Speaking to staff illuminated little, and they suspected that their interpreter was paraphrasing, and even not passing on information in some instances. The interpreter had been recommended by the director of Clinik Stamenov and in the end Jack decided they would be better off without him.

Megan and Jack returned to Clinik Stamenov. The director looked less than pleased to see them, without a crew, but he had given his consent so what could he do?

'We'd like to go through the records again. Ideally we're looking for an unusual couple of cases,' Jack explained. The director smiled, phoney but comfortable. Megan was convinced that the records concealed a multitude of sins, they'd just not found them yet, and she was increasingly frustrated that the director appeared confident they could not pin anything on his practice. She was determined to prove the arrogant shit wrong.

This time they dug deeper, more carefully, and found reference to a couple from Wales, spelt in Welsh, incorrectly. Cumree instead of Cymru. Megan had stopped searching for Hannah and Owen by name – it was clear that they had used aliases – and was searching via country of origin, then county, then town. Also, this time, they trawled through paper records, a task they were unaccustomed to, and progress was slow.

In the winter of 2019 the centre took an enquiry from a Mr and Mrs Roberts of Gwynedd. And in January 2020 a Mr and Mrs Bevan of 'Chester, near Cumree' had checked in and stayed for five days, returning one month later for a 'follow-up' and then again in the March. Megan remembered that she arrived early, at about thirty-five weeks, Elizabeth guessed. March would fit almost exactly. After then the references to the couple disappeared. Mrs Bevan was described as 'a little older' than the usual client and the date of birth column listed her age as fifty-nine.

'That doesn't fit. She was in her early seventies,' Jack said, looking up from the mountain of paper in front of him. A ream slipped off the desk, floating to the dusty floor. 'Christ! Have they never heard of environmental protection laws here? All this bloody paper's driving me nuts. My eyes are hurting, the mulmed's finding the translation difficult, there's no natural light in here and I'm dying for a fag!' He kicked the table leg.

'Have one. Who's to know?'

They were in the bowels of the clinic, in a room with a torpid, stale aura, a couple of ancient mulmeds, and a filing system with row upon row of paper records. Neither Megan nor Jack had seen so much paper before.

'I'm afraid I'll set this place alight,' said Jack, sheepish.

'Be careful. And you can roll one for me too.'

They sat with their feet up on the desks enjoying the illicit pleasure of the tobacco. Megan had crafted an ashtray from the torn off corner of a cardboard file divider. She looked at the sheet in front of her.

'Hannah'd have been seventy-three at the time of the visit. But she'd have lied about her age, surely? There were age limits on fertility treatments here, weren't there?'

'There were. But who's to say this lot adhered to them?' Jack pointed to the ceiling. 'I don't trust him, our director. Not one bit.'

'She looked good for her age, judging by the photographs. It wouldn't have been difficult,' Megan said.

'What about him? Any age listed?'

'Why would there be? Hannah was having the baby.'

'No donor?'

'No.'

'If it is them…'

'It is.'

'There must have been a donor. Hannah was too old to have any eggs left.' He dragged hard on his cigarette. 'How can you be so sure that it's them? They can't have been the only couple who came here from North Wales.'

'Hannah's first husband was called Robert. And Elizabeth's husband, the one that died during the plague, was called Bevan. By all accounts Hannah idolized Andrew Bevan, almost as much as Elizabeth. It's as if she was trying to honour their memories by taking their names.'

'Or she lacked imagination.' He finished his cigarette.

'Or she didn't want to bury all trace of herself,' Megan snapped. She sat up and stubbed out her cigarette.

Jack placed his hand over Megan's. Megan jumped at the contact. Jack withdrew his hand immediately, checking that both cigarettes were out before kneeling to collect the fallen paper and return to work.

'I'm going to speak with our director,' she said.

'Want me to do it?'

'No. I'll get more out of him.'

'Be careful.'

It was late when Megan approached the director. Although the lights were on, the administrative section of the centre was quiet. Energy saving appeared to be less of a priority here than at home. Most of the staff had gone home. Jack had returned to the hotel earlier and Megan wanted to leave as quickly as possible. She was exhausted.

The centre and its director gave her the creeps; it was a place where people were altered, where healthy people underwent surgery. The director was lecherous and he was suspicious. While he professed a lack of interest in her and Jack's background work, he appeared often, fiddling in corners of rooms they were working in, as if monitoring their work, studying their reactions, listening to what staff reported.

Megan rolled back her shoulders before knocking at his office door. A low, irritated-sounding voice growled 'Enter' in Romanian. He was sitting at a large, empty desk, staring at a state-of-the-art mulmed. When he looked up and registered Megan his countenance altered and a smile snaked across his features. An old woman with a severe curvature of the spine was struggling to clean the enormous glass window that during daylight hours looked out over the westerly quarter of the city, the commercial district.

Too tired for the formalities Megan dispensed with them. She said, 'I've been going through the records again. There are some inconsistencies and I'm hoping you may be able to help.' She remembered to smile.

'I will certainly do my very best,' he said, standing and gesturing to the far corner where a pair of easy chairs and a low table sat.

She took a seat and folded her legs around each other. 'There seem to be significant numbers of clients who do not appear to have needed a donor. Is there any reason why this might be, Director?'

'Of course.' His smile was slow, deliberate, his whitened teeth gleamed in his tightened face. 'Many women had their eggs frozen when they were young and at their most... How can I say this...'

'In their prime?'

'Precisely.'

The cleaner's cloth was making a low squeaking sound as she pulled her arm back and forth across the glass. He barked at her in Romanian.

'Then why is it that when I follow the records back to when your clients were…'

'In their prime.' He spoke the words salaciously, his meaning clear. Megan thought he would have loved to get his hands on her ovaries. Little did he know.

'There are no such records.'

'Mysterious.'

'Indeed.'

'Not all clients needed to have a stock of frozen eggs. Part of the deal was that 'extras' would be taken and donated to women who were themselves incomplete, so to speak.' He rubbed his hands down his parted thighs.

Megan shifted in her chair and much as she fought the impulse, she could feel her eyes being drawn to his crotch. What's the matter with me, she thought. This man is repulsive. Turning away, she watched the cleaning woman who had moved from the window and was wiping down his already spotless desk. Megan changed tack and said, 'As a former surgeon you must have treated many women yourself?'

'I did.'

'Are there any you remember in particular? Who were especially grateful for your help, your skill?'

He seemed perplexed. She added, 'Viewers love anecdotes. It helps bring a story alive, the human touch.' He was making a show of giving it some thought. She said, 'Anyone particularly young? Or desperate? Unable to find anyone else willing to help?'

He shrugged coolly and replied that he saw so many English couples it was impossible to remember them all. That it was such a long time ago.

'But not all your clients were English. I came across records of a Welsh couple this afternoon,' she said, casually.

He shook his head, failing to disguise his irritation. She knew she had rattled him.

'Welsh, English, all the same to us.' He waved his hands dismissively, sweat appearing on his brow.

She needed to tread carefully. She smiled, 'Of course.'

Visibly relaxing, he said, 'I will give it some thought though, and come back to you. Now, can I get you a drink, Miss Evens?'

She glanced at the jug of water on the table.

'I have something stronger in my cabinet. You should enjoy the view. The city looks magical from here at night.'

Standing, she said, 'It does. Perhaps another time. It's been a long day.'

'Another time,' he said, touching her on the shoulder. She tried not to flinch and smiled through gritted teeth.

She collected her belongings from the cloakroom, frustrated and miserable. The director was slippery and volatile; he could turn against them very easily, and it was hard enough without adversaries. Where had Hannah and Owen got their egg donor? There had to be another way.

Megan was about to leave when a figure appeared in the doorway. She jumped. Rheumy eyes gazed at her. It was the woman who had been cleaning in the director's office. The woman opened her mouth as if to speak, then closed it again at the sound of a slamming door and scurried away. There was something about the way she looked that fired Megan; adrenaline raced through her veins, eradicating her exhaustion. It was almost as if the woman recognized her. But that would be impossible. Wouldn't it? Megan grabbed her bag and ran after the cleaner. As she turned the corner she almost crashed into the director.

'Miss Evens, you look as if you've seen a ghost. Are you all right?' he said.

'I'm fine, thank you. I...' she lifted her hand in the direction of the cleaner and then thought better of it and in one clean movement drew her hand to her head and smoothed down her hair. 'I'm late meeting my colleague, that's all.'

'The exit is this way.' Blocking her route he raised his hand in front of him and pointed in the opposite direction.

'Yes. Thank you.' Megan knew when she was beaten. For the time being.

Outside she leant against the wall. Exhaustion overwhelming her once more. The icy air pinched at her face and she felt the skin on her scalp tighten. She looked out over the city. The director was right – it looked magical, a fairy kingdom spread out before her, glittering and promising. But it was vast, so many souls resided there, and she was looking for just one woman. It was an impossible task. The magnitude of her search was staring her in the face and she felt profoundly depressed, powerless and small. What if she couldn't find her mother? What then for Cerdic? The sound of her breathing fractured the silent air and she thought of the muscles moving within her, forcing her lungs open, filling them with oxygen, pushing out the carbon dioxide, and repeating the exercise again and again. And she thought of Cerdic, some day in the future, struggling with this most instinctive, thoughtless of tasks, and she tried to imagine a world in which he did not exist, but could not. She felt as if she might break in two. Her knees buckled and she slid down the wall. It was too heavy a thought to bear. She held her head between her knees for a while; she felt sick and faint, but the feeling passed. She lit a cigarette and exhaled loudly, watching the smoke mingle with the steam of her breath in the night air. I need a genie, she thought.

She saw the cleaner's face in her mind's eye. It was as if she wanted to say something to her. But that was ridiculous. The woman spoke no English, how could she possibly have understood the conversation with the director in his office? Megan stubbed out her cigarette on the brickwork, clambered up and headed for the car park before remembering that the easiest place to catch a cab was at the rear of the building. She could feel the chill in her bones.

As she walked through the carefully landscaped gardens to the rear she heard voices. At first she thought it was an argument, then she realized that one person was doing all the shouting. She recognized the voice: the director's. Almost subconsciously, she slipped across the grass and behind the trunk of a large tree, hiding herself from view, before peering round surreptitiously. The director was yelling at the cleaner. Although Megan could not understand the words she recognized the tone well enough:

threatening, bullying. At first the woman sounded as if she was defending herself, but soon she appeared to concede defeat. Not quite begging, but almost. The director's voice had fallen to a menacing bass.

Megan knew when someone was being silenced, whatever the language. Damn the man. He had something to hide, she knew it, and she would find it. She waited.

The click of the director's heels fell into the distance. Megan stepped out from behind the tree. The cleaner was shuffling along the path, head down, her shoulders stooped and low. Megan ran after her.

'Please, please,' she called, before realizing her foolhardiness and lowering her voice.

The woman turned, startled, her eyes wide with fear. Megan whispered, 'May I talk with you? I think you know something, you're being silenced?' Megan pulled her hand across her mouth in an imaginary zipping movement. The woman shook her head vigorously and waved her hands. Her fear was almost tangible. She turned to go. Desperation seized Megan.

'You know why I'm here, in Romania? You've heard the talk?' She spoke the words slowly into the thin air wondering why she did so. The woman could not understand, and even if she did she might not help. She is frightened, but she is the key, Megan thought. I feel it, and I cannot explain how much I need her. The cleaner began to walk; Megan felt her son slipping away. She uttered a low, guttural cry and covered her face with her hands, and when she pulled them away the woman had stopped. She stood still.

'My son,' Megan mimed, cradling a baby, 'will die,' she crossed herself and pointed to the heavens, 'if I cannot find my mother...' Her voice cracked, then caught. 'I think you can help me. I feel that you can help me.' She was crying now, shaking and sobbing, her frozen nose running. 'Please, please,' she said in Romanian.

The woman looked over her shoulder, back at the clinic. The woman cradled a baby and pointed at Megan.

'No, no. I have a baby,' Megan said. 'An old woman, like you.' She bent over, as if with a stick, then pointed to the woman's grey hair. 'Here, for baby?' She flashed ten fingers three times and waved her right hand over her shoulder. 'Thirty years ago?' Megan said.

The woman nodded, and though Megan wasn't sure that she had understood, she said, 'Thank you, thank you.' The woman smiled, her face lit by the overspill from the clinic. She had only a handful of teeth, stained brown-yellow and crooked. She wouldn't have any in a few years time.

Megan wiped her nose with her gloved hands. 'Can you meet me? Not here? With a friend, family member who speaks English, or Mandarin? I speak Mandarin. I am staying here,' she took out the hotel's business card, 'I can buy you dinner.' She shovelled imaginary food into her mouth and chewed. The woman seemed to understand. Megan pointed to the nine on her watch and the woman nodded.

'What is your name? Me: Megan. You?'

'Teresa. Teresa Micu.'

'Thank you, Teresa Micu,' Megan said, hands on her thumping heart. 'Thank you.'

As she sat in a cab speeding back to the hotel Megan clasped her hands and prayed.

Please God, don't let her change her mind. Megan thought of Elizabeth and wondered what she would make of her faithless daughter resorting to prayer.

Chapter Twenty-five

Jack looked at his watch. Megan knew it was nine o' clock.

'You took a risk, breaking your cover like that,' he said.

'I had no choice.'

'What if she doesn't show?'

'She will.'

'She'll want money.'

'Let's see.'

Minutes later Teresa Micu and a young man bearing a striking resemblance to her walked into the hotel lobby. They lifted their heads, looking around, taking it all in, like children entering a Christmas grotto. It was clear that the boy was a grandson and that Teresa Micu must have been a beauty as a young woman. Although the hotel was not especially opulent, the EBC empire was notoriously frugal when it came to expenses, Teresa and her grandson looked distinctly out of place.

Megan and Jack sat in a bar area tucked in the far corner of the reception. They lounged on wide couches and were hidden from view by a tropical plant with leaves as large as umbrellas though their own view was unimpaired. Teresa stopped well before the desk and its officious looking occupant and looked around again. A porter dashed over to them, a self-important air in his stride. Megan leapt up. For one dreadful moment she thought they might be expelled from the establishment before she reached the porter. Her insensitivity shamed her. Of course they would feel out of place. She was a cleaner. This was a four-star hotel designed for wealthy tourists. She should have waited for her by the revolving doors or spoken with the doorman. She greeted them with heartfelt apologies and thanks.

The young man worked in telecommunications and spoke clumsy English with a heavy accent. But they could understand him. Megan was glad English was the chosen language, her Mandarin was rusty. Teresa was visibly proud of him, and told them that one day he would run his own company, a worldwide operation, and take care of his elderly relatives. The boy flushed a salmon pink and shook his head.

'I am her one grandparent son. She blind to my problems.'

They wouldn't accept dinner, or even a bar snack, and Megan respected their pride. Teresa was not here for any personal gain. It was a long-winded, complex conversation with frequent misunderstandings, but Teresa was keen to share her story. That much was clear.

Teresa had worked at Clinik Stamenov for over forty years. As a young woman she worked on reception but as the flow of western clients increased, and her grasp of English did not increase with the same rapidity, she was removed from the front desk and offered a position behind the scenes. Her first employer, the previous director of the clinic, was an honourable, decent man who cared for his employees and whose attitude was paternal. But he died in a road accident in 2015.

Teresa remembered it well because his death was so shocking, so sudden. It affected many people in the community. And it was made more poignant because of reports of what was happening in Western Europe and America. Of the deaths there. Commonplace, young and old alike. Especially the young and old.

A few years later, when Clinik Stamenov was growing in size and reputation, when western couples flocked to Romania for babies, Teresa recalled an attractive woman with shoulder length grey hair visiting the clinic. At first Teresa assumed the woman was in her late forties, prematurely grey from the shock of what had happened to her country. She was British Teresa thought, definitely not American.

'How can you be sure?' Jack said.

'She didn't look right. Too small, not fleshy enough.'

But the second time Teresa saw the British woman she was much closer and she realized that this woman was older than forty-something. Much older.

Megan showed her a photograph of Hannah and Owen. Teresa shrugged and said that she couldn't be certain, but that yes, this might be the same woman.

'This is the woman who gave birth to me. She was seventy-three years old. The man may be my father. But I am less interested in him, I can never be sure of him. I have a little boy who is very, very sick and my biological mother, family, are the people most likely to be able to save his life. I need to find out where this woman,' she pointed at Hannah, 'got the egg, or he,' pointing at a picture of Cerdic on his third birthday, blowing out the candles on a cake cut into the shape of a starfish, 'will die.'

Teresa crossed herself and touched Megan's brow. Her fingers felt arid against Megan's soft flesh. It was an intimate gesture that, ordinarily, would have made Megan uneasy. Teresa took hold of Megan's hand and covered it with her own.

'He will be saved. I feel his spirit. Your spirit. There is something in you.'

Jack turned to Teresa's grandson and said, 'Can we stick to the facts. There are few records of donors at the clinic. Yet there must have been loads judging by the numbers of people treated, the numbers of pregnancies forged. Do you have any ideas where the donors came from? Who they were? And how we might trace them?'

Teresa sighed. She said that after the kind director died, a younger, greedier man replaced him. Clinik Stamenov altered. Its marketing became more aggressive and only a couple of years after the new director took over she noticed that the clinic started advertising in the city for egg donors.

'They offered handsome reward for donation. People are poor here, especially then. Difficult to make that kind of money,' Teresa nodded and gesticulated, and wrung her hands as her grandson spoke, making clucking sounds with her tongue against her remaining teeth.

'So women were paid to donate their eggs? How were they paid, per egg or per visit, or batch?' Megan asked urgently.

Teresa and the boy nodded in unison. She spoke rapidly to her grandson.

'I do not know how they were paid. I am not important there. I was not told such things, but I did notice that the director kept large amounts of cash in his office, and these girls and women left with white envelopes.'

'Girls?' Jack interjected.

'Yes, girls. Some as young as thirteen, fourteen. There were rumours. Clinik Stamenov gave cards outside schools. The principals tried to stop them, to warn the girls of handing over their future for a few lei. What they were risking was priceless, irreplaceable. But they were young. What did they care? They had plenty of eggs. They took no notice.'

'God, how awful. It's pretty unpleasant, taking the drugs, the procedure to remove the eggs. I hope the money was worth it,' said Megan.

Teresa didn't believe that all of the girls were there of their own accord or understood what was happening to them. Familial pressure played a part for many. It was a way for families to get out of trouble.

A dull ache spread over Megan. It was horrible to think that young women, children, were cajoled and forced into undergoing an unpleasant procedure that later in life might have affected their ability to have children of their own. She was disgusted with her country's capitalism, its exploitative nature. The clinic director was far from blameless but had there been no demand, had people asked more questions, he would not have needed his ill-gotten supply. And Clinik Stamenov obviously did not check the medical history of donors. It was sickening.

'My son has a rare genetic condition, AMNA, passed from mother to son. Daughters are unaffected. If there are other sufferers here, in the city, their mothers have to have been possible donors.'

Teresa shrugged and muttered to her grandson.

'She knows nothing of this disease. You ask doctor for this,' he said.

'I understand.' Megan grasped Teresa's hand, 'Please tell your Grandmama, thank you. We are very grateful for this, and tell her not to worry. The director will never know where we got our information. And I'm going to ruin that slimy bastard just as soon as I've saved my son.' The words came easily, and the sentiment, but Megan knew that her task had just got even harder.

As they crossed reception with Teresa and her grandson Megan turned to Jack and said, 'Where on God's earth do we start with this? No wonder there are no records.'

'Let's sleep on it and talk in the morning, Meg. You need some rest,' Jack said. They had reached the revolving doors.

Jack said to the boy, 'Let's get you a taxi home.'

Teresa touched Megan's cheek with her leathery palms and murmured in Romanian.

'What did she say?' she said to Teresa's grandson.

'She said you are one of us.'

Megan stared at Teresa. 'How can you be sure?'

The boy and his grandmother spoke rapidly to each other. It sounded like an argument. Megan and Jack looked on. Finally the boy offered his grandmother's reply. 'There is a woman, a girl, who my grandmother knows in a neighbouring district who looks like you.'

'And you know this girl? Her mother?' Megan said.

'The mother has not been a well woman. She has many problems. Health problems. She drank too much, too much drugs.'

'Why did she drink so much, Teresa? Do you know why or suspect why? I think you know. Please tell me.' Megan was shaking.

'She has been sick for many years. Off and on. Up and down. Good times, bad times. She used to come to the clinic, drunk, accusing the director of stealing her children. Saying in her dreams he took them away. Everyone laughed. Said she was a mad woman but I was never sure. I thought she was a sad woman, but not mad. I saw too much to believe she was crazy. The rumours.

'And then she disappeared. Stopped visiting, and for a while some of the staff missed her. She gave the empty-headed idiots something to gossip about,' Teresa clucked as her grandson gestured to his head and the air, 'and then she was forgotten. But not by me. I remembered her and thought on her from time to time. And then six months ago I was visiting a friend in a neighbouring district, she is sick with the cancer, and I saw her: the sad woman. She had not altered much in all these years. A few grey hairs, a little fatter. Nothing more. She was arm in arm with a girl, seventeen, eighteen years old. She recognized me, as I had her, though I fear the years have been much less kind to me and we said a polite, hesitant hello to each other. She was sober, happy, and she introduced the girl as her daughter. It was such a very special moment, for me. To see her content, with a child. She was at peace.

'We did not talk much more. After all, what was there to say? I was nothing to her. I worked at a place she used to visit. A place that pained her. I said how good it was to see her and she repaid the compliment though I could not see how. I was a reminder of a painful past. At this point the girl said that they must get home, so and so would be waiting, and they had three blocks to walk. The girl was serious looking, severe but beautiful. I would not forget a face such as that.'

Megan looked at Teresa. 'You think this woman is my mother? That one of her eggs was donated to Hannah, the old woman from Britain?'

'Seeing you. Closer. Time with you. Maybe. Probably.' Then the boy spoke for himself, 'But my grandmother is old, it was a long time ago. Nothing is certain.'

But Megan didn't hear him; she didn't heed his words. She said to Teresa, 'I have a sister? A half-sister?' To Jack she said, 'A chance for Cerdic, a good chance. She may not be a carrier?'

A couple barged past the little group and flounced into the doors. The movement snapped Megan from her thoughts. She snatched her mulmed from her bag, pressed record and began to babble into it, flying questions at Teresa as she did so. Did she know the woman's name? In which district of the city did she bump into her? How long ago was this? Did she call her daughter by name? And so on. The old woman flinched at the sight of the recorder. Megan put it away.

Teresa's grandson spoke again, 'I must take Grandmama

302

home. It is late. She is not young. She must work tomorrow. You understand. We talk again.'

The old woman spoke again to her grandson. Then he said, 'She says her name is Monica Petrescu. The sad woman.'

Megan wanted to jump around she was so happy. A name! She had a name! Controlling herself she apologized for bombarding Teresa with more questions, for using her mulmed without asking permission, ashamed of her thoughtlessness. Then she and Jack chaperoned the Micus through the exit and hailed a taxi.

They stood on the steps, shivering in the cold air, watching the cab speed off into the night.

'I need another drink,' Megan announced.

'And so do I.'

Megan ordered vodka, Jack whisky, and flopped back on the lounger. She gazed at the ceiling mesmerized by the droplets of the chintzy chandelier that hung from it. They reminded her of raindrops and she longed to feel Welsh rain on her face, splash in puddles with her son. Soon. She was getting closer to the truth.

'So my mother was a thirteen, fourteen-year-old kid whose eggs were farmed without her consent or understanding. But somewhere inside she knew she had been robbed. That something had been stolen from her. And it drove her crazy. It's disgusting. Hideous. I wish I didn't have to find her, to remind her. But I must.'

'You're leaping to conclusions. There's a lot to check, double check. One old woman's opinion. Not fact.'

'Oh come on, Jack. You feel it as much as I do. Don't give me that. I know you.'

'Then you'll know it's my job as your older and wiser mentor—'

'*Former* mentor.'

'To insist on facts, other witnesses, an opposing viewpoint—'

'But what a story! This isn't only about Cerdic. This could be huge. There might be hundreds, thousands of people out there like me, like Cerdic, who have all sorts of unanswered questions, problems, because these people stole eggs to line their pockets.

303

And not only that, or probably because of it, they didn't bother with all the normal checking stuff. They probably lied to people. Told them the donors were all gorgeous, intelligent, sporty, confident, healthy people. When most of them were spotty teenagers abused by so-called life savers.'

Jack took a deep breath.

Megan stared at him. 'What?'

He coughed.

'Come on Jack, out with it.'

'You are, of course, correct. It could be a massive, important story.'

'But?' she said, exasperated.

'But nothing. Well, nothing to do with the story. The story's good. Great. A career maker, or saver.'

Megan took in his unkempt hair, the day old stubble, the shabby jumper. It was unusual to see him like this. If he was scruffy occasionally it was studied and contrived; he was proud and vain. That evening he looked like a tramp. He had worked so hard since they'd arrived in Romania. Perhaps even harder than her. She had slept for four or five hours each night, slipping into oblivion despite herself. He looked as if he hadn't slept in weeks, let alone days, and she knew he was on the mulmed to London every night after they'd finished, keeping up with what was going on at EBC. He was a workaholic, as she had been. But he couldn't afford to let up. She'd heard the rumours. That Jack North had lost his touch; he was all dried up. Time to make way for younger, sharper journalists.

'Your name on the byline. I don't care about that anymore,' she said.

'You think that's what this is about? Christ.'

Momentarily, Megan thought he looked hurt.

He ran his fingers through his hair. 'I'm worried about you as it happens.' He continued, unusually hesitant, 'Have you thought about what all this means for you? I know that Cerdic is your number one priority, but you must care for yourself too. How do you feel about meeting your biological mother? Are you okay? It could throw up all sorts of things.'

He looked concerned, and Megan was surprised he brought it up. Neither of them did heavy emotional stuff. It wasn't that kind of a friendship. He acted like her dad most of the time. Formal, reserved, detached. But she was good at distance too. For much of her life she'd felt like an observer of it. Reporting her inner, never-ending monologue. Was this detachment created by the void of her motherless state? Her parentless state? Had this detachment been created by a deep sense of not-belonging?

'Have you thought about it? Because if you haven't you must now.' He took her hand. She noted how strange it felt to be held by him, how embarrassing. She slapped his knee.

'Thanks for caring. I have thought about it. Not a lot. But a bit. Difficult to put into words. I'll need another drink or four.'

'Look, why don't we go to my room? Raid the mini-bar. And if you feel like talking you can. You can cry without fear of public embarrassment.' He pulled her up from the couch.

'Without fear of embarrassing you more like, Mr North.'

'You know me well, Ms Evens. C'mon.'

He released her hand and she followed him across the lobby to the lifts.

Chapter Twenty-six

Megan's head pounded. Her body was a dead weight. She had lost sensation in her legs, paralysed in her dreams. She focused on her toes, trying to move them. It was such a supreme effort. Then a tingling. She followed it up her calves and to her thighs. Not paralysed then. Sunlight bored through her eyelids. Daytime. She could not bear to open her eyes. With them closed she could continue the falsehood she had built since she came round several minutes ago.

Although she hadn't yet turned her head or moved her limbs she knew she was lying on the right hand side of the bed. The side closest to the window. She forced her left eye open, turning it sharp left, straining until it hurt. She didn't move, she was as still as a rock. A shock of straw coloured hair.

Closing her eye again she lay rigid in the bed and rifled through her scrambled brain for fragments of the night before. They came in a rush. His hand on her skin, stroking her lower arm, on the soft side, pushing up the sleeve of her cardigan, tracing the purple-blue tracks of her veins. The brush of his lips against the crook of her elbow, the melting in her abdomen, her craving for touch, tenderness, her desire.

Jack's room, late in the evening, sitting on the floor leaning against the wall beside the mini-bar, drained from mixed emotions and too much vodka. He brushed his fingers against hers, a deliberate, conscious move. She asked him to stop.

'Because if you touch me, I will want to touch you and then there'll be no stopping it,' she'd said.

He withdrew only for her to reach out and squeeze his shoulder. She meant it to soften the rebuke, but he bent forward and kissed her hand. This time she did not ask him to stop.

'Megan, Megan, Megan,' he whispered, more to himself than to her, it seemed, 'if things were different I could tell you that you have the most beautiful skin. The most sublime skin.' She could feel his breath on her wrist. He took hold of her again and ran his fingers, firmly, up her arm then kissed her at the elbow. She watched as he did it, gazing at his crown, the flaxen fringe obscuring his face. So familiar and yet so strange. And then she was lost. She sank into the careless world of desire, allowing herself to forget. She closed her eyes and felt the blood in her veins rush to her tips. As oxygen flowed through her, lifting her, rendering her weightless, she took his face in her hands and kissed his forehead, eyelids, nose and lips. It was clumsy and tender, hasty yet lingering. His hair smelt of crushed almonds, he tasted sharp, and fresh, and creamy.

They stripped where they sat, kissing, caressing, exploring. Like finding a secret chamber in a house you've lived in all your life. They didn't remove all their clothes. She pushed him back, down onto the floor, fumbling with his belt, drunken, awkward. He grappled with the metal button at the top of her jeans. She pushed his hand away, released the waistband, pushed her trouser legs and knickers down to her knees, pulled one leg out and lowered herself onto him. He gasped as she did so and opened his mouth as if to speak. She covered his mouth with a sweaty palm, closed her eyes and began to roll. Her hair swung backwards and forwards as she moved, sticking to her face. He swept it away. She felt his hands, smooth like a woman's, on her breasts, thighs and neck. He tried to slow her down but she pushed harder and faster, the energy within her volcanic and dangerous.

Megan was perspiring. She wasn't sure if it was the alcohol, a hangover sweat, or panic and shame. She couldn't remember getting into bed. She felt under the sheets for remnants of clothing. She had knickers on and a t-shirt. One of his judging by the amount of fabric bunched around her middle.

The persistent thumping in her skull took over and dulled her mind. She concentrated on visualizing herself without a headache and just as she thought the pain was subsiding, her heart palpitated wildly. She remembered some more.

Now the yellow wall was hurting her eyes. Already her physical memory was blurring, like a dream it slipped away. It hurt so much. She felt the beauty of the night and wanted to remember every tiny, intimate moment of it. It all began with talking, the sharing of her fears and doubts. But once she'd done with words a physical need took over and she was powerless to stop it.

Megan fought hard. She would not let them come, those tears. She would shake and crumple and wake him. She was confused and frightened and hung over. And vulnerable. The feeling unsettled her. She felt powerless and stupid.

She could lose his friendship and the thought was unbearable. She would not allow that to happen.

Megan slipped one leg out from under the duvet and placed it on the ground. The wooden floor felt cool against the sole of her foot. She pushed the duvet from her body, sat upright and swung her other leg over to meet the one already resting on the floor. A breath slipped out from her sore lungs. She had smoked too much, again. They both had. Her throat hurt. She had talked and talked.

Anodyne and sparse the hotel room offended her eyes. Jack's room was a replica of her own, though a little larger, and she doubted that others in the hotel differed in any significant way. It should have looked better, with the winter morning's soft sunshine pouring through the thin curtains, but in fact it high-lighted the room's insipid qualities. Megan thought wistfully that perhaps she had slipped into another dimension and that she would return to her room and the real world and all would be well. That it had never happened, and that she and Jack would continue as normal, searching for her mother, the key to Cerdic's survival.

Megan heard the squeaking of a trolley from the corridor. The rattling of mop and bucket. It was getting louder. It stopped. She glanced at the clock on the bedside table. It was 10.30am. They had slept late. She realized with horror that the trolley would have a pusher and that pusher was a cleaner, doing the rounds, and Jack's room could be next, and if the cleaner knocked Jack might wake up. She scurried across the room, not daring to look back, and carefully clicked open the door. She peered out and motioned to a bored-looking maid to come back and clean the room later. The maid, a woman in her mid-twenties, nodded her consent disapprovingly. Though she knew it to be irrational Megan felt annoyed with the woman for her waspish disposition and knowing nod, and threw her a scowl before pulling the door to, immediately feeling foolish for her puerile behaviour. Of course the woman must have seen it a thousand times. Women in stranger's rooms. Men in rooms they shouldn't be in. All part of hotel life.

Draped neatly over one of the chairs by the desk were Megan's clothes. She couldn't remember tidying them up, it wasn't her style, and realized that Jack must have done it after she passed out. She picked up her bra, catching sight of her reflection in the long wall mirror as she did so. She had altered again. A stranger stared back at her. A foolish woman who had sex with friends in hotel rooms. A woman who no longer belonged, who wasn't who she thought she was. A woman with no mother, a father (father? She wasn't certain about this) she could picture but never know because he died a long, long time ago, an unknown history. A changeling. A foundling. A mystery.

Jack was right. She hadn't allowed herself to think about what all this meant to her. But it was a distraction, this discovering. The quest was about Cerdic. Elizabeth had raised her, Elizabeth was her mother. Nothing had changed for Megan. But she was deceiving herself that it didn't matter who her mother was.

Everything had changed. Not that she felt a strong, over-whelming urge to discover her true identity, her origins. She didn't. Hadn't. She wasn't sure what she felt about the very real possibility of meeting her biological mother. She expected to feel little, even nothing. The woman was a stranger to Megan and she to her. Why should they feel anything? Let alone some nebulous, mystical bond simply because some code, a random strand of DNA, had been passed from one to the other.

But her perception of Elizabeth, and Elizabeth's story, had altered everything. How could she have held that lie? Had she lived with it for so long that it became truth? At least to Elizabeth.

Megan felt like a forgery. Someone created to fulfil a fantasy. Stolen to replace another.

A door slammed along the corridor. Megan turned away from her reflection and pulled on her jeans. She smoothed her hair against her head and swathed herself in the long, thick cardigan. As she twisted the door handle she turned to look at the bed. She couldn't leave like this. Creeping out like a thief. This wasn't an ordinary one-night stand. This was Jack and it would be appalling to leave this way.

She tiptoed to the desk and searched for some paper. Surely there would be some? Hotel rooms always had paper and pens. Always had, always would. Surely? The drawers were stiff. Megan could feel her patience and resolve evaporating.

'I used the paper the other day. There wasn't much,' said Jack, his croaky voice floating across the sunbeams.

Megan gripped the desk edge before replying, as casually as she could muster, 'Jack! I didn't want to wake you. Sorry.' She didn't turn round, still fumbling for the non-existent paper.

'You didn't wake me.'

'Oh.' Her heart thumped, sweat oozed from her pores. She thought she might be sick. She must turn and look at him but her feet were glued to the spot.

His obvious regret cut deep. So deep that she didn't feel the pain immediately. That came later, much later.

'What idiots we are.'

Megan hadn't the faintest idea what he was talking about. She said, 'Sorry?' She was still facing away from him, let alone meeting his eyes. She saw him running his fingers through his hair in the reflection and wondered if he could see her as she could see him. She lowered her head, and wondered how he had ever found her attractive. She was so embarrassed.

Megan turned and remembered to smile. She nodded her head. Jack was sat up in bed, his hair on end, eyes puffy.

'God, I was drunk,' he said, filling the silence. 'Can't remember a thing.'

'Nor me,' Megan said, complicit in the lie.

'Would you like some coffee? There's instant in the tray.' It was a ridiculous thing to say. He coughed, trying to cover his embarrassment, Megan thought.

'No, thanks. I think I'll head off back to my room. Shower and stuff.'

'Good idea. I'll make some calls and we can get together a bit later. Decide on a plan of action.' Jack clapped his hands together, rubbed them, and rested his chin on his knuckles.

'I'll buzz,' he said.

'Okay.'

'Bye then.'

'Bye.' She waved before closing the door behind her. She heard a muffled groan as she skittered down the corridor. She wondered if he'd tell Julie.

Hailstone-hard water flayed Megan's back. She'd been standing in the shower for so long that it was running cold and she was shivering. The temperature gauge was useless. She didn't care. Though she tried to focus on the day's task, ways of finding the woman Teresa talked about, the night kept coming back to her. She replayed the evening over and over, beat by beat. How it all started.

There was only one easy chair in Jack's hotel room. So they'd sat on the floor next to the bar, leaning against the wall, legs splayed out in front of them like students at a party. They didn't speak for a while, content with their thoughts. Megan had been swinging her feet from side to side. They were big, like a clown's. So were Jack's. Then he broke the silence.

'When I was younger I often daydreamed that my parents were still alive, that the Millingtons had adopted me after I was given away as a baby. You know how it is as a teenager. Everyone fantasizes about being adopted because they hate the parents they've got. That particular fantasy was denied me because I knew I was adopted, so I'd dream about the Norths still being around and me looking them up.'

The air was charged and sparking.

Megan had never hated Elizabeth enough to dream that she might have other parents to look up. That Elizabeth was so different to her they couldn't possibly be related.

'I knew people who talked like that. I never felt it. Not if I'm honest,' she said.

He leant in, a faint whiff of almonds. 'So you never longed for another mother after you guys had a fight?'

'We didn't fight much. There were tensions but I didn't ever not want her to be around. Not to be connected to her. I wanted to be more connected if anything. But I did long to escape Wales. I felt it was too small for me somehow, that I didn't fit in, that I was different.' She paused, then said, 'I sound like a twat.'

'Most teenagers are confused. Comes with the territory,' he said. She could smell the whisky on his breath. Smokey, warm.

'Elizabeth is my mother. I feel nothing about the fact that she didn't give birth to me, that I'm not a part of her. I wish she was my biological mother. That she matched. Life would be a lot simpler. This is absolutely about Cerdic.'

'Honestly? Your nature might have driven you to seek her out even without a need. Aren't you intrigued?'

'Not really.'

She'd bitten her bottom lip, then admitted, 'Perhaps a little.'

He raised an eyebrow and half-smiled. She returned the grin and said, 'Well, yes, okay. You're right. But intrigued, that's all. Just to see her. Them. If it is them. I don't actually feel anything about it all. Like discovering another part of myself, the missing link, or other kinds of crap.'

'You told me you were interested in the mystical, once.'

'I was a teenager then.'

'You felt different. Perhaps the universe was trying to tell you something. You got older, and cynical, buried your instincts?'

'Don't give me that, Jack. You don't buy into any of that crap either. You've never expressed any great longing to have known your real parents, to find out more about them. You loved the Millingtons like I love Elizabeth.'

'I have concrete, clear memories of the Norths. I know where I come from and it's impossible to say how I might feel if I didn't. I might want to discover the real me.'

'There's nothing real about memories, Jack. Memory is the great trickster. An illusion of reality. We form and mould and shape our memories to suit ourselves. Other people create them for us too. Parents, friends. Sometimes it's impossible to know what is real, what really happened. We believe what we wish to believe. What others want us to believe. We make our own histories.'

'And what about the fact that Elizabeth lied to you? That must make you feel something. Betrayed? Let down. Baffled?'

'I don't know. I was angry at first. Because of Cerdic. And then I saw that the woman I should be angry with is Hannah. She was the selfish, careless one. She chose not to ask too many questions about the egg donor. She chose not to confront the fact that she was an old woman, that she was unlikely to see her child into adulthood. Elizabeth was trying to protect me.'

'Perhaps.'

She rolled a cigarette as she spoke, working the tobacco and paper with her fingers. 'And then I thought about the random quality of life, of creation. Why do we do it? There is little, if any, certainty despite all our scientific and technological knowledge. We're doing our best to control Mother Nature, genetic engineering, cloning and so on, but she can still outwit us. There are still imperfect people in the world, incurable diseases, mutating viruses. And that's good. Life should be unpredictable, challenging, extraordinary and mundane, beautiful and imperfect. It is right that we rail against nature but it is equally right that she reigns.'

He stared at her.

'What?' she stared back at him, a wry smile slipping over her features.

'Nothing. Carry on, Ms Evens. Fascinating argument.'

She raised an eyebrow, licked the cigarette paper, took another gulp of vodka and continued, 'What I'm trying to say is that once I calmed down I realized that no one can foresee everything. That's the gamble of life. And if Hannah had known more about her donor and hereditary conditions and so on, I would not have

313

been created, which means that Cerdic would not exist, which is completely unimaginable and unacceptable.'

'God, yes. No Megan Evens. Unbearable.'

Megan thumped Jack's shoulder. 'What is this drive, this instinct to reproduce? If parents could see into the future... The work, the pain, the sleepless nights, the fear.'

'Don't ever think of applying to work in population protection. You're not sounding like an advocate for parenthood,' said Jack.

'Oh, for sure there are the small everyday pleasures. The pride. The love,' she said, choking with emotion, thinking of Cerdic, before controlling herself and continuing, 'but on paper the negatives outweigh the positives. And we don't need that heir thing anymore, and no parent in their right mind expects their kids to look after them when they get old. It would be nice, but it isn't a sure thing. So why do we still do it? The rational side says no, but procreation is a thing of the heart, not the head. It's all about love. The giving and receiving, but mostly the giving, because every parent loves their offspring more than their offspring loves them. And perhaps it's more nebulous than that. It's a primitive drive. And for all our sophistication we are deeply primitive. So who am I to berate Hannah for her need, her drive? Or Elizabeth for her nature? For her need to love and be loved. I've come back to nature haven't I? Have I argued against interfering with nature? God, I'm drunk. Perhaps it's all shit.'

'You did say that we must rail against Mother Nature. She can be horribly cruel,' he said. 'We'll save Cerdic, Megan. I know it.' He tapped his foot against hers. That was the first touch.

An arrow of icy shower water hit her right eye. She squealed in pain but was glad. She deserved it. She stepped out of the shower.

The softness of his skin had surprised her.

She brushed her wet hair and rubbed her battered flesh with the luxuriant hotel towel. Her skin was pink, orange and purple. Blotchy, covered in goose bumps.

His lovemaking had been skilled and tender. The skill was

314

unsurprising given his reputation and endless lovers. The tenderness shocked her. It wasn't like sex. More like love-making. After she came she lay on the floor, spent. But he had more to give, and he gave and gave. As she dried between her legs she could still detect a trace of him.

The humming of her mulmed broke her thoughts. She pushed the talk button and then quickly pushed the vision off. She was naked and felt doubly exposed.

'Hi, Mum. Good, good. Not much to report.' The lie slipped out. 'How are things there?'

Megan listened to Elizabeth rattling about the weather, the birds visiting the garden.

'And Cerdic? How is he?' Just the shape of his name in her mouth made her entire body throb. His absence actually hurt.

'He's lovely. And he's dying to speak with you.' Elizabeth called him over and Megan wondered if her mother realized what she'd said.

'Hello, Mummy.' The slight lisp like a balm.

'Hello, handsome. What you playing?'

Chapter Twenty-seven

Jack looked down the street. It was narrow and dark. Washing hung from one balcony to another, row upon row of laundry formed a strange bunting. Jack wondered if it would ever dry in a temperature that rarely strayed above freezing. Although there was no snow on the ground the frost was so heavy that bald trees bore white leaves. A feral tabby cat meandered from one doorway to the next, then stood, frozen, and glared at Jack. The creature unnerved him.

Earlier he'd called Megan and explained that it might be best for him to locate and visit the woman Teresa Micu had talked of, the sad woman, alone. It would be a shock to be confronted with Megan even if she didn't turn out to be related, the physical resemblance to the daughter and the mother's history of mental health problems might have a less than desirable effect. What he didn't say was that they needed to put some space between them. He was confused and hurt, and surprisingly guilty. He had betrayed Julie and not been truthful with Megan. He'd acted like the old Jack North and he didn't like it. Megan sounded hung-over and embarrassed. Regretful. No doubt she was relieved not to have to see him.

In the breast pocket of his jacket was a photograph of Megan taken when she was a girl, sixteen or seventeen years old, sent over by Elizabeth and printed out in the hotel reception.

Elizabeth had sounded nervous and fragile when Jack spoke with her. It hadn't surprised him that Megan hadn't told her about the Petrescus, though he wished Megan had warned him. Breaking the news to Elizabeth made him feel like a complete bastard.

'You've found her then, that's a relief, I knew that you would, you're both marvellous you are, marvellous. Wonderful news, wonderful, for Cerdic, for Megan. She didn't say when I called the other day...' Her voice trailed away. 'How is Meg? Is she looking forward to meeting her?' Elizabeth said brightly, too brightly.

'Steady on, Elizabeth. Early days. We don't know for sure that it's her, the donor, and even if it is she may not match. She'll almost certainly be a carrier herself, and then we'll need to find and talk to other family members, if there are any, before we find a match,' he said.

'Of course. How silly of me.'

Jack softened and ended, 'Don't worry, Elizabeth. Megan loves you, nothing is going to alter that. Nothing.'

When the hotel receptionist handed over the photograph of Megan Jack thought he would find it difficult to look at it. Every time he thought of her a sharp pain skewered him. With each stab he bled a little. What a mess.

You should never have let her in. You fool, Jack North. You promised you'd stay away from the complicated women.

He took out the photograph in the cab on the way to the market district on the other side of the city. She was exactly as he had imagined she would be. Almost the same girl he remembered traipsing across the EBC canteen floor fourteen years ago: gauche, as ill at ease with her striking beauty as she was confident in her intellect. Could it be possible that there was another like her? Jack didn't think so.

He looked up the street again. The one running parallel to this had proved fruitless as had many others. Jack's feet throbbed and every step felt like a descent onto broken glass without shoes. He had worked quickly and efficiently that day and he was exhausted. The high brought on by their lovemaking had faded. Often he found labour the best way to work off a hangover and push distracting thoughts from his mind. He had been back to Clinik Stamenov to check records for a donor named Petrescu. It was a common name and there was mention of a number of Petrescus though none matched the timescale or profile of the woman Teresa described. He checked the electoral register. There were no records of a Monica Petrescu living in the district, but when Jack called on Teresa and her grandson to double check she was adamant that this was the district she had seen Monica in.

'I was shopping in the meat market,' she'd said. 'She said

they were close to home.'

So Jack had knocked on doors. He had no other option. Mostly he was met with suspicion, understandably he thought. And then a young woman, a girl really, had suggested the street next to this. But that too proved useless and as a last stab before darkness fell completely he'd banged on a cheerful red door in the adjoining street. A solemn young man opened it. Jack asked if there was a family called Petrescu nearby and Jack's heart leapt when a spark of recognition flashed across the man's face. He nodded slowly, gravely, and pointed three doors up.

As he stood before a dark green door Jack had no idea what he would say to whoever opened it, assuming there was someone at home. The blood rushed in his head. He clutched a Romanian phrase book, a promotional postcard from Clinik Stamenov and the photograph of Megan. Pictures of Cerdic and more up to date images of Megan were on his mulmed. He knocked hard, three times in quick succession. There was no reply. He tried again.

He was about to leave when he heard the bolt being eased from its hold. There was no doubting the resemblance between the young woman stood before him and Megan. Tall, lean, pale yet dark, she was both wicked witch and fairy princess. Like a manicured Megan, sharp edges filed away, rounded off, polished. More conventionally pretty, less arresting. Jack was so taken aback that he was unable to speak. The words locked in his chest. Finally he pushed out a stumbling hello and asked if her mother was at home, Madam Petrescu. He had practised his Romanian whenever he could. He was about to find out if it was passable.

'Mama! Mama!' Words tumbled from the girl's mouth, tripping over one another. A middle-aged woman appeared out of the darkness, gliding into the feeble light of the doorway, the haze of the streetlights throwing an orange glow on her rounded cheeks. She too was tall with dark hair, though the jet was shot through with ribbons of grey. A tight mouth and sharp nose, penetrating eyes. The resemblance was much less marked than in the girl but Jack thought it was there. He felt as if he'd found the pot of gold at the end of the rainbow.

In terrible, broken Romanian he pushed out his carefully rehearsed speech: that he believed a friend of his could be related to them. Her name was Megan. He hoped what he said was at least an approximation of this. The woman looked blank, he wished he had waited for an interpreter; his impatience had got the better of him and now he was paying for such haste. He took out the photograph of Megan. The glow on the mother's cheeks faded, their curved shapeliness seemed to have collapsed. She babbled to the girl, waving her hands, then the girl shooed her mother inside before stepping forward and pulling the door behind her. She spoke slowly and deliberately, enunciating every syllable, shaking her head violently. 'She has only one child. Go.' And with that she stepped back inside and slammed the door in Jack's face.

He stood there a while, remembering her words, her expression, referring to his book, checking his understanding of her words. Of her tone. He had made no mention that Megan might be a daughter, another child of her mother. He had said relative, he was sure of it. He was also sure that Monica Petrescu was Megan's biological mother and the girl her sister. But why did the girl keep her mother from him? She had virtually shoved her back inside the house.

Back at the hotel Jack went straight to his room; he did not call on Megan to tell her his news. He would wait. He wondered if he had been foolish. If another approach would have been more effective. The girl disturbed him – there was something immovable about her. He was worried. On the balcony he lit a cigarette, the first of the day. You stupid bastard, Jack North. I hope to God you've not blown it, he cursed. Megan will never forgive you.

They ate a light supper of soup and potato cakes at a restaurant close to the hotel where local musicians entertained the diners; Megan had wanted to get out having spent most of the day in her room, and, Jack suspected, chose the restaurant because the wandering minstrels in it would provide a welcome distraction from talking to him. It was snowing when they left. Inside the restaurant Megan was taciturn. When the musicians put down their instruments for a break, Jack rambled, filling the awkwardness with trivial nonsense: anecdotes from his day, gossip from the EBC offices. Megan smiled and laughed politely, though she barely looked at Jack. He wondered if it would always be like this between them from now on.

On the short walk back Megan said again, 'So there was no one home?'

'No. Lucky really. I'll have an interpreter tomorrow,' he said, kicking the dusting of snow on the ground. 'Do you think we'll see snow in the south of England again? In our lifetime?' Current affairs was safe, unlike affairs of the heart.

'Greenhouse gas emissions fell dramatically after 2015...'

'In the west...'

'But we were the main culprits. We've kept them kind of low since, though we're relaxing a little too much lately... It takes time but earth will recover to some degree. Left alone nature repairs.'

'It's rather lovely, isn't it?' Jack was desperate to cheer her up.

'I'd like to have a snowball fight with Cerdic one day. I remember it snowing one February in Wales. I must have been eight or nine, I'd never seen it before, and I was so excited that I lay face down in it and rolled around like a newly washed dog in dirt. It was crumbly and fine, it wasn't great snow for making snowballs Mum said, and when I ran it through my hands it reminded me of flaking butter into flour, like pastry making.'

As she reminisced Jack collected a ball of the snow from the bonnet of a parked car and lobbed it at her. It hit her in the face, and she squealed and said, 'That's it, North. This is war.' She ran after him, throwing badly aimed snowballs.

Small puddles of melted ice collected at their feet in front of the hotel reception. As they collected their cardkeys Jack asked Megan what she would do while he went to call on Monica Petrescu the following day.

'I'm going to check out the sperm donor records. Assuming there are any, which I doubt,' she said, without enthusiasm, her joviality fading rapidly.

'Why not wait until I feedback?'

They moved to the lifts. 'Because I can't bear waiting around. You sure I shouldn't come?'

'Sure.' He hoped she wasn't going to push it. She could be very persuasive and he didn't think he could resist.

'Even if she is who we think she is, she might not agree to help, she might be a carrier, she probably won't match, there might be no other relatives, and before I contact Owen's son we need to be sure they used Owen's semen. God, I feel nauseous just thinking about it…'

Jack was dismayed by Megan's pessimism, though he'd had similar doubts that day. Pessimism frightened him, and despair. Too close to depression. He remembered Eleanor, his first wife. He tried to lift Megan's mood. 'There's the daughter. We know that,' he said, forgetting that he'd lied and said there was no one home.

'We think that.' Her brow furrowed.

'Slip of the tongue. Trust me, there's hope.' He wondered why he said that. Hope was a dangerous thing. He'd hoped for everlasting love once. After Eleanor went he'd sworn never to do so again. In the absence of the real thing a semblance of love would do. And Julie was as good a catch as he could hope for.

They bade each other goodnight rather formally and went their separate ways, both lost in their own private woes. Jack headed to the bar.

Jack met his interpreter, Gyl Savu, a fellow journalist, early the next morning. He'd found it difficult to rise and even then, thirty minutes after he'd dragged himself from the comfort of his bed his eyes were still bloodshot and surrounded by dark, puffy skin. Gyl was a cheerful character with a confident, ever so slightly sleazy aura. Jack had worked with him in the Balkans early in his career and they had stayed in touch ever since, helping each other out from time to time with background, sources and contacts. But this wasn't a favour; Gyl was interested in the story from a professional point of view also, and though Jack was loath to share it, he needed him. Megan and Cerdic needed him to get it right this time and they were more important than the story. He doubted he would get another chance. Nevertheless, Jack told Gyl only as much as he had to. In the cab to the Petrescu house they agreed that it would be better if Gyl approached Monica alone. Jack's presence could be a barrier; Monica might trust another Romanian. And the daughter needed to be kept well away.

'I've a feeling she's encountered journalists before, and is, perhaps understandably, guarded,' Jack said.

'I will pose as a middle-man from one of these agencies that reunites people,' replied Gyl, chuckling.

Jack asked the cab to stop a few streets away; they would walk the remainder of the journey. The day was sunny and bright; by the looks of things it had snowed all night and a thick layer had transformed the area. Jack hardly recognized it. He gave Gyl the address and they agreed to meet in a coffee shop a few blocks away.

'Ask her to come and meet me. Any time, she can name the place,' Jack said, as he waved Gyl on his way, wishing he felt as optimistic as his words implied.

Jack ordered a drink and sat at the window watching the world go by: children on their way to school, heads down, dragging their feet, creating train tracks in the snow, adults on their way to work, faces locked in concentration, trying to avoid slipping and falling on the treacherous sidewalks, old ladies walking their dogs, streams of yellow piss deflowering the virgin snow on the verges. He finished his coffee and ordered another despite the exorbitant price tag.

A brass bell above the door announced the arrival of each new customer and with every tinkle Jack turned from the window expectantly. When he saw Gyl pushing his way in a little later he knew the visit had not gone well.

'She was on her way to work so the timing was not good—'

Jack interrupted, 'But?'

'I do not think it would have made any difference if she had

had all the time in the world.' Jack sighed; Gyl continued, 'She is not interested. She is a very stubborn woman.'

That figures, Jack thought. He said, 'Did you suggest she might be mother to your client?'

'That is not the word I used. Relative, I said, as we agreed.'

'I'm a fool. Too soon after my visit. Her guard is up.' But there was no option. Time was something they didn't have. 'You offered money?'

'She virtually spat in my face.' Gyl smiled at the memory, and Jack realized that the grubbiness of the act didn't trouble Gyl as it did him.

'She's so defensive it has to be her. She doesn't want to acknowledge her past,' Jack said.

'She was very upset, very angry. It was a violent reaction, I have to say. We are on to something. I have done some digging of my own, I have names, women who donated at Clinik Stamenov. The director there is shifty, I do not trust the fellow. I was sniffing around a few years back, but did not get anywhere. I heard your people were too.' His use of 'we' made Jack nervous. This was his story. Jack's.

'Did you see anyone else there?'

'Should I? I thought you said she lived alone?'

'There are friends.'

Gyl ordered more coffee, and after his third cup Jack was feeling more jittery than ever. He needed Gyl for a while but he didn't want him too involved. Gyl had made it so clear he was a journalist, and the woman found this off-putting. Jack needed to appeal to Monica on a human level: Cerdic. He needed to get rid of Gyl.

'Look, why don't you go to Clinik Stamenov? Say you're working with Megan and me. You may turn up something we've missed,' Jack said, confident that Gyl would find nothing of any significance. Gyl thanked Jack profusely and left as soon as he'd finished his drink.

Rather than hailing a cab Jack decided to walk back to the main square; he needed to think. He checked his mulmed; there was no message from Megan. He walked and walked, following the mulmed's instructions, and it was only when he came to a dead end that he admitted the machine had let him down. He was lost. It was a narrow street, half in shade, not far from one of the university colleges. He guessed he wasn't far from the hotel, but he wasn't sure of the direction and his legs were beginning to ache from the exercise and the cold. He spotted a café and decided to go in; he could get a warm drink and ask for directions. If he could make himself understood.

The café was rustic in character, with plain wooden tables and benches, and a canteen style counter where the dishes of the day were displayed. Jack's mouth watered at the sight and smell of food; he'd risen too late for breakfast and was famished. It was late morning and the place was almost deserted. A serious-looking woman in a dark green cardigan and gold rimmed spectacles sat hunched in the corner, reading and picking at what Jack assumed to be a pastry of some sort. He sat down at a window table and picked up the menu. He longed for a piece of red meat: a steak or lamb shank smothered in a thick, rich sauce. There were no such luxuries on offer, only the usual cold climate stodge. A shadow appeared beside him and without looking up he pointed at the menu and ordered potato soup and a roll.

'You are American, yes?' the waitress said.

'I'm English,' he smiled and looked up, into the eyes of Monica Petrescu's daughter. She looked as surprised as he felt. She looked so pretty in her black shirt and trousers with her long hair tied back in a ponytail. So very pretty, and so very like Megan. Jack's heart pounded so hard he thought she must be able to hear it.

'We do not serve lunch until noon, Sir. You must choose from here,' she said, stumbling over her words and pointing to another section of the menu.

'Miss Petrescu?'

'Would you like a few minutes to decide, Sir?'

'We met, briefly, yesterday, at your house.'

'What do you want?' She seemed frightened now and Jack

resisted the urge to touch her.

'I am a friend. I wish you no harm, or your mother. I am trying to save a little boy's life. May I talk with you, please?' A man appeared behind the counter and called out something to the girl.

'I have to work. What can I get you?' she said.

'What time do you finish?' he said.

'I have college after.'

'What are you studying?'

'Medicine. What would you like to eat?' She licked the end of her pencil, poised above the note pad sat in her palm.

'It must be difficult, studying and working,' he said. Jack saw two routes in: she was a life-saver, and she needed money. He wanted to punch the air with his good fortune.

'You must order, Sir. Otherwise I get in trouble. Working, no chatting.' She glanced over her shoulder towards the counter, and Jack longed to hear the funny way she said chatting again.

'You agree to meet me, I'll order,' he said. The boss hollered across the café.

'Okay, okay. You win. Order,' she said.

It was dusk when Jack went back to meet the Petrescu girl. Megan had called, sounding low and looking tired; she had discovered nothing and he chose not to tell her what he was up to. He lied again and said that he had a lead on where Monica might work and was following it up.

The café was empty, another waitress wiped down the tables, and Jack wondered how on earth the place made any money. He stirred two heaped spoonfuls of sugar into his fruit tea and pushed back the cuticles on his fingernails. She was late. She could easily break her promise. He finished the tea and was toying with ordering another when she came through the door. She waved at the waitress, who was now hovering behind the counter, fussing with napkins and cutlery, and sat down opposite Jack.

She checked her watch and said, 'We do not have long, the café will be closing soon.'

'I wanted to talk to you about something that might have

happened to your mother when she was young, a teenager, like you,' he said.

'You said it was about a boy.' Her English was excellent.

He brought up a photograph of Cerdic and showed it to her and told her of his condition. He did not mention Megan.

'You are a reporter. We have your kind here before, years ago. We talk,' she corrected herself, 'my mother talked, about difficult, bad things. Very upsetting for her. Heart broken twice now. Promises were made. The people who did these things will be punished, they said. Then nothing. She will not talk again, she was very ill. I will not let that happen to Mama.' She straightened and folded her arms holding his gaze, defiant. You are so like Megan, he thought.

He felt a bit guilty. Journalism was a messy business. But necessary. 'I'm sorry,' he said, wondering how on earth this other journalist had found the Petrescus. Jack decided to break the habit of a professional lifetime and be entirely honest.

'I'm Jack North, a senior reporter with a large European news conglomerate. And although I believe there may be a story, a way to help your mother bring those who damaged her to justice, I am here on behalf of my friend, Megan Evens. The boy's mother.' He offered his hand and said, 'I don't even know your name.' He saw her eyes soften.

She said, 'I am Stela. Stela Petrescu.' Her arms remained folded across her chest.

Jack ran through the story once more, the sick boy who needed a donor, that she might be related to him, the image of Cerdic open on his mulmed. He asked Stela what she knew of her background. Stela was polite, but terse. She was the child of Monica and an unnamed father. There were no other children. Monica's parents were dead; she had no brothers or sisters. Alone, aside from her child. Like Megan, he thought, forgetting Elizabeth for a moment.

'I am sad for the boy, for your friend, but how can you be so sure? The other reporter said there were many, like my mother, not just here but in other towns and cities too. At first I did not understand, I was young, but I have heard the rumours.'

'We have some evidence. You look alike—'

'My mother needs to forget.'

'Your mother was ill? After the visit from the reporters?'

'They made promises, then nothing. She has been sick before I was born. I was her salvation.' Stela smiled at the memory, and Jack felt her loneliness. He imagined her childhood must have been stifling.

'Sick?' Jack said, as if this was news.

'The alcohol, drugs.' She added quickly, 'But she is a good mother, the best. I will not hurt her.'

'I don't doubt that, Stela. But if you are related, there are serious implications.'

She shook her head and frowned, puzzled.

He continued, 'You are young, but one day you too might be a mother. You could carry AMNA. Or your daughters. I'm sure your mother would want you to know.' The boss man came out from the kitchen rattling keys.

'We have to go, the café is closing,' Stela said briskly. 'I have to get home, Mama will worry.' She stood and collected her bag. She had not removed her coat.

'May I walk with you?' Jack said.

She looked unsure. 'Mama would not like me talking to you. I already say too much.'

He had to persuade her to meet with Megan. To convince her mother to test, to talk, about what happened to her, and others. This was not just about a headline; it was about a life. He needed to move quickly, time was running out. She would be gone soon and he doubted he could persuade her to meet him again. He followed her to the door. 'It must be difficult – working and studying,' he said.

'I would like more time for the studying. But the fees, they are costly, and my mother works as hard as she can.' She waved to the proprietor and stepped outside. 'I go now.'

The street lamps threw a haze over the snow. Icicles hung from bare branches. Jack shivered, pulled his coat around him and watched her go. Soon she would disappear round the corner. He was losing her. Damn it. He ran, shouting, 'There would be money. You could use it to help—'

'You think you can buy me, and my mother?' Her cheeks blazed and her nostrils flared; she stared directly at him before turning on her heels and marching on.

He shouted after her, 'I'm only asking that you meet my friend. Listen to her story. Make your decision then.'

She stopped again and turned, livid now. 'She is a reporter too, no?'

'She's a mother. With a son who is dying,' he screamed, his voice cracking at the edges.

Stela bowed her head. Jack hardly dared to breathe.

Finally, she said quietly, 'I will talk to my mother. Give me time. No promises.'

He walked towards her. 'Here are my details. Call me.'

He stood on the frozen corner, not feeling the cold at all, and watched her figure growing smaller as she disappeared into the night.

Chapter Twenty-eight

Two days later Stela Petrescu called. It was late in the afternoon, the sky was the colour of pewter. Megan sat opposite Jack in the hotel café attempting to compose a message to Cerdic and her mother, struggling to find the right words. She hadn't felt up to speaking with them, and writing wasn't proving any easier: the message was taking several drafts. Time had slowed to point of being almost stationary.

Megan had spent most of the day pacing round her room, gawping out of the window. In the morning, she'd followed an impulse to visit church, but when she stepped into the hushed air she'd felt like a fraud and left almost immediately. It reminded her of childhood visits to chapel. She'd hoped to offer a prayer, calm her nerves, but she wasn't a believer, and so she returned to the hotel and gazed into the clouds instead, wondering how anyone could believe there was something out there, controlling everything. Life seemed so random, and cruel.

Jack's mulmed purred and he leapt up and walked away from the table. She knew it must be Stela. She did not dare follow him; she sat still, her right hand clutching her left, pressed between her clenched thighs, as if she were trying to stay warm. She followed Jack with her eyes to the exit, where Jack leant against the arched wall, head down, looking into his mulmed.

As he closed the console and lifted his head Megan half stood, but her shaking knees forced her back down. He jogged back to the table, and she could not read his expression. His cheeks were flushed pink as if he had been drinking.

'Good news. We've had a stroke of luck. But we've got to play it carefully, very carefully indeed.'

'What did she say?'

'Monica Petrescu lost a baby, a boy, before she had Stela. The child died within hours of birth,' he said.

'Poor woman.'

'Stela says that Monica is extremely fragile. Stela's worried old wounds will open, wounds that Monica has spent half a lifetime trying to heal or forget. Or that old notions of her lost children being returned will destabilize her, especially if it turns out that you and Cerdic aren't related. The disappointment will be too much.'

Megan's heart was palpitating, her emotions jumbled. What if Monica Petrescu wanted Cerdic to replace her lost boy, for him to become part of her life? He has a mother, a grandmother, she thought, if anything he needs a male relative, a role model, not another cloying woman.

'I only want her to donate, or lead us to other relatives—' she said.

'You can't pick and chose like that Megan, it's not that simple. Or fair.'

'What if she is my mother? What if she wants to be part of my life? Fuck, that would be awful for Elizabeth. It would kill her. I'm not sure I'm ready for this, Jack.' Megan's fingers were shaking.

'You might be underestimating Elizabeth. Let's stick to the facts. Nothing is certain yet.'

Megan took a deep breath. Jack continued, 'Stay calm. Don't get emotional, unless you feel you need to, for leverage. "Do not break my mother's heart. She cannot take it," Stela said. I mentioned money.'

Megan pulled a face and said, 'Jack—'

'Quit the sanctimonious look. If it works...'

'Maybe this is Stela projecting stuff onto her mother? She might be jealous. After all, she's been everything to her mother for eighteen years and now, suddenly, there's the prospect of at least two other people who may have a claim on her mother?'

Jack shrugged. 'Possible.'

'When can we meet them?' Megan said.

'Tonight.'

'Great. No time to change their minds.'

'They want you to go alone.'

'Fine.'

'She asked how they would know it was you. I said, "Trust me, you'll know." '

Megan spent the next few, never-ending hours swerving between elation and fear. She couldn't allow herself to believe that this might be it. But her hope was hard to contain. Like a butterfly it fluttered from her net, wings spread, colourful and bright and beautiful before flickering out of sight again.

It took her ages to get ready. She fussed over what to wear in a way she hadn't done since her teenage years, trying on every item of clothing she'd brought. Nothing felt right. She wished she'd given herself time to go shopping, to buy something new. She applied her make-up carefully, touching up her eyeliner and lip gloss endlessly, chastising herself for her vanity. What did it matter what they thought? Everything it seemed. Ready early, she paced her hotel room waiting, fantasizing.

At the appointed time, Megan stood at the heavy green door of the Petrescu home. Her mouth was dry, her stomach churned. Unable to find a bell or knocker, she raised her fist but before she could strike the door creaked open. A young woman stood in front of her, apprehension and anticipation lurking in the shadows of her dark eyes.

'Stela?' whispered Megan, barely audible.

'Megan.'

It was like looking in a mirror, in a dream. Where everything appears normal. Until one looks a little closer and realizes that everything is a touch skewed. Megan quashed the urge to reach out and touch, to verify the veracity of the reflection in front of her. The dream could so easily have turned into nightmare. For here was another Megan. As she stared at her second self she saw a hint of a furrow in the brow, between the eyebrows, and recognized it as something that would develop with the passage of the years into a wrinkle, just like the fine line between her own brows.

She scanned the girl's face for differences. They were there: the hair a shade lighter, rinsed with red-brown, the almost imperceptible freckles on the bridge of the nose, which spilled out onto fuller cheeks. But the similarity over rode all else.

Moments passed then Stela said, 'We are like sisters.'

Megan thought a myriad of emotion should be swarming over her, but, in fact, she felt nothing. She looked and looked without self-consciousness. Stela did the same. Megan saw herself as the world might and it fascinated her. She jumped when Stela coughed and indicated that she enter.

Megan stepped inside and waited for Stela to pull the door to before following her down a dingy hall into the main living area. The room was drab, sparsely furnished, with an angry fire crackling in the corner. A shabby rug, the only adornment on the bare tiles, collected embers. Stela invited Megan to sit and she perched on the edge of an easy chair next to the fire. Another chair sat opposite and next to that a low stool.

'I will fetch my mother,' Stela said.

Alone in the room Megan opened her coat and removed her gloves. Her fingers were naked; she had forgotten her ring. Panic drenched her. When had she seen it last? She couldn't remember and she was afraid. It was a bad omen.

In an attempt to calm her rising panic she stood and looked around. Under no other circumstances would she have attempted to trace Monica. And yet, here in this little room, she longed for these women, these strangers, to like her. She sat and returned to watching the flames flickering, mesmerized by the golden tongues. She worried her bare finger. She heard footsteps on the tiles and swivelled to face the woman she believed gave her life.

Monica Petrescu stopped in the middle of the room and raised her hand to her mouth. Tears formed in the corners of her grey eyes and she muttered something in Romanian. Stela translated. 'She said everyone told her she was crazy, years ago, when she knew she had been robbed but had no proof.'

Megan shifted uncomfortably on her seat; she didn't know how to behave. She stood and offered her hand. Trembling, Monica took her hand and then pulled back, as if she had received an electric shock. Monica ran from the room. Stela went after her,

332

slamming a door behind them.

Unsure what to do, Megan waited uncertainly, shifting from one foot to the next, the sound of voices rising above the noise of the fire. She felt so uncomfortable but she couldn't leave. She pressed her thumbs into her palms over and over, looking round the room. She shivered despite the fire.

Megan noticed a picture on the mantelpiece and bent in to study it. It looked like Monica with a girl of ten or eleven: Stela, dressed in a crisp uniform. First day at a new school, Megan guessed. She thought of a similar photograph of Elizabeth's, taken outside Tŷ Mawr – Megan's first day at high school. Monica had an arm around Stela's back, the other hand resting on her near shoulder. Megan could almost see herself in the picture, standing to Monica's left: the proud older sister. She felt her Adam's apple harden, her throat constricting, tears threatening, and was confused by this spring of emotion. How different her life might have been had she been born of Monica here in Romania. What might have become of her? Would the faulty gene have made itself known? Would she have loved this woman as she loved Elizabeth? More than likely. But Monica had Stela and Elizabeth would have had no one. She wondered did Monica spend hours, days, months, years waiting for, even expecting, the eager knock at the door? The lamb returning to the fold. Did she imagine the people her eggs might have gone on to become? The lives that may have been led. Had she hoped that one day, it might come to this? Such hope had almost destroyed her, and now that she was better Megan was here, stirring it all up again. Megan felt terrible, and guilty, and humbled by the power of such loss. She wondered if she was a disappointment to Monica. She turned from the photograph and tried to blink away the thoughts. She was here to save Cerdic not to discover a long lost family.

Stela and Monica's voices rose. It sounded like an argument, jagged words thrown across the air, penetrating the walls. The words held rage and tears and retching sobs. Like a child's. Megan heard the sound of Cerdic crying and her heart flipped. She could wait no longer. She stood in this miserable, bleak house that reeked of loss because her son was dying and these women might be able to help save him from a lingering, undignified death. Not because they were good, or special, or unique. Because they might be compatible. Have good blood. Shared DNA, not experience.

She stepped towards to the door that led, she assumed, to the kitchen, then took a deep breath and tapped before pushing it ajar. Both women stopped and looked at her with eyes glassy with surprise and emotion.

She had no idea what to say. Then, addressing Stela, she said, 'Your mother has had a shock. She didn't expect... We all look so alike—'

'We cannot be sure of anything,' Stela barked.

'I didn't mean—' Megan looked at Monica who was leaning against a cooker, shaking, her foundation streaked and mascara running down her cheeks, and smiled. Monica stumbled forward and clasped Megan's hands, babbling unintelligible words, all the while looking into her eyes. 'What is she saying?' Megan said, turning to Stela.

Stela did not reply and when Monica began to stroke Megan's cheek she lunged forward and pulled her mother away, whispering in her ear. Monica crumpled immediately and her body shook with convulsive sobs. Stela led her past a stunned Megan back to the living room where she lowered her into the easy chair before throwing a blanket over her lap as if Monica were an old woman or an invalid.

'Go. Now. You see how my mother is.'

Megan discerned brittleness in her tone, and it dawned on her that Stela was frightened, not only for her mother, but for herself. Monica sat perfectly still, as if in a trance, or drugged.

'May I come back? Please?'

Stela shook her head.

Megan felt Cerdic's life slipping away, and in one final, desperate, and later Jack would say inspired, act she took out her mulmed with the image of Cerdic on the beach at Harlech on the home screen and held it in Monica's direction. Crying, she

334

whispered, 'For my boy, please?'

Monica said haltingly, in English, 'We help.'

Stela shouted at her mother in Romanian, but Monica ignored her and repeated, 'We help.'

Megan reached out and touched Monica's arm, 'La Revedere: thank you.'

As she stepped on to the pavement Megan turned to Stela and said, 'I understand that you are afraid for your mother.'

'You understand nothing…'

'If tests prove that we're not related it will be another dreadful blow. She'll fall back into old habits, you'll have to care for her, abandon your dreams of university success and a career in medicine—'

'You are not looking for a mother, and she will not try to be your mother, it is too late for that perhaps, but she will want to get to know you. Are you ready for that?'

Astonished by the younger woman's perception, Megan pulled her hat down over her ears and said, 'Are you?'

'I will help if I match because you will pay me, and this will enable me to finish my studies, to give up waiting tables.'

'I'm glad we understand each other. I'll be back tomorrow to collect samples for a DNA test. I'll take them back to Britain.' And with that, she left.

The first thing Megan did when she returned to her room was search for her ring. It didn't take long. A cleaner had been at work – the bed had been made, the scent of laundered sheets filled the room, and the ring sat on the dressing table next to a vase of plastic flowers. It was a good sign, and as she slipped it back on her finger she realized that Stela had never doubted that they were related. She'd said, 'If I match.'

Chapter Twenty-nine

'Here we are, home, sweet, home,' Jack said as the fasten seat belts sign flashed and pinged for the third time.

Megan leant across him to look out of the oval window; she misjudged the distance and banged her head against the plastic. She could feel his breath on the back of her neck; he was nervous. She pushed her nose up against the glass. Wisps of white-grey cloud faded to reveal a spread of patchwork green fields, and though the view was impaired by the rain splashes and grime on the windows it was unmistakably Britain. Megan's heart surged. She sat back up and said, 'For Christ's sake, doesn't anyone, anywhere, clean aeroplane windows? One day, I'd like an untainted view. It's not too much to ask, is it?'

'Indeed not. It's always the little things, isn't it? That make life worth living,' Jack said.

And Megan thought of the way Cerdic sat in front of the mulmed watching his favourite programme, back impossibly straight, wrapped in a moth-eaten blanket, no matter what the temperature; the way his tongue moved in his mouth when he read in bed at night, struggling to sound out the letters. She heard his slight lisp. In her mind's eye she saw the look Elizabeth gave him before dishing up a sweet treat. 'Yes,' she said, 'the little things.' Tucked in the side pocket of her suitcase, carefully wrapped in layers and layers of protective padding were two carefully labelled tubes of hair and saliva. Human fibre and waste on which a life hinged.

'You'll be with him soon,' Jack said.

'Can't wait.'

The plane began its descent, and Megan gripped the armrests. It was habit but it gave her energy and excitement a focus. Jack went to place his hand over hers; he didn't like flying, never had. He drew away at the last moment, afraid to touch her she imagined. As casually as she could, she took her hands off the armrest. She watched him squeeze the plastic rests so hard she thought they might break under his grasp. She remembered the mound of his belly, the gingery blonde hairs trailing from his chest down beneath the elastic waist of his underpants. She'd laid her face on that spongy white belly, enjoying the flesh enveloping her cheek. As they drew to the end of the runway the engines revved defiantly for the last time before settling to a harmonious hum. Jack's knuckles were white.

The journey through the airport seemed interminable. Passport control was easy; Romania was a country of federal Europe so they breezed through, but there was a delay with baggage, and then Jack was pulled over at customs. A regulation spot check the official claimed, though Megan tried to make light of it and said Jack was shifty looking. The official remained straight-faced, and Megan fell to an edgy waiting. Jack told her to go on ahead; he would find her in the arrivals lounge, but Megan would have none of it. She needed him – for moral support.

Megan was apprehensive about seeing Elizabeth again. They had not spoken since she left a brief message after meeting the Petrescu women. She had stated baldly that there was a 'higher than average chance' that Monica was the donor of the egg implanted into Hannah, and that she, Megan, was looking forward to getting home. Elizabeth had responded with a stark note saying that she too was looking forward to Megan's return, as was Cerdic, who missed his mummy dreadfully, and that they would be at the airport to meet her if she could forward the flight information.

The contents of Jack's bags lay scattered across the table, dirty laundry, a twisted, near-empty tube of toothpaste, a battered history book. Jack never read fiction. He remained nonchalant, and when the official gave him the nod he began to fold his clothes, placing them carefully back into his bags. The official asked him gruffly to speed up. Megan went to help, but Jack said, 'Leave it.' And she stepped aside, waiting patiently while Jack repacked his bags. The official was less patient as other passengers streamed past.

'I have a quota. Can't stand here all day,' he said, and Megan saw Jack slow his pace further, tormenting the man deliberately.

At last Jack was done. 'C'mon, Ms Evens, your mother will be waiting, getting nervous,' he said, heading towards the exit, as if it was Megan who had kept them waiting. He jostled and steered the trolley with its wonky wheel through the exit and out into the short corridor which led to the arrivals lounge, 'Sorry, sorry, excuse me, so sorry...' he said, colliding with other home-comers.

Megan knew that her mother would be anxious. Hence the trip to London. She needs to see me as soon as I arrive, Megan thought. After all, the journey would not have been easy, especially with a small, excited boy to entertain. She remembered Elizabeth's words before she left for Romania.

'I know what you think, Meg. But I wish you luck. Don't hold back. I will not blame you if you love her as you have loved me. It's natural – the love between parent and offspring. It's uncondi-tional, like discovering another part of you—'

'You'll always be my mother.'

Elizabeth had not looked convinced.

It was many years since Megan had come through an arrivals gate, and back then she rarely had anyone to greet her, anyone to look out for, and never family. It was chaotic: people stretched forward across the barriers to touch loved ones unable to wait the few minutes until they were clear of the tape, others shouted names and waved and screamed, professional greeters with impassive faces held their signs and waited. Trolleys were abandoned in the gangway.

Megan saw her mother first; she was removed from the core of the crowd, waiting in front of a bureau in her unfashionable coat and leather knee-high boots, back straight, chin high, holding onto Cerdic's hand. Dressed in an elf costume he looked impossi-bly cute and Megan realized that Christmas was fast approaching. She'd forgotten all about it. Cerdic was standing very still, as if on his best behaviour. She beamed at the sight of him. Jack saw them and told Megan to go on ahead. She stopped for a moment, ignoring the tutting of crabby, harried people behind her.

She was taken aback by her mother's appearance. In the weeks they had been away Elizabeth had all but disappeared. Like a ghost she was virtually transparent, transforming to gas before her eyes. In a flash Megan saw Elizabeth as a young mother, bereaved and bereft. A ghost of her former self, lacking substance. Everything, and everyone, that Elizabeth had loved had been taken from her. No wonder she was so frightened of Megan finding her blood mother. The need to reassure her mother of her love was overpowering, almost as strong as her need to hold Cerdic.

Megan abandoned the luggage to Jack's care and starting running, shouting, 'Mum! Cerdic!'

Elizabeth looked round, her lips quivering, rooted to the spot. As Megan strode across she mouthed, 'Are you still mine, Megan? Are you still mine, cariad?'

'Always.' And she flung her arms round them both.

Cerdic laughed and Elizabeth wept in Megan's arms.

Megan could not open the mail on her mulmed. She asked for Jack's number instead. It rang several times before he picked up.

'I've got the laboratory report,' she said.

'And?'

'I can't open it.'

'You have to.'

'Stay online.' She touched the screen and the mail opened. Chest pounding she scanned the document and let out a small gasp. 'Monica Petrescu is my biological mother.' She had found her.

'I'd have been amazed if she wasn't,' Jack said. 'Marvellous. Bloody marvellous.'

'Now all we have to do is establish if either of them is a suitable donor. All. Huh?!' She laughed, but she couldn't contemplate the possibility that they were both carriers.

'I'll bet Monica matches.'

Glad he was keeping things light, she said, 'How much?'

'Look, I've got to go. Busy here. Keep me in the loop.'

'Yeah, sure.' And he logged out. Unsettled by the brevity of their call Megan went downstairs. He'd reacted as if she'd told him she'd just got a new book, and then she dismissed her feelings as irrational. Of course he cared; he was busy, that's all. She told Elizabeth.

'When will she come over? You'll forgive me if I don't meet her just yet?'

'As soon as possible. Stela too.'

Megan offered to meet the Petrescus at the airport, but Stela insisted they made their own way to Bangor. Secretly, Megan was relieved. She had not relished the idea of a long journey with two women who were, despite what the test results said, strangers. And there would have been no escape on the train. At least here, in the restaurant of the city centre hotel where Megan had booked them rooms, the meeting could be brought to a close whenever it felt appropriate.

The restaurant was quiet. Christmas decorations still hung around the room, like stragglers at a party's end, adding to the slightly tired January atmosphere. Megan sat at a table, fifteen minutes early for the appointed lunch, fiddling obsessively with her ring, worrying how best to greet the women when they arrived. A hug was out of the question but a handshake seemed so formal. These people might turn out to be her son's salvation. She had no idea how to behave and had nothing to quash her nerves. She'd ordered wine, but as she raised the glass to her lips the smell turned her stomach and she replaced it immediately with water. She regretted organizing the lunch at all. The idea had been to break the ice, rather than meeting for the first time at the hospital where tensions would be running high.

When Megan stood to greet the Petrescus her thighs caught the edge of the table, spilling the wine and smashing a glass. A waiter rushed over and in the minor commotion that followed all forms of address were forgotten. Megan's lap was wet but she didn't care. The little drama provided conversation.

Megan ordered lunch, though no one ate much. Monica tore a

bread roll to shreds, reducing it to a mound of crumbs on her plate. Stela sipped at a glass of fizzy water and pushed pasta round without putting much into her mouth. Megan didn't eat at all; she thanked them profusely for making the trip, agreeing to take the tests. She asked if their journey had been comfortable, their rooms satisfactory. Her voice echoed round the near-empty room. Stela nodded and translated. Megan looked at her watch. Monica muttered to Stela.

'Mama would like to see your son.'

Megan's heart flipped. Surely Monica had not expected her to bring him?

'You have photographs?' Stela said.

Megan brought up images on her mulmed: Cerdic on the beach, in the garden at Tŷ Mawr. The photographs loosened tongues. Megan answered empty questions about their lives: birthdays, favourite toys, first word, favourite colour, movies they liked to watch. Questions that revealed nothing, not really. But Monica seemed content with the answers. It felt rather like a strange job interview, or an interview for a house-share like those she'd attended in London as a teenager before deciding she could not share a home with strangers.

With little to do the waiter was overly attentive and hovered throughout like a shadow. Megan wondered what he made of the threesome. So alike and yet so ill at ease. She asked him for the bill. There was no point looking at the desert menu – the main course had been barely touched. When the bill arrived Monica looked embarrassed, as if unsure whether or not to offer to pay. She leant towards her bag; Stela put her hand across her mother's lap; Megan whipped out her plastic.

'I will cover all expenses,' she said. 'And should either of you be suitable I will pay for every cell, blood, plasma donation. It is possible to harvest more than we need, to freeze for later. It will be uncomfortable, but in the long run it will save time, avoid you having to travel backwards and forwards.' She heard the words and regretted how harsh and greedy she sounded. How cold. She hadn't meant it to be this way.

Monica grew very agitated. Stela said, 'She is bunică to Cerdic. Grandmother. She does not want money.' Then, 'She would like to meet him.'

Megan's stomach churned; she had anticipated and dreaded such a request. And she knew Elizabeth would have considered this possibility too. Then there was Cerdic – he didn't even know of their existence.

'Can we do the tests first? There'll be plenty of time.'

Megan knew that even if neither Monica nor Stela matched they still had the right to request a meeting. Monica was Cerdic's grandmother, Stela his aunt. Nothing could alter this fact.

The visit to the county hospital was brief. Bloods were taken. Megan paid to have the tests prioritized. Afterwards she ordered a cab to take the Petrescus back to the hotel, but they insisted on walking. To have a look at Bangor. Megan wondered what they would make of it.

Early the following day the three women sat in a row, straight-backed and silent outside Mr Barnet's office. The sounds of hospital life growled in the background. Megan spotted the reflection of the three of them in the glass of a picture hung on the wall opposite. Their faces were indecipherable but what struck her was the similarity of form, of posture and attitude. Touching her ring, she hoped the similarities were not internal. The office door moved and Mr Barnet's head and shoulders slid out.

'Do come in,' he said.

There were only two seats, so Megan stood behind the Petrescus clutching the back of each chair.

'I'll not beat around the bush. I'm sure you want to know the results immediately,' he said. Still trotting out the clichés, Megan thought. All three women nodded.

'Mrs Petrescu is a carrier and will not make a match.' Megan heard the words but the sound did not come from the doctor's mouth. They swam round her head as his mouth moved, mixing with the pulse of her heart, the blood in her head. She dared not breathe. 'But the good news is that Miss Petrescu has escaped,' he continued.

Stela shook her head, and he reiterated, 'You do not carry AMNA, Miss Petrescu. You are young and healthy, you will make a fine donor. I see no reason why young Cerdic shouldn't live a long life. And we will store donations for future male children, Mrs Evens. Just in case. Technology… Such a wonderful thing, eh?' But Megan was no longer listening, the words faded away.

Monica turned to her daughter, eyes wide, chin nodding. Stela spoke and Monica threw her arms round Stela. Megan looked on, heart beating wildly, relief consuming her. Stela remained dry-eyed despite her mother's tears.

Outside Megan called Elizabeth and told her the good news. Then she brought up Jack's number.

'Fantastic, fantastic news! Give the little chap a squeeze from me, won't you?'

'Thanks, Jack. I couldn't have done it without you. I don't know how I can ever thank you.'

'Work on the story with me. I'm going back. Gyl Savu has more names, women who'll talk. I reckon it went on here too. It's huge.'

'The support group in Chester?' She felt her antennae twitching; he was right, and it was tempting. 'I can't. There's Cerdic, Stela—'

'I'm not asking you to go back to Romania. Just do some digging, between hospital visits and so on. Do the Petrescu interview. Get her to talk.'

'I'm not sure I can persuade her. You know how painful it is for her—'

'Not now she's found you, surely? C'mon Megan. You're tempted, I know it. We make a good team.'

At the mention of her and Jack as a team Megan remembered their night together, and another sharp pain skewered her. 'I'll think about it,' she said.

Over the following weeks Megan, Stela and Cerdic attended the various consultations and meetings with specialists. Monica insisted upon coming too. They spent interminable hours in hospital waiting rooms. Stela spent hours undergoing a number of uncomfortable and lengthy procedures. To Megan's surprise she was good-natured throughout. Megan marvelled at Monica's growing mastery of basic vocabulary and phrases. She discovered that they had a wicked sense of humour, particularly Stela, and she never tired of watching these women who reminded her of herself. And they were good with Cerdic, so very good with Cerdic. He enjoyed the extra attention and accepted without any awkward questions that Monica and Stela were 'like aunties'. Megan feared he might miss them when they left. She feared she might. A warmth stole into her when she thought of Monica and Stela. Something she couldn't put into words. It wasn't a connection as such but there was a hold, a sense of having found the pack. Something had shifted and to Megan's great astonishment it felt good. A tentative friendship blossomed, but still Elizabeth had not met them.

Stela thawed. Megan made a payment into her bank account after the first donation, as she lay recovering in a hospital anti-room. She studied the remittance message on her console and said, 'I feel guilty now, for taking this. He is a boy, it isn't much to save his life—'

'Imagine it's payment for talking to EBC. I may even get some cash out of them—'

'That almost feels worse,' Stela said.

'Then accept it as a gift, from one sister to another, to help you through medical school. And when you are a doctor, make time to do some research.'

Stela looked puzzled.

'Into AMNA. How to prevent it. Cure it.'

'Deal.'

And they shook hands.

Two nights before the Petrescus returned to Romania, as Elizabeth and Megan cleared up after supper, Elizabeth said suddenly, 'Invite them to lunch. Tomorrow. We'll say twelve-thirty till two.

344

They'll want to see where you both live before they leave.'

'You don't have to do this, Mum,' Megan insisted, but Elizabeth was adamant. She bent to load the dishwasher. Megan scrubbed at a burnt oven dish. Neither spoke, concentrating on their tasks instead. Scratching and crashing filled the air. Megan took a knife to the dish.

Then Elizabeth said, 'It's good that you've found your family, Meg. Good for Cerdic naturally. After all, Stela will save his life. But it is good for you too.'

'I don't need another family – I've got you. And Cerdic.' Megan wiped her brow and a drop of dishwater dribbled into her eye, stinging and blurring her vision.

'You mustn't worry about me, about hurting my feelings. I am sure of your love, I can't believe I ever doubted it – I couldn't ask for a better daughter.' Elizabeth finished loading, stood upright and rubbed the small of her back as she spoke.

'And I couldn't ask for a better mum.' Megan couldn't look directly at Elizabeth. She continued to scrub away at the brown stains on the dish, though it was as clean as it was ever going to be.

'I won't be here forever, Meg. I'm an old woman. Monica is not, and Stela… Well, she is a sister. A grandmother and an aunt for Cerdic. Don't block them out for fear of hurting me. It pleases me to see you grow fond of them.'

'Am I that transparent?' Megan choked, fighting back tears.

'Open yourself up to possibility, don't close yourself off as I did. You may get wounded, you may not. And you have so much to gain. As does Cerdic.'

And for a few seconds Megan thought her mother meant more than her relationship with the Petrescus. She wiped her cheeks with the back of her wet hand, and pointed. 'You are a remarkable woman Elizabeth Evens. Christ, I sound like Jack North!'

In a flash she returned to that night in Romania. She thought of it often, turning the memory over and over in her head. Obsessively. An attempt to stop it fading. As if she were in love, infatuated.

They laughed. Then Elizabeth turned to leave. She paused at the doorway, looked over her shoulder and said, 'I'm a Bevan really. Deep in my heart I will always be Mrs Andrew Bevan.'

And then she was gone.

Chapter Thirty

The sky was duck egg blue the day of Elizabeth's funeral. White clouds surged over a restless sea. A flock of highly-strung choughs soared from the cliffs, their loud 'kweeow's' drowning out the delicate call of the kittiwake.

They stood in the grounds of Holy Island's bird sanctuary looking out over the Irish Sea. Megan spotted puffins landing on the grassy slope to the side of the lighthouse. The clowns of the bird sanctuary, Elizabeth said. Comical waiters with their carrot coloured parrot beaks and over-sized feet. It was thanks to Elizabeth's hikes and patient waiting that Megan noticed and recognized these creatures. Reluctantly dragged on walks and watches as a teenager, complaining vociferously in front of peers, she'd secretly enjoyed the thrill of the chase and discovery. And while Megan didn't inherit Elizabeth's passion for these creatures that fly, and skim, and soar, and swoop, and roam the open skies she was glad that she noticed their existence. And she understood why her mother loved them so.

Her mother: Elizabeth Bevan, née Evens.

Megan wondered if the suddenness of Elizabeth's death had made it more difficult, or easier, to deal with. There had been no warning signs, though Megan learned later that Elizabeth had a heart condition, one she had been aware of for years, but kept secret from Megan. Probably hereditary, her doctor said. One day Elizabeth was gardening and eating and nattering as normal. The next a massive heart attack stopped her in her tracks, on the path underneath the ugly fir tree she had always meant to have removed.

It was dusk and Megan thought Elizabeth was on the bench watching the blue tits feasting on the titbits she left for them each day. It was almost dark when Megan realized that Elizabeth had been outside for a long time. Normally she'd have been in for another cup of tea to hold off the chill, despite the unseasonal warmth that March. Peering out of the window as she filled the kettle Megan saw a mound on the path. At first she thought that Cerdic must have left some dressing up clothes out there. She stepped outside to collect them. She ambled over the patio, across the lawn, enjoying the budding daffodils, the promise of spring in the air. She had taken only a couple of steps on the slate path when she understood what she had seen.

Megan's hand came to her open, silent mouth. She ran even though she knew there was no point. Elizabeth was so very, very still. Down the path she went, her house shoes flip-flopping on the purple stone. The birds had stopped warbling. She could smell hyacinth on the breeze. Nuts and seeds were scattered across the path. In Elizabeth's right hand a packet of bird food, split at the seam. A carer to the end. Megan kneeled down and placed her head on her dead mother's shoulder and wailed.

Jack stood a short distance behind Megan on the peninsula. Her vermillion scarf danced on the breeze, like an exotic seabird diving and fishing, a life all of its own. The sea choppy and green.

'I like the scarf. Don't often see you in colour. Never, really,' he said.

'It's for Mum. She liked bright colours, even though she rarely wore them herself.'

'She nagged you about your wardrobe?'

'Endlessly! You look like a witch, Megan! You are young, celebrate it, wear something gorgeous!' She mimicked Elizabeth's shrill Welsh tones.

A clammy hand wriggled in Megan's palm. She tore her eyes from the puffins and looked down. She said, 'Can you see the puffins, Cerdic? The little birds, like parrots, with orange noses, feet and eyes.'

'Birds don't have noses, Mummy. They have beaks.'

Megan laughed and crouched to face her son, looking into his deep yellow-green eyes. Dizzy from the sudden movement, she placed her hand on the ground. She'd been suffering from light-headedness for weeks. Must remember to eat, she reminded herself.

'You're quite right, silly me. Nana would be proud of you.' She brushed his caramel cheek and thought she might burst for the love of him.

'Are you sad that Nana is died?' he said, suddenly.

'Are you, cariad?'

'You never called me that before. That was Nana's name.'

'Saying it reminds me of her and how much she loved you and how much I love her and how much I love you,' she said, as a solitary tear fell down her cheek. Cerdic swept it away with chubby fingers before Megan wrapped her arms round him.

Her living, breathing son. Her son who would have a long and rich life with all the usual ups and downs. She felt so happy and so sad that she thought she might implode, turn into dust and blow away across the sea, or melt into the earth.

'Come on sunbeam, let's do it!' she said, releasing her boy and picking up the small box at her feet. It was hard to believe that this handful of dust had once been a life, once been her mother. She knew these ashes were merely the shell. Her mother would exist for decades to come – in her memory, in Cerdic's memory, in Jack's and in the hearts and minds of all whose lives she had touched. The box was made from pale wood with slim silver handles. It was just like Elizabeth's coffin. Megan recalled the service.

Along with Jack and two professional pallbearers sent by the funeral parlour, Megan had carried her mother's coffin from the cart to the municipal crematorium service hall. Jack advised against, but Megan was insistent and, as ever, she got her way. Her primary concern was not that she might be too emotional to carry the coffin, but that she might find it too physically demanding and drop it, and create a terrible, macabre scene in which Elizabeth's coffin plummeted down the walkway, the horrified faces of the small crowd of mourners looking on, mouths gaping, waiting for the wood to split and the corpse to roll out, teeth bared, eyes milky and bulging.

In the event Megan was shocked at how small it was, and how light. Though diminutive in stature Elizabeth retained her weightiness to the end. She was squat and solid, heavy in the leg and hip. Megan could not believe that death rendered her so weightless and insubstantial, like puffballs. As she walked she doubted if the coffin contained anything at all, let alone her mother's body. And then she realized that it didn't matter to her if it did not. This was not Elizabeth. Megan hoped that Elizabeth was a puffball, floating on high with her friends the birds. She would be so happy up there.

Megan removed the lid from the little box and took hold of one handle. Cerdic took the other, and together they emptied the contents to the wind.

'Goodbye, Mum.'

'Bye-bye, Nana.'

They turned their back on the sea and walked towards Jack who was brandishing a spade, looking ill at ease and unsure what to do with it. It looked like a toy in his hands.

'This is for you. To put the last bit of soil around the tree,' Jack said, as if answering a question, 'if you want to that is?'

Megan raised an eyebrow and smiled. He'd carried the spade all the way out here only to lumber it back. She thought about reminding him of this folly, then thought again. He seemed vulnerable, different from his usual assured – some would say arrogant – self. Perhaps it was the constant presence of a woman in his life.

After Megan had told him Stela was a potential donor Jack told her that his relationship with Julie looked like it might be serious after all. 'She wants to move in. We're thinking of the spring,' he said. Megan had guessed already – the hairgrips and face wipes in his bathroom – but she was glad Jack told her. After all, that's what friends do, she thought, they share news. She'd felt odd about it though; Julie simply wasn't right for Jack. Megan didn't want to see him hurt.

It was quite a trudge to back to the sanctuary visitor centre and its garden. None of the trio spoke. Jack insisted on carrying the shovel and by the time they got there it was clear his shoulder, as well as his pride, ached. He led them to the freshly planted silver birch.

'It looks small. Thought it would be bigger when I ordered it,' Megan said.

The tree did look pathetic. It stood just over a metre, a spindly trunk and no foliage. More like a twig. They all leant in to inspect it. The tree held promise, buds were plentiful.

'It looks big to me,' Cerdic said.

'You're right, Mr Boy. It's a fine tree and it will grow. Be even finer,' Jack replied, nodding sagely.

'You're both right,' Megan said as she took the spade from Jack and plunged it into the earth. 'I'll make a hole for the plaque. You do have it, don't you?'

Jack disappeared into the centre building, returning with a slate plaque mounted into a large sand stone. Megan placed it in the space she had created a metre or so away from the foot of the tree. They stood back to admire her handiwork.

Carved into the slate in a gothic font the white lettering read:

Elizabeth Bevan, née Evens, 1978 - 2053
Much loved daughter, sister, wife
Grandmother to Cerdic
Mother to Matthew, Luke, Robert and Megan.
'And death shall have no dominion.'

'It seems odd now, seeing it there. All wrong. In the cold light of day. Like I mattered to her more than anyone else,' Megan sighed.

'Nonsense. You, and Cerdic, were everything to Elizabeth. You're last because you're still alive. The natural order. You outlived her,' Jack reassured her.

'And Cerdic will survive me,' Megan whispered.

'Thank God,' Jack whispered back.

'Thank Stela.'

Megan wondered if she would attend Monica's funeral in years to come. Would she grieve her second mother as much as her first? She couldn't imagine grieving like this a second time, though who could say how their relationship might develop. Megan's heart was open and, if she was watching, she knew Elizabeth would be pleased.

Chapter Thirty-one

'I have a bottle of fizz at home. I was saving it for a special occasion. And today feels special,' Megan said, as they walked away from the little birch.

'Righto.' Jack nodded.

After a walk through the gorse, which crackled underfoot, Megan drove Elizabeth's battered car across the lumpy flatness of Anglesey. It was such a clear day the Menai bridge was visible in the distance. The ash box sat next to Cerdic in the back. Jack sat in the passenger seat clutching the door handle. He was a nervous passenger and Megan's driving, always erratic, was especially bad that day.

'I feel like celebrating. Mum's life, Cerdic's life, my life. Yours too.'

'It's a fine idea, Ms Evens,' he replied, and in spite of his words Megan noted a distinct lack of joy in his tone. She wondered if he was thinking of his parents.

'You okay?'

'Always.'

She knew he was fibbing but didn't press him. 'Then stop clinging onto the fucking door. It hardly inspires confidence you know,' she scolded, half-serious. 'Never repeat words like that, Cerdic,' she added, hastily.

Jack let go and sat on his hands, to ensure they didn't stray back to the handle Megan presumed. She continued, 'How long are you planning to stay? I never did ask when you arrived. Always seems so rude, asking someone when they're going the moment they walk through the door.'

'Not sure. Depends how it goes.'

'What does that mean exactly, Jack North? How scintillating my company is!' She laughed and almost hit the kerb. Jack grabbed hold of the door and Megan didn't reprimand him.

The box sat on the kitchen table. Megan didn't know what to do with it, now that it was empty. Jack was in the study making a call. Cerdic had raced to his room to play with a toy Megan had bought him in compensation for her lack of attentiveness over the past week. There had been so much to do, and she'd been feeling lousy. Megan would never have imagined death would be so all consuming. She remembered that Elizabeth would have organized five or six funerals. Too many for one person. No one should have to go through the heartache and painstaking organisation more than a couple of times in a lifetime.

Tŷ Mawr felt desolate. Like its soul had gone.

Megan glanced up at the bookshelf next to the Welsh dresser. Packed with well-used, dog-eared cookery books vying for space with heaps of scrap paper. On the paper were scribbled notes and recipes copied from the mulmed and, before that, the radio and television. Page upon page of Elizabeth's sloping, curled hand-writing. Written in blue ink with a treasured fountain pen: a gift from Hannah on her eleventh birthday. The botanical themed pottery on the dresser, her teapots, wedding gifts to Elizabeth and Andrew. The telescope aimed at the sky in the bedroom with the rose pink walls, the binoculars on the dining room sideboard. The ivory elephants on the fireplace. Megan closed her eyes and wandered through Tŷ Mawr in her mind. Elizabeth was every-where, like dust. Megan smiled, opened a cupboard and brought out two champagne flutes.

Jack paced the study, she could hear his footsteps. She could-n't hear his voice, so he wasn't making a call. What was he doing up there? He'd said it was quiet at work. It was why he was able to come up for the funeral.

'Nothing big on right now,' he'd said when she told him the date of the ceremony. 'Planning for the documentary. Waiting for a juicy news story.'

But he didn't need a big story. He was hot property again. How quickly things changed. Jack's career was not only salvaged when he broke the rotten eggs story, it was propelled to new heights.

The story headlined on the EBC homepage earlier in the month, and most other news-sites, as well as hitting the number two slot on the premier channel's ten o' clock evening news. It ran for days as more and more women and their descendants came forward – from Clinik Stamenov, as well as countless others throughout Eastern Europe, India and Australasia. Megan had helped out as and when she could, as Jack had requested. He'd been commissioned to make a documentary, and Megan wondered if he might ask her to work on it.

She was at a crossroads: where next? In theory there was nothing to hold her here. Cerdic was responding well to treatment; he wouldn't be ready for school till September. Part of her wanted to leave, start afresh. But this felt like home. Could she build a life here without Elizabeth? Loneliness came in a sudden rush.

Jack caught his shadow on the study wall. He noticed the curve of his collapsing belly, the slight droop at the jaw line. No lines, no grey hairs, but it was a middle-aged shadow, no mistaking. He was crumbling.

He was playing for time, rehearsing his speech for the umpteenth time. But time was running out for him. He could hold it in no longer. He wondered if this growing inability to contain his emotions, this loss of control, was age related, like his failure to stop the spread across his torso. He had to get out. He cursed himself over and over for suggesting Megan help out on the rotten eggs story. Not because she'd lost her touch; she hadn't – she was a great journalist. But they'd been in almost constant communication and he needed distance. They spoke frequently, sharing ideas, facts, impressions. Sharing everything but the one thing he wanted to share with her.

He'd broken up with Julie soon after he'd said things were serious between them. He'd no idea why he lied to Megan. To provoke a reaction probably? After Romania he saw his relationship with Julie for the sham it was; the sham he was, and ended it quickly, brutally. Single once more, he'd returned to dating women he found physically attractive but unchallenging and fundamentally uninteresting. Women he could never fall in love with. Safe women. He'd been through two women, girls really, in the past month alone. He felt sickened by his actions.

He stared at the far end of the garden, unused to such rural expanses. The trees were budding. He remembered Eleanor, his first wife. He'd been doing that more and more since that night with Megan. He remembered the little things that made their marriage good. The way she brought him tea in bed in the mornings, the sexy, filthy mails, the strange little noises she made when he returned from assignments in the dead of the night and slipped into bed next to her. And then the big things: shared dreams for four, maybe five, children; the way they made each other laugh, and cry. He remembered the bad times – when she fell into those black periods of despair, and how he came so close to following her there, when she died and he considered taking his own life too, and when the rage took hold. But there was no longer any pain or anger, just a faint, distant sadness and a longing for love, with all its ups and downs, again. For years – decades – he'd shielded himself; he'd kept away from the clever, complex women. He'd done so well, for so long.

Poor Julie, he'd hurt her so much. He'd wanted it to work, he really had. On paper she was perfect: good-looking, intelligent, healthy, with plenty of child-bearing years left. Parenting was the one area where he thought he might meet with resistance. Julie was so desperately ambitious. But she'd surprised him when he mentioned kids. She burst into tears and said, 'I'll be a gorgeous mummy, gorgeous! We'll make beautiful, perfect children, Jack.' He felt queasy when she said this; she looked anything but perfect with her red nose and bloodshot eyes, but he pushed his doubts aside. By then she'd starting leaving underwear at his flat. He'd found moisturiser in the bathroom cabinet.

And then Megan slipped in. And she simply wouldn't go away. And now, here he was: middle-aged, in love, longing for a family.

There was something different about Megan. She'd lost weight again; she was almost skeletal but, strangely, there was a bloom about her. Grief accentuated her aching beauty, God damn her. God damn Romania. If only he'd not gone, he'd not be in this mess. And now she was talking about possibly returning to London.

He opened the window and leaned out of it, smoking. He heard her calling from the mezzanine landing.

'Jack? You're very quiet. Come down. I'm about to open the champagne. We can sit in the garden. You can have a smoke.'

She clattered down the stairs. Jack stubbed out his cigarette and crept across the room, shaking. Pushing the door open wide he stepped out, took a deep breath and called, 'I'm right there, Ms Evens. Just nipping to the lav.'

Outside Megan sat on the bench, the champagne bottle at her feet. She tapped on the seat beside her, but Jack pulled up an ornamental wooden toadstool and perched on it, facing her. Megan wondered why. It was uncomfortable to sit on the toadstool for any length of time with its rounded top and rough surface. 'Don't want to look at the garden? It's gorgeous today. Mum would have loved it.'

'I need to look at you.'

Megan was embarrassed, and thrown, by the comment. It was so unexpected. He referred to her looks rarely, and Megan liked it that way. When she thought about their night together she was filled with longing and confusion. It threatened to spill over into something she couldn't understand or control, like liquid released from a container struggling to find a shape. She relived it in her day dreams. She told no one. Jack was complicit in the glossing over, the ignoring, of this event and Megan assumed he regretted it. After all he was seeing Julie Brookings; she knew he'd not told Julie about his infidelity.

Blushing, Megan raised her glass and said, 'To Mum, Elizabeth! All there is to say and more.'

'To Elizabeth. A formidable woman, and one who made you what you are today.'

Megan flushed again and took a gulp of the sharp bubbles. They fizzed round the delicate flesh of her cheeks, shot over the roof of her mouth and sent shivers down her spine. It always did that. Like an aphrodisiac. And then it frothed up her nose and made her splutter. She'd taken too greedy a sip.

They sat in silence for a while. The alcohol had made her feel sick; she tried to ignore it. He offered her a cigarette. She shook her head.

'Been right off them recently.'

He lit up, inhaling deeply.

Megan held her glass aloft and watched the sunlight bouncing through it. She couldn't face another sip. The queasiness felt familiar but she couldn't quite place the memory. 'I love the way it softens things, blurs the edges. Alcohol during the day I mean.'

He didn't respond, shifting on the seat instead, gripping its edges. 'Bloody hell!'

He had a splinter in his palm. Megan went upstairs to fetch tweezers and cream, and as she opened the bathroom cabinet she caught sight of a box of tampons. She hadn't had a period in months. It's the weight loss, she thought, it's happened before. But as she closed the door, she knew, suddenly, with such surety that she threw up, only just making it to the toilet. Still trembling, she staggered downstairs. Fuck, fuck, fuck, she thought. What am I to do?

She hadn't sat down before Jack said, 'I'm leaving. Leaving EBC, leaving London. The UK actually.'

'Oh.' Megan said, motionless, as if in a state of suspended animation. 'What about Julie?'

'I can't do this any longer. Pretend to be your friend.'

'Pretend to be my friend?' she echoed.

'I want more. Shocking isn't it? Jack North, the bastard allergic to love. Got hit so hard once, lost it, nearly died. Swore never to get that close again. Except that sometimes it's just so bloody powerful that it's impossible to stop. Even for me. I'm healed. Ready to love again. Only took a couple of decades.'

'You've told me about Julie,' she whispered, stunned, wondering how to tell him. If she was going to tell him.

'Friendship is good, friendship is fine. It was okay by me for years. But having tasted possibility I want more and I can't have it and it's killing me,' he said, as if she'd remained silent.

Megan felt a quivering in her gut and thought she might be sick again.

Jack was still talking. 'Why now? After all this time? I hear your questions. What took you so long? Why can you no longer bear to be my friend? If I'm honest, I'm not entirely sure. It's been painful for a while. I thought I could control it. But, in fact, it's got worse – much worse. And I can't move on while you're around. It's hard to look for something else, when the one thing you really, really want is right there – in front of you – but you can't quite reach it. Touch it again. Possess it. You held it once and it was gorgeous. More gorgeous and precious than you could ever have imagined. You have a glimpse of a possible future, like an exquisite garden, only to be shut out by an impenetrable brick wall that gets thicker and thicker as time goes on. It gets covered in moss, weeds, then roses with vicious thorns. I can't spend my life looking at that wall. I have to get away. Move on.

'Elizabeth's death triggered something in me and I can't go on like this. Life's too short. I don't want to be lonely any longer. Having meaningless fucks with women I care nothing for. They'll get harder to come by anyway. Hell, I want kids. I refuse to spend years pining for someone I can never have, as Elizabeth did, as I did. And Elizabeth had you. I have no one, Megan, no one.'

'What about Julie?'

'Over. Kidding myself. She's not my kind of woman.'

Megan thought she might explode. She collapsed onto the bench. She said, 'You'll never find another Eleanor.'

'I don't want another Eleanor.'

'Why can't you be my friend?'

Jack looked into her eyes. His pupils were dilated. He continued, 'I need to move on and the only way is to have no contact with you. Sorry. I really am. It's self preservation.'

And despite trying not to, Megan began to cry. She said, 'You can't do that. You have to stay.'

'I don't want part of you. I want all of you. There. I've said it.'

'I can't imagine life without you,' she said.

Jack shrugged and went as if to say something but no words came. Megan saw the tiny blue veins in the dark circles around his eyes throbbing. He ran his fingers through his hair. Slender, strong fingers.

And Megan knew why she couldn't imagine life without him. She fell to her knees, knocking over the champagne, the clatter of glass on stone echoing around the patio, ringing in her ears. Wood pigeons flapped their wings in shock and fled from the coverage of the fir. The air reverberated around them. Megan wiped her face and leant in. She held his face in her tear drenched hands and said, 'Take me, keep me. Stay.'

His eyes met hers. 'What?'

'I love you, Jack. I always have. It's just that I never knew it till now.'

He looked at her.

She said, 'Romania... I thought it was the drink. You never said anything.'

'I thought I had said something. Maybe I dreamt it,' he said.

'What did you say?'

'That night?'

She nodded.

'I love you.' And he held her face.

'Did you know?' she said.

'What?'

'That I wouldn't let you walk out of my life.'

'Not for certain. It was a gamble. Either way life would be bearable. It's the not knowing that's the killer,' he said.

His embrace was firm and passionate, and as they kissed Megan felt like she had come home.

'Mummy, mummy!' Cerdic hurtled onto the patio.

They snapped apart. Megan clambered to her feet while Jack coughed and stood up from the stool.

'Hello, Mr Boy,' Jack stuttered, 'Your mother and I were just whispering a secret to each other.'

'No you weren't. You were kissing. Like mummies and daddies kiss. Have you been doing this a long time?'

Megan hugged her boy and said, 'Not very long.'

'Does Jack love you?'

'Yes. I love your mother,' Jack smiled and took hold of Megan's hand and then Cerdic's.

'You going to be my real daddy now?'

'I'll try. Let's have some food, Mister. I'm famished,' Jack said.

Megan led them up the concrete stairs through the French windows to the front rooms. Red and blue squares of light from the coloured glass at the corner of each door danced on the carpet as they walked across it hand in hand. And Megan felt the energy within her, the cells multiplying and growing. Jack's baby, Cerdic's brother or sister, on the treacherous, miraculous journey to life. A herd of ivory elephants sitting on the mantelpiece watched the little family's progress with bead eyes.

Additional Material

The Inspiration for BloodMining

Discussion Points for Reading Groups

WARNING: THERE ARE 'SPOILERS' IN THIS MATERIAL

The Inspiration for BloodMining

BloodMining began as a piece of flash fiction written after reading a news item on the BBC website about a sixty-three-year-old Sussex woman who was having a baby. One baking July afternoon my sister Helen and I sat on Shoreham beach discussing my micro story – we both agreed that it didn't work in its existing format. This was a much bigger yarn. A novel sized one.

At this time my second son, Cameron, was almost three and, like all little boys, running around like a mad one. Having only just recovered from years of chronic sleep deprivation, now I was exhausted chasing after him and big brother Morgan. I wondered how this woman a few years shy of retirement would cope with the physical demands that a newborn inevitably brings, let alone an energetic toddler. What would it be like on her child's first day at school, surrounded by much younger parents? How would her other children – all adults – feel about it? With eggs in such short supply how did she persuade the doctors to impregnate her? Would she even survive the birth itself?

Like many of my generation I was in my thirties before I started my family; ten years older than my own mother had been when she became a parent. But I have friends who started much earlier than I did, and we have spoken of the advantages and disadvantages of raising a family as younger or older parents. Also, I have friends who have taken advantage of reproductive science without which they would not have the precious gifts that are their children.

Advances in reproductive science have given us freedoms and choices that earlier generations could only dream of, but, I speculated, where will it all stop? Digging about – I was a journalist and researcher for the think tank Demos before turning to fiction – I discovered that the British woman was by no means the oldest mother on record. At the time a sixty-seven-year-old Romanian held that honour. Since completing BloodMining – over two years ago now – older women still have given birth, some for the first time. In India, where motherhood is more revered than in the West, there are even clinics specializing in helping the seventy-pluses fulfil their dream and cultural expectation.

So the story began with Hannah and Elizabeth. And the tension created by Elizabeth's grief at the loss of her family and Hannah's decision to have another child. Elizabeth cannot imagine trying to replace her lost children, but when Megan is born and Hannah dies, Elizabeth steps in as mother quite naturally. So naturally, in fact, that she cannot bring herself to tell Megan the truth about her origins.

The ethical framework behind our scientific and technological advances and issues of reproductive choice is shaky and differs widely from country to country. The laws around surrogacy and egg donation are still evolving. Stepping into a not-too-distant future, I imagined a scenario in which the guidelines and laws would be open to abuse and corruption. And the effects this might have on the children born as a result of such abuse, and subsequent generations followed. Children like Cerdic.

English born, I grew up in North Wales. Like Megan I was pretty desperate to get away at eighteen, but it was an idyllic area to spend a childhood and I wanted to honour this. Many of the settings in the novel – Harlech, Shell Island, Bangor, Anglesey – were places I visited for holidays as a child and young adult. I take my own boys there now, and though I live hundreds of miles away Wales still forms part of my identity. Unlike Megan I am not well travelled and though I have visited Paris, I have never been to those places which act as backdrops to the novel's progress: China, the Middle East, the Arctic and Romania. Only in my dreams.

Although BloodMining is in no way autobiographical it would be fair to say that my life experience influenced the exploration of identity in the novel, and what it means to be a parent. As a child I knew little about my biological father; he died when I was five years old. My memories were scant and somewhat vague, gleaned mostly from photographs and the odd conversation with my mother and grandparents. Always the 'good' girl I sensed that to ask too much would be courting trouble. It seemed that to attempt to dig deep upset my maternal grandparents, and to a lesser extent my mother. I steered clear of the subject. By contrast, Helen probed and questioned, and during one such interrogation, when we were in our teens and Mum was out, our stepfather told us the truth about our father. He was surprised that we didn't already know.

Many years passed before there was a meaningful conversation with my mother. I do not mean this as criticism; it happened when it happened, but after a weekend in London when she talked about her first husband, our father, and the subsequent letter she wrote to me and Helen – a love story, a beautiful eulogy to his memory, and testament to the enduring power of love, through life and death – I felt more complete. Knowing where I came from was more important to me than I had realized. And I wish I'd had the chance to get to know him a little.

But in the nature versus nurture debate, as in all things, opinions differ. I have friends who were adopted as babies and young children. There are those who have traced their biological mothers and at least two who have no desire to do so whatsoever. And I can understand this. I could not have asked for a better father than Mike Williams, the man who raised me. But I do not know what I would have done if I had had the option of tracing my father. Of course, Megan has no choice but to trace her biological family.

My mother says she can see aspects of my father in both me and my sister, and I'm sure there are many aspects of Mike in there too. I wrestled over the dedication at the front of this book, and though in the end I opted for my nuclear family, this book is as much for Marian and Mike Williams. With love.

Discussion Points for Reading Groups

- Discuss the main themes of the book and look at how integral they are to the plot.

- The author sets the story in the very near and near future. How did this affect your response to the novel?

- The story is not told chronologically. What do you think this structure brought to your experience of the novel?

- How did you feel about Elizabeth's decision not to tell Megan of her true origins?

- Did you relate to Elizabeth's initial response to Hannah's actions? Do you believe Hannah was acting responsibly having a baby in her 70s?

- Elizabeth is almost destroyed by the loss of her family, yet Hannah bounces back with relative ease. How did you react to the two women's very different responses?

- Megan is a somewhat detached, lonely character. How does her relationship with Elizabeth compare to Elizabeth's relationship with Hannah?

- How does Megan change throughout the course of the novel? Do you believe she will be a better mother as a result of what she discovers about herself?

- Jack was also raised by people other than his biological parents yet he has a secure sense of self. Why do you think this is?

- Can you comment on the relationship between Megan and Jack and how it evolves throughout the novel?

http://laura-wilkinson.co.uk

Other novels by Bridge House

Calling for Angels

by Alex Smith

Em tries to avoid the annoying clones – the girls in her year at Philiton Comprehensive who spend all their time thinking about clothes, make-up and boys. She worries about her aging grandparents and her older brother Ollie, who seems to be behaving in a distinctly odd way.

Then three new people come into her life: the mysterious woman who gives her a beautifully carved figurine, Kai whose own story has a touch of sadness, and Zak, the new guy who causes a stir amongst the girls.

And she discovers she needs to call for angels.

Alex Smith is 16 and lives in Hertfordshire, England. She started writing when she was just four and says, "to me, writing is like breathing." She finished her debut novel, Calling For Angels, at the age of 14, "as a way of relaxing".

Winner of *The Red Telephone's* 2009 novel competition.

Order from http://theredtelephone.co.uk
The Red Telephone – an imprint of Bridge House
ISBN 978-1-907335-09-9

Voices of Angels

edited by Debz Hobbs-Wyatt

Do you believe in angels? This collection of fictional short stories explores encounters with angels – in whatever form they take. Some stories are sad, some are funny; all will touch you. The collection includes a new story by Laura Wilkinson.

The foreword is written by TV and Radio Presenter, Gloria Hunniford, and for every copy sold a donation will be made to her cancer charity: *The Caron Keating Foundation* – set up in her daughter's memory.

Order from www.bridgehousepublishing.co.uk

ISBN 978-1-907335-15-0

Do you have a short story in you?

Then why not have a go at one of our competitions or try your hand at a story for one of our anthologies? Check out:
http://bridgehousepublishing.co.uk/competition.aspx

Submissions

Bridge House publishes books which are a little bit different, such as *Making Changes*, *In the Shadow of the Red Queen* and *Alternative Renditions*.

We are particularly keen to promote new writers and believe that our approach is friendly and supportive to encourage those who may not have been published previously. We are also interested in published writers and welcome submissions from all authors who believe they have a story that would tie into one of our themed anthologies.

Full details about the submissions process, and how to submit your work to us for consideration, can be found on our website
http://bridgehousepublishing.co.uk/newsubmissions.aspx

Lightning Source UK Ltd.
Milton Keynes UK
UKOW021222300911

179537UK00002B/6/P